BOOK TWO

SOUL BOUND

ЯuniK Press

ISBN: 979-8-3303-4515-1

The book is a work of fiction. Characters, events, and locations are the product of the author's imagination. Any resemblance to other events, other locations, or other persons, living or dead, is coincidental.

BOUND BY

A
WEB
OF
WYRD

TRILOGY

RENATE ROWLAND

Runik Press

Author's Note

Dear reader,

Thank you for picking up my book. At this point, I would like to warn you about the content of this book. If these are in any way detrimental to your mental health, you might want to reconsider.

This book is a suspenseful urban fantasy romance. It contains explicit sexual content recommended only for an audience of 18+, as well as scenes of violence and torture.

I hope that you will consider following my characters in their fight for love, destiny, and honor.

Thank you,
Renate

Playlist

What's Gonna Be — Asking Alexandria

Another You — Danny Worsnop

Blue Eyes Blind — ZZ Ward

Beg — Emphatic

Natural Born Killer — Highly Suspect

Heavy Is The Weight — Memphis May Fire

Fade Out — Zero 9:36

New Blood — Zayde Wolf

Alone — I Prevail

Adrenaline — Zero 9:36

Dial Tone — Catch Your Breath

Love Falls — Hellyeah

Safe And Sound — Point North & The Ghost Inside

So-Called Life — Three Days Grace

Another You — Of Mice & Men

The Past Is Dead — Beartooth

Eve — Asking Alexandria

Werewolf — Motionless In White

Gorgeous Nightmare — Escape The Fate

The Answer — Beartooth

One Turns To None — Asking Alexandria

Hated — Beartooth

Circle With Me — Spirit Box

Painkiller — Three Days Grace

Never Know — Bad Omens

Brand New Numb — Motionless In White

Lightning Strike — Escape The Fate

Chemical Prisoner — Falling In Reverse

High On Me — Saliva

Pain — Three Days Grace

Love The Way You Hate Me — Like A Storm

Bad Things — I Prevail

Antisocialist — Asking Alexandria

Take What You Want – State Of Mine

The Death Of Peace Of Mind — Bad Omen

…To Be Loved — Papa Roach

I Stand Alone — Godsmack

The Red — Chevelle

Soak Me In Bleach — The Amity Affliction

Throne — Bring Me The Horizon

Animal — Magnolia Park, Ethan Ross & PLVTINUM

Parasite Eve — Bring Me The Horizon

Puppets — Mike's Dead

Self-destruction — I Prevail

Heartache — From Ashes To New

A Grave Mistake — Ice Nine Kills

Carry On — Falling In Reverse

Brighter Side Of Grey — Five Finger Death Punch

Another Life — Motionless In White

Saviour II — Black Veil Brides

Said & Done — Bad Omens

Would You Still Be There — Of Mice & Men

Back To Me — Of Mice & Men

Til The Casket Drops — ZZ Ward

Best Bad Habit — Danny Worsnop

Pronunciation Guide

Ǽgishjálmr – Aeyish-yaulmr (Helm of Awe)

Ǽsir – Ayesr (Ásgarðr faction of Gods)

Ásgarðr – Ows-garth

Askja – Ahskia

Bifrǫst – Be-fruhst

Dynja – Dun-ya

Fenrisúlfr – Fenris-oolfr (Fenrir)

Fólkvangr – Fohlk-vangr

Freyja – Frei-yah

Frigg – Frick

Hǫðr – Huhrth

Huginn – Hooy-in

Iðunn – Eathun

Jǫrmungandr – Yuhrmun-gahndr

Kjan – Ki-an

Kjartan – Kiahrtan

Kría – Kri-a

Kristján – Kristiaun

Miðgarðr – Mith-gahrth

Miðgarðsormr – Mith-gahr-thyomr (Midgard Serpent)

Mjǫllnir – Miuhtll-nir

Muirchertach – Muirk-tahk

Muninn – Moo-nin

Mýrkjartan – Mýrkiahrtan

Óðinn – Oh-thin

Ragnarǫk – Rahg-nah-ruhk

Skuld – Skoolt

Sleipnir – Slehpnir

Týr — Teehr

Urðr – Oorth

Valhǫll – Vahl-huhtll

Vanr – Vahnr (Vanaheimr faction of Gods)

Verðandi – Vehr-thahndi

Web of Wyrd – Web of Veert

Yggdrasil – Eekdrasil

Þórr – Thohr

Þórunn/Thórunn – Thohrun

Runes:

ᛒ : Bjarkan – bierkaan

ᛇ : Eihwaz – eye-whas

ᛦ : Algiz – ahl-ghiss

ᚴ : Kaun – cown

ᛏ : Ár – owhr

ᚱ : Reið – rhight

ᛏ : Týr – teehr

ᚬ : Áss – us

ᚾ : Nauðr – neuyth

"NEVER SWEAR FALSE OATHS.
GREAT AND GRIM IS THE REWARD
FOR THE BREAKING OF TROTH."

—Völsunga Saga, c. 21

EIHWAZ
(Yew Rune)

It represents:
- Strength
- Reliability, dependability, trustworthiness
- Enlightenment
- Endurance
- Defense, protection
- Transition

It symbolizes:
- An honest man who can be relied upon
- Life, death, and change since death carries the possibility of rebirth
- Light as well as shadow since one cannot exist without the other

It signifies:
- The timeless, eternity, immortality
- The driving force to acquire
- Providing motivation and a sense of purpose and indicates that you have set your sights on a reasonable target and can achieve your goals

PROLOGUE

The man lay on his back before him, his chest bare, his arms and legs outstretched.

His latest victim.

Bands of runic script and other familiar symbols ran in black ink over his skin, peeking out wherever the dried blood did not cover him.

Like the others, the mortal had entered the glacier through the grotto's portal, seeking to slay the monster, only to become the hunted themselves. No one ever escaped him. He was the shadow. The darkness that haunted this place.

The sweet taste of fear made him salivate. The man remained still on the icy floor despite being unbound. There was no need for restraints; the torture had drained the fight from him.

Twelve times, his captor had killed him. Twelve times, he had ripped him back from the brink. It happened so rarely that he received a visitor. It was only appropriate to draw the occasion out.

The warrior's fingers twitched with desperation to feel his axe in his grasp. Alas, it had landed out of reach.

"Worry not. You shall not die herein," the Ancient One told the man, crouching beside him. "Your soul is not bound for Valhǫll." Only those who died with a weapon in their hand would be allowed entry to the *Hall of the Fallen* in Ásgarðr.

He drew another strained breath, his eyes unfocused and useless in the darkness of the cave. The Ancient One observed him with persistent excitement. His own vision was not impaired by the lack of light.

The man's hair was dark. As were the braids in his beard— no signs of gray. He appeared young. Much younger than the others.

And yet he had ended up like the rest of them, lying in a pool of blood. His own, of course.

The bladed weapons the warriors carried with them were inadequate to cause him injury. He had learned early on that not even the rocks or glaciers of the cave he called home could harm him. Only his own fingernails had the ability to penetrate his skin. They were long and sharp, like the claws of a beast, always ready to tear away at his prey's flesh.

He remembered the first time they had tasted the blood of an unfortunate creature who had stumbled into his domain. Long before his tongue ever had the pleasure.

And what a pleasure it was. With ease, he cut the trespassers open. Watched them bleed out before healing their wounds by forcing his own immortal blood on them. He repeated the process as many times as he wished, studying his subjects with insatiable curiosity, snapping bones, tearing flesh, breaking their bodies over and over to watch them mend.

CHAPTER

I

Winded, they stumbled into the condo. Eve moved backward as she adhered to Kjan's nudging, his tongue leading a bold tango. Her hands ran up his chest, right into his hair, meeting him eagerly.

It was a dance of sorts. He made the steps up as he went along, but she followed effortlessly, their combined shifts fluid and in perfect unison, as if choreographed.

With each click of her heels on the hardwood, she pictured the layout of the new place in her head: a subtle tilt to her left to avoid the corner of the island's granite countertop, a little further down past the spacious kitchen. They both knew it so well that they found their way blindly while reveling deeper in each other's kiss.

Melting against her mouth, he walked her toward the open wall space beside the rows of shelves in the living room. Nimble fingers traced her curves, the sensation as exhilarating as the first time.

The notion of his body being so close to her own still held something forbidden, considering how it had started. Running off into the unknown with your significantly older neighbor was usually frowned upon.

And here he was, Kjan Murphy, the phlegmatic loner from upstairs, running his greedy paws all over her; no more boundaries. He had been all over her on the elevator ride. Hadn't been able to keep his hands off her since they left the car.

Drifting beneath her layers, the velvet pads of his fingertips left a searing trail. She felt him everywhere as their breaths fell into rhythm with each other. He was a buzz across the little hairs on her skin. Sparks fizzled in her belly and crept lower to the junction of her legs.

Eve took the final strides leading up to the dead end behind her. He ripped the sweater over her head, and in a flash, his grasp was back at her neck, firm and confident, raw desire burning through his touch.

His mouth crashed down on hers, trading more air and heat with greater urgency.

Keeping their lips locked, Kjan got busy unzipping her jeans. He yanked the two halves apart and slipped his hands inside against her bare skin.

On a groan thick with erotic charge, he gave her ass a thorough squeeze, making her arch toward him in response. Eve's breath shuddered at the sensation of his broad, warm palms kneading her muscles. The heat spread to where their bodies were joined at the hips, and a very distinct, hard ridge pressed into her.

Breaking from her kiss, he dragged the denim down her legs, the black satin strap of her G-string included. Her ankle boots went flying over his shoulder before he rid her of the fabric entirely.

Settled on his knees, his hungry eyes flipped to hers. The undeniable magnetism of his stare immobilized her. Hooded, deep green eyes riveted to her as he took her in, pupils dilated, breaths heavy.

His tongue licked over his lips, and she bit back a whimper. With nothing but her bra left, he had her pinned between himself and the wall. No escape. No chase. No playing 'hard to get'.

And he knew it.

Kjan was all dominance. He loved to tease her. If her body had a voice, it would be calling his name and begging him to fuck her senseless. Which he'd happily do. Eventually.

She didn't have to articulate her neediness with words, though. He knew the ins and outs of her cues.

The smacking sound of wet, sloppy kisses filled her ears, giving the impression he couldn't decide which part of her to devour first. It was probably an accurate guess. He wanted all of her. And he wanted it now.

#SAME!

"Kjan…"

His name danced across her lips in a plaintive moan. Full-scaled flames licked through her gut, igniting a fire between her thighs as he slowly rose, his palms trailing up the sensitive backside of her legs, tongue at the front, mapping her curves.

The three weeks' worth of scruff along his jaw chased a burn across her skin. Then there were his fangs, pointy and sharp, digging in ever so lightly, not to break the skin but to leave shallow pink marks in their wake, which she was already familiar with. But thanks to him, she healed quickly.

When he reached the underside of her breast, he sank his canines deeper, right through the black lace of her bra. The endogenous morphine secreted by their fangs numbed the pain from his bite, the pressure behind it coaxing a moan from her instead. Fingers twisting roughly through his soft locks, Eve was far from complaining. Kjan was harsh. He was savage. And she ached for it.

Gratified sounds of pleasure escaped his throat as he suckled the welling blood, then a skilled swipe of his tongue sealed the wound.

A mix of heat and moisture flicked across her nipple before rising higher up her front.

Her heartbeat accelerated when his lips stalled at her jugular vein. The unspoken question behind the gesture was loud and clear. Offering your throat meant submitting yourself to another. It was a sign of trust, and it was never to be claimed by force.

Eve tipped her head, baring herself to him. She trusted him with all her heart.

But he didn't bite her. His beard shifted against her skin. Fangs sheathed behind his lips, he pressed a tender kiss to her throat instead. All he wanted was her consent.

"Your blood is too precious, Dove," he reminded her. "You take from me. I don't take from you."

At least not much. She couldn't provide for him the way he did for her.

Yes, they needed blood to survive, preferably of the human variety, but the blood of any vampire older or stronger would do. Having been sired almost a millennium ago in Iceland,

Kjan's blood was as powerful as it came. Powerful enough to sustain them both. Hers, on the other hand, was useless to him.

"You nourish me in other ways." His teeth nipping at her jaw, Kjan straightened to full height, towering over her again.

Gripping the outside of her thigh, he hiked her leg up over his hip. With his other arm coiled around her waist, he worked himself against her.

Breaths sharp, heart racing just like her own, he had her trembling, chasing the sparks in her core until they triggered the longed-for release.

His dark, husky chuckle reverberated across her skin. "You are too easy. I hardly touched you."

"Oh well. I'm sure you'll give me a chance to redeem myself."

Eve never fought the climax. He felt too good, and Kjan wouldn't be satisfied unless he got her off at least three times.

The second he loosened his hold on her, she slid her hands under his shirt and pulled it over his head, exposing his tattoos. She loved touching them and tracing the lines of the designs all over his upper body.

Lazily, she dragged her nails along the shapes on his chest, his eyes following her movement with anticipation. She didn't mind doing a little teasing herself.

Kjan's scowl came down on her, hard, and two heavy thuds followed at either side of her head simultaneously, where his splayed palms slammed into the wall.

He leaned in, leveling his glare at her. "Quit gawking. They haven't changed since the last time you admired them." Then he lowered his lips to the shell of her ear in a taunt. "Do you want me inside of you or not? Because I'm going to finish either way."

"Hypocrite!" He didn't like the shoe on the other foot, did he?

Meeting his impatience, Eve ventured lower. She let her fingertips trace the waistband of his jeans.

His hot breath feathered over her cheek, and a gentle hand angled her face to meet his eyes as his thumb found her bottom lip. Nudging it down to dip inside, he said, "Touch me already. I need to feel your hands on me, Dove."

Hands? She was a breath away from falling to her knees and taking him into her mouth.

As much as he loved to bend her over any piece of furniture readily available, he had yet to make a demand of her in that direction. Eve was happy to fulfill all his desires. Voiced or unspoken.

Why was he holding back?

Was he worried about pushing her too far? Yes, she was new to the rough handling, and he was big, but she could take him.

And to show how eager she was, she closed her lips around his knuckle and sucked. One hand anchored on the waistline of his pants, she popped the button, then released the zipper to free him.

Holding his unrelenting stare, she reached her hand in—

Yay, commando. No fuss.

Eve teased him with a lazy swirl of her tongue as her fingers closed around his thick, pulsing shaft. She swiped her own thumb across the slick bead of pre-cum at the head and didn't miss the shiver that raked through him at that.

His eyes flared. His thumb popped out.

Kjan dipped with a deep growl. He hoisted her up by the back of her thighs, then wrenched her legs apart to brace her against the wall.

Settled in between, he reclaimed her mouth with fervor. Panting with impatience, Eve didn't miss a beat and wrapped herself around him, heels locked at his back, her breasts squished to his chest.

She focused on the poignant friction of his skin against hers, rubbing her sensitive parts. The length of him slid across her slippery entrance every time he drove his hips forward, teasing and taunting.

Eve whimpered. Her nails dug into his shoulders, drawing him into her. The torture was too much.

His strong hands cradled her hips. "Eyes on me, Dove," his voice reminded her.

She met his dark gaze, enlarged pupils leaving only a thin ring of green.

With one swift, almost brutal thrust, he speared her. Not slow. Not gentle. He was possessive when he claimed her, and in that short moment, he needed to see her eyes. Needed to see the pleasure he brought her revealed in them as it reflected in his own.

In that small moment, he claimed more than her body. He claimed her soul. Or maybe reclaimed his own; who knew? What they had was unique. Their love made it extraordinary.

Eve's lips parted in a gasp, the only chance at air he granted her before his mouth crushed back down on hers, feeding her his moans instead. He was no longer careful with her. Knew what her body could handle.

And she let him in. Her contours molded to his, he captured her breath with his mouth, swallowing the whimpers spilling from her lips as he rocked his hips into her, smooth and steady. Their movements aligned without any conscious effort.

Finally acknowledging the dire need for air on both sides, he released her lips. "Don't pass out on me," he rasped rather heavily himself against her cheek.

Eve groaned, "Oxygen is overrated," and then inhaled deeply when Kjan kissed her neck. Softly at first, increasing the urgency as he matched his pace below, tightening the grip on her ass.

More of the squeezing…

…the rolling…

…grinding.

Eve closed her eyes and relished every second, every determined thrust of his hips. His muscles flexed beneath her touch with each powerful stroke, pure and raw masculinity radiating from his body, delving deeper.

"Hold on tight. I'm not going to last much longer. I need you hard and fast."

"Hard and fast," she echoed his words breathlessly while her hips rocked to meet his thrusts.

"More!" His growl burned through her skin straight to her core, with him grinding against her. "That's it, Dove… so good."

Blinding lust peaked in her belly again, viciously racing toward another climax. The itch in her gums flared. She nudged her fangs free, welcoming the relief.

"Come with me," she gasped, deep, heaving breaths sawing in and out of her.

She sank her teeth into the vein at his neck, and the taste of him instantly ricocheted through her like a shock wave down to the very marrow of her bones. The rich wine of his blood, with the distinct flavors of dark chocolate and black cherries, tantalized her senses. The subtle nuance of whiskey tingled on her tongue, burning smoothly down her throat.

Their connection was so much deeper than the physical act. The sliver of his soul, the piece of himself that he'd inadvertently shared by siring her, ignited in her chest as the two halves merged for a brief moment, making him whole.

But they had also consciously chosen each other. Bonded their very DNA by pledging their mind and body to a single mate. With each conscious bite, the vow was reaffirmed.

Eve could hear his heartbeat in her own head and knew exactly when his orgasm hit. The sweet sting of her bite sent him over the edge. He reared back and relented, filling more than her veins. Greedy as she was, she took everything he could give her, and then her own climax detonated in her body like a bomb. Exploding up and out, the flames flooded her veins.

A soft curse spilled from his lips, muffled by the crook of her neck, and his body shuddered against her. She took that as a compliment.

Pressed close, his pace tapered down to a slow grind until they both regained their breath. "You still with me?"

"Like I'd miss this? No way. There is nowhere I'd rather be."

Eve wiped her hand across his forehead. His cheeks were flushed, his eyes alive.

She sucked in her bottom lip as her gaze dropped down for a second. "I love it when you fuck me with your boots on."

They weren't his usual 6-inch Timberlands. He was wearing the taller ones in the work boot style. He looked so hot with them half-laced, his black jeans stuffed inside the loose tops. The eye-catching ruggedness oozed sex appeal.

Kjan snorted a laugh and rolled his eyes at her crude expression. "Heat of the moment," he mumbled, nipping at her lip.

Releasing his hold on her, he let her feet slip to the ground. He gathered her hands in his and drew them to his lips, kissing each one in the center of her palm like he was performing some sort of ritual. Then he placed them at his temples.

"I can feel you... in my head," he says, dipping his forehead to hers, his voice hoarse, their hearts pounding in sync. His hair fell around her face, tickling her cheeks.

"Funny. I was just thinking the same thing."

His warm chuckle made her heart swell. His arms looped around her waist, holding her tightly against his bare chest.

Legs entwined, they ended up on the shaggy rug a little while later, which was so much softer than the hardwood floor of the new place.

Kjan had sold his penthouse in Seattle and taken up permanent residence in Portland, but Eve's 3rd-floor apartment in the University District was hardly worth his standards. He'd moved them into a high-rise in the South Waterfront area on the other side of the Willamette River. The one-bedroom was again on the top floor, and the views of the park and river were amazing, so Eve really didn't mind giving up her place.

Just last week, he'd hired movers to clear out his studio at the farmhouse. Most of his stuff was in storage now until he'd get a chance to sell it.

Of all his old furniture, the black leather wingback was the only piece he kept. For sentimental reasons. Eve had inherited Eleanor's matching chaise lounge—they were an inseparable set after all—and the wicked-looking pair currently sat in their living room.

"I love you," he said for what seemed like the millionth time tonight.

And Eve couldn't get enough of hearing those three words ever since the first time he'd spoken them down in the tunnel.

They were more than just words, though. When she looked into his eyes, she could see his love for her.

"I love you too," she replied.

He'd changed so much in the past month. He seemed to always be smiling now, cracking jokes, and generally glowing. Like he'd been carrying the weight of the world on his shoulders before.

She sighed and frowned.

"What?" he asked, nuzzling her cheek.

"I wish Eleanor could see you like this. So happy. She always wanted this for you."

"I wouldn't be here now if it wasn't for her."

Eve gave him a bittersweet smile. "True. She kept saving your ass to make sure you'd eventually end up here." She paused briefly, remembering their friend. "Will you take me to Paris someday?"

"I will take you anywhere you want, Dove. Just say when."

She brushed her fingertips over the scar on his chest, which he never talked about, and then drifted up to the Helm of Awe tattooed on his right pectoral. *Ægishjálmr*, he called it.

His mouth tightened before he answered, "Except there," shutting down her unspoken request.

Renate Rowland

CHAPTER

2

His chest clenched. *How do we always end up here?* And he didn't mean on the rug. Sooner or later, she would always circle back to his past. To all the things he just wanted to forget about.

He could never go back. A crippling fear chased the memories that still haunted him. Eve was like a damn dog with a bone. Tenacious. He was running out of ideas to avoid the answer.

Kjan pressed his forehead to hers. "Oh, Eve, relentless little dove. What am I going to do with you?" He kissed her again, fangs affectionately biting her plump bottom lip.

"Punish me?" she cooed, grinding her hips into him.

"Hmm, sex is never a punishment. It's a reward."

"A reward for what?"

"For being alive," he replied, still nipping at her lip. "Every time I touch you, I feel this jolt of electricity in my chest." He clasped her hand and placed it over his heart, mimicking the process. "Like defibrillator pedals." Not that he had ever actually been subjected to that, but he knew what it was like to be statically charged to the nth degree.

Eve frowned against his forehead. "Can't those kill people?"

"Not if you're flat-lining. You keep bringing me back to life. That's why I can't keep my hands off you."

"And here I thought I was *your* slave."

His chuckle was soft. "You have it backward, Dove. I'm entirely at your mercy, driven by the need to feel your walls grip me, your body claiming mine. Every day, you choose me anew."

"And sometimes twice," she let out with a laugh.

She wasn't wrong. When he was inside her, that was when he felt truly whole.

"You're addictive. I'll never get my fill." Each touch breathed air into him while leaving him breathless at the same time. She craved his proximity, but he was the one dependent on her. She was his lifeline.

"And you don't have to ask for punishment, Dove." He picked back up on her fetish. "If you want me to spank you, just tell me. I'm open to anything you want to try, and you never have to be shy or embarrassed around me. I'm more than happy to feed your kink. Just know that it will never measure up to mine."

The sound of her laugh flooded him with warmth. "We should hit the nightclubs more often if they have this kind of effect on you. I barely made it out of there with my clothes on."

She moved to get off the floor.

"It's not the clubs that have this effect on me." He pulled her back down, making her crush into his chest. "But I admit I wanted to bend you over the cushioned seats with or without your clothes on," he added, brushing his lips against her neck.

Eve purred in return. Her fingertips skimmed the front of his body and, yep, right down into his pants, which were still unbuttoned.

Ah fuck. He could do this all night.

Rocking his hips into the velvet touch of her palm, he met her halfway. She closed her grip and started stroking him, gently moving her hand up and down, creating a maddening rush of hot and heavy in every fiber of his body.

Kjan couldn't help it. He moaned against her cheek, rolling his forehead lazily across her temple. One hand weaved in her hair, he cradled her head.

He had indeed been tempted to take her right there. It would have been easy, too; he always went commando, unless he wore a suit. There were plenty of dark corners. All he had to do was drag her jeans down over her perfectly-shaped ass and bend her over.

His mind promptly drew up the detailed image, and, what do you know, the throbbing ache increased.

With other women in his past, he had not cared, but with Eve, everything was different. He wanted her all to himself. Didn't want to share their intimacy with anyone. The sweet sounds she made were for him alone to enjoy.

Kjan bit his nails deeper into her lovely thighs as the friction got to him. Fire blazed beneath his skin, spreading fast.

"You're going to make me come again." His breath was choppy. The ragged texture of his voice expressed tenuous restraint.

Eve nudged him onto his back with a ravenous look in her eyes, and for a moment, he thought she was going to mount him, but then her mouth started skating south down his chest—waaaay south—her palm still riding his shaft from head to base.

Fuck no. Not like this. Not while lying on his back.

The sensation surged. The red warning light came on in his head, and his fingers curled into fists, clenching the rug's long shags underneath him.

Even after Anne had escaped her prison, the nightmares from her PTSD had affected them both through his Sire-link. Suffering from it for months had revived his own suppressed trauma. He locked his jaw. His neck stiffened. His whole body grew tense.

"Eve…" Her name left his lips on a groan, the sound hoarse in his throat.

"I want to taste you." Her voice rasped against his skin as she nipped at him.

She went past his abs, her tongue circling his navel, her fangs grazing lower, and Kjan hissed through his teeth. The whisper in his head turned into a roar, and he squeezed his eyes shut to block it out. The need to seize control of the situation was overwhelming. He didn't like being pinned down, feeling defenseless. Every muscle in his body quaked at the familiar sensation. All that rage, and pain, and shame came rushing back.

Well, he wasn't technically defenseless. He knew he could toss her off if things got out of hand, but he didn't want to.

He really, *really* didn't want to.

The fist of his left hand loosened on the rug's shag, and his palm found the fragile back of her neck. Cradling it gently, he forced his eyes open to focus on her.

This was real. *This right here*, not the cave.

He watched while her warm breath feathered across his hypersensitive skin, going lower. One wet kiss at a time, he willed his body to relax and fought his natural urge to take over.

As the slick feel of her tongue met him in a swirling motion at the tip, he let himself go. His hips moved on their own accord before she brought her mouth down on him.

The heat from the seal of her lips fusing them together, she pulled him farther in each time she retreated. He was so close already.

Pleasure exploded behind his eyelids like fireworks when she swallowed to adjust. The back of her throat narrowed, squeezing around the sensitive head, and she took him deeper still.

Tears glistened in her eyes while she held his stare. *So beautiful.*

Fangs sheathed, her tongue greeted him in more languages than even he could speak, and he lost himself in the slow rhythm as she worked him to climax.

Blood whirring in his ears and every muscle in his body a taut wire, threatening to snap, he didn't last. On a violent jolt, he arched off the floor, holding back the curse as he came hard down her throat.

The razor-sharp release raked through him, rendering his limbs useless and his mind senseless for a moment. Or two.

Eventually, he jerked his body off the ground and grabbed Eve's wrists to pull her into him.

"Let me return the favor," he uttered, his breath slowing.

Eve groaned. "As much as I would *love* to continue this, I have to get some work done tonight. I'm pretty sure you do too."

Kjan let her slip out of his grip. "But I do need a shower first," she tacked on.

They had done nothing but screw their brains out for the last three days since he had gotten back from Seattle. He found himself buried inside her the moment his eyes opened at sunset, and when it began to creep over the horizon, he wanted to be inside her again. Any time in between, he still couldn't peel himself off her. Couldn't stop touching her. His body craved the feel of her against him.

Giving her one more chance to change her mind, he called after her, "Want some company?"

"Nice try!" she chirped over her shoulder before disappearing down the hallway.

He sighed deeply, forking his fingers through the matted strands of his hair. It was getting long. It had grown another inch and was now almost resting on his shoulders.

She was right, however. Neither of them had gotten much work done, and they were falling behind. At least she had dropped the issue from before. *Good girl!*

Swiping his shirt off the floor, he changed into something more comfortable and powered on his laptop. As he waited for the thing to respond, he absentmindedly rubbed his neck where she had sunk her fangs into him. The skin was smooth and immaculate. Kjan hadn't fed on blood since leaving Vegas two months ago.

He used to gain a small degree of nourishment from drawing on others' emotions. Fear was particularly satisfying, but hate had always been the one he flocked to. Self-loathing was one of his specialties. Deep hatred was such a strong emotion. He had never met anything close to it.

Then Eve came along. Turned out that her love surpassed it all.

When the computer's screen finally flickered to life, his inbox was already in the triple digits with the usual development contracts and consultant work he kept himself busy with. Eve was looking at pursuing a career in media by branching out her psychology degree into marketing and advertising. She was raking up a nice collection of bachelor's degrees while doing side jobs as a remote intern at various companies.

She had quit her job at Jack's pub but stayed close with her friends and still stopped by regularly to hang out. Kjan was glad she had made a life for herself here, and he couldn't be prouder of her.

Like in Seattle, he had chosen another high-rise condo by the river. The view of the water had always given him a sense of peace, and the few parks in the city broke up the gray landscape. He had always preferred nature over large concrete structures.

Being already familiar with the Portland area himself, he was looking forward to taking Eve to the Colombia River Gorge, which was one of his favorite places. The waterfall reminded him of home, although he would never admit it to her. After that, he was taking her on the aerial tram to watch the sunrise as a sentiment for their first date on the Great Wheel in Seattle. Plus, the view of the mountains here was stunning. Even at night.

He was planning the trip for March 8th, still three months away, but he couldn't wait. He had been thinking about the night he turned her a lot lately. It would be a year to the date, their anniversary, and there was so much more he wanted to show her.

They had time now.

An eternity.

Renate Rowland

CHAPTER

3

Tender kisses grazed the length of her throat, mingling with his coarse beard and the tip of his nose. Grabby hands explored the rest of her curves.

Eve gave a grunt of disapproval, keeping her eyes closed. "It's early."

"It's four thirty in the afternoon," he murmured enticingly, rolling his body into her backside.

"Your sundial tell you that?" She could feel him hard against her hip without him making an effort to point out what he wanted.

A laugh burst from him that tickled the hairs on her nape. "The sun is going down. I can't sleep."

"Well, I can. So, sounds like a personal problem to me."

Kjan didn't appreciate her snark and nudged her onto her back, trapping her underneath him. "I will make it your problem," he cautioned suggestively, his voice thick.

Her eyes flipped open to greet him properly. They both slept naked. For obvious reasons.

"Indulge me." He ran the tip of his nose along the bridge of hers. He was the attention-seeking cat again. A very large, very persuasive cat.

A tingling raced all the way down to her toes. His dark, almost shoulder-length hair fell around his face as he leered down at her. It was starting to rival her own.

Eve's fingers brushed the soft locks back behind his ears. "Wanna borrow a scrunchie?"

"Your jokes are not the kind of entertainment I'm looking for," he remarked impatiently, rubbing his erection against her sweet spot. "Are you going to make me spell it out? I want you. So. God. Damn. Bad."

"*Goddamn?* Come on, is that the best you can do? We both know that's not the word you were thinking of. Don't hold back on my account, I'm not easily offended. Say it," she dared him. "Tell me exactly what you want to do to me."

"Never," he growled with conviction, pressing his mouth to the dip below her jaw.

He acted like he didn't cuss, but she'd heard him let the big one slip on occasion.

"Prude—*huh!*" Her taunting chuckle was cut short by a sharp inhale when Kjan curved two fingers up into her slick passage.

She whimpered, her nails biting into his bicep at the sudden but welcome invasion.

Braced above her, his heave of breath poured hot against her throat, his teeth trailing higher up her chin. Her heart skipped. The pressure of a third finger met her walls as her honey coated him, creating a smooth glide on the steady in-and-out of his motion.

Eve tipped her head back with a prolonged moan, and he brought his mouth down on hers, devouring her breath. Her lips quivered against his. He purposely cut the oxygen reaching her lungs in half. If she wanted to breathe, she'd have to come first.

Which she did on cue, her body answering the unspoken command of his.

Satisfied, his fingers retreated to ready himself at her soaking-wet entrance. With every flick of his tongue, he slid deeper against her pulsing walls. They collared him after the orgasm.

They'd had sex a million times by now, and yet her body never felt used to his size. He forced the last bit in a final sharp thrust, relieving them both of the torture from the anticipation.

"I heard that," she said, acknowledging the nearly inconceivable curse that tangled in his choked breath.

"You want to hear it again?" He retreated, only to plunge right back into her again. "Want to hear how fucking good you feel, Dove. Hot. Wet. Squeezing me and pulling me deeper. Claiming my cock like you own it."

Left hand clasping the front of her throat, he slid her leg over his shoulder, folding her in half while railing into her at a deeper angle.

"But we don't fuck, Dove," he said without stopping. "Fucking is the physical need to get off as quickly as possible. When I bury myself inside you" —*thrust*— "we feed" —*thrust*— "we heal" —*thrust*— "together we are invincible."

Thrust after thrust came at her, harsh like his graphic language, as he wound her body up to another climax.

Eve's eyes rolled back. Spine arched, muscles tight, her own moaning droned on inside her head, blending with his strenuous breaths.

Her orgasm arrived with vicious force, making her toes curl, but Kjan pulled out before he finished.

Her weak leg dropped from his shoulder. Sitting back between her thighs, he spread them apart with his knees, a wicked little grin dancing across his lips. One hand on her hip, he reached for his slick shaft to stroke himself in front of her.

Eve's jaw slackened in awe. The view of him was so much hotter than she'd ever expected. The wolf tattoo on his right arm contorted in sync with the Ægishjálmr on his pec through the flexing of his muscles while his palm worked his length. He was glorious to watch. His ripped abs contracted, head tipped back, lips parted.

On a feral growl, his body shuddered, and hot jets hit her belly, coating her skin as if marking her. She couldn't pry her gaze away. The sight of him finishing like that was intoxicating.

Kjan's eyes met hers, then dropped down to admire his work. "It's a shame I can't keep you like this," he expressed in regret. "You look perfect. Like a masterpiece. I should sign my name under it."

He bit his bottom lip with an accomplished smirk and ran his hand through the mess he'd made on her, spreading it more. Then he dragged it to the traitorous little nub between her legs, which was still tender.

Eve's hips jerked up. Two long fingers slid up into her, and Kjan leaned down, pressing his lips to hers.

"You're so *fucking* perfect," he hissed through clenched teeth.

"So that's your dirty talk?" Eve pressed her hands to his smooth chest, feeling his heart thunder against her palms.

"I prefer to let actions speak." Pulling his slick fingers out, he moved them further back, circling the sensitive rosette of her other opening like a hungry vulture. "Call me prude one more time, and I'll bury my cock somewhere else. I'll make you beg me to give it to you hard and deep before I let you finish. I want to feel your body claiming mine, Dove, over and over, your tight cunt squeezing my fingers in front as I fill you from behind. I'll break you in the sweetest ways before I put you back together."

Shifting his mouth over hers, he spoke so low his voice was all heat, no sound. And yet she heard him loud and clear. Heard his crude words.

Why did they excite her?

She couldn't fight the effect they had on her. The tiny muscles in her core responded to his call—responded even when he didn't voice his desire, and it remained a thought behind that wicked gleam in his eyes.

"You sure are playing fast and loose with your tongue now."

"I could do even more with my tongue." He teased the seam of her lips in a slow circle to prove his dedication.

"So you do have dirty thoughts?"

"I have all kinds of thoughts about you," he drawled while continuing his avid game of 'Ring-Around-The-Rosey' at her rear. "But what exactly makes them dirty? Who gets to decide what's socially acceptable and what's taboo?"

He applied more pressure, as if pointing out that she'd already let him stake his claim there, too. His thumb pressed down hard on her clit at the same time, and the jolt darting through her freed another whimper from her lips.

"Nothing is forbidden between us, Dove."

"Because you made me?"

"No. Because you offered yourself as a gift of your devotion. You gave yourself over to me."

Her body had made that choice when her brain released a high dose of oxytocin, the love hormone, to trigger her instinct to bite him during sex.

His thumb made another rough pass over her button, and she twitched in response. "You're mine," he stressed, his words a fact, not an assumption. "Your body belongs to me."

He had a point. She couldn't shake the authority he held over her. His voice enthralled her like a spell. "So, that's why I have this undeniable urge to please you?"

Her dilemma drew a soft chuckle from him. "The submission must come willingly. You can't possess someone by force. It would never hold." His arm snaked around the small of her back, arching her into him. "A part of you chose this. *That's* undeniable."

His lips hovered above hers. Eve's fingers curled on reflex, her nails clawing his chest.

"And I can't fight the pull any more than you can." Since he had likewise given himself over to her. "But everything you feel, I feel tenfold because I sired you."

His coaxing tone of voice rippled down her throat while he tortured her body with his exploration. Every nerve tingled. Eve felt herself unfurl in his embrace.

"Every bone in my body calls out for you. I get off just watching you come for me. And next time I take you… I won't pull out. I'm going to bury myself deep inside you. Make you scream my name until you're hoarse, and there's no air left in your lungs. I will have you dripping wet… trembling… your legs quivering to hold your body up as I force a chorus of agonizing moans from your lips. I will shatter you into a million pieces, little dove."

Pleasure twisted in her womb. She was so close, his play and his words nudging her toward the edge—

His glorious touch pulled away abruptly right before making good on the promise. A cold, hard wave of disappointment crashed down on her, thwarting the heat of her passion.

"You tease," she cried spitefully.

"Payback! You threatened to deny me. It's only fair I make you wait a little." He gave her mouth a gleeful peck. "Let me wash you first."

A spark of hope rekindled between her thighs at the prospect of picking things up in the shower. He'd likely give her double what he'd withheld just now.

"We have over fifteen hours until sunrise. Plenty of time for me to work your body in any way I can imagine and still get some work done.

Kjan rolled off and reached for her hand to tug her along. "I might even throw in a game of blackjack. Give you another run for my hard-earned money," he offered pretentiously.

The card game was just a sly ploy. It had taken him 0.5 seconds to turn it into strip-blackjack. She could never beat him, so it was a double win for him: he got to keep his money *and* get her naked. Not to mention, they'd end up right where they'd started.

"I might as well not bother putting any clothes on," Eve suggested when he dipped down and scooped one arm under her knees. The other hooked around her back, then her feet lost the feel of the rug.

"But then I would never get any work done." He picked her up as if she weighed nothing. "I only need a few hours, try to keep your clothes on for that long."

"Highly unlikely," she said, linking her hands behind his neck. "They can't seem to stay put in your presence."

Kjan growled, swinging toward the master bathroom. "And you call *me* a tease."

Half an hour later, her boobs smashed into the cold shower tile, his strong arm snaked around her front, angling her hips. The force of the intense orgasm lashed at her muscles. If her toes had been touching the ground, her legs would've given out when it detonated in her core. It was so powerful. Her body had never felt more alive.

Eve's vision blurred, and it wasn't from the water raining down on them. The raw emotions he was able to stir in her left her a wailing mess.

Kjan's forearm, braced against the dark marble next to her face, had kept him from ramming her straight through the wall. He slid free and set her feet down.

"Did I hurt you?" His voice held sincere worry when he spun her around and inclined his head to kiss her forehead.

The fact that he even considers the possibility…

"Never," Eve replied. "I don't think you could if you actually meant to."

"Are you saying I'm taking it too easy on you when we spar?" His eyes had that mischievous twinkle they always got at the prospect of torturing her. "And here I contemplated letting you off the hook tonight after the workout I already gave you. Alas, your big mouth just changed my mind." He reached around her to shut the water off.

"Uhm, I was thinking more along the lines of yoga at the gym in the morning," she said, trying to save herself. She needed a good stretch after all the *exercising* they'd done. And that would still be hours from now.

Grinning from ear to ear like she'd made his night for the third time, he ripped the door of the spacious shower open and tossed her a towel. "Too late."

Crap. She should've kept her trap shut.

∫

Kjan watched her shoulders sag. "How am I supposed to fight someone bigger than me?"

When he was sparring with her, neither of them held back. There was no tapping out. No safe word needed.

They did, however, have a safe *combo.* Eve was good and had put on a noticeable amount of lean muscle mass over the past few months to keep up with him, but sooner or later he would always pin her on her back. That didn't leave her without options: if she bucked him off and reversed the position, they would keep going; if her body went lax, they were done. With the sparring, anyway.

It was always her call.

"Don't be intimidated by size. Remember, pressure points. Eye sockets and groin are the most obvious choices, but there are others you can use against a seemingly superior opponent."

He reached for her right hand and stretched her dainty palm over the front of his deltoid. "Drive your thumb into the brachial plexus above the armpit right here." He demonstrated by pressing down on her thumb with his, digging it deep into the muscle tissue. "There's an intense network of nerves running underneath. Pressure will cause pain and numbness in the hand. A hard blow can even break the clavicle and sever the nerves, causing paralysis."

He lowered her hand but held onto it, readjusting his grip. "Another good pressure point is in the hand. If an opponent is holding on to you, press down on the area between the thumb and index finger."

"Ow-ow-ow," Eve whimpered, immediately collapsing onto her knees as he demonstrated that one on her.

Kjan smirked. He liked the way her brilliant blue eyes were looking up at him. Almost pleading.

"He will likely weaken his grip after that, so be prepared for your next move," he said, pulling her back up to a stand. "Manipulating joints will also work well in your favor. To lock your opponent's joint, push it in an unnatural direction. Take the elbow, for example."

"Wha—" Eve only sucked in half a breath. He didn't give her time to brace for the attack.

His dominant hand firm on her wrist, he gripped the back of her neck with his left before she could anticipate it and gave it a sharp pull. As her head lurched toward the ground, Kjan locked her arm behind her, twisting her wrist outward and forcing her elbow in the wrong direction, just enough to make her wince.

"Immobilize your opponent before he can strike," he suggested.

"Oh, bite me."

She glared up at him from beneath her scrunched eyebrows. Kjan couldn't resist the retort. "With pleasure. But we're not done here yet."

Eve groaned some more. Her anguish amused him.

He released her arm and let her straighten. "You can't rush progress. It takes time. Patience."

"Yes, master."

"Much to learn you still have, young Padawan."

Eve cracked first. Then he joined in, the uninhibited melody of her laughter so bright, so genuine, so *her*.

Kjan had no words to express how much he loved this woman. She was more radiant than any sunrise, her glow and warmth unyielding.

Fisting the front of her t-shirt, he pulled her in for a kiss. Not one that was filled with a lot of heat. He simply needed the taste of her on his lips.

"I don't see you as Yoda," she said with that adorable nose scrunch. "You're more of an Obi-Wan. And I'd rather be Anakin than Luke."

He released her shirt and let his hands skim down her sides to her waist. "You choose to be the villain?"

"I believe he's misunderstood. I like the anti-hero. And I'm a sucker for redemption arcs." Her idle fingertips traced the shape of his pecs, and her touch lingered over his heart.

Kjan raised his brows. "What if *I'm* Anakin?"

"And I'm Ahsoka?" Squinting one eye, she cocked her head to the side, looking up at him. "I can live with that. Just don't go 'dark side' on me." Her tiny fist gave his chest a blow.

He saw her more as his Padmé.

"How good is your pop-culture knowledge?"

"Eh, so-so." He kissed her forehead. "Depends on the decade. I'm pretty good with 90s movies."

"That's a little before my time."

"Yeah, rub it in, *youngling*," he mused, nuzzling the hairline at her temple.

A furrow formed in her brow. "Joe made me watch some of his favorites. He called them *classics*."

Kjan noticed the change in her expression as soon as she mentioned her uncle. Her mood took a drastic turn he hadn't anticipated when suggesting they spare tonight. It was the quiet, pondering moments in front of the laptops he tried to avoid.

Why would she put herself through this?

CHAPTER

4

A queasy sensation uncoiled in his gut.

Kjan shut his laptop. Elbows resting on the counter, he raked his fingers across his scalp.

Eve had gone to the gym on her own and was due back a quarter past seven. The digits above the stove to his right read 07:54 a.m.

She was late. And it wasn't like her to run errands without letting him know.

Eve still insisted on going to the gym once a week, although he had made his opinion on the matter clear numerous times. He had offered to take her, not wanting her out alone, but she had shut him down. The argument had caused so much tension between them two weeks ago that he had simply given in to prevent another fight.

He understood that she wanted to be independent and agreed to give her more freedom. As long as she kept him in the loop, he wouldn't control every aspect of her life.

Even if it went against his nature.

His leg bounced on the footrest of the bar stool as he tried her phone again. She hadn't answered the first time, nor had she replied to his text.

He wasn't going to stay home and wait any longer. The yoga class was over at seven, and she always came straight back. His worry felt justified.

Kjan handled the Charger with the usual lead foot and shortly pulled into the gym's parking lot, which by now had started to fill up.

He didn't glimpse her baby blue Beetle in any of the spots and circled around for a second time just to make sure, but he couldn't sense her presence. She was too far out of range.

With little hope but not much else to go on, he dialed her number a third time.

No answer.

Fuck!

He hated this feeling. The unknown. Too many variables. Too many threats. *If anything happened to her…*

His leg started twitching again. Eve had clearly left the gym already and should have been on her way home. Perhaps she took a different route, and he had just missed her.

His eyes shot to the cell in his hand. That wouldn't explain why she wasn't picking up her phone.

As he tightened his grip around the useless gadget, the Charger's engine sputtered. The unhinged rage flaring in him required something other than blood for fuel, and if he didn't cool his temper, he would end up sucking the juice out of the car.

He pinched the bridge of his nose. The bright sunlight aggravated his corneas. He preferred the dark.

Discouraged, Kjan exited the parking lot, taking the long way home by avoiding the Interstate. He passed a black pickup truck on the side of the road that was facing the wrong direction and missing most of its front end. Traffic was slow, but not too bad anymore. He figured the accident must have happened a little while ago.

His adrenaline spiked again. He could see the lights of an ambulance flashing up ahead.

An icy jab of panic shot through his nerves. Kjan slammed on the brakes, his scalp tingling as the blood drained from his face. He recognized the crumbled blue mess, no longer obscured from his view by the truck.

He swerved the Charger onto the shoulder and jumped out. Ignoring the other vehicles, he rushed toward the flashing lights. His heart had a bad case of the hiccups, loud enough to drown out the noise.

This was it. His worst nightmare.

∫

Eve sat in the back of the ambulance, feeling like the child who got sent to the principal's office. The sky was a clear, bright blue this morning, and the unhampered rays prickled her skin.

She was supposed to have been home at sunrise. Kjan didn't want her outside during the day. Especially not without him.

She'd heard the Charger approaching from half a mile away and knew that he must've been out looking for her. She didn't want a lecture.

"Are you okay?" He studied her appearance with the most scrutinizing expression, and she knew he was looking beneath the surface, reading her aura for any signs of distress.

Eve rolled her eyes. "I'm fine."

"She was lucky," the paramedic mentioned over his shoulder. "Not a scratch."

"Can I go now?" She'd been sitting here for far longer than necessary, considering the glorified nurse had just confirmed she was unharmed. She'd given the police officer her statement too, and they would handle the beetle's tow. Her presence was no longer required.

"Yep. You're all set."

She hopped out of the back, catching the grim look on Kjan's face from the corner of her eye as she beelined for his car. No doubt she was about to get an earful.

"I'm sorry," she started as soon as he got behind the wheel. "I would've called, but my phone is somewhere in that crushed tin can of a car. I didn't mean to worry you."

He kept his eyes on the road in front, hands firm at ten and two. "You shouldn't have gone out," he said in that judgmental tone of his. The 'I told you so' was implied.

"Oh, like you knew this was going to happen? The guy was going the wrong way and hit me head-on. That could happen to anyone," Eve argued.

"But it happened to *you!*"

'The fuck? Was he blaming her for attracting bad luck? "What's that supposed to mean?"

His hold on the steering wheel strained, knuckles turning white as he clenched and unclenched his grip. "I don't care about anyone else, Eve. I only care about *you*," he clarified, eyes still facing straight ahead, his voice no longer reproachful.

Eve sighed loudly, folding her arms, clutching the parka to her chest. She decided not to give her defense any more airtime, and they rode the rest of the way in silence. She'd have better luck talking to a wall.

As soon as they were through the door, Kjan yanked her shirt up to inspect her for injuries.

"The paramedic already checked me, and you do know that I can heal, right?"

"Doesn't matter. I don't like the idea of you getting hurt. Besides, I can do a much more thorough inspection of your body." He grabbed a hold of her wrists and drew her into his chest, staring down into her eyes with those deep green emeralds of his.

"You're doing it again. Patronizing me," she tacked on in case he didn't know what she was referring to.

"I'm sorry. I don't mean to, I swear." Kjan cradled her face and leaned down to kiss her. So soft, so gentle, as if he were suddenly afraid to break her or shatter her with his touch. "When I saw your car… it scared me to death."

Eve eased forward to lean her head against his chest. His arms closed around her, hugging her tightly to him, and his lips brushed against her hair in another tender kiss.

She relaxed into the warm comfort of his embrace. She knew he meant it and couldn't blame him for being concerned about her safety. She *did* have a record of attracting bad luck. But he made her feel delicate—fragile even—and she was neither of those.

Her opposition dwindled. She didn't want to argue anymore. "I'm tired," she said, pulling away.

Kjan took her hand and led her to bed. He seemed as exhausted as her when he chucked his boots and pulled her down next to him.

"Take my vein," he offered nonetheless, sweeping the loose hair behind her ear and brushing her cheek.

Eve wasn't going to argue with him, even if she didn't feel the need to. She knew it was more for his peace of mind than out of necessity. He always put her first, sacrificing himself in a heartbeat.

She was his number-one priority.

5

Her eyes focused on the clock beside him. They had both passed out shortly after she'd fed from him, and Kjan seemed to still be asleep next to her now.

At some point during the day, he'd taken off his shirt. Lying on his chest, he was facing away from her. She stretched across his huge upper body and slithered her arm underneath him.

He stirred. Lacing his fingers through hers, he dragged their hands up to his chest.

Eve felt the even beat of his heart and automatically matched her breathing to his. With her eyes closed, she kissed the inked branches of *Yggdrasill* between his shoulder blades, the tree of life and death that connected the *Nine Realms*. Its roots formed the shape of Thor's hammer, *Mjǫllnir*, in the middle of his back. She'd rather not try to pronounce the name herself, but from his tongue, it came effortlessly.

He was right. She did admire his tattoos any chance she got. She remembered the night she'd first asked him about them. It wasn't a subject he liked to talk about, but she couldn't understand why. He'd told her everything about his former mate Andromeda, the first one he'd sired before her, and shared a lot of the time he'd spent as a vampire, yet she knew nothing about him as a human.

Her fingertips found the distinct irregular texture of the somewhat egg-shaped scar beneath the Muninn tattoo right above his heart. She'd notice the minuscule variation in the ink on his arms. They looked like touchups he'd gotten over the course of a millennium. Where the skin healed, the artwork obviously did not.

The ink of both his ravens appeared in a slightly different shade if the light hit it just right. It was more like her own, a mixture of crushed aspirin and salt to seal the design into their resilient skin without healing right over. It was clear he'd added those *after* becoming a vampire.

Most of his tattoos were older, though. From the time he'd still been human, she gathered. But that scar…

No human could have survived that.

Eve thought of the wooden stake he'd used on Andromeda. Splinters had left scratches on the inside of his palm that were still visible. Any knife wound she'd ever seen on him had healed flawlessly in comparison, but that specific type of wood caused permanent damage to the skin tissue.

What connection was she missing? What was he hiding?

"Kjan," she said quietly over his shoulder, resting her chin on top of her free hand on his back. "What were you like? When you were human? I want to know—"

"Eve," he tried to cut in, but once she was on a roll…

"You always avoid my questions. I know you don't want to talk about it, but it's part of who you are and who you used to be," she rambled on before he'd interrupt her again. "Andromeda said you used to be different, but nothing in your past can ever change the way I feel about you. I want to know all of you."

Kjan remained silent, the way he always did when she touched on a topic that he wasn't entirely comfortable sharing with her. For a reason she couldn't explain, it irked her that he didn't trust her with his secrets. It was the final layer he wouldn't let her penetrate.

Eve waited. Hoping. She knew he could feel the tumult in her. Taste it in the air like a fog between them.

He exhaled slowly. Then the muscles in his back contracted beneath her.

When Eve lifted off him, he shifted, his head turning to face her. "That's not what she meant."

He paused, trying to figure out the right words to say, his darkened eyes darting back and forth between hers. "After I turned her, I kept her isolated for too long. Only had her feed from my vein. No human contact. We hid underground most of the time for nearly a century."

He averted his gaze in what she assumed was shame and rose onto his elbows. "I wanted to keep her safe, but I couldn't protect her from myself."

Twiddling his thumbs, he chewed his lower lip. The tip of a brilliant white canine flashed for a split second. "I killed a lot of innocent people, Eve. Women and children, too. I didn't care. I didn't care much about anything back then. I was angry. I was in a really bad place… for a really long time. Long before I corrupted Anne."

Andromeda had been his mate for 180 years until he took her out of commission for overindulging in humans. Eve had assumed their falling out had led to his depression. He'd spent another 120 years trying to cope with the guilt of betraying her, punishing himself, believing he didn't deserve to be happy. This was the first time he made it sound like his issues preceded the psychotic blonde who'd attempted to kill her to get revenge on him. According to his own words, he'd never truly loved Andromeda. Not the way he loved *her*. But if not love, what else could bring on a state of self-destruction the likes of his?

"Why were you angry?" Eve wondered. Did he become a vampire by coincidence, like her? Would he have preferred death?

"A lot of reasons." Refraining from refocusing his eyes on her, he shook his head as if he were clearing it. "I was angry at things that were beyond my control. Anne was a distraction from that. She was only seventeen when I met her. Hunting came naturally to her. She looked so young, men underestimated her. Saw her as easy prey when, in fact, it was the other way around. She was ruthless. Especially when bored. But I had no right to judge her. I was just like her in the beginning."

"Your Sire didn't teach you?"

"I had to learn on my own."

She blinked at him. "So you killed to survive," she justified.

That must've been so hard. For the eleven years she'd known him, he'd never once appeared to take pleasure in hurting others. Feeding without taking too much required skill. How long had it taken him to master it? He had to carry that burden alone.

Eve imagined herself in his place. How many humans would she have murdered? Would she have been able to master control the way he had?

Being responsible for the deaths of others? Eve shuddered.

"I was so much worse," Kjan went on. "It even earned me a few nicknames."

"Like the *Ancient One*?" She recoiled. The memory of her ex sent an uncomfortable shiver through her spine.

His muscles tensed, and his gaze shot back to her, narrowing. "Where did you hear that?"

"That's what Jordan called you." Right after he'd kidnapped her to use as his personal battery, *and* just before Andromeda had ripped him to shreds. "He said he had been tracking you for a century and finally followed the trail to the States. I mean, I get it. You know… you're *old*," Eve teased.

But Kjan wasn't laughing. A dark shadow flickered across his face, and he looked serious, as if brooding over something. He rolled onto his back, his slow, apprehensive motion a sign of dread.

She didn't like it. "What's wrong?"

"I have been called many things, Dove, but never that," he explained.

"What do you mean?"

"I don't think Jordan was talking about me."

"Then who?" Eve couldn't be sure, but his face showed more than just concern. Kjan looked scared. His jaw tensed underneath his beard.

"I think, he was talking about my Sire," he replied, the wheels in his head spinning visibly faster. "He mentioned he followed him to the States? Are you sure?"

"Yes, that's what he said." Eve nodded her head with conviction. "Why? Is that bad?"

ᚴ
⟨HAPTER

6

K jan sat up straight with his back to Eve and rubbed his face. Besides Andromeda, Eleanor, and Charlotte, there had been one other significant woman in his life. The one he refused to ever think about. She was the one who had put him on his immortal path.

Or rather, her death had.

He swallowed hard. He couldn't believe he was really going to do this now, but like his inevitable confrontation with Anne, he couldn't avoid this any longer either.

How would Eve react?

He tried to take a deep breath to rally up the courage to get through it, but his lungs were tight. The weight on his chest was so heavy the air caught in his throat. His whole body went numb.

He squeezed his eyes shut, then he saw them in front of him: the mother and child.

"I was married," he blurted.

It sounded so strange to hear the words out loud. It was so long ago. A lifetime.

"When I was human… I had a wife."

A ragged sigh rushed out of him as his shoulders dropped a little. His most coveted secret was finally out in the open.

"She died in childbirth," he went on with a faint rasp. "So did our daughter. She was too small to live."

No heartbeat… couldn't claim her as his own… couldn't even give her a name according to the old laws…

"She was dead before I ever held her."

Yes, he had loved once, with all his heart, and he had lost everything. He couldn't do that again. Couldn't face that endless abyss again. That was why he had never let anyone in. Not even Anne, whom he had claimed as his mate. That had been desperation and guilt, but not love. He couldn't make himself vulnerable to that kind of pain again.

"I-I couldn't handle the loss. I was so desperate to join them."

He felt the tremble in his voice as much as he heard it. "Back then… I still believed. I believed in the stories of our Gods and that they walk among us. If I took my own life, I would never be allowed entry to reunite with them. I had to find a different way."

He recalled the sliver of hope that had sparked when Charlotte poisoned him. The hope of a reunion after all, because he had not succumbed to taking his own life. There had been a chance of seeing her again.

"I had heard tales of an immortal being… something evil, roaming the glacier. People who ventured too close would suddenly collapse, their strength drained by a force surrounding it. They woke weakened, with no recollection of what had caused the exhaustion. The ones who dared to enter were never heard from again. I thought… I thought if I fought the creature and it killed me, I would die a warrior's death, and the doors to Valhǫll would open for me."

Nothing but blackness in front of him, Kjan paused and swiveled his head, reliving the pain he had felt then. "I was wrong. Instead, the doors would forever stay closed."

The bed creaked as Eve shifted closer. She looped her arms around him, and her chin dropped onto his shoulder. He could feel her stare burning into him, but he regained his composure and managed to open his eyes.

"What happened in the cave?" she asked with apprehension.

His vision out of focus, it traveled over the sheets, unable to lift to her. He was somewhere else in his head.

He felt alone again.

"I remember how dark it was down there. No way for light to force its way through. I never saw his face. He was only a voice. His words echoed off the walls like he was the cave itself. He told me who he was. Told me his story, claiming to be the illegitimate son of Hǫðr and Iðunn."

"Who?"

He sensed Eve's question more than he actually caught the sound of it in his ears. Sometimes it baffled him that people had forgotten the Old Gods so easily. Christianity was practically based on Pagan traditions; although nobody chose to acknowledge the facts. Tweak a myth here and there, *et voilà*, you've got Christmas. Who did they believe was Santa Claus?

"A son of Óðinn," Kjan went on. "Hǫðr is the God of Darkness, who killed his own twin brother. Iðunn , the Goddess of Eternal Youth, in charge of caring for the *Apples of Immortality*. Supposedly, they had a secret child together, whom she kept hidden in a cave in our world, raising him on the apples. Frigg, mother of the twins, discovered the child's existence after the death of Baldr by his brother's hand and put a curse on the boy.

"The stories are rather vague about Frigg, but she is often believed to be a different form of Freyja, a Vanr Goddess with powerful magic. She used a spell to confine him to perpetual darkness and bind him to the cave. According to the legend, he became the first vampire."

Okay, some of that wasn't official lore, so he couldn't fault anyone for not knowing the sagas.

Eve stayed silent, listening to his story and clinging to every word. It took another moment before he was ready to face her, but when he did, there was no judgment in her eyes.

Kjan turned his body, dropping his forehead on hers. His breaths smoothed out. Her presence was his comfort. It seemed contradictory to believe a woman's gentleness could become a man's armor, and yet that was how she made him feel. She *chose* to let him in. *Chose* to receive him. In her arms, he felt invincible.

Reaching up to cup the back of her head, fingers splayed through the silk of her hair, he breathed her in, the scent of spring flowers and sweet berries soothing his pain.

When she spoke, her voice was barely more than a whisper, as if she didn't want to break the trance he had slipped into. "So, if he's the first vampire ever, does that mean you're the second?"

"No."

He may be different, but Kjan didn't consider himself that significant. "Too many cultures have their own myths, and they could be just as true."

And just because he hadn't met anyone like him in a long time, didn't mean they didn't exist. He had kept himself fairly concealed for over 950 years. Who was to say others didn't as well?

"Besides, he said he had turned more before me and suggested I seek them out. After leaving the cave, I followed a trail of rumors leading back to Ireland. I eventually did track down a few vampires there, but none of them were over a century old. Most of them had been turned within the last few decades. They confirmed the myth and told me stories of humans hunting some of us down and others being killed by our own kind over quarrels." He scoffed, forcing a smirk. "Turns out, vampires are fickle and have quite the temper."

"Surprise-surprise," Eve joked sarcastically.

Kjan let out a long sigh and pulled back, giving her space. His hand dropped down to hers, and he rubbed his thumb across the center of her palm. "He is considered a God among our kind, Eve. Nobody knows how old he is, but he never leaves the sacred caves. He's bound to them. Jordan must have made a mistake and gotten his intel wrong."

But if Kjan was so sure his Sire couldn't get out, why had he been running his entire life?

"Probably. He wasn't the brightest." Eve snorted a laugh. "He had this crazy theory that his sperm kept women from aging."

Kjan looked her dead in the eye, no hint of amusement. "That's the dumbest thing I have ever heard." If the guy wasn't already dead, he would very much enjoy tearing him limb from limb for laying a hand on Eve. He should have thanked Anne for ridding the world of that asshole.

"I know, right? But then I had to think of Eleanor and how she didn't look like an eighty-year-old lady."

Huh. Perhaps the son of a bitch had been on to something. Hell, every time he'd fed on Eleanor, the healing proprieties of his saliva entered her bloodstream, and the high white blood cell count wasn't just in his blood. It was in other transmittable bodily fluids too.

Kjan pursed his lips, then shrugged, stifling a sly grin. "I like to think it was my magical presence that kept her young."

Eve let out a weak laugh, then her expression turned grim. "But he called him Kjartan. *Your* name."

"I don't know. As far as I am aware, the bastard son of Hǫðr doesn't have a name."

His own father's name, Mýrkjartan, was an Icelandic appropriation of the Irish name Muirchertach. It was specific to the region, so whoever Jordan had been tracking had a common past with Kjan.

Cold dread snaked beneath his skin like icy tentacles. Where did their paths cross?

Eve's full lips twisted to one side. "Hmm. So if he's been stuck in a cave for that long, how does he feed?"

"He doesn't."

"I don't understand."

Join the club. "He's different, Eve. Nothing like other vampires. The rules don't apply to him." He was an immortal. The son of two Gods. For all they knew, he couldn't be stopped.

Or killed.

Eve glanced down at his hand in hers. She could tell his fingers had gone cold. He could barely feel her touch anymore. Her questions kept riding his panic button.

"But what if he suddenly decided to leave and show up here?"

"Highly doubtful." No. He was trapped. Imprisoned. Had to be. Kjan tried to connect the dots another way. Any other way. There had to be a different explanation.

"Shouldn't we at least consider it and maybe do our own research?" She quirked a brow, lips pressed into a thin line.

Kjan withdrew his hand and raked it through his crown, rubbing the top of his head. "I'm pretty sure Jordan just got his information mixed up along the way and confused me with him."

Perhaps if he heard the words out loud, he could believe them too. He gave her a quick half-shrug and moved toward the edge of the bed, retrieving his shirt from the floor.

"But—"

"Please, Eve. I'm begging you, let it go," he said without turning around, shoving his head through the hole and tugging the fabric down over his ribs.

He couldn't go there. Couldn't give her any more details. The nightmares had haunted him long after and were the reason why he had never turned anyone before Andromeda. Unlike turning her and Eve, his personal *experience* had been much different.

Kjan remembered the stories about the Blood Eagle ritual being performed as part of certain Viking executions, during which the ribs of the prisoner were severed from the spine and spread out like wings. He imagined what he had been through was similar to that—unimaginable pain that lasted for an eternity.

He had no idea how long he had been down in that glacier… trapped with HIM. Sprawled out on his back on the uneven ground of the dark grotto. Paralyzed, presumably from loss of blood and shock, he had been utterly helpless as the *Ancient One* had taken his own axe to cut him open.

But he had felt the invisible hand reaching into his rib cage, closing his grip around his heart, and squeezing it slowly.

With his nail, the creature had made a cut, slicing through the thin tissue of the organ. Kjan had been able to track the event by sound alone but lost consciousness after that.

Eve could never know. He would take this secret to his grave.

⎰
CHAPTER

7

Wow! She finally understood why he'd held back about his past this whole time.

Eve stood at the kitchen island. Her back toward the patio, she leaned across the cool granite top, chin propped on one hand. She couldn't concentrate on school tonight. Her mind fixated on Kjan. It had taken a lot of guts to confide in her, but the weight was finally off his shoulders, and his honesty meant everything to her.

Frigg—Eve had seen the Goddess's name in books before. He'd pronounced her name with a sharp *ck*-sound at the end, despite the spelling. She wondered which other names she'd ignorantly mispronounced.

A steel arm hooked around her waist from behind, jerking her body upright. As if he'd read her thoughts, Kjan had sneaked up behind her, trapping her in an embrace. He'd been on a work call outside. All wrapped up in her head, she hadn't even heard the door slide open.

Amused by her high-pitched squeak, his bright, elated laugh had a weightlessness to it that almost seemed juvenile. The heavy darkness from earlier had thankfully dispersed.

"You stick your bubble butt out like that, and I might just forget my manners. I grind you right through that granite if you let me."

Eve cringed. "Yeah, let's put a pin in that one."

"Scared, Dove?" he growled softly. His teeth raked her throat just below her ear, offering a shiver of pleasure. One hand wedged between her thighs in front, the other tightly around her rib cage, he locked her in a snare against his chest.

"Never." Her steady voice validated her confidence. "I trust you completely."

He took that as a challenge and spun her around. Fingers twirled in her hair, he jerked her head backward and crushed his lips to hers, kissing her viciously. With his arm around the small of her back, he raised her up to him. His hold on her was as unrelenting as ever. He showed her no mercy.

Not even when she heard the ringer on his earpiece go off, which reminded her that she needed to replace her phone and text Tanya.

With a quick press of the button, he rejected the call, then plucked the bud from his ear altogether and blindly tossed it somewhere onto the counter to give her his undivided attention.

But no matter how much Kjan physically dominated her, she had him wrapped around her finger. She brought this out in him, and she could take it away. When they were together like this—in bed, on the table, or on the floor—he would hand over control to her. Never took it further than she wanted.

Eve knew it wasn't easy for him. Control was his safety net. He thrived on it, always afraid something bad would happen if it slipped from his grasp. Her voice was the only control he granted her—because her body was so unreliable; it simply couldn't say no to him. But if she asked him to stop, she knew he would. Or at least she was convinced that he would. The word had yet to pass her lips.

"How about we hit the Pearl District tonight?" Eve suggested, once he let her come up for air. "Or maybe just a walk by the river? I feel like stretching my legs for a bit. I can't sit anymore."

Kjan's nose pressed against her cheek. "Sounds good."

"I hope they put up some Christmas lights by now."

Eve got quiet, remembering her uncle back home. She hadn't seen him in months. She still believed she'd made the right decision by cutting all ties to her old life, but that didn't mean she didn't miss Joe. He'd raised her after all. Christmas was especially hard, even with Kjan doing his best to cheer her up.

"What's wrong?" he asked, letting her weight slip through his hold. He had obviously felt the shift in her mood.

"I was just thinking about Joe."

Kjan slid his left arm around her shoulders, bowing his head towards her. His lips grazed her forehead as his thumb stroked up and down the side of her arm. He knew how hard the decision had been for her, and there was nothing he could say to make Eve feel better about it. Instead, he just pulled her into a hug, and that was better than any words.

She could feel the warmth of his breath on her skin before he kissed her temple, and then she practically melted into him.

ſ

Kjan kept a leisurely pace, their hands linked.

"Is there actually anything you're *not* good at?" Eve asked while they strolled along the Eastbank Esplanade.

After getting her a new phone, they had taken a couple of rounds at the ice skating rink, but she had called it quits after making a '*complete fool of herself*'. Her words, not his.

"Why would you ever challenge me in a winter sport?" he mocked her. "I learned to ski the day I could walk. I practically invented that."

"Okay, you're right, that was on me. Still, I didn't intend to land on my butt." She winced. "Twice."

The walkway on the east side of the Willamette River was almost deserted at night now, one week into December. But neither of them minded the cold. It was much more peaceful this way, and Kjan could see why Eve loved the view of the skyline from the east side of the river. There were thousands of lights everywhere: on the bridges, trees, and even on the rails and buildings.

"Are you okay? You're awfully quiet tonight," Eve observed after they had been walking for an hour.

Through their bond, she could sense his surface emotions just as easily as he could sense hers. He had meant to cheer her up and take her mind off Joe, but instead, he had been the one distraught all night while dealing with the aftermath of his confession.

He forced a smile, trying not to let it show and kill her buzz. "Fine. Just enjoying the view."

Kjan stopped and leaned back against the floating bridge's handrail, gently tugging on her hands to join him. Whisps of her hair blew in the light breeze, and her cheeks were flushed from the cold. He watched the twinkling lights around them dance on her skin as her eyes sparkled like little stars.

"Beautiful," he said under his breath, still gazing at her twin set of blues. Her face was glowing, and he wanted to remember that look on her forever. Burn it into his memory. Never let himself forget.

The guilt was eating him alive. *How could I let this happen?*

He kissed first her right and then her left hand before releasing them to wrap his arms around her waist and pull her closer. Her parka was open at the front, just like his coat, and the heat radiating from her pressed against him, penetrating every cell in his body.

"Told ya." She winked, tilting her head up. A chestnut-colored strand drifted across her forehead.

"I never doubted your judgment, Dove." He swept her hair back behind her ear because it obstructed his view. He couldn't envision living without the image of her.

Her flowery fragrance flared in his nose. He considered bottling it up to preserve it.

One more thing that faded, like all the other little details that once seemed so insignificant.

Her soft smile vanished, her sharp gaze searching his. "Are you sure you're okay?"

His thumb grazed her jawline, and he tilted her chin an extra inch. "Perfect," he whispered against her mouth, leaning down to kiss her.

Words couldn't convey all the feelings surging through him. His tongue teased the seal of her lips, and they parted to let him in.

Eve got up on her tiptoes to link her arms further around his neck, and he tightened his hold on her. His body lit up like a torch. It wasn't close enough. Voracious desire twisted his gut. He wanted her naked against him. Feel her warm skin under his touch.

His voice was a starving rumble as he pleaded, "Home?"

"Yes!" Eve agreed without hesitating.

Kjan forced himself to ease up on the gas pedal. Getting her home at a reasonable pace sounded inconceivable, but being pulled over would cause a most tragic delay he had no desire to face. His muscles ached thinking about everything he wanted to put them both through. They screamed with the need to take her up to their bed and savor every glorious inch of her.

Back at the condo, his patience strained again. They had company on the elevator, and he hated having to keep his hands to himself.

Fuck being decent.

He took the spot in the corner and backed Eve into him, keeping her tight against his front. She didn't need to see his face to know how badly he wanted her. Her delicious little gasp at the contact confirmed her awareness.

Kjan's hand dipped under her sweater. He dragged it slowly higher until his fingertips brushed the delicate lace of her bra. From his high angle, he could see her biting her bottom lip to keep from making a sound and drawing the attention of the other couple. They had their backs to them, and he wanted to keep it that way.

Watching her was such a turn-on. He wanted to sink his teeth into the soft flesh of her neck, where it protruded from her parka.

He lazily trailed his kisses lower down her neckline until he found the right spot. Then he grazed his fangs over her sensitive skin, giving her a fair warning.

Eve caught the hint. Her hands reached back, twisting her fingers around the hem of his shirt, preparing herself for his bite. Her body tensed in his arms, but she didn't make a sound as he sank all four canines in.

Such a good girl.

The other couple got off on the next floor, and Kjan withdrew his teeth, licking his tongue over the puncture wounds to seal them in case there were other prying eyes on them. Drunk on the rich, exhilarating taste of her blood, he spun her around and crushed his mouth to hers, cradling her head in both hands, lips parted, perfectly ravenous.

The elevator doors opened again as they reached the top floor. Unlike his old place in Seattle, there were two penthouse suites in this building. Kjan dragged her to the right while fiddling with the keys and nearly took the door off its hinges.

Eve slipped from his grasp. She chucked her coat and made a run for the bedroom.

He was right on her heels, however.

Catching up with her inside the doorway, his arm snapped around her waist in a firm grip, effortlessly picking her off the ground. The swell of her ass tucked neatly against him, she wriggled and squirmed in his hold. He savored her weak attempts. Savored the whimpering objections. Savored every little sound escaping her lips as he tossed her onto the bed.

Eve scrambled up, reaching for the fly of his pants, but he cut her off. Grabbing her behind the knees, he gave a sharp pull, and she plummeted onto her back.

He took hold of her wrists and locked them over her head, leaning down, hovering over her. "I have all night. I don't want to rush this," he said softly, nuzzling her neckline.

He needed to hold on. Needed to remember. Another thousand years from now, her image had to remain branded into his memory.

She wrapped her legs around him and rolled her hips to meet his. "Good luck," she challenged, working herself against him.

He accepted with a moan that sounded more like a deep growl, but when it came down to it, he knew he had more self-control than she did.

He skimmed his fangs down the column of her throat and sank them through her knit sweater into her shoulder. She climaxed right then and there, her body convulsing underneath him as she arched her back.

One down, he thought, inhaling her sweet berry and spring flower scent. He would keep her going until sunrise.

♪

Eve's head was spinning. That orgasm had come out of nowhere. She hadn't even realized she'd been so close.

He had known, though, hadn't he? *Damn.* He could really read her like an open book.

"*Soooo* easy," he emphasized again.

His dark and wicked chuckle had a direct line to her core. The sound coiled in her belly. She couldn't help it, she loved this man. It didn't take more than a look from him to make her wet.

Kjan released her wrists and pulled away to shrug out of his coat, then he reached behind his head, grabbing the back of his shirt and removing that, too. With her legs still shaking, he had no trouble slipping out of her pathetic trap.

Sitting up, he placed his knees on the outside of her thighs to keep her from wriggling her way out. "Just so you don't get any wild ideas," he justified with a smug grin as she pouted.

His large, warm hands slipped underneath her sweater and around her back, lifting her off the bed to do the up-and-over. He dipped his head and reclaimed her mouth, undoing the front clasp of her bra and gradually sliding the straps down her arms.

The slow suspense sent a shiver of impatience down her spine.

He nudged her back onto the pillow, kissing her throat and the stretch of her sternum. His long hair tickled softly, the scruff of his beard rougher in comparison as he suckled her breasts. His gratified moans hummed through her rib cage.

With the pop of the button on her jeans came the release of the zipper. Kjan scooted down, stripping the rest of her clothes, then did the same with his, kicking off his boots as a result.

Eve opened her mouth to voice her complaint.

"Dealer's choice," he said with a cocky tip of his head.

She screwed her mouth shut without further objection and watched him undress at the foot of the bed, his massive pecs flexing as he moved. The muscles in her thighs twitched in response. He was magnificent from every angle.

Eve reached for his shoulders the second he drew near again, her hands too small to grasp them fully. The skin on skin contact set her aflame. She wanted him closer. Wanted to feel more of him covering her.

Despite another groaning protest from her, he stayed true to his word about keeping it slow. He rolled onto his side and laid beside her, entwining their limbs.

With his leg wedged in between her thighs, he shaped her contours into his. The friction became slick.

As his mouth and hands mapped every inch, her motion grew more fierce, ruthlessly chasing another surge in her belly. Countering her movement, his touch roamed the curves of her body at will, from the tender mounts of her breasts down to her waist, squeezing her hips while she rode his thigh.

Her pulse quickened. She could feel the second wave rising to swallow her up.

"Come for me, Dove. I want to hear you," he breathed against her lips.

Eve came apart with a shuddery cry as another release washed over her, the throbbing ache between her legs sending ripples of pleasure through every fiber of her being.

Kjan granted her no rest. One arm tightly coiled around her waist, he guided his dominant hand down between them until his moan told her he found what he was looking for.

His thumb rubbed over her in little circles, and Eve winced. "I'm too sensitive."

"You want me to stop?"

"No."

"You sure?"

"Yes. Please don't stop."

His chuckle was dark and sexy. "Say that again."

"Please, Kjan, don't stop touching me."

"I love it when you beg me." He paused. "And when you give me full control of your pleasure." His thumb made another slick pass, then pushed down on her, pressing into her hard enough to draw whimpers.

She clutched him as her body trembled. Flicking over her, he made her come again so fast her head swam.

Kjan kept the rhythmic motion going to help her ride out the climax. Eve held on to the sensation as long as she could, but once the adrenaline ebbed, she started shivering.

Bracing his weight off the bed, he rolled onto her and found his place between her legs. His skin was like the heat of the sun spreading across her body, warming her instantly.

He circled her nipple with his tongue, and another whimper escaped her. Eve was getting impatient. She rolled her hips, squeezing her thighs around his waist to urge him on.

Kjan got the hint and laughed. "Do you want me so badly?"

"Um, yah! Isn't it obvious? Why are you holding out?"

"I'm not." He looked up at her with hooded eyes from beneath his long, dark lashes. "I'm studying you."

Eve grimaced. "I'm pretty sure you've memorized every inch over the last five weeks."

"That's not nearly enough time to fully appreciate all your lovely qualities." He chuffed another laugh, scrutinizing more of the crook of her neck and the crease below her jaw.

Eve sucked in a sharp breath when he finally quit messing around and answered her plea. Prodding at her, he rolled his hips, inching deeper.

A zap of pain came with the last poignant thrust to bury himself inside her, and she cried out, closing her fist around a handful of his hair. He devoured her tortured wailing with his mouth as he gathered momentum to wind her up.

She clung to him, arms cuffed around his neck, heels stabbing into his lower back, arching up to meet him. One arm hooked at her shoulder, the other hand gripping her hip, he resumed his pace, hard and rough, grinding his hips deeper into her on every drive.

Eve quivered beneath him, mustering her breath. Muscles stiff with urgency, she could feel the release culminating.

He worked her inside and out until the shuddery cry from her climax ricocheted off the walls. Kjan locked into her in one last backbreaking thrust, and they both splintered apart.

Utterly spent, they collapsed onto the bed as soon as he released her. *Perfect bliss.* There was no other way to describe the feeling in her head.

Eve was exhausted. Physically anyway; her mind was still racing. Kjan was fast asleep next to her within minutes, his soft snores filling the space between them. The sun was already coming up.

Married? Eve couldn't stop thinking about it. She knew it was silly to be jealous of a woman who had lived a thousand years ago, but she still couldn't help the feeling.

Why had she never contemplated the possibility until now? It made sense, of course, that he'd had a life before he was turned.

CHAPTER

8

"*Marry me.*"

Kjan was back in the meadow. *Their* meadow. The one that stretched far behind the cottage.

"*You are funny, Kjartan,*" she said with a soft laugh that was a distant melody in his head. "*That's why I love you.*"

He watched her pick up another rock and turn it over in her small hands. "*If you love me, why do you continue to refuse me? I mean it, Thórunn. I want to marry you.*"

Her tone lost its cheerful lilt. "*No man in his right mind would want to marry me. They do not think me a proper wife.*" With a skilled flick of her wrist, she sent the rock skidding across the water. It bounced six times, one more than his.

"*I do.*" He shifted his body toward her. "*You are perfect the way you are. I would never dare change you. Marry me,*" he implored her again. "*Tomorrow.*"

She shook her head and averted her gaze. "I will not marry you, Mýrkjartansson. You would soon grow tired of my sharp tongue, and I would die of a broken heart," she said with her eyes downcast.

He cupped her cheek and tilted her chin toward him. "I like your tongue," he replied. "And I like your strong head. I do not want anyone else. If you will not have me, then we shall both die of a broken heart. I have loved you since the first day and will have no one but you."

Thórunn's pale eyes glistened with tears as she looked at him. "Swear it. Swear you will love me until my breath leaves my body."

"Until the last beat of my heart." He dipped his forehead to hers. "I swear it, kona."

CHAPTER

9

When Eve woke in the middle of the day, Kjan was no longer beside her. She found him sitting on the floor with his back to the bed, head low, elbows propped on his knees.

She slid out, snatching his shirt from last night off the ground to put on, and took a seat to his right. He raised his head at the contact of her leaning into his side but kept his gaze straight ahead.

His mouth was set into a pained line.

As he stared off, brows drawn together, he took her hand, lacing their fingers. "I'm sorry," he said in a mournful tone, gently brushing his thumb over her knuckles.

"You don't ever need to apologize for your pain." She could see that his mind had slipped into a memory. Who was this woman who still had such a hold on him after all this time? How much had she meant to him?

"Tell me about her. What was she like?"

The creases across his forehead deepened while he gathered his thoughts. Eve got the sense that he chose his words carefully because he didn't want to hurt her feelings.

He wet his lips and looked at his left hand, resting on his knee. "She was stubborn. And fearless. Braver than most of the boys in our village. Tougher too. She never backed down from a fight."

He cut himself off with a little shake of his head. His jaw flexed. A few dark strands shifted against the chiseled lines underneath his beard as he worked it.

Eve watched him swallow. When he cleared his throat and spoke again, his voice was no longer calm and steady. "We... we used to hunt rabbits together. She was a skilled archer. I always preferred blades," he said hoarsely. "I loved her since we were kids—"

The words caught in his throat.

Eve had never seen him so vulnerable. So raw with emotion. The love for his wife was still there, simmering beneath the surface. How could she possibly compete with that?

"What did she look like?" Eve wasn't sure why she wanted to know, but she had the sudden urge to put a face to the phantom. She needed to picture someone.

A shadow crossed his expression. He bit his bottom lip and took his time to answer.

"I used to dream about her. All the time. I had to lock her away so deep... I don't remember. Eve, I can't remember!"

His voice trembled with anger and sorrow at the same time. Eve saw that he was holding back tears.

"How can I remember everything about her except her face? Her hair, her eyes... the little details. How could I let myself forget? When I dream of her now, her features are always a blur. All I see are her pale irises… but no color in them."

The sharp points digging into his lips drew blood as he stalled.

Eve felt a twinge in her chest. *He's still dreaming of her?*

"I have never told anyone. Not Anne. Not Eleanor. I haven't even let myself think about her since."

So it was the guilt about forgetting the woman he had loved with all his heart that haunted him?

Eve couldn't imagine the pain he was going through. It broke her heart that she was helpless to comfort him.

"I'm glad you told *me*," she whispered. She didn't know what else to say.

Kjan lifted his head and brought her hand up to touch the back of it to his lips. Then he turned to meet her eyes. "I love you. You know that, right?"

"I know you do." She smiled at him, raising her free hand to his cheek.

He covered her hand with his own and touched his forehead to hers. "You mean the world to me, Dove."

Eve believed him. And prayed that his heart was big enough for both of them.

♪

Kjan rubbed his bleary eyes. Eve was curled up in his lap, her head tucked under his chin, when the buzz of her phone woke them at 6:45 p.m., according to the alarm clock on his nightstand.

After initially passing out cold for only an hour, he had woken up from the dream, unable to go back to sleep. He had been awake all day, and then Eve had found him on the floor.

Fuck!

He felt like punching a hole into the wall. He didn't want her to see him like that. Ever.

Eve went around the bed to check the message. "Tanya is asking if we want to meet her and Colby at *Jack's* tonight?"

"You should go," he encouraged her, his smile set into a thin line.

She watched him, her narrow blue eyes clouded. "I don't want to leave you."

He let out a chuckle. "Why, I appreciate your concern, Dove, but I'll be fine. I promise. Go have fun. I got some more work to finish anyway." A weak excuse, but not a lie.

Then he remembered her car. "I'll drop you off. And might get a haircut while I'm out," he tacked on.

Kjan rose to his feet and just now noticed that she was wearing his gray shirt. The look of her sent a thrill up his spine, reminding him of last night—the way her body fit so perfectly against his, molded to his chest, not the trip down memory lane.

She hung on to the frown, but her shoulders came down. "Don't worry about it. I'll just get an Uber."

Over my dead body. Kjan scowled, shaking his head in solid objection. "That's not even up for debate. I'm not letting you get in a car with a stranger. I'm taking you."

"Well, there is another option." Eve twirled her hair around her finger. He already knew where she was going with this, and his answer was a hard *no*.

"Okay, hear me out—"

"Not gonna happen." Kjan cut her off, then disappeared into the closet.

Eve huffed. "I haven't even asked yet."

"There is no way you're taking the Charger."

"The accident wasn't my fault."

"I never said it was," he clarified when he returned to the room.

Hip cocked defensively, she folded her arms over her chest. "So you trust me with your life but not with your car?"

He let out a sound of frustration. "It's not about you damaging the car. It's about the damage it can inflict on *you*." His eyes zeroed in on her, and he forced his voice to soften. "I don't want you to get hurt. The engine has more power than you can handle."

"*Hellooo…* Vampire!" She did the jazz-hands thing, waving her hands up by her head, and then pointed at herself. "I can't get hurt, remember?"

"Wrong! And don't get sassy with me. Just because you heal fast doesn't mean you can't still get hurt."

He sank onto the edge of the bed, his eyes steady on her. "We are not that different from humans, Eve. Yes, we survive solely on blood, but we are susceptible to injury just like they are. And let's not forget poison." He arched his brow.

Plus, the fact that their mutated genes rendered them infertile and, in his eyes, inferior to the human race in that aspect. But perhaps not everyone considered that a setback.

"We don't age, and our cells repair faster. That's all. We are not Gods. We are far from immortal."

"I've seen you heal. You're pretty damn close."

"Give it a few centuries, and you'll learn some new tricks too."

Eve opened her mouth. Closed it. Opened it again.

She seemed tempted to continue the argument but then threw her hands up in defeat. "Fine, you win. I'm sorry I even brought it up."

"Eve, please…"

She didn't respond, flying past him to get changed. Kjan's jawline tightened as he slammed his molars shut. He knew this wasn't over. He wished she would understand his point of view. She could be more than a little reckless sometimes and didn't need his car to increase her prospects.

With a sigh, he flung himself back onto the bed.

"Do you mind if I keep the shirt on since you're not coming?"

His head jerked up, and to his surprise, she had not changed out of it. Only added a pair of dark blue jeans and black heels to the outfit.

His body snapped back to attention. She looked so damn fine.

Walking toward him, presumably no longer cross, she stepped in between his legs and placed her hands on his shoulders.

Kjan looked up, his lips curling into a pleased grin. "No, I don't mind."

He hooked his arms around her hips and kissed her belly through the thin fabric of the shirt. Hiding his face in the folds, he simply held her there, sagging into her embrace, and breathing deeply. The scent that clung to the cotton fibers was an exhilarating combination of them both.

"I don't want to fight with you," he murmured.

"I know. I don't want to either."

The lazily drag of her fingers up his nape shot a spark straight down to his groin. And she wondered why he couldn't keep his hands off her?

"I just need a few more minutes, and then we can head out," she said, breaking away.

Yeah, a few minutes was all he needed to finish too. If it were up to him, they would never leave the bed.

He adjusted the constricting front of his jeans. *Damn this woman.*

Kjan dropped her off at the pub, and she promised to give him a call later. He was dead serious about her not getting a different ride home, but he felt relieved that at least she wasn't going out still mad at him.

He took a detour through the Pearl District, stopping off at the jeweler to pick up the Christmas gift he had specially commissioned. It was so perfect, down to the deep green emerald he had chosen himself, and he couldn't wait three weeks to give it to her.

Leaving the store, he ambled through the alleys. He wasn't ready to head home. The echo of last night's confessions still haunted him. Out in the cold, he felt more able to breathe and shake the demons.

A few people passed him on his way, most of them hurrying along to get someplace warm. A scrawny boy with raven black hair stood in the dim glow of the streetlamps, leaning against the glass window of a tattoo shop.

He kept his head low and didn't pay Kjan any attention. He didn't appear older than twelve, but it wasn't too unusual to see kids his age around here at night.

Kjan shrugged it off as he walked past him.

"You insult me with your disrespect."

A jab of panic shot through his nerves. He froze. The words spoken in the old language thrummed in his head, their comprehension as natural to him as breathing air.

"I have found you at last, my elusive son."

CHAPTER

10

A warning prickled up his neck. The child's face might not have been familiar, but the recognition of his voice felt like ice down his back. His pulse started racing, and shrill alarm bells went off in his head.

Muscles rigid, Kjan was immobilized by his fear. He closed his eyes at the sound of light footsteps approaching.

They stopped short in front of him. "FACE ME!"

Against all instincts, Kjan complied with the command and pried his eyes open.

The boy's rather young-looking face didn't match his authoritative tone, but he knew better than to underestimate the seemingly fragile appearance. He could feel the raw power hiding under his exterior now, emanating from his skin, almost as if he had flipped a switch to avoid being detected prior to his official introduction.

"Why are you here?" Kjan gritted his teeth, hands balled into fists. He wasn't sure he wanted to know.

"You ask the question, and you are the answer."

"I don't understand. Why would you come looking for me now? After all these years?"

The boy sucked in a sharp breath and went on a pace, slowly circling Kjan, his tiny hands clasped behind his back. "Actually, I have been looking for you for quite some time. Two hundred years, to be exact. You are a very cautious and meticulous creature. You have indeed been hard to find."

"Then how did you track me down?" Kjan didn't sense the link between them anymore.

His Sire stopped and turned to face him, cocking his head to one side. The color in his eyes glinted an unnatural electric blue. "It is a rather curious thing, is it not? The way we give away a little piece of ourselves every time we choose to share our gift? Unfortunately, that line is disconnected once our offspring sires the next generation."

So, by turning Anne, Kjan had freed himself from his Sire and linked himself to her? But then how—

He's coming for you, her last words. She had known. She had been the key to finding him.

"It was *you* who freed Andromeda!" Kjan shouted. There was no one around to see or hear them. Even the tattoo shop was empty.

She must have taken *his* vein. That was why she had been so strong and why her emotions had been blocked from Kjan. His Sire's blood must have cloaked them somehow.

"Yes. I recruited her to track you. She had the means I lacked. But even after she regained her strength, it took her months to locate you in Seattle."

Fifteen months approximately. Fifteen months, during which he had suffered from her nightmares.

"What do you want from me?" Kjan's tone grew more cautious now.

"I am a God, but my power is limited by my body. Unlike you, I am still trapped by the light, condemned to eternal darkness."

He exhaled long and slowly. "I desire salvation. You see, I need a new body. Since the curse remains stitched into this." He hiked a thumb at himself, then jabbed his index finger at Kjan. "And you, my *son*, you possess the supreme vessel."

Vessel? What's he implying?

"I have a proposal for you." The immortal's eyes drew into narrow slits. "I am suggesting a transfer of my essence, my mind, into your body. You and I together. We will be unstoppable. You will be a true God amongst mortals."

Kjan scoffed, crossing his arms over his chest. He no longer felt cooperative. "Why the hell would I agree to that?"

His Sire took another step toward him, and the pendant at the end of the leather cord around his neck caught Kjan's eye. White-hot rage ignited in his blood.

"THAT'S MINE!" He lunged himself at the boy's throat, nostrils flaring, lips curled into a sneer.

A blast shot from the kid's splayed palm and hit Kjan square in the chest, knocking him back a couple of feet.

His head collided with the unforgiving cobblestone when he landed. Fireworks ignited in his vision, and a sharp ringing blared in his head. "That doesn't belong to you," he groaned through the pain. "You had no right to take them."

He started to push himself off the ground but only managed to get onto his knees before his body seized. His spine caught in an electric current, paralyzing him in place. He couldn't move. His muscles didn't respond to his commands. It was the same unknown power he had felt back then.

The boy wrapped his small fist around the object. "Finders keepers."

His grin stretched wider while choosing his next words carefully. "I think you will find me very persuasive. The new female you turned…" He paused to give the comment time to sink in. "Yes, I know about her, of course. What if I told you I would let her live? You have my word that I will not harm her as long as you agree to the bargain."

Kjan's heart kicked behind his ribs. He knew about Eve. He had been watching them.

"Why me?" he snarled, the invisible reins still holding him at bay. Beads of sweat began to trickle down his forehead from his efforts to break free.

"Because you are the only one left. The last and most valued of my *Firsts*. All the others were traitors. They renounced our faith and turned their backs on the Gods." The muscles in his small body flexed, and his eyes flashed in anger, illuminating the alley with a red glow.

"Your blood is strong, and you are still a believer in the Old Ways. I saw it in your memories."

"You're wrong! I stopped believing in the Gods a long time ago." Kjan's voice shook with surging fury.

The memories his Sire spoke of had been plucked from him almost a thousand years ago in the same fashion he could reach into a human's mind when he took their vein. But they were a different man's memories. That man was long gone. He had died in that cave, and so had his prospects of a life beyond.

"Two souls can't inhabit a single body. There is only one way for you to claim me as your vessel." Kjan wasn't fooled. "Don't sugarcoat it. You're going to kill me."

His body would be no more than an empty shell for the immortal to possess. To use as he pleased.

"Indeed, two spirits cannot coexist within the same vessel. But I can offer you the one thing you always wanted." His voice softened enticingly. "A way home."

Could it be true? Would he really be welcomed into the Realm of the Gods?

Kjan didn't trust the offer. The runt in front of him didn't have the means to back it up. His father—a prince of Ásgarðr, and the God of Death? Possibly.

"If you're so powerful, why don't you just take my body then? Why come here to bargain at all?"

"I cannot possess you by force. I need a sacrifice," the immortal said coldly. "As you well know, it is impossible to sacrifice another's life because you cannot give something that is not yours to give. It renders the sacrifice worthless. The lamb has to offer its own life. *Freely.* In other words, I need you to surrender your body willingly."

Kjan laughed and shook his head. "You want my fealty but you're blackmailing me to get it?"

"But I am not forcing you." The small immortal raised his skinny finger to Kjan's face to emphasize the minor technicality.

The silence between them stretched an eternity, his muscles still twitching from the jolts.

Kjan ground his teeth, battling the pull of his restraints. A slow trail of sweat trickled down the side of his face and in between his shoulder blades. It left a chilly path in the frigid

December temperatures. He couldn't see a way out of this; he couldn't fight him, couldn't beat him, couldn't gamble with Eve's life.

A lump formed in his throat. He racked his mind, wrenched at his thoughts... but there was no escape.

Sudden hopelessness pierced his heart. Angry and defeated, he hung his head. "What do you need me to do?"

The question burned on his tongue like acid.

Finally, his Sire released his hold on Kjan's body, and he collapsed forward onto his hands.

"Are you familiar with the significance of a lunar tetrad?"

Unfortunately. "Yes."

It was a series of four total lunar eclipses over the span of two years, Kjan recalled. There were usually no more than four or five total eclipses transpiring within a decade, making the occurrences of a tetrad quite rare and providing them with special magical power.

"Lucky for me, there happens to be a lunar tetrad coinciding with this year's Winter Solstice," the boy went on elaborating. "One, more significant, more powerful than any other because all four events will occur within only twenty-eight weeks of one another. The first total lunar eclipse within a fortnight will mark the beginning of the cycle. Return here on the night of the blood moon," he instructed.

"I have one condition." Kjan glared upward, meeting the boy's expectant stare, which was back to its electric blue. "You have to leave Portland and make sure that she will never lay eyes on me again."

Because it wouldn't be *him* anymore. No part remaining of the man she knew.

"Promise me that, and I will do what you want."

"Deal." An expression of utter superiority and pride decked the boy's features. "I will forget about her so long as you hold up your end. But if you break your word, she will pay the price."

Then his Sire turned away and disappeared down a dark passage between the buildings, leaving Kjan alone in the deserted alley to let the consequences of the agreement he made sink in fully.

He was going to die.

For a millennium, he had covered his tracks, running from the evil that cursed him into this immortal existence. The stories of his ancestors had been passed down for generations. Although Iceland converted to Christianity almost a hundred years prior to the end of the Viking Age, his family had stayed true to the Old Ways and continued to worship and honor their Gods in secret.

Kjan might have stopped worshiping them, but he had never truly given up his beliefs. His Sire was right. It was in his blood, in his very nature. He had changed his appearance by cutting his hair and even trimming his beard down to a few millimeters, only to blend in with a modern world that was constantly evolving. In his heart, he still believed in the Heathen Faith, and not just because he was raised to do so.

No. It was because his own personal experience had proven it to be true when his blind faith had turned into reality.

Renate Rowland

CHAPTER

II

K jan had been sitting in his car for hours when the buzzing of his phone caught his attention. The scene through the windshield in front of him shuttered as he blinked rapidly.

He couldn't fathom what had happened. He had gone from being convinced he would spend eternity with Eve to having a mere two weeks.

"Hey," he answered, his breath catching in his throat.

"Where are you? Did you fall asleep?"

He could hear the smile in her voice and automatically pictured her face. It was like a knife in his heart.

"N-no, uh, no. I'm sorry. I'll see you in ten."

He clenched his fists hard until he felt the cut of his nails and the blood collecting in the center of his palm. He couldn't tell her. It would ruin the little bit of time they had left together.

The only way he was going to get through this was in complete and utter denial. He wiped his hands on his dark jeans and turned the key.

Eve hopped in the Charger the second he pulled up to the curb and leaned over to kiss him.

"You seem to be in a good mood," he said, keeping his tone neutral.

"It was nice catching up with them, but I'm ready to go home." Her eyes sparkled when she smiled at him. "What happened? Did you change your mind?"

His eyes shifted nervously. "On what?"

"The haircut."

"Oh, right. Yeah. No. I mean, I did... change my mind." *Wow,* that was soooo smooth he almost fooled himself.

"Are you alright?" She shot him a skeptical look.

Kjan expelled a hard breath. "I am now." He kissed the knuckles of her hand, returning her smile.

"What have you been up to—Oh my God! Is that blood on your hand?" She dropped her smile in shock.

Crap.

His heart sputtered. "It's nothing." Keeping his eyes on the road, he gave her a dismissive shrug.

Please don't make me lie to you.

Eve didn't seem entirely convinced, but she thankfully dropped the Q&A.

Back at the condo, they actually did good on their word about sticking to work for once. Eve finished her paper well before her deadline, and he fixed the issues he had been having with some of the new contracts while a movie was playing on the TV.

When Kjan looked over to check on her, he noticed that she had fallen asleep at some point before the end of the second movie. He couldn't remember the last time that had happened. He turned off the TV and powered down their laptops, then carried her to bed.

Nestling close beside her, he kissed the top of her head and erased the last eight hours from his mind.

Renate Rowland

CHAPTER

12

Head in the crook of his shoulder, Eve woke up in bed, not recalling how she'd ended up there. The last thing she remembered was watching John Wick Chapter 2 in the living room while Kjan was still buried in his laptop.

"What time is it?" She could tell by the rhythm of his heartbeat that he was awake, too.

He rolled over on his side to face her and ran his fingers through her hair. "Why? You have somewhere more important to be?"

"Never," Eve drawled with a sly grin.

He burrowed his face into her neck, his lips exploring her throat, licking and kissing a hot, wet trail.

"Do you have a particular agenda this evening?"

"Mm-hmm," he purred in her ear, nipping at her lobe. The dark timber in his voice vibrated through her chest, making her thighs twitch.

"And what's that?"

"You know, your fluids… my fluids… *mixing*." He dragged out the *m* with emphasis.

She suppressed a giggle. "Sounds filthy."

"It's sex, Dove. It's supposed to be."

He pressed his mouth against the front of her throat, forcing a moan from her lips, and what started with a hungry kiss turned into an extra hour well spent in bed.

"I missed you last night." Eve rubbed her hands across his back. His arms were wrapped snugly around her rib cage, head down on her chest. "As much fun as Tanya and Colby are, I did feel a bit like a third wheel."

"You're right. I'm sorry. I should have gone with you." He propped his chin on her sternum. "How about I make it up to you?"

Her curiosity was piqued. "I'm listening."

"I take you out tonight," he proposed. "If you want, we'll stay up and hit the market in the morning."

"A date on a Friday night and Old Town in the morning?"

"We can even make it to Bridgeport before the shops close," he added.

"If you're in a generous mood, we shouldn't have wasted the last hour in bed. Let's go." She shoved him off, gunning for the closet to get dressed.

He called after her, "What do you mean *wasted*?"

Twenty minutes after Eve reemerged from the closet, they were strolling down the busy streets. A lot of people hustled around trying to finish their Christmas shopping early this year, and most of the shops stayed open late despite the brisk weather moving in. The promise of snow was in the air. The forecast predicted the first flurries any day now.

Kjan gave her hand a gentle squeeze. "Are you sure you're not cold?"

"No, I'm alright." She smiled up at him, leaning into his shoulder, and hugging his arm.

As they weaved through the herds, Eve welcomed the distraction. In the quiet penthouse suite, she constantly found herself thinking about her uncle.

"Thank you," she murmured

"For what?"

"For trying to cheer me up. I couldn't get through this without you. I was really dreading the holidays."

A jitter of discomfort reached her as Kjan appeared to tense at her words. But then he turned to her with his usual grin, his tone instantly reassuring her. "I would do anything for you, Dove. And on the danger of sounding like a broken record, are you sure you're doing the right thing? If you miss Joe so much, you should call him—"

"I can't." Eve shook her head adamantly. "I wouldn't even know what to tell him. I don't want to lie."

"You don't have to lie. You can tell him the truth. I don't care."

The sincere look in his deep green eyes implored her. Why was he suddenly so determined to sway her?

"Joe is your only family. He's worried. He misses you, too. Neither of you has to go through this alone."

"I doubt he's alone. And I have you." She saw the disappointment in Kjan's expression and quickly changed the topic. "I don't suppose you have any Christmas traditions?" They had never even mentioned exchanging gifts.

"No," he sighed in resignation, dropping his gaze to the cobblestone in front of his steps. "I usually hung back when Eleanor threw one of her big parties."

"What about before?" Eve tried to recall if she had ever seen him in the farmhouse around that time. Did it mean anything to him? It was, after all, originally a Pagan holiday.

Kjan shook his head sullenly. His arm with their clasped hands hung stiffly by his side, his other hand was shoved deep into the pocket of his black wool coat. He probably didn't want to go down that road again, but Eve had to wonder how he'd celebrated important events with his wife.

Her mouth fell open on a gasp when a sudden realization struck. "When's your birthday? I mean, I know the year. 1039, right?" She'd done the math: 953 years ago, he'd been 28. "But what day?"

"I don't remember." He shrugged, his voice apathetic.

"You don't remember? How can you not remember?"

"It's not something we celebrated."

"What *did* you celebrate?"

"The change of the season. Summer, winter, their midpoints... we only had the two."

"No fall or spring? What about Easter? That's a Pagan holiday, isn't it? What's the deal with the rabbit and the eggs?"

He smiled and swiveled his head at her ignorance. "Spring means the return of life after winter. Rabbits and eggs symbolize fertility."

"Huh, that actually makes sense now."

"Do you know where the tradition of decorating evergreen trees comes from?"

"Ah, nope."

He laughed softly. "It was believed that the spirits living within the trees hide away during the cold winter months but could be coaxed back with offerings like little trinkets, food, lights. Mistletoe and wreaths are Heathen traditions too."

Eve squeezed his arm tighter. "I like your traditions."

Something flickered in his eyes, but his smile never faltered. "Where do you want to go next?" he asked, presumably to change the topic.

"I don't know. I think I've had enough of the crowds. How about somewhere a bit more private? Maybe the park?"

"You read my mind," he whispered in her ear. "The beach officially closes at midnight, but I might know of a few places to stay out of sight. Come on." Kjan tugged on her hand to pull her through the crowd back to the car.

South Waterfront Park was deserted when they got there, and even though there were no more flowers blooming, the Christmas lighting more than made up for it. Eve loved coming here and walking along the riverbank at any time of the year.

"I can't wait for it to snow and everything to be covered in a white blanket," she said as Kjan pulled her down by a tree out of view from the main trail.

Sitting down, he wrapped his arms around her and rested his chin on her shoulder. Music played from hidden speakers in the shrubs.

"Why did I ever want to move to a big city?"

"Beats me," he replied, brushing his lips against the sensitive skin of her neck. "I was perfectly happy in that little house with your uncle. Cities are overrated."

"I found what I was really looking for." She nudged him. "And it wasn't the thrill of the lights or the noise at all. Maybe we should leave Portland. Go somewhere else."

Eve turned her head, waiting for Kjan to say something, but he kept his gaze on the ground, avoiding her stare. Something seemed to be on his mind.

A sudden sense of distress echoed through her.

"Anywhere," she said, trying to snap him back. "The place doesn't matter. Wherever you go, I go," she vowed in a whisper, leaning her head against his.

He tightened his embrace as his lips touched her temple.

"You know, this is not what I thought you had in mind when you dragged me off the path and into the bushes," Eve joked to lighten his mood.

A laugh broke from his throat. "You expected indecent exposure? I prefer to have you all to myself. Away from prying eyes."

"That's funny because I clearly remember you wanting to bend me over at the club the other night."

Eve yelped when Kjan knocked her down onto the grass. "Don't tempt me, woman. You continue to test my restraint in public. I'm afraid one of these days I really will bend you over and take you right where you stand. If it hadn't been for that couple on the elevator…"

His words cut off as he slipped his hand under the back of her sweater. Searing heat met her cold skin. He was definitely hot-blooded, always ready to warm her, and when he kissed her passionately, she felt like catching fire.

"I love you so much." She grazed her fingers through the stubbles of his beard along his jawline.

Kjan leaned into her touch, kissing the inside of her hand. "I love you too," he replied with a wide grin, his green eyes shimmering in the dark. "How about we watch the sunrise from the sky?" he proposed as he hoisted her off the ground.

"The tram? Hells yes!"

The entrance to the aerial tram was only a short distance away. The view from up there was always spectacular, and Eve had not been afraid of heights since the night on the Great Wheel in Seattle. The sunrise was an added bonus.

As there was no one else in the car, he stretched out on the seat, and she curled into him. The first rays were already coming over the horizon. They were so bright against the blue sky that she had to close her eyes and bury her face in his chest.

It didn't matter, though; she just wanted to be close to him. Lose herself in the rich dark chocolate and black cherry nuances of his natural scent.

Eve reached deeper, searching for the hints of whiskey that completed the irresistible concoction. It was the scent she had always associated with the forbidden truffles she once sneaked from her uncle when she was younger. Eve had never tasted anything so heavenly. Kjan was everything the desirable treat represented.

"What do I smell like to you?"

She'd never asked him before. Nor had she admitted her guilty indulgence in his scent. Did she trigger a personal memory for him?

His head dipped down over hers, the tip of his nose brushing her hair as his hard chest expanded against her back. "Wild berries and spring flowers."

"Hmm." Eve felt a twinge of disappointment.

He swept strands of hair behind her ears to see her face, his touch featherlight and tender because there was another side to his roughness. Maybe they made love harder than other couples, but he had his way of being gentle. Though he probably wouldn't use those exact words to describe himself, and maybe others wouldn't either, Eve knew his touch by heart.

"Are you okay?" She cocked her head toward him and noticed the reflection of the sun giving his eyes a stunning glow. The golden bursts in the center of his irises were utterly mesmerizing.

"Perfect." He kissed the top of her head and returned his gaze to the window. "Look, you can see them setting up the stands at the market."

Eve straightened and followed the direction of his eyes.

"Do you still want to go?"

"No." Brushing her fingertips over his hands as they encircled her, she knew she was ready to head home. "We can go another time. I'd rather snuggle up with you under a warm blanket."

"Snuggle?"

"Alright, fine. Snuggling is not what I had in mind. I want to f—"

Kjan smacked his hand over her mouth. "You don't have to twist my arm. Why do you have to phrase it that way?"

"Because it's true," Eve replied blatantly when he let her speak again. She glanced up and caught him rolling his eyes with a bashful smirk.

His searing touch dropped to her throat, his thumb stroking the side of her neck affectionately. "Besides…" she drawled.

"Hey, that's *my* line."

"My point exactly. Couples who live together adopt the same vernacular over a period of time. I mean, have you heard yourself lately?" His speech pattern wasn't so snobbish anymore since he'd ditched the social elite of Seattle.

He gently tilted her head back with a nudge of his fingers along her jaw. "Not going to happen, Dove."

The low rasp in which he spoke the endearing term sent a warm tingle of pleasure through her. His thumb brushed her cheek, and a dark hunger filled his hooded eyes.

Yeah, they needed to get home stat. *And maybe...*

"Will you keep your boots on?" She mentally crossed her fingers.

He winked, biting his bottom lip before answering. "We'll see."

∫

Kjan tensed under her scrutiny. Her fingers skimmed the side of his hand as her sharp eyes tried to read his emotions. Not just the ones on the surface but the ones that crawled further down.

He hadn't missed the look of disappointment his reply had painted on her face. She had hoped for a more significant answer. A personal trigger.

Cinnamon had been one for her uncle because of the Snickerdoodles they used to bake together when she was younger. Kjan had never caught a trace of it himself. The warm spice was her personal, unique connection to home.

It hurt to keep the truth from her. Little did she know, her scent was anything but ordinary. The berry fragrance was, in fact, not her shampoo at all. It was the wild strawberries and bog berries that grew in the region of Iceland where he had been raised. Her blood had the distinct taste of sweet crowberry wine that was native to the country.

As for the flowers?

Spring was a symbol of the life she had given back to him, and when he closed his eyes, he could still see the little white flowers that had bloomed every year in the back of the house—his home.

Eve was his home.

But he had to keep his emotions at surface level now. For both their sakes. Telling her would only make things harder, and he wasn't sure he would be able to get through what he had to do next.

On his brief trip back to the farmhouse for the move, he had made a point of checking in on Joe in person. He had promised her not to divulge her whereabouts or his direct involvement with her, but he had managed to give her uncle enough peace of mind by offering to track her down for him, should he ever wish to. It had been incredibly hard to look the man in the eye and keep the truth from him. Kjan was forced to do the same to Eve now, and the lie was draining the life out of him.

He wouldn't be able to keep his promises to either of them.

CHAPTER

13

An arrow whizzed past his head, too close for comfort. Cursing, he whipped around and then dodged behind the nearest boulder as she drew up the next one.

"Did you bed her?" she shouted, her voice dripping with rage.

Sucked into the flashback by his dream, Kjan's memory filled in the blanks of that pivotal night. He was a teenager again.

"Who?" he heard himself ask in a juvenile tone of voice.

Another arrow zipped over his shoulder and disappeared into the thicket behind him. He dug his heels into the dirt and shuffled closer to the large rock. Her aim was deadly, even in the dark.

"You know who!"

Ah, so she had seen them. He peeked around the boulder and instantly felt the air pass by his ear. "Stop shooting at me."

"Did you?" Thórunn asked again, her tongue as sharp as her projectiles.

"I did not touch her."

"Liar!" A fourth arrow nearly caught his foot. She was closing in on him. *"I saw you kissing her."*

Actually, the girl had kissed him, and he had kept his hands to himself, so technically, it was not a lie. He wasn't interested in her, but he hadn't turned her down either. He was 16—Thórunn almost a whole year older than him—and his actions were dictated by raging adolescent hormones.

"Do you deny it, then?"

A self-satisfied snicker erupted in his throat. *"I do not deny it. I kissed her."*

Truthfully, he had hoped she would catch them. He tried to get a rise out of her. Thórunn was the only one he wanted.

"What is it to you? You said you do not want me," he teased her in a jaunty undertone.

She didn't reply, and he couldn't hear her footsteps over the crackling of his fire. He dared to poke his head out from behind his cover—

The tip of her arrow appeared in his vision, pointed right at his left eye, bow taut.

He held his breath, gazing up at her. Her chest rose and fell with the agitation he had brought out in her, eyes burning with emotion. He had her right where he wanted her. He was at her mercy and didn't flinch.

"Jealous, elskan?"

"Do not call me that," she sneered. *"I am not your sweetheart. I do not belong to anyone. And I will be no one's wife."*

"You should be mine."

The words slipped out, and he let them hang in the air for a moment because he knew them to be true. She was perfect in any way he could imagine. Beautiful. Smart. Bold.

"I did not lie with her. I swear it. Nor with any other," he admitted, rolling his eyes. "I want you, Thórunn. How many times will you make me say it? I want to marry you one day."

"I will not marry you. I will not marry any man."

"But you are alone. You have no family." She had been living by herself on the outskirts of the village since her mother died a year ago. She had cared for the sick woman all on her own. Never complaining.

"I do not need a husband to take care of me. I would rather fend for myself than rely on someone else. I make my own decisions."

She lowered her bow and then dropped it altogether. "And I take what I want."

Her hands clasped his face to capture his mouth with her own, her legs on either side of him as she dropped down to straddle his lap.

His lips parted, reveling in her passionate kiss. "I would never ask you to change," he rasped, his voice hoarse and out of breath.

His palms rubbed along her sides with reverence, up to her breasts and down to her hips, rocking her tender shape into him. He had been aching for her for so long. The feel of her body against his was everything he had dreamed of.

Mouth still locked to his, her movements made haste, hands shooting down in between them, feverishly fumbling with the ties of his pants.

Yes, Thórunn took what she wanted. Her fingers reached between the lacing, and her grasp tightened around his throbbing flesh to stand him up. Nothing had ever felt this good.

Eyes closed, he felt her weight shift. Her breasts surged into him as she briefly rose onto her knees and then came back down on him hard—

Sharp pain erupted where they were linked, halting them both in their panting.

Thórunn winced, her body tense on top of him. Her legs quivered from the shock, and she hid her face in the crook of his neck, trying not to let her pain show.

With a curse on his tongue, his grasp tightened around her waist. "Why would you do that? Why force it?"

"To get it over with," she sobbed quietly, too afraid to move.

His lips brushed her collarbone. "I do not wish to hurt you, Thórunn."

"But it is supposed to hurt, is it not?"

He straightened her with gentle hands, sweeping her long hair behind her ear to look into her eyes. They were bright and clear in the light of the fire. "No, elskan. Not like this." He wiped her tears, and his thumb lingered on her chin. She was the most beautiful woman he had ever seen.

"Tell me that you trust me," he beseeched her.

"I trust you. You know that I do."

"Say it again," he urged. "Use my name."

"I trust you, Kjartan, elskan mín."

Her frustration fled as she spoke the words out loud, and her body relaxed at last, melting into his touch.

He drew her to him, whispering against her velvety lips. "I love you with all my heart, Thórunn. I will never purposely hurt you... this way or any other. I want this to feel right. For the both of us."

Sealing his vow to her with a kiss, he shifted his weight, holding her against his chest.

Still joint at the hips, he laid her down in the grass and covered her body with his own.

Renate Rowland

CHAPTER

14

Eve shut down her laptop and pulled the tie out of her hair, releasing the too-tight ponytail. Elbows on the counter, she forked her fingers through the tangles and rubbed her scalp.

She'd been working too much the last two weeks, and it was starting to catch up. She felt exhausted. With Christmas only days away, her mind kept circling back to Joe. Her eyes darted to her phone, and she stared at it for a long second, phrasing out the awkward conversation in her head from the forced *"Hey, how have you been?"* to the *"I'm having an illicit affair with our upstairs neighbor, who is much older than me—much, much older. Oh, and I'm also a vampire now. Just like him. How are things with you?"*

Eve expelled her breath and turned her gaze in the other direction. Kjan was outside on the patio in nothing but his sweatpants. The little black earpiece was no longer in.

She'd once listened to him go off in a burst of rapid French, the syllables pouring out of him. She had no clue what he was saying. For all she knew, he could've been declaring his undying love or ripping his contact on the other line a new one. It sounded beautiful.

Last week, she'd listened in on a phone call from Hamburg, Germany, discussing the details of a large shipment. Eve had picked out enough words to put the gist together.

Usually, his phone rang off the hook, but he'd only taken two calls tonight. It seemed the more work she'd put in to keep herself busy, the less time he'd spent on his own.

Bent over with his back turned to her, elbow resting on the steel rail, he was brooding like some kind of superhero watching over the city.

Wasn't she the one with the holiday blues?

Over the past few days, he'd gradually turned inward and regressed to his former pensive state. As if the heavy, black cloud hanging over his presence had split open just for a second to let the light peep through.

She'd brought this on. She'd forced him back into his past, and that had refreshed his feelings for his wife. She might have died a long time ago, but in his heart, she was still very much alive.

Eve rose from the barstool at the kitchen island and crossed the living room. When she slid the glass door open, he looked over his shoulder. "You done?"

"Yeah. My eyes hurt—"

Her jaw dropped to the floor as he straightened to face her. "You're drinking?"

She'd seen him enjoy the exquisite bouquet of his beloved Bourbon before, but his lips had never actually touched the amber liquor in her presence. Why now?

"I am," he confirmed blithely.

He set the small glass with the wide belly and narrow rim down on the table beside him to free his hands, then pulled her close.

Uneasiness trickled down her back. Along with the heat of his body, a ripple of tension wafted off him. It wound through the muscles at his shoulders, raising alarm rather than excitement in her.

"Any particular reason?" she prodded.

"Nope." His embrace closed tighter around the small of her back, and his head dipped, his lips skimming along her shoulder as though he were trying to distract her from something.

The gnawing sensation in her stomach sank deeper. He was thinking of *her*, wasn't he? She could almost feel his wife's presence between them. No longer a specter but a solid manifestation of the woman standing between them, keeping them apart.

Eve wished she'd never asked. She felt like she was living on borrowed time, but she'd be damned if she didn't savor every second she was granted to hold onto him.

"You know, it's really not fair that you *can*, but I *can't*." Getting smashed sounded really good right now. She was already nauseous.

"You'd regret it, trust me."

"I drank Patrón."

"And then you passed out." He nuzzled the curve of her neck up to the soft flesh of her ear, evoking a delightful twinge in between her thighs despite the knot in her stomach.

"Because it was laced with Lorazepam."

"No, Dove, the drug kept you sedated. The tequila sent your system into shock. Alcohol is essentially a poison. True, the effect doesn't last, but when you're unconscious, you're vulnerable. Your body just can't tolerate it."

"But yours can?"

He sighed in exasperation. "We're not... the same."

"You're saying I'm a different vampire than you?"

"Is that what we are? Sometimes I'm not sure," he whispered, his head shaking against hers. His long hair tickled the side of her face.

"You're not making any sense. Maybe you're drunk."

The distance in his voice kept her from diving deeper into the dread stretching across her bones. If he didn't want to talk, then she would play the game of ignorance.

"I can *drink*, but I can't really get *drunk*," he pointed out.

In his next breath, his arms unlinked from behind her, and as he eased back, a wicked glimmer shot across his eyes. "How about a compromise, then?"

His offer came out more like a challenge. Eve watched him reach for the Glencairn on the table with exhilarating curiosity. He raised it to his lips, knocking the rest of his drink back in one gulp. His throat bobbed, and her mouth went dry, unable to pry her eyes away from the veins that ran up the side.

Kjan had barely set the glass down when his right hand snapped to the base of her skull, snaring it in his large palm. A spasm jerked her leg muscles. His head dipped, and hers tilted toward him automatically in anticipation.

The instant his lips met hers, his fierce heat raced through her, setting her cells aglow with all the force their bond could generate.

The insistent tips of his fingers delved deeper into the soft tissue at her nape. He kept his grip firm but his kiss gentle, running his tongue over her lips before nudging past the threshold of her teeth. He licked his way into her. Explored her mouth with diligent patience.

Eve let out a soft moan, and her body went lax. His strong arms around her waist were the only thing keeping her upright.

"Do you feel it?" he breathed hotly against her cheek, his voice inching closer to her ear.

The breeze dancing across her skin, the prickle at her scalp, the pounding inside her head... she felt everything.

The stars in the clear sky overhead were swiveling. With every pump of her heart, more of the liquor pulsed through her veins.

"It's so strong. Why is it so strong?"

"You're extremely sensitive to the effects, but it won't last long. Your metabolism will burn it off in seconds," he explained. "Breathe with me."

The cool metal rail bit into the curve of her backside as he braced her up against it. Palms at either side of her neck, he cradled her face in his hands, running the tip of his nose along the narrow bridge of hers.

She got lost in the perfect little moment, chest to chest, hearts beating in a matching rhythm. This was what she would remember.

"Better?"

Eve gave a silent nod.

"Good. I want you to be sober when I make love to you."

"Make love?" she echoed. "That's so sweet."

He stifled a laugh against her mouth. "Would you rather have me use your explicit vernacular?"

"Mmmm," she hummed contentedly, eyes closed. "You don't have to use words at all. I'm perfectly capable of translating your body language." Tugging on the waistband of his sweatpants, she arched her hips against his erection. "It's the only other one I'm fluid in."

"Not true. Your French is on point."

She chuffed in a retort. "I hardly ever cuss." It wasn't like she dropped F-bombs left and right. She only used it for emphasis.

"I was referring to your extracurricular tongue work, Dove," he clarified in a sultry timber voice.

"Oh, right. Well, that's one of *your* specialties too." She grinned.

His mouth slanted down on her in a ferocious kiss that she felt down to her toes. One arm snaked back around her waist, his other hand gripped her thigh to carry her off.

ʃ
⟨HAPTER

15

51 hours until the eclipse.

Two weeks had flown by, and Kjan could no longer ignore the emptiness growing inside him. He had successfully managed to keep Eve in the dark, making no changes to their usual routines, but his denial was nearing its inevitable end.

After keeping her awake well into the early morning hours, he slid out of bed and got dressed, trying not to wake her...

...and failed.

"Where are you going?"

Damn. His shoulders sagged, not from the weight of the boots in his hand.

He let go of the door and turned back to the bed. Eve was lying prone on her chest, hugging her pillow, half of her face buried. The silk sheet covering her body only reached the middle of her back, giving way to the perfect bend of her spine.

He lowered himself down on his side of the bed, brushing his fingertips along the curve and observing the twitch of her lips into a subtle smile. The strong muscles in her back tensed as she stirred from his touch. Arms raised and wrapped around the pillow under her head, she was flashing him some sideboob.

He quickly pressed a kiss to her shoulder and tugged the sheet higher. "I have to take care of something."

"In the middle of the day?" Eve didn't open her eyes as she groaned.

"Sunset's in an hour." He chuckled. "I won't be long. I promise."

His smile faded the second he turned his back. Then he was out the door and on his way to the jeweler.

As she had not expected him to return, the woman was concerned about any problems with his purchase, but Kjan assured her it was perfect and that he simply wanted to make an addition.

He stuck around while the owner took care of his request, and then there was one more stop he had to make before heading home.

The two errands on his list stole time he would rather have spent with Eve, but they were a necessity. She was huddled under a plush blanket on the chaise, already hard at work once he made it back.

Her eyes lifted toward him, and a grin stretched across her face. She looked so beautiful in the antique piece, with the nearly full moon rising behind her.

Kjan grabbed his own laptop and joined her. "Do you have a minute?"

"What's up?"

"There is something I want to run by you." He turned his screen toward her.

Eve looked puzzled. "What is this?"

"My personal accounts and finances. I want you to know the basics of how it works." He had already taken care of everything in advance. The final shipments under his supervision had cleared customs, and the new CEOs he had appointed were eager to pick up the slack while ownership remained under his assumed names.

"Why?"

"Just humor me." He tried to sound casual. "You're the one always lecturing me about not treating you like an adult, so here is your chance to shine."

Eve narrowed her eyes at him, and he wasn't sure if she was buying the false pretense.

"Alright, good point. Teach me." She straightened with an excited smile on her face that made his heart ache.

She picked up the details quickly, and he even ran her through a few different aliases he still used. The passive income would continue. It was one thing she didn't have to worry about.

"I got you something while I was out."

"A Christmas present? I didn't think we were doing that." Eve closed her eyes and held out her hands.

Kjan fished the set of keys from his pocket and dropped them into her open palms. She looked at him, confused.

"What are these for?"

"Your new Tahoe." He grinned.

"A Tahoe?" Clearly not the new kind of wheels she expected, but the size upgrade in the vehicle was for safety reasons. "Why didn't you just get me a tank?"

He matched her sarcasm with derision. "Because those aren't street legal."

"Fair enough." She shrugged. "Thank you."

Eve put the keys down on the side table and grabbed her phone. "Come on, snow." She was checking the weather report again in anticipation. "Ooh, there is a total lunar eclipse tomorrow night at 7:22. A blood moon. The full moon is going to glow pink. How pretty."

The hollow sensation in the pit of his stomach returned. Her lips kept moving, but Kjan stopped tracking them after that, the few syllables from her mouth cutting him to the bone. They left his emotions raw.

He closed the laptop, not even bothering with shutting it down properly, then grabbed her phone and tossed it onto the floor.

"What are you doing?"

"No more work," he replied, closing the distance between them. He yanked off the blanket and tugged on her precarious bun to release her hair.

"No more work? Who are you?" Her words seemed to object, but her body was very much in agreement as she grabbed him by the front of his shirt, wrapping one leg around him.

The shot of adrenaline her enthusiasm triggered sent his blood thundering in his head. His breath fell into shorter, faster huffs.

Keeping her eyes steady on him, she took his hand and brought it up to her mouth, sucking his finger in between her lips and rolling her tongue around it.

A prickle ran up his nape, recalling the feel of her mouth on him. Sparks of pleasure ignited at every nerve ending.

As he retracted his finger to replace it with his tongue, her lips parted in surrender to welcome him. Licking his way deeper into her, he lifted her onto his lap with one arm, splitting her thighs over his hips.

She inhaled sharply at the bold contact between her legs, but it wasn't really a surprise. She knew how badly he ached for her. Tasted it in his kiss as much as he did in hers.

He found her lips again, with a gnawing hunger to match his own, and all but growled when she rolled into him.

Skimming his hands lower, he followed the soft curve of her body, fingertips sinking into the muscle of her ass. Eve got with the program and rocked herself against him, the thin fabric of her leggings, not being enough of a barrier to obstruct the friction.

Kjan broke from her kiss. He ran his fangs over her skin, his nose brushing the curve of her throat. One arm ensnaring her, his free hand left her hip and moved across her thigh, sliding inward.

With his greedy fingers repositioned, he forced pleasure and shivery moans from her, making her tremble on top of him. She was so wet to his touch that he nearly lost focus. Fortunately, she was in complete control of the situation. He didn't mind being used like this.

Drunk on each other and both of them panting, her body shuddered through violent spasms. His restraints snapped, the rosy flush of her cheeks fueling his ache.

Not enough, he thought, his breath sawing in and out of him faster still.

The flutter in his chest increased to a painful need to touch more of her. He ran his hands up her back, pulling the shirt over her head. Then went for her bra.

He bit right through the front, springing the two halves open like a treasure chest to reveal the prize he was after.

More…

He slid the scraps off, latching onto her pink nipple without a warning. His tongue lolled around the tender peaks. He sucked them into his mouth, one at a time, his grabby hands mapping every curve of her.

Quivering as she did with shallow breaths, she arched into him even more, compressing him beneath her with each rocking motion.

MORE!

His palms skated up and down her body more aggressively as he nipped at the underside of her breast—

Kjan froze. He had cut her. Drawn blood unintentionally.

He was spiraling. Fast. His body was moving, but his mind couldn't focus. This was all wrong. It was not how he wanted to spend tonight.

"I'm sorry," he choked out, his voice trembling.

"What's wrong?"

"I didn't mean to."

"Don't worry." She shook her head. "I'm fine."

"No, it's not… it's not right." His throat tightened, and he felt the panic attack coming on, smothering him, blurring his vision.

He swallowed, blinking rapidly, and straining with each erratic attempt for air. "I don't want to hurt you."

"Kjan stop. You're scaring me. What are you talking about? I'm not some porcelain doll. You're not going to break me."

The words stung in his chest. He *would* break her, though. Crush her little heart to pieces.

She scrambled off his lap, but he didn't let her get far. With shaky hands, he held on to her wrists, took deep breaths, and forced his lungs open.

"I'm alright. I just got carried away." He smiled, trying to downplay the fact that he was going off the rails. His nerves were frayed.

He pulled her off the chaise and led her into the bedroom. "This is what I really want." His thumbs traced her jawline as he cradled her face, keeping his kisses light and soft when backing her up against the bed.

He sank in front of her, stripping the rest of her clothes before he released her.

Eve watched him undress, He didn't rush that, either. He drank in her hungry gaze. Her eyes chased his movements while her teeth tugged at her lush bottom lip.

With his hands at the back of her thighs, she held onto him, and he lifted her off the ground, moving slowly and taking his time now. He didn't want a quick fix. He wanted to memorize every freckle, every inch of her body.

He worshiped her with his touch. His tongue. He led her to the peak of ecstasy before taking any for himself. She was so beautiful, so perfect, and he relished the moment she came with him, from the way she arched her back to the divine whimper leaving her lips. There was nothing more beautiful than watching her splinter apart.

He didn't hold back. He needed to fill her again. Receding to flip her onto her front, Kjan dragged his tongue and fangs from the crook of her ass up her back, tracing her spine to the base of her neck. She quivered beneath him, hands twisted in the sheets.

Settled on his elbow, he snaked his arm under her waist and hauled her onto her knees. "Let me in, Dove," he whispered, lips grazing her cheek, eyes squeezed shut to focus on his other senses.

His hold firm on her hip, Eve exhaled a stuttering breath, relaxing her muscles, her knees spread wide for balance. He wrapped his arm around her chest and pulled her flush against him as he found his rhythm. Bracing their joined bodies, his fangs at the side of her throat, she ground back into him, rocking to meet his thrusts.

Kjan's thoughts threatened to drown him. Enveloping her small frame with his, he focused on the cries she made when she shattered beneath him. Still locked in his embrace, her body shuddered through the pleasurable throes again and again.

The first light of the morning was just prickling across his skin when he climaxed a third time, Eve's legs quivering, unable to hold her own weight any longer. The shoulder that supported him started to tremble too.

Kjan released his grip around her rib cage and lowered her onto the bed. "Take my vein," he urged, rolling her onto her side and settling next to her. "Please, before you fall asleep."

She could barely keep her eyes open, so he pulled her across his chest, gently guiding her to his jugular.

Cradling the back of her head in his hand, he felt her lips brush against his skin, right before the light punch of her fangs.

Relief washed over him as she drew his blood for the last time. Kjan closed his eyes to fight the tears and burrowed his face in her hair, holding her closer, breathing her in. He didn't want her to see him breaking down. He couldn't let her know that he was falling apart. He didn't want to die.

He felt like was drowning, and there was no lifeline... no escape.

"You seem tired." Eve circled her fingertips over his heart. "When was the last time you fed?"

"I'm fine." Kjan brought her hand to his lips and kissed the center of her palm.

It wasn't technically a lie. There was nothing wrong with him physically. Although she was right about him being tired. He hadn't slept in days. He was running out of time to spend with her, and he was not going to waste it sleeping. Even if he had the option.

Instead, he settled for watching her, holding on to the steady rhythm of her heartbeat, and praying that she would be alright.

Renate Rowland

CHAPTER

16

E ve felt the movement of the mattress. "You're leaving again?" she asked, her question a sleepy mumble.

Kjan didn't answer, but the weight of his body settled back on the bed behind her while she kept her eyes closed. His arm slid around her waist. His breath warmed her neck with a kiss.

"I love you."

"Love you too," she whispered back as he pulled away.

Wait, where did he say he's going? Eve was too tired to remember asking.

It was 3:15 in the afternoon when his feet carried him to his destination. Kjan couldn't wait until sunset. He was like a ticking time bomb already, and his hands were shaking uncontrollably.

He had slipped out of bed to shower the moment Eve had fallen asleep. He had washed every trace of her off, but he couldn't bleed her from his veins. She was still in his head, buried deep beneath his skin.

Slouched on the steps of the tattoo shop, he waited until the full moon crept over the roofs. With his eyes on the sky, watching the first snowflakes of the season fall, a hollowness grew in the place where his heart used to beat.

Two human women eventually approached him, and he looked up from where he sat. *An escort?* Didn't that make him feel special.

"Come with us," the taller one ordered him like she was in charge.

Her honey-colored eyes reminded him of whisky as she focused on him and made him wish he had reconsidered his decision to stay lucid for this. She spoke English, but she had a familiar accent. She was not American.

The other woman, with a mop of auburn curls framing her face and pale skin, natural for a redhead, avoided his eyes altogether. But he recognized her nonetheless. She was the waitress who had offered him a drink at Eleanor's fundraiser at the Glasshouse.

What was in the drink?

If she had been working with his Sire instead of Andromeda, she wouldn't have tried to poison him with deadly nightshade. A drug that could have subdued him, perhaps?

It didn't matter now. Kjan refrained from asking any questions and meekly trailed them to a car. They were on the road for an hour before they turned down a dark, uneven road that led them to the entrance of a hidden cave around Mount Hood.

The couple exited the vehicle first, and he followed behind, approaching the large gate where a young man awaited them. His appearance was that of a street kid. His features were harsh, and his hair was shaved down to almost nothing, but Kjan could tell his hair was brown. His eyes were deep navy blue, almost black, and seemed hardened by tough life experience. He didn't say a word when unhinging the heavy iron and jerking his head toward the mouth of the tunnel.

Claw marks, probably made by bears, scarred the entrance walls before the passage constricted into a narrow stairwell. It dwindled into the cavern's heart, a seemingly endless abyss where a choking darkness awaited him.

Kjan's throat tightened. He reached out to the side, his hand grazing the bumpy stone wall as he made his descent into the unknown. He didn't like the idea of going underground. He wasn't claustrophobic, but he much preferred the view of the city from above. That was why he always chose places on the top floor; high-rises were much more his thing.

The sounds of the wind lessened until only the deafening echo of their footsteps remained. Along with the cold, damp air, the foreboding feeling of being trapped washed over him. The icy chill of fear crept deeper into his bones.

So familiar.

The dreadful sensation squeezed tighter around his throat. He pushed the images out of his mind.

At last, the steps came to an end. The bottom, scarcely lit by torches, opened to various small catacombs and one very large chamber. Heavy double doors stood wide, waiting to swallow him up like the maw of an ancient beast.

Kjan had to wonder how long this had been here and who had used the caverns before. Unlike the smuggler tunnels beneath Chinatown, where Andromeda had taken Eve, he had never known about the existence of the extensive underground maze in the mountains. There were too many tunnels and chambers to count.

His legs balked for a moment. A heavy, repulsive smell hung in the air that triggered a faint memory. *Smoldering henbane.* The seeds burned over coal to produce the toxic fumes, which had a sedative effect similar to that of belladonna. Kjan tried to recall what he remembered from the old rituals involving the herb. It was supposed to endow *Spirit Flight* by easing the soul out of the body and guiding its crossing to the otherworld, bringing a swift death.

The Norn Verðandi, who represented the present, was often associated with it. Along with her two sisters, she weaved the threads of destiny. Woven by Urðr, Norn of the past, the thread was passed through the hands of Verðandi and would inevitably be cut by Skuld, Norn of the future, at the moment of the individual's death.

Crossing over the threshold, the smoke scorched Kjan's lungs as he inhaled, and the sickening odor forced him into a stupor.

"*Welcome!*" the voice greeted him kindly in Old Norse.

The small figure was wearing a large, blood-red ceremonial cloak. It looked heavy and dragged on the ground behind him, dwarfing his delicate shape even more. Bile rose in his throat, knowing now that he had been tortured by the puny hands of a runt.

The *child* turned toward Kjan with a satisfied smile as he addressed him. "I am glad to see you have not changed your mind. I would have very much disliked tracking you down and holding you to your word."

He could practically feel the threat in his bones, even though the words were spoken softly in a gentle tone.

They weren't alone. The three humans from earlier and one other male, all dressed in similar robes, joined them in the main chamber. The two women who had escorted him sealed the doors behind him from the outside.

"I hope you enjoy this dwelling as much as I do. I thought it would be the perfect place to choose as the residence of my—" He chuckled as he corrected himself. "I mean, *our* new coven. I assume you recall how it worked the first time?"

Minor details that Kjan had deemed insignificant were starting to come back to him. Like the fact that a blood moon had also risen over the glacier that night before he entered.

"How could I fucking forget?" he gnashed, adding a little 'French' to his American.

If only Eve could hear me now.

The boy looked briefly irked by Kjan's disrespectful use of profanity, perceiving it as the personal attack that it was. His jaw ticked with contempt before he recovered his gleeful smirk.

"Good. The physical part of the ritual will be much the same. Only this time, you will have a front-row seat." He made a big show of pointing out the many candles and torches up against the stone walls.

Unlike the icy cave the last time he had been through this, this hall was illuminated by dozens of tall black ceremonial candles on iron stands, each of them at least four inches in width and one foot tall. Kjan's vision would not be obscured by darkness.

Fan-fucking-tastic.

His eyes canvassed the chamber, taking it all in. A Helm of Awe was etched into the stone on the floor a few feet in front of him. It was identical to the one on his right pectoral, except it was the size of a pickup truck. Mainly a magical symbol of protection, its purpose was also to strike fear, and it was doing a formidable job at that.

Two chains were fastened to anchors in the stone floor on either side of it. At the end of each was a handcuff. The modern design had a rotating arm that engaged with a ratchet and didn't fit the medieval-torture-dungeon look, but an unnatural power radiated from the shackles. Kjan had to assume they were competent to hold him should he choose to put up a fight.

Surrounding the Helm was the design of Jǫrmungandr, the world serpent, which also snaked up the entire length of Kjan's left arm. It too held special meaning in the Heathen Faith. Generally, the snake biting its own tail and forming an eternal circle represented the cycle of life with no true beginning or end. It signified that everything simply transformed into something new. The ancient symbol was still popular today, but most people were more familiar with the Greek name Ouroboros.

A large stone slab in the far back of the room served as an altar. Two dead ravens with their wings spread were pinned on top of it, and a long golden dagger was placed in between them.

Kjan felt a jolt in his chest when the immortal took the blade from the altar and approached him. The voice in his head told him to run. Ravens signaled reflection, recovery, and healing. They were supposed to ease moving through transitions by casting light into darkness. However, the birds on the altar were dead. This was all wrong. The ancient rites and rituals, twisted to be used for HIS purpose.

He built himself a temple. He has no intention of leaving Portland. Kjan's thoughts scrambled.

"Kneel!" The Ancient One's words echoed through the great hall as he pointed the dagger at the center of the Helm on the ground.

Kjan felt himself frozen with fear. Yet not for himself. Although he knew the pain would be unbearable, he only feared for Eve. He didn't trust the immortal. There was no doubt in his mind that his Sire would resort to using her against him. Of course, killing her wasn't an option without losing the only leverage; Kjan would never agree to the transfer willingly. But the monster wouldn't hesitate to torture her and make her suffer in his place.

He had no choice.

Tearing his shirt over his head, Kjan stepped forward and fell to his knees. His heartbeat pulsed frantically at his throat. He closed his eyes and tried to control his breathing as the chains were linked around his wrists, stretching his arms out wide.

When he heard the light footsteps coming to a halt right in front of him, he lifted his gaze.

With an impassive expression on his face, the boy aimed the golden tip at Kjan's right shoulder and dragged it along the inside of his arm down to his wrist.

A searing trail followed its path through his skin across his bicep and forearm, but Kjan refused to turn his head to acknowledge the wound.

His Sire repeated the same on his other arm. "You heal so much faster than the last time I had the pleasure of torturing you," he said, marveling with pride over what he created.

"Then what's the point of it?" Kjan raised his chin higher. "Quit fucking around and get on with it already." Not that he was in a hurry, but the suspense sucked more than the papercuts on his arms.

"Call me nostalgic. The last time, I forced you to let me in. Tonight, you embrace your transformation willingly. I want it to be special," he replied, stepping back to the center.

Dangling the golden dagger by his side, the small figure raised his left forefinger to his chest. As he began carving a long line down the center of his own flesh using his nail, he spoke in the old language, "*I call to you with an open heart. I pray to you with open eyes. Hear me, Baldr, most beautiful, bright-shining God. You, who rule over Ásgarðr, guide me out of the darkness, for there is no other being who burns with your fire. Hail Baldr, living amongst the dead. Yours is the tale of what must be, and of what must end. I honor you, Fallen Son, great God of Light.*"

To the first vertical stave, he added the bellies of the B-shape that were pointed instead of round, creating a ᛒ—*Bjarkan*, the Elder rune for birth and growth. It was the symbol associated with the Light God.

After closing the shape at the bottom, he brought his hand back up. He wasn't done. Kjan narrowed his eyes with apprehension.

"*I call to you with an open heart. I pray to you with open eyes,*" his Sire went on, extending the vertical line at the top of the *Bjarkan* with the branch reaching down and out to the right like a reversed number one. Then he added the short horizontal branch to the left at the center of the B-rune, pointing upward like a check mark, to create a bindrune out of *Bjarkan* and one other: ᛇ—*Eihwaz*, the symbol for regeneration, rebirth, and death.

How fitting.

The rune was assigned to the yew tree, Yggdrasill, which connected the world of the living with the world of the dead. The vertical line symbolized the world pillar, and its two hooks represented the link to life and death. The shape as a whole was the union of both universes, hence giving power to exchange and travel freely between the two.

Kjan's blood curdled. Eihwaz signaled a turning point in life. It was considered a rune of endurance as well as transformation, and therefore a herald of profound change. It was believed to show the true destiny of a person, and if one was ready to dare a new beginning, the rune stood with its whole force and protection in the quest, granting the strength of resistance and determination. Kjan knew there was no derailing his Sire's ambition.

The boy wet his lips. *"Hear me, Hǫðr, father, God of Darkness and Winter, peerless warrior, and prince of Ásgarðr, companion of Baldr and Hel in the underworld. Hail Hǫðr, who bore the burden alone and followed his twin in death. You, who now rule by your brother's side as his advisor and council, I honor you, God of the Accused, of Atonement, and of Redemption."*

Locking eyes, he switched the blade from his right hand into his left and pointed the tip at Kjan, who coiled his fingers around the iron links in preparation for what he knew was to come.

He didn't blink. The double edge plunged into his abdomen, the force of the low blow lurching him toward the attack as the restraints held him in place.

Curling inward, he pulled on the chain but made no sound. A cry was a sign of dishonor.

His vision blurred, framed by his hair that had fallen forward. The metal scraped against his lungs. He felt the slow drag of the upward motion all the way to his sternum.

Still, he stayed quiet.

Over his body's screaming pain, he heard the clanking sound of the dagger dropping to the ground, but he knew it wasn't over. He didn't remember all the details; he had been going in and out of consciousness from pain and blood loss. The things he did recall, he wished he didn't.

When he forced his head up, the boy had taken a step back and opened his arms to the sky, continuing the prayer. *"I call to you with an open heart. I pray to you with open eyes. Hear me, fair Frigg, wise and knowing Goddess, Lady of Ásgarðr, judicious one, watchful and aware. Hail to you, beloved Frigg, Guardian of Children, Defender of Family, Holder of Harmony, and Heart of the Home."*

He paused and waited, his stance stiff.

Nothing happened. The chamber remained immersed in silence.

"No one is going to answer your call. Haven't you heard? The Gods are dead," Kjan sneered through the pain. A spark of hope flickered inside him.

"Yes, Ragnarǫk. I am aware. But not all Gods are gone." The corner of his lips curled up. "Some of them still live."

The Ancient One stepped back up to Kjan, prying his bony fingers into his rib cage just like he had done 954 years ago, almost to the day. Kjan could feel the grip on his heart. His body trembled in panic.

"I call to you now," he spoke again, his little fist clenched. *"I implore you. Grant me justice, for I was condemned for the*

shortcomings of others. Let me make amends. I have served my penance. Bless me with deliverance from my exile."

This time, when Kjan felt the slicing sensation of the organ's tissue, he recognized the shape. It was an exact copy of the bindrune on his Sire's own chest, carved into Kjan's heart. The ritual signified a timeless connection between the two of them, giving the vessel a truly eternal purpose, and since the vow was to be taken willingly, it would prove Kjan to be loyal and trustworthy.

A coldness started to spread from his fingertips along his arms, which were now only held up by the restraints. He had no more strength left. He was so close to passing out. Feeling his body going into shock, he willed his eyes open.

The floor beneath him started to shake. Gusts of wind filled the grand chamber as the light of the torches expanded toward the ceiling.

A grip in his hair tipped his head back. Matted strands stuck to his forehead, impeding his already-fading vision.

"The Gods have accepted my request." He heard the childlike voice in his head. "*Do you concede?*"

There was no air left in his lungs. He felt the life slipping out of him as he lost the fight to keep his eyes open. The oath left his lips without a sound, "*I concede.*"

As he exhaled his last breath, he wanted to hold on to every memory he had of Eve. Every little detail about her. The fear of forgetting what she looked like sliced through him, yet he knew the only way to keep her safe was to lock those memories away forever.

Her smile, her touch, the sparkle in her eyes—he would bury them so deep where HE could never find them.

Renate Rowland

CHAPTER

17

E ve rolled over onto her back apprehensively, expecting the aftermath of last night to sink its teeth into her muscles any second.

It didn't.

She woke up from her half-coma fully recovered. Her body felt amazing, and if it wasn't for the vivid pictures replaying in her head, she wouldn't have believed they'd spent the entire night in bed. She'd passed out stiff and sore. In a good way.

Correction. The best way.

She craned her neck toward Kjan's side of the bed. He wasn't next to her, and she vaguely remembered him leaving earlier but couldn't for the life of her recall what time it had been. In the dark bedroom, the bold white numbers of the alarm clock on the nightstand popped in contrast against the sleek black wood design: 7:08 p.m.

How long has he been gone?

She slipped out of bed, then showered and got dressed, picking out a dark blue pair of comfy leggings and one of Kjan's hoodies that was a size large but fit her like a triple XL.

As she crossed the living room to look for her phone, she noticed the unusually bright view from the window.

Snow!

It must've started a little while ago. There was already a thin white layer settling on the balcony. She eagerly opened the door to step outside, the soles of her bare feet leaving perfect little footprints.

With the flurries still coming down steadily, she looked up at the full moon as it crept into the earth's shadow and turned a gorgeous dark shade of red against the black sky.

The eclipse, she remembered. It was so beautiful, it almost felt magical. She wrapped her arms around herself to keep from shivering, wishing Kjan was here.

Returning inside to warm her toes, she finally found her phone on the kitchen counter. Next to both laptops and the keys to her new wheels.

A queasy sensation roiled through her insides. It was odd, almost as if he had arranged the whole setup.

When she checked the screen, there were no missed calls or messages. She instinctively dialed Kjan's number. To her surprise, the call went straight to voicemail.

That was unusual.

She had no other option to reach him. Sending him a text was pointless if his phone was turned off.

Clutching her cell, Eve got the sudden sense of a flashback: the night Kjan had returned from Charlotte's. Dying.

Where the hell is he?

The instant her mind formed the question, there was a pulling sensation in her chest, like two magnets being forced apart against their natural attraction. Her pulse began to speed up, heart pounding seemingly for no reason.

But there *was* a reason. The vacuum. Something was wrong. She just knew something was—

With an abrupt lurch, she felt her body slump, the warmth of the stable flame inside her blown out in a single breath.

Dread crept into the void left behind.

Suddenly overcome with despair, Eve staggered back through the living room. She wasn't sure where her feet were carrying her until she landed on the soft, tufted leather of Kjan's chair.

She curled up into it. The tall sides of the wingback towered over her head, absorbing her tiny figure as she craved comfort.

She felt silly for being so melodramatic, but it wasn't like him to just vanish without notice. And then there was the way he had acted last night.

From her refuge, Eve watched the blood moon rise to its peak in the sky. The snow had stopped falling, and the city looked so peaceful in its pristine glow. There was still no news from Kjan, and her worry grew with every hour that passed.

Zoning in and out, she heard people moving about in the suites below, and by the time dawn brought on the beginning of a new workweek in the city, she was sure something had happened to him.

Eve chided herself for not going after him sooner. She should've followed her gut. Should've known better than to just sit around and wait. But where could she possibly look for him?

She rose from the chair, unable to sit still any longer and started pacing, trying to clear her head, rubbing at her temples.

She couldn't wait until sunset, even though the bright snow was irritating her retinas. It made her want to scratch the inside of her eyeballs. Sunglasses wouldn't do with the blanket of snow.

Eve was struck by a sudden weariness, her head pounding in alarm. How was she going to make it through the day with this nagging feeling chasing her? Her hands started to shake, and she clenched them into fists, focusing on calming herself down.

Screw this. There was no calming down or getting any sleep. She put on her shoes and snatched up the keys for the Tahoe as well as her set of house keys from the little table by the door.

She made it down to the garage and stopped short. Kjan's black Charger was parked in its usual spot.

If he left hours ago, how is his car still here? It didn't add up.

Her mind reeled, grasping at explanations. Dizziness made her swayed, and Eve leaned her shoulder into the concrete pillar to keep her body upright. Her breath came quicker now as she started to panic and tightened her grip on the keys, one set in each hand.

Then a suspicious feeling struck.

She looked down at them, opening her hands slowly in front, and inspected the ring that still held the key for her crashed Volkswagen as well as a key for the garage, condo, and mailbox. Her heart stopped at the sight of the black key that wasn't hers.

That was when the truth came crashing down on her. Kjan hadn't told her where he was headed or when he would return. That should've been the first red flag because it was so unlike him. She'd been too tired to question him, almost as if he'd anticipated that.

Or planned it.

Her shoulders sagged. Eve felt sick. He wasn't coming back. The key was proof. Why else would he have given it to her after being so adamant about her not driving the Charger?

He was gone. She'd felt the exact moment his soul disconnected and the presence of her mate was ripped away from her.

Brokenhearted, Eve took the elevator back upstairs and threw herself on the bed. Clinging to his scent that still lingered in the sheets, she pulled the blanket over her head.

She hadn't seen the signs, but they had been there, hadn't they? It was all coming together now. The way he'd made sure she knew how to handle the finances, for example, and other things too. Little things, like the way he'd looked at her last week. He'd acted so strangely, keeping her in the dark.

But Kjan had sworn that he would never again attempt to take his own life. Would he really break his oath to her?

∫

His eyes refocused on the ceiling as he blinked.

Once.

Twice.

He was lying on his back on the rough ground of the cave's grand chamber, his memory returning slowly.

The transference.

He staggered to his feet, clutching the sides of his skull, in an attempt to get his bearings. In front of him, a momentarily small number of acolytes dropped to their knees, bowing their heads to him.

His mouth curled into a twisted grin. *Yes!* His plan had worked. After spending millennia trapped in the cave as punishment for simply being born, he finally had true freedom.

CHAPTER

18

E ve huddled on the chaise lounge, computer in her lap. It was snowing again. The large flakes fell and fell, flurries curling and dancing carefree in the gentle wind.

As it filled the harsh edges of the concrete jungle, a clean, white blanket settled on a world of grays. It covered up the past and present, wiping the slate clean.

Days had passed with her in denial, refusing to accept the truth. A part of her was still clinging to the hope that she was wrong. If he wasn't dead, he was going to find his way back to her one day. She'd wait a thousand years if she had to.

Her phone buzzed with another text from Tanya, begging her to go out tonight. Like she needed to be around happy couples and people in love right now.

Eve didn't feel like answering. And she didn't feel like partying either, New Year's or not. Her plans were the same as they had been for Christmas: locking herself up at home.

She inhaled a deep breath and forced it slowly out through her nose. Tanya and Caleb were good people and the only friends she had. They had quickly become more than coworkers in the short time Eve had worked at *Jack's*. She considered herself lucky to have met them. If she pushed them away too, she wouldn't have anyone left.

Keeping up appearances, even when your body is little more than an empty shell, is important.

Eve grabbed her phone and replied to the text, promising to show. She could manage to drop by for an hour, couldn't she?

She got changed and headed down to the garage. The sight of the Charger twisted her gut, and she tried to ignore the feeling. She couldn't see herself ever driving it.

In her brand-spanking-new white Tahoe, she drove down to *Jack's* to meet up with Tanya and Colby. The streets were packed with people cheering, and Eve instantly regretted leaving home.

Fighting back the tears, she took another deep breath. She was not going to cry. Instead, she pushed her grief down and got out of the car to join her friends inside.

"Yo, Eve! Over here," Colby called out to her from a table near the bar, his black, 4-inch Mohawk a beacon above the crowd, adding to his height.

She forced a smile on her face and gave him a big hug when Tanya came around to take her turn.

"I'm so glad you showed. We haven't seen you in ages." Her blue hair was a few inches longer than the last time she'd seen her.

Eve hoped they wouldn't bring up Kjan. After Jordan, he was the second guy to disappear on her without a trace in less than two months, according to the general knowledge of her friends.

She'd come up with a story about him leaving for a job somewhere else, and honestly, she didn't even remember which city she'd told them. As long as they didn't mention his name, she could make it through this without having a complete meltdown.

"Were the walls finally coming in on you at home?" Colby teased. "I told you, you need a distraction. You look like you could use a stiff one."

Eve cringed.

"Uh, I mean drink," he tagged on when receiving an elbow in the side from his girlfriend for the comment. "You could use a real drink. That's all I'm sayin'." He threw up his hands apologetically, his bull piercing glinting with the twist of his mouth.

Tanya shot him another dark look from beneath the silver barbell in her right eyebrow, her usually warm brown eyes almost as black as his.

As students at PCC, the two were in their early twenties and had been dating for three years. Eve had to admit they made a great couple. They had the kind of chemistry that would last, with similar tastes and interests. Tanya's ears were gauged like Colby's but much smaller than the double-zeros in his earlobes. Cobalt blue tunnels sat in hers, where his matched the titanium coating of the ring beneath his nose. He looked like the type of guy who had metal hidden in other places, but Eve had never confirmed her theory with her friend.

His facial piercings didn't distract from his good looks, though. His mixed Native-American features were quite handsome, and his smile was genuinely kind. Eve wondered if he inherited that from his mom, along with his dark, almond-shaped eyes and high cheekbones.

"Let me get the next round," he offered.

Colby had been trying to persuade her with his comments about working at a pub and not partaking in the *advantages it provided*—meaning the free booze. The table was already littered with an impressive collection of empty shot glasses.

"I appreciate the effort, but I'll stick to water as usual. I'm driving anyway."

"Buzzkill. Why wouldn't you just Uber here? It's freakin' New Years!"

He threw back a shot of tequila, and for a second, Eve had to think of Jordan. She remembered the burn in her throat and almost heaved.

Nope. Not going there, either.

She swallowed hard and pushed the thought back down as Colby bit the lemon. He was right about the distraction, of course. She had to admit that it felt good to be around people.

The *high* didn't last, though. The cacophony of people laughing and all the shoving eventually became too much. The mix of beer and hot wings stung her nose, making her stomach turn over in disapproval.

Eve called it a night around 1 a.m., when for most people, the party was far from over. She got in her Tahoe, trying to avoid the crowds dancing not just on the sidewalk but also in the street. A lot of them were wearing masks or costumes.

A chill chased down her spine, and she slammed hard on the brakes as a guy stumbled in front of her truck.

She managed to bring the vehicle to a stop before colliding with him, but he hammered both of his fists down on the hood, giving her a threatening glare through his shaggy brown bangs.

A golden shimmer in his eyes struck her, and she knew without a doubt the alarming chill she sensed was emanating from him. He was a vampire.

And so was the small female next to him.

Eve wasn't sure how she knew. She just did. Much like Jordan had known back then.

Thankfully, the two of them moved on without another glance, and she was clear to hit the gas.

Eve made it home, still a little shaken. She'd never seen other vampires in the city except for Jordan. He'd mentioned friends, and there was the one who owned the tattoo shop, but she had never actually run into any of them. Almost as if Kjan's presence had kept them at bay.

Or maybe he'd just known how to avoid them, probably sensing them from a distance.

Eve stretched out on the bed and focused on schoolwork until the sun started coming up. She was about to power down when an email notification came in. It was an automated end-of-the-month bank statement from one of Kjan's accounts.

She opened the record, wondering why the email was addressed to her directly instead of him. She found nothing out of the ordinary until she caught the recent modification in the account holder section.

Her name was listed in bold letters. Kjan must've made the change to put it in her name after walking her through the process.

He's gone. And he's never coming back.

She wished she could convince herself that Kjan had vanished with a reasonable explanation. That maybe there had been something he wanted to protect her from. That he would never have left her unless there had been no other way.

But none of that was true.

Two days after his disappearance, she'd noticed Andromeda's stake missing from the shelf in the living room. The bullet made from the same poisonous tree had turned her body into dust. That had to be how he'd done it. Driven the length of wood through his heart to end it all.

Kjan *had* broken his oath. He'd pledged his life to her—his body, mind, and soul—and she'd believed his words. Believed his actions, too, until something changed and he'd pulled away again, closing himself off. Eve had pushed him to relive his worst memories, and in sharing them with her, it had brought back all his pain.

No, not just the pain. The love for his wife had still been there as well.

In the end, she had not been enough to make him hang on, and the realization overwhelmed her, filling her with regret, disappointment, and anger. She felt betrayed. But not by Kjan. His own feelings had betrayed him, reversing his conviction and commitment to her.

And what was worse was that she couldn't blame him. It was her fault.

Yes. As harsh as the truth was, he had broken his oath to spare her more heartache in the long run from helplessly watching him succumb to the darkness within himself the same way Eleanor had.

Sometimes love just wasn't enough to save someone.

Not *her* love anyway.

∫

It had not taken him long to determine the sudden decrease in his godly abilities that resulted from shedding his body.

But what good is all that power if the one thing you desire more than anything remains out of your reach?

The sacrifice was well worth it. For so long, he had been convinced that Kjan was the key, the missing link he needed for his plan to succeed. An inexplicable bond tying them together.

And his scheme had proven successful in the end. Even if he had to do it himself.

The first step on his agenda after awakening had been turning his acolytes and securing their irrevocable fealty. This new generation was quite unique. Having used his vessel to create them, they were unlike his first neophytes. But they were not exactly like the one Kjan had sired, either. The essence that gave them new life was very much his own and not his host's. The Ancient One could feel the connection between them.

Which ones proved superior remained to be seen.

Renate Rowland

CHAPTER

19

E ve couldn't believe she was really going to do this. *Flying to Europe on my own?* She had never been overseas before. Had never even traveled outside the North- and Midwest of the US on trips with her grandparents.

She was nervous and excited at the same time, but there was no place she wanted to go more in the entire world.

Not even Paris.

Kjan's knack for being overprotective used to drive her nuts. Now, she had to admit, she kind of missed it.

Of course she missed his smug grin and his heartfelt laughter. Missed his mouth on her skin and his hand in her hair. She missed the quiet moments when she'd caught him staring at her full of affection, as if he couldn't get enough.

But she missed all the little annoying things too. Like the way he would've insisted on planning out the whole trip down to the very last detail. If she'd ever been able to convince him to take her, that was.

So, since he wasn't here to be her guide on this adventure into the unknown—and wasn't here to stop her either—she had to find her way on her own. Just like she'd done these past few weeks.

Eve now fully understood the depression he'd gone through during the separation from Andromeda. Their pledge of commitment to each other had triggered an oxytocin addiction that manifested physically. The withdrawal was agony.

It had been nearly three months since she'd finally come to terms with Kjan's absence, but the glimmer of resentment for his decision remained.

Why was my love not enough? Why did he choose death over me? What did I do wrong? The questions kept repeating in her head, and maybe they were part of why she had to go on this trip. Something was calling to her.

Eve had made up her mind and been counting down the days ever since researching everything she could find on Iceland, geographically and historically. Kjan's tattoos had already piqued her interest, but she still needed to know more than the little bits and pieces he'd fed her. She'd practically devoured every book she could find, from Viking history to Norse Gods and mythology.

She'd always been somewhat of an agnostic and, at times, had felt more at peace walking through a forest than sitting in a church with her grandparents. There was this connection to nature that lingered in her bones.

Spiritual rather than religious, Kjan had called it. He'd unlocked her *Heathen Heart* and paved the way to something she couldn't put into words. Iceland was *his* home, and yet it felt like their roots were now intertwined. The spark of his soul was her conduit, and she felt a hunger, a yearning, that would never be satisfied unless she saw it with her own eyes.

It was March 8th. Eve had started to think of this date as their anniversary. It was the night Kjan had turned her in the woods one year ago, and she'd been wanting to come to Iceland for almost as long. He'd been resolute about never going back, but now she felt like this was the only place she could be close to him again. When the memories became too painful, she couldn't even find refuge in the home they used to share.

After her arrival at the airport, Eve rented a car to get around easier. The scenery of the country was simply magical, and coming alone wasn't too bad either. Sure, it would've been nice to share it with someone, like Tanya and Colby, but in the end, this was a journey she had to make on her own.

Over the next few days, she found her way around the various ice caves, waterfalls, and geysers and checked off all the typical touristy stuff she could possibly fit into her short trip to Reykjavík. The famous Blue Lagoon hadn't made the cut. She'd purposely crossed it off her list, deeming it way too romantic for her trip, with or without catching a glimpse of the breathtaking Northern Lights.

The hike to Brúarfoss had been her favorite, though, the view of the rambling waterfalls so stunning, it had made her want to weep.

Standing on the bridge above, enchanted by the sound of the tirelessly rushing water with its vivid turquoise coloring, Eve had spread her arms wide and closed her eyes. With the wind whipping through her hair, she'd heard his voice, whispering lovingly in her ear as if he were standing right beside her, his spirit the air beneath her wings.

It had seemed so real. A memory she could almost touch.

A scream had snaked beneath her skin then, threatening to tear her in half. *This is your home! This is where my heart belongs. Why would you choose not to share this place with me?*

The voice in the wind had not replied, and with her nerves frayed, she'd pried herself away from the scenery.

For her final night, Eve decided to give the nightlife a try, having avoided it all week. Her inner clock was a mess. With the jetlag and then taking tours during the day, she'd spent the nights actually sleeping.

She knew she had to hold off on feeding until she got home, and she'd managed to stretch the time in between to almost two weeks, preparing just for this trip. It was all worth it. She was exhausted, but she didn't care.

After spending an hour at a salon to give her hair a traditional makeover, Eve wasn't really in the mood for a bar crawl. She'd done some online research beforehand and was able to narrow it down to two clubs she wanted to check out before getting on the plane in the morning. Luckily, the nightclubs were open super late on weekends. Some of them didn't close until almost 6 a.m.

The first place she'd chosen was rather small, and though the music was right up her alley, she didn't stick around for more than an hour. It was too much like home, and she wanted something different.

Walking down the main street of the small city, she made it to one of the more notorious nightclubs. While waiting patiently in the long line outside, she tried to catch little conversation pieces from the crowd around her but failed miserably. Though she didn't have to worry about the language barrier being a problem since most people she'd had exchanges with spoke

English very well, she still wished she could pick out more. The Icelandic tongue was beautiful, and she wanted to retain as much of it as possible.

Kjan had been fluent in sixteen languages, so naturally, she felt a little behind. Even Andromeda had known at least three that Eve was aware of: Italian, English, and her native Greek.

After the long wait, Eve stepped through the threshold of the club, and the hair on her arms stood instantly on edge, buzzing as the music flooded her ears. From the volume of the sounds to the smell of alcohol and smoke invading her nose, down to the taste on her tongue, the scene was intense and incredibly overpowering. Even the ink from the stamp irritated her hypersensitive skin. It glowed a bright neon green in the black lights.

This place was a lot more extreme than Eve preferred. She loved Hardcore Punk Rock and Metalcore, but this was straight-up Death and Thrash Metal. The décor pieces on the walls featured pictures and logos of bands she was unfamiliar with and alienated her more by the minute.

The odor of cigarettes hung thick in the air, and Eve fought the urge to hurl. There was something artificial about it, and she'd always hated the smell. It was more chemical than the natural scent of tobacco leaves.

Why am I here?

She looked around, trying to get her bearings. The club was huge. There was even an upper level, but she couldn't see any access stairs; crowds blocked her view, screaming in each other's ears over the blaring music.

Jerking and spastically flashing lights in all colors of the rainbow left her disoriented and dizzy. Her hair was starting to stick to the back of her neck and her shoulders, but at least it wasn't plastered to her forehead, thanks to the braids keeping her long, rogue locks in check.

Strangers rubbing up against her was the final straw. She wanted out of here.

Eve squeezed through the gyrating mob of people grinding on each other and found her way past the lush seating area way in the back, only to encounter more clusters of bodies making out and getting busy in between the cushions.

The sight of the couples made her physically nauseous, and she was about to turn away when something in the midst of the colored lasers caught her eye. She wasn't sure what exactly had gotten her attention, but the familiar shape slowly lifted his head out of the woman's cleavage, where she was sprawled out beneath him.

Eve's heart stopped the moment their eyes locked. She couldn't breathe. As she stood far away in the crowd, it should've been too dark for him to see her, and yet he was looking right at her, his glowing red stare burning a whole into her.

He cocked his head.

Assaulted by the noxious air clogging her lungs like a hand around her throat, the world went on a spin. Eve whipped around so fast that she tripped over her own feet and faceplanted right into the chest of a really tall man, solid as a tree.

Without looking up or waiting for a response, she pushed past him and weaved back through the crowd toward the exit. Elbows jostling from every side in the dim interior, shoulders bumping into her, she was caught in a torrent with no way out. Everything was a blur.

Air.

I need air.

Bursting through the front door, totally uncoordinated, Eve stumbled onto the sidewalk. The cool night breeze came to her rescue, easing the burn in her lungs, and she inhaled deeply as she recovered her footing.

Next thing she knew, she was running without slowing down until she was around the corner and out of anyone's view. Then her legs gave out.

Eve collapsed to the ground. Bracing her shaking hands against the cold, hard concrete, she broke down crying. Her heart shattered into a million pieces all over again.

Those eyes! Oh God, those eyes.

The memory of them sent a shiver through her nerves. They haunted her still. But it couldn't have been him. There was no way.

If it weren't for the tug in my heart…

This was a mistake. She shouldn't have come here. What was she doing, chasing ghosts? She wanted to go home.

∫

His nostrils flared when he caught the scent of fresh spring air inside the club, as though someone had lifted the roof right off the building.

He became enthralled with it as it seemed to flow through his very veins, turning into a physical experience: the gentle touch of a hand, a soft caress along the nape of his neck, and down the center of his back.

The bouquet of delicate flowers inflating his lungs brought an image of sunshine to his mind, and he lifted his eyes, darting, searching the crowd until he locked onto its source.

Impossible! There she was. He saw her now. Clear as day.

Heart pounding, he charged toward the female, but by the time he made it to where she had been standing, she was gone.

He sorted through the various nuances of different fragrances and picked up on her fading scent. With growing urgency, he shoved people out of his way, bolting for the exit to follow her trail.

He burst out into the cold breeze, still in high-speed pursuit. Around the corner of the building, he slowed his chase and finally came to a full stop.

Frantically, he scanned the vicinity, turning his gaze left, then right, then left again, but to his misfortune, her scent had dissipated. She had slipped away. Taken flight like a spooked snow owl.

Anger flared in his chest, and he curled his lips in frustration. His heightened vision was overstimulated by the reflective cover of the night's fresh snowfall. He would have to give up the hunt. For now.

A sting of reminiscence pierced his heart. He had seen this woman before. A long time ago, in someone else's memory. As he had drained the man's blood, he had sucked the fresh memory from the mind of the human who had come in search of death. Of *him.*

He had never experienced an emotion this powerful. It had fascinated him so much that with every drop he had taken, he had absorbed the feeling into his veins, making it his own. It had left such an impression on the numbness of his existence that it had become a part of himself.

He felt the same tug toward her again now. The love for her was still burning inside of him. There was no doubt in his mind…

…he would find her again.

Renate Rowland

CHAPTER

20

The incident in Iceland was a fluke. There was no other explanation for it. Her heart wanted to see something that wasn't really there. Like a transference of her feelings onto the next closest thing or person.

Yes. That had to be it. It was the only logical reason.

Case closed.

Two weeks had gone by since Eve scraped herself off the sidewalk in Reykjavík, boarded her plane back home, and returned to her *normal* routine. Feeding had cleared her head, but her verdict hadn't changed.

She was hitting the gym five days a week again, less yoga and more weights, taking her frustration and anger out on the iron, blasting music into her ears. She'd also taken on another internship position and was still playing catch-up with the new material while simultaneously assisting in advertising, market research, and sales for three different companies.

She kept herself busy with anything as long as she could work remotely from home. Overworked, she usually passed out quickly once the sun came up. However, today was not the case. Some jerk in the parking lot was revving the throttle of his motorcycle, keeping her from getting some well-needed shut-eye.

How did nobody call the police yet? It couldn't just be her sensitive hearing. The crescent shape of the two connecting condo buildings framed the parking spaces from one side, making his racket echo all the way to the top floor.

The asshole circled the complex for an hour before eventually taking off. Eve was so pissed that it took her another hour to relax and finally fall asleep.

She got up early in the evening to make a blood supply run and checked her reflection in the mirror before leaving. She looked exactly how she felt: exhausted.

Little braids ran along the side of her head, keeping the loose strands out of her face that had bugged her for way too long. The hair on top was teased for maximum volume, and Eve loved the look. She'd tried to recreate it as best as possible, but it didn't make up for the dark circles under her eyes. They were part of her edgy new look now.

Drawing attention with her flashy Tahoe was a clear no-go, so she usually went on foot. Bag slung over her shoulder, she sneaked in through the back door of the building, making a few left turns and then one right at the end to find the unit she was looking for. She knew her way around well by now and always avoided showing her face to the cameras.

Connor was the same supplier she'd made contact with one year ago. He took his payment without asking questions, and since he wasn't much for small talk either, it only made the matter easier. A flawlessly executed transaction. Eve stuffed the two one-pint bags into the insulated compartment of her tote and left.

Back out on the street, she stepped off the curb at the crosswalk, wondering how long she could stretch the supply this time. *Calm thoughts*, she reminded herself. *You're the one in control.*

Fate, however, had a different idea. She was only a few feet from the other side when the roaring sound came up on her right. She didn't have time to dodge it. With a deafening whir, the motorcycle shot around the corner at full speed, darting toward her and never slowing down.

Her breath exploded out of her in a high-pitched scream as her hands jolted up, thrashing in the air. The rider of the bike was so close, he actually clipped her, sending her on a whirl. Her bag swung in an arch.

Eve took a tumble and all but collapsed on the sidewalk. Pain flared in her hands and knees.

Nerves on edge, an eerie thought crossed her mind before her pulse could even settle. It had kind of sounded like the one from this morning.

But it couldn't possibly be the same guy. That had to be too much of a coincidence. Besides, she didn't know squat about motorcycles.

Eve rose and dusted herself off. Straightening the bag's strap on her shoulder, she moved on. Trepidation lingered in her steps. So much for making her supply last.

She was a straight shot from the condo when she saw the motorcycle again, idling in front of the garage's entrance. The visor of his helmet was down, but the man on it appeared to be staring at her.

Her body prickled from head to toe. She instinctively looked around herself to make sure that his attention was not directed at someone else.

Nope. It was a standoff between the two of them. No one else was around.

The rider tilted his helmet to the side as if this were some inside joke that Eve didn't seem to get. Then he revved the engine twice and gunned toward her.

She watched him speed closer, hands glued to the bars, no sign of changing direction. *Sadist-much?* Playing Chicken with pedestrians seemed hardly fair. She had to jump out of the way and lunge behind a parked car to avoid getting hit.

What's this guy's deal?

Still shaken by both incidents, she stored the blood in the fridge and took a hot shower to calm her nerves before getting back to work. The new ads were coming along nicely, and Eve was really fond of the colors she'd chosen for the upcoming collection.

She put the final touches on them ahead of tomorrow's deadline and made her usual check into this month's bank statements. Other than the accounts under the name Kjan Murphy, the ones with the most transactions were his aliases Kai Garret and Finley Keane.

Eve continued to track them all regularly for any suspicious activity. When she found nothing new, she powered down her laptop and fell asleep.

Rumbling thunder ripped through her. She jerked up in bed, eyes wide.

HE WAS BACK!

This was clearly personal now. Heart thumping, she kicked the covers off and flung the curtains open, not bothering to shield her eyes from the sun.

There he was, sitting on his bike, revving the engine. Black jeans, black leather jacket, and black helmet, just like before. Even without seeing his face, Eve felt his gaze on her all the way up to the 46th floor.

How could that be possible? He shouldn't be able to see her in the window of the penthouse.

Her heart dropped into her stomach. Unless he was a vampire. But Eve hadn't felt any indication of that. Not like that night on New Year's, or back at the club in—

No!

Eve froze. The rider cocked his head to the side, and she immediately recalled where she'd seen the gesture before.

In utter disbelief, she leaped back from the window, tripping over a pair of shoes and planting her butt firmly on the floor with a hard *thud*.

Pain shot through her.

Eve's body started shaking, and she felt sick again. She scrambled onto her feet, barely managing to make her way to the bathroom.

Without taking her pajamas off, she tripped into the shower and turned the water on in hopes the ice-cold spray would help her fight the urge to throw up.

It did not.

Huddling in the corner, she gave into the shivers taking over and closed her eyes.

♪

Kjartan wished she could see the satisfied grin on his face. He was truly enjoying the torment he was putting her through. The little scare he had given her earlier was only the beginning; he wanted to get under her skin. He did not believe in coincidence. Fate had sent her to him, Norns be thanked, and following his gut feeling, he had tracked her here.

Already too complacent in his new role, he was looking for a new kind of thrill. The initial exhilaration of being worshiped had swiftly faded. It was not what he wanted after all.

He had added five more to the ranks of his chosen acolytes, bringing them to a total of eleven, with him as the twelfth. The number represented perfection and maturity in the Old Ways and also carried special symbolism for him personally. A boy was considered a man at the age of twelve, and that was when his curse had taken hold, his own body never growing past the stage.

His mother had stopped coming around by then, too.

Being stuck in the shape of a boy for eons had been as infuriating as the rest of his endless suffering. But he had more than made up for that in the past five months.

Even initiating his followers had been much simpler than turning his first generation of neophytes with his child-like body. He did not need to drain them of their own blood to immobilize them anymore. They had been willing. Now, all it took was a cut at his wrist and a few drops on their tongue instead of directly onto their hearts.

Savoring the moment, he looked up at the penthouse one more time with a smile. Then he took off, returning to the place that had become his new residence. The caverns were perfect for ceremonial purposes, of course, but he much preferred to dwell above ground these days.

Kjartan pulled the Harley into the empty underground garage. Picking his host's brain on ordinary things about surviving in this modern world had been as easy as opening a book and flipping through the individual pages as needed. He had accessed information on Kjan's bank account in his memory and had also tried on a few of the man's alter egos to see which personality suited him most.

The cabin, for example, was bought under one of his many aliases, a drug dealer from Vegas, and a pretty big fish too, as it turned out. *Convenient.* The official authorities tended to leave one alone if they were shaken by the mere mention of the name *Donovan Morgan.*

The man was smart, however. His intelligence had clearly been wasted on a bladesmith in his human life. But the ease of access made Kjartan wonder if it was some sort of defense mechanism to keep him from scratching at the walls in his mind.

Containing his ancient immortal lifeblood, the vessel no longer had the need to feed. Not on blood. Kjartan was still fueled by energy. Specifically, the kind of energy that was emitted by human emotions. Fear, being his personal favorite. He had quickly developed a taste for it.

The truth was, he finally had everything he had ever desired, and yet he was not content. Throughout his whole existence, he had always worked toward the next step, and now that he was at the top, he was unsure where to go from here.

What more could he want?

Renate Rowland

CHAPTER

21

Nightmares plagued her relentlessly. Eve couldn't get his glowing red eyes out of her mind. Why would the vampire have followed her halfway around the world?

She wasn't going to cave and let him terrorize her. Wouldn't give him the satisfaction. She was angry, *not* afraid. And if he really wanted to harm her, she'd given him plenty of opportunities by now. She'd gone out with Tanya two nights ago, but he'd been a no-show for over a week.

What are the odds he went back to Iceland after all?

Probably slim to none, but Eve felt like pushing her luck some more.

"Hey, Shorty!" Jack hollered at her over the crowd at the bar. "Look at you stopping by twice in one week?"

The edges of his long, black beard tickled her neck when he came in for a one-armed bear hug, the air puffing from her parka and his enthusiasm knocking her slightly off balance. With a man of his stature, it really was like hugging a bear. Her hand hardly reached the middle of his broad back.

"I know, I know. I'm sorry," she told him. "I've been too much of a stranger lately, but I'm going to change that. I swear."

Her former boss gave her a crinkle-eyed smile and another pat on the back, then retreated behind the bar.

Eve shrugged out of her coat. She draped the fluff over the stool next to Tanya at the bar's short end and plopped down on it. Colby was working tonight, but she had the night off, so it was kind of a girl's night out. The trip halfway across the world remained their favorite topic.

"I'm so jealous. I wish I could've gone with you." Her friend reached for the pretzel bowl in front of her and shoved a handful into her mouth. "Maybe the two of us should go to Las Vegas for Halloween this year," she suggested while chewing. "That would be epic."

Eve propped her chin on her hand. "What about Colby? I don't think he would like the idea of you in Vegas without him."

"Come on, Eve. I want to see some of those infamous strip shows." Tanya nudged her with her elbow, and they chuckled, a slight flush rushing to Eve's cheeks. Then her friend's face turned somber again. "Honestly, though, how did it feel going alone? You haven't really talked about it."

Eve knew the 'it' she was referring to was not just about her travels. Her throat went dry, and she didn't respond, letting her eyes wander over the crowd to avoid Tanya's question. She desperately wanted to change the subject.

"Kjan seemed really nice. We just didn't know him much."

No one did, her inner voice added on reflex.

"I'm glad you went. You can't coop yourself up like that. And if you ever need someone to talk to, you know I'm here, right?"

Eve's heart hiccupped as she watched her dig into the snack bowl again. Only the added beat to its usual rhythmic pattern had nothing to do with her friend's offer. She'd felt a shove. Not the graze of a shoulder from someone accidentally bumping into her either. It was an utterly internal force, perceived by no one but her. It was a familiar recognition.

But it can't be… it simply can't—

The invisible hand nudged her a second time as if to say, *Look at me.*

A chill skipped down her spine. Pulse racing, she held her breath, and then slowly turned, eyes leading the way, head gradually following behind.

The icy touch that had brushed her a second ago made the blood in her veins run cold before she spotted his face.

There he was, standing off to the side of the door, right under one of the bright neon advertisements. The light flickered spastically, as if to point out his position in the mass.

A maliciously dark smile of recognition twisted the corner of his mouth. She could feel his stare on her even through the dark sunglasses he wore.

Eve pulled her posture straighter. *How long has he been standing there?*

Some guy at the bar shouted at the TV and threw a handful of pretzels, snapping her out of her daze.

"Eve? Hello?" She heard Tanya's voice chiming over her shoulder. "What are you staring at? Wow! Who's the intense guy with the shades? He's H. O. T." She silently mouthed the letters, overemphasizing them.

"Someone I met on my trip."

"Like a vacation romance? Look at you getting back in the game. Good for you."

"No!" Eve choked. "Nothing like that."

She craned her neck to look back toward the door. One of the servers weaved through, jerking his tray high to avoid a near collision. He was still there. Smiling. Blocking the only way out.

"But he followed you to the states? *Stalker-alert!*"

"Tell me about it," she muttered, barely moving her lips. "Hey, you mind keeping an eye on him? I think I'm gonna hit up the restroom."

"Go ahead. I got you covered."

Eve hovered over the sink. She was shaking, sweat beading on her forehead. Hands planted on either side, she stared down the drain. She would not be intimidated by him. She just needed a few minutes to breathe.

The woman to her right, reapplying her lip gloss, squinted at her from the corner of her eye. Eve ignored her. She splashed cold water on her face and gave her hair a quick rake with her fingers before getting back out.

As she squeezed back through the crowded hallway, Tanya came rushing at her.

"I'm so sorry," she burst out. "I swear I took my eyes off him for a split second, and he was gone. I don't know where he went. I *think* he left." She grimaced apologetically.

"It's alright." Eve jerked a shoulder, then shoved a path for them back to the barroom. "I think I'm gonna take off anyway."

"Okay. I told Jack and Colby too, and also gave them a description of the guy," Tanya said, keeping pace. "Be safe. And text me when you get home," she called after her as they parted at the bar.

Out the door, Eve checked down the street. When she didn't see him, she made a run toward her truck.

Approaching on the passenger side, she rounded the tail end, then sucked in a startled breath. Less than five feet from her, there he was, leaning against the driver-side door. And she didn't sense him at all. He was a ghost.

Was it possible for him to turn it on and off as he pleased?

He slowly removed the sunglasses, and the dim light of the parking lot was more than adequate to assess him properly.

Eve gasped again. Her heartbeat sputtered. *It's really him.*

He had Kjan's face: his sharp, angular cheekbones, his defined nose, his full lips... all his features.

Except for his eyes. They were an unnatural electric blue, much brighter than Andromeda's had been. Eve thought of lightning as they connected with her.

He looked bigger, too. Huge. Like he'd put on fifty pounds of solid muscle. Thirty in his chest alone. His dark brown hair was tied into three braids on top of his head that were gathered up by a single tie high on the back of his head. The sides were shaved down to skin, revealing a set of brand new tattoos: a rune band with a bird underneath it, one on the left and one on the right. Óðinn's ravens, Huginn and Muninn, Eve presumed.

The dark stubble of his full beard no longer lined his jaw. It was shaved down to a modest mustache and goatee that matched the mohawk style on his head and revealed his chiseled jawline.

"Kjan?" Eve whispered, her fingertips brushing her lips as she covered her mouth in shock.

He shook his head slowly from side to side, his lips twisting into a haughty grin. "I am afraid Kjan had to check out, but he was kind enough to hand his body over to me before leaving."

His words came out so matter-of-factly, another icy tingle slithered through her bones, so much worse than inside the bar. Her pulse doubled, which was saying a lot considering how fast it had been going to begin with. His voice was the same, but his tone was too harsh. Too cold.

She blinked. "Then who are you?"

Eve hated how shaky her voice sounded. She didn't want him to know how terrified she was.

But she had a feeling he already knew because that slow, dark smile from earlier stretched his lips at a crooked angle. "You can call me Kjartan."

There it was again, the unseen surge hitting her like a wave, nudging her backward. Raw power and dominance emanated from him like a warning.

That name. He'd not only taken Kjan's *body.* He'd taken his *name*, too!

A hand clamped around her lungs, strangling her from the inside out. It had to be HIM. The Ancient One Jordan had been looking for. The one even Kjan had feared.

∫

Kjartan watched her thoughts scramble.

"I don't understand. What did you do to him?"

"He conceded his body to me," he said, pushing off the car.

His leather jacket split open in the front. He was fully aware of his imposing appearance, even before the girl took a step back, cowering.

"You're lying. He would never do that."

"Oh, believe me, he did it quite willingly." His lips twitched, and he restrained a smirk, stretching the credibility of his half-truth. His memory was sketchy on the specifics, but he recalled blackmail of sorts.

"No. No, I don't believe you." Her voice quivered again, her eyes glossy from the tears she was unsuccessfully fighting. "He wouldn't leave me like that. He swore he wouldn't—"

"Wouldn't take his own life?" he finished for her. "He did not. I took the liberty of doing it *for* him."

Her expression went slack. Her plump lips parted on a soft gasp, inciting a flicker of glee in him. "Are you really surprised that he never stopped looking for an exit strategy? I presented him with an opportunity, and he practically jumped at the chance. He wanted out; I wanted in. So, we made a deal. I transferred my mind into this vessel."

He took two steps closer and was on her before she could react. He clamped his hand under her jaw to make her look at him and focused on her delicate diamond-shaped face, his stare darting across every detail: her flawless skin, the dainty tip of her nose, perfectly luscious lips, and those brilliant blue eyes that reminded him of the first time he had seen the sky in daylight.

Something writhed under his skin as he drew in her scent, stirring an insatiable hunger. It was intoxicating. Addictive.

"I remember you now. You are the female he turned a year ago." He brushed her lower lip with his thumb, raking his brain for more details. "Aw, you two were lovers," he drawled with false pity. "How. Cute."

Her throat jerked in his grip, and her eyes widened. "You have Kjan's memories?"

Kjartan stared at her for a moment, his teeth on edge. His memory since the merge was deficient, as though parts of it had been erased.

He narrowed his gaze on her dilated pupils. "There are certain things I cannot seem to recover. You, for instance. I had no knowledge of you until now."

He scrutinized her face again. "No, let me recant. Curious, did he ever tell you that you look just like her."

She tore herself free from his hold. "Like whom?" she bit out.

He swept his tongue across his lips, savoring the taste in the air as her emotions flared. His body hardened. His grin grew wider. "You even have her spirit. A spitting image, really. Except for your eyes. Yours are blue. Hers were green, with little flecks of gold." He paused, thinking back on his host. "He really could not remember her face, could he?"

Kjartan felt the anger surging within. The heat burning in his chest. But the unrest was not his own. His passenger was fighting back. Again.

Facing away from her, he closed his eyes to gather himself, extinguishing the flame at its source. Then he turned his attention back to her.

"You cannot blame him for forgetting after repressing the memory of her for so long," he continued casually. "The human mind is a weak thing. Memories fade. But I am able to hold on to them far better. When I first consumed his blood, I was gifted a glimpse of his most recent memories. Things that he would forget over time became burned into my mind."

He felt no remorse for lying to her about Kjan. Of course, he was still very much around, making himself known now and then. He refrained from sharing that little detail with the female.

"If Kjan is gone, why are you here? Why even come back to the States?"

He crossed his arms over his chest. "Reestablishing dominance. I believe I am exactly where I am meant to be. What about you… *Eve*?" He searched her face for a reaction as he addressed her by name for the first time. "Do you have faith? Do you believe in destiny?"

"No. I believe in making my own destiny," she sneered.

Kjartan snickered. "I believe our fate is already written in stone. Or woven by the Norns, according to *my* faith. You and I are connected somehow, and I am determined to find out how," he said, wagging his forefinger in her face.

The rush he felt was exhilarating. He could smell her fear practically seeping out of her pores. And it was delicious.

"The only connection we share is Kjan. Without him, there is nothing between us."

"Perhaps. Perhaps not. Either way, I will see you again, Eve," he promised with a wink, and then stalked past her around the car.

Unfortunately, he was forced to cut their official meet-cute short. He had to attend another valuable rendezvous tonight. The meeting was taking place with the usual buyers, and the details were already arranged. Everything was expected to go smoothly.

'We had a deal! You swore to me!'

Ah, yes, he was back. The voice in his head. He would hear it occasionally. Feel him wriggling around in there, biding his time, and hoping to break free. His efforts were feeble, of course.

Kjartan remembered the other woman's name now. Thórunn.

'Don't you dare use her name.'

"Hush," he spoke to himself. "I know you are withholding things from me. Locking them away so I cannot access them. You will not be able to keep this up forever. She is mine," he growled through clenched teeth.

And he would have her. One way or another.

CHAPTER

22

Eve got in the Tahoe and locked the doors, but she didn't press the button on the ignition. Having come face-to-face with the God who sired Kjan, rendered her in a state of disbelief and confusion. She'd expected to die of fear the moment he touched her. She was still in shock. Her entire body trembled, unable to process what she'd seen.

She'd been looking for another explanation for why Kjan had left her, and maybe she'd found it. Or rather, *he* had found *her*.

Did he really agreed to the transfer voluntarily?

Eve had found one answer. She would figure out the rest, too. Her hands sweaty, she pressed the button for the ignition and put the truck in drive.

At home, she searched the entire condo for the millionth time, only to come up empty-handed again. She stepped into the closet and ripped the mirror panel open, revealing the embedded wall safe.

3-1-1-2-1-0-6-7

Eve entered the eight-digit code into the pin pad when suddenly something clicked, and it wasn't the lock. No, something in her head registered.

December 31st, 1067.

The pin for the safe was a date, European order, with the day before the month. It was the day he'd been sired. *Reborn.* It was as close to a birthday as she was ever going to get. A Re-birthday, so to speak. His 954th.

The safe door unlatched at the press of the key symbol. The first thing her eyes fell on was his handgun on the top shelf and the cases of ammo beside it. Her focus dropped to the ginormous black lacquered watch box below. Through the glass porthole in the center of the lid, she saw the rose gold watch.

She lifted the wooden cube off the middle shelf and flipped it open, staring at the skeleton dial-type face with its little gears. Only the even clock numbers were displayed. The color of the casing wasn't actually rose, but it had a warmer hue than typical yellow gold.

Eve knew it was expensive. Why else would he keep it in a safe? Plus, the size of the box kind of spoke for itself.

He never wore it, though. She'd seen him wear it only once. The night he'd come for her in her old apartment. He'd shunned it ever since, almost as if it belonged to a different persona, and he didn't want to be associated with it. Kjan had the money, but he didn't show it off. Flashy wasn't his style.

An image of him in his distressed baseball cap jumped into her mind. That was who he'd been to her. Casual. Vintage. She didn't know the man this watch belonged to.

Eve flipped the case shut and slid it back onto the shelf, then relocked the safe. She wouldn't find any more explanation in here than the last time she checked.

How could he do this? It was so damn frustrating to know that someone else held all the answers now.

∫

"*Da.* I will deliver on time," his counterpart affirmed with a thick Russian accent before shutting the lid of the briefcase. Then his large hand dragged it off the table.

Kjartan's eyes lingered on the man's tattoos. The ink covered his arms all the way down to his knuckles. He thought the sturdy brute looked more like a soldier than a businessman, matching his own approximate height and weight. He was casually dressed in a black t-shirt, cargo pants, and military issue boots— clothes for combat instead of a pressed suit, leaving the firearm at his hip unconcealed. Kjartan respected that.

Behind the one in charge were two more of the sort who, for all he knew, could have been the man's biological brothers based on the similarities in their faces. It made him pity the mother who birthed the trio.

Arms crossed over his chest, Kjartan gave a nod, concluding the deal. They kept the pleasantries brief.

With his own backup flanking him, he watched the three men turn and vacate the premises. This was his turf. Contacts came to him, not the other way around.

Their steps echoed. The warehouse was currently little more than an empty building. Things moved quickly, and merchandise never stayed put here for long. Whether he was buying or selling, the secluded location outside the city was ideal for the kind of transaction that had best remained under the radar. For either party.

Once the sound of their vehicle faded into the distance, he dismissed Kristján and Lucas. He had his own ride out back and would be the last one to leave.

After locking up behind them, Kjartan faced the empty warehouse. The muscles in his neck tensed involuntarily. Rows of shelving racks created a maze of shadows before him, but it was not the dimly lit isles that triggered his nerves. It was the dead silence.

He released a sharp breath and crossed the floor to the rear exit, where he had parked his bike.

Boots scuffing along the rough concrete, he stalled when the bell chime from his back pocket made him pull out his phone. He knew it was a motion activity alert from the security system; it was the same he had dismissed when the clients arrived. Although there was little to steal at the moment, the warehouse remained under 24/7 surveillance.

What set it off?

Kjartan checked the notification on the screen. The motion alert came from one of the cameras mounted in the backlot of the warehouse. He watched the soundless, black-and-white feed show a sudden burst of white from an undefined source.

A flashlight, perhaps?

Lifting his gaze, he let his senses do a sweep of the area, but they came back with nothing. He was still alone in the warehouse. No sign of a trespasser.

He wrote it off as rats. The tech was sensitive, and he had encountered the occasional rodent scavenging for scraps. And the flash of light? Could have been a glitch.

Turning toward the exit, he gave his phone another scroll to check the status of his latest purchase. An impulse buy, but he had no doubt that a purpose for the pointy end would arise sooner or later. He hoped for the first.

He shoved the phone back into his pocket without giving the camera feed another thought until he was outside. Something— no someone—streaked through his periphery.

Kjartan spun toward the sound of motion, like the flapping of a coat, but the only thing meeting him were darkness and an icy gust.

He stilled, his senses back on high alert. His gaze scanned the shadows. It was not so much a physical presence that registered but malicious intent. Whoever had been here was gone, but the scent of hatred still tinged the air.

Renate Rowland

CHAPTER

23

Eve went to bed, hoping to give her mind some rest, but sleep evaded her for days. She felt depleted. And no amount of blood could fill the void. What usually lasted her a month was gone within 72 hours.

Stressing herself out, she had run through her supply at an alarming rate, and a check in the fridge confirmed that she had to go back to the clinic today.

Eve barely stepped foot out of the building when she sensed someone watching her.

Vampire! Definitely!

Nothing like the intense energy Kjartan had thrown off three nights ago, yet it felt familiar somehow.

The presence clung to her all the way to the med clinic, never getting any closer or further away. Tired of playing along with this silly game, she exited the building on the other side, trying to catch a glimpse of whomever was stalking her.

She pushed the heavy door open with her shoulder and peered outside, holding her breath...

Nothing.

Not the slightest bit relieved, she took the first step outside. She stayed close to the brick wall, flattening her back against it until she was able to peer around the corner and...

Still nothing.

Fear pounding in her heart, she moved as quietly as possible. There was no one there. When she tried to hone in on the presence again, she couldn't sense it anywhere.

She leaned back against the wall and closed her eyes for a moment to gather herself. She couldn't let her emotions get the better of her.

After a few deep breaths, she was ready to head home, and once the O-negative hit her tongue, Eve finally relaxed.

She felt like a goddamn drug addict. She despised him for turning her into this. It was so pathetic—

The sound of a motorcycle snapped her to attention. She rushed to the window but found no sign of him in the parking lot. She was furious now. The slow simmer of her blood increased to a boil. She refused to humor his cat-and-mouse game.

Eve stormed out, her pulse rattling through her veins. She took the elevator to the garage, where she sensed the other vampire's presence again. She caught the shadow on the ground before he turned around the corner, staring right at her. Hands in the pockets of his jeans, he leaned casually against the pillar.

She didn't believe her eyes. She recognized the shaggy brown head of hair. It was the vampire from the New Year's party. He was one of Kjartan's. And he'd been here in Portland right after Kjan disappeared.

Eve stumbled back against the wall, her shoulders bumping against the cement. He had a big smile on his face, taunting her. He knew that she'd been trying to catch him at the clinic.

The bike's engine roared outside on the street, and she turned her head at the sound on reflex. When she looked back to the pillar, the boy had vanished.

Dammit! Eve felt her blood bubbling in her veins. This had gone on for way too long. If they thought they could use her for their own personal entertainment, she would give them a run for their money. She was no pushover.

She would have to wait for him to make a move first, but the next chance she got, she was determined to confront them. Either of them. Special powers or not.

The next week went by without any incidents, but Eve wasn't fooled. She had a deadline to keep for tonight, and after that, she was officially on spring break. She hadn't left the condo since her adventure down in the parking garage and was looking forward to meeting up with Colby and Tanya. She wasn't joining them for the camping trip but had promised to stop by for the party on the island tonight.

Her phone went off, and she answered it on the first ring. "I'm just finishing up. I'll be on my way in ten, I swear." The words spilled directly out of her mouth, assuming it was Tanya checking in.

There was no reply from the other end of the line.

"Tanya? Hello?"

Maybe the reception at the campgrounds was shotty? Eve shrugged it off and reviewed her work one more time before submitting it. Her laptop had been running slowly all day, but now that the paper was done, she just felt relieved that it didn't crash on her.

On the elevator ride downstairs, her stomach suddenly twisted into knots. She got into the Tahoe when her phone rang again. This time, she checked the screen:

unknown number

"Hello?" Eve waited for a response, but the line stayed silent.

She hung up and dialed Tanya's phone from her contacts. Her friend picked up after a few rings. "Hey, girl. Are you here yet? Where are you?"

"I'm just leaving now. Sorry, it took me a bit longer than I expected," she apologized. "My laptop was having issues. Hey, did you call me earlier?"

"No. We've just been walking around the trails. The place is packed." Eve could hear loud music playing in the back. "Call me when you get here, so we'll find you, okay?"

"Sounds good. See you in forty." Eve hung up and pulled the Tahoe out of the garage. Turning up the volume on the radio, she tried to get herself in a party mood.

Traffic on the bridge was backed up and took twice as long as usual to get across to the island. By the time she found a parking spot, it was already 3 a.m.. She tried calling Tanya back but couldn't get a dial tone.

First my laptop, and now my phone's on the fritz, too?

With the parties far from slowing, there was no way she'd be able to find her friends in these crowds. After searching for an hour, she gave the cell in her hand one more shot. The call still didn't go through, but she sent a text just in case.

Frustrated, Eve headed back to the truck to drive home. So far, spring break was a total bust. Hopefully, tomorrow would be better.

Her phone started ringing again. She was still miles from home. At almost 5 in the morning, the streets were deserted. Not a single car in sight.

She reached for the cell to check the screen, and sure enough, it was the unknown number calling for the third time. She didn't answer and tossed it onto the passenger seat next to her instead.

Eve lost focus on the dark intersection for only a split second. When she looked up, her foot slammed down on the brake. A black Dodge Ram merged onto the highway in front of her at full speed without minding the stop sign. It cut her off as it veered into her lane.

She cursed, watching it accelerate and disappear from view.

Her clammy grip tightened around the steering wheel. The highway wasn't well lit, and she hated driving this stretch of road. Due to the lack of lights and thick tree lines, it was always pitch black out here just before sunrise, making it impossible to see wildlife crossing until the very last second. If at all.

High-strung and twitchy, Eve shrieked when the ring of her cell went off yet again, startling her half to death. She jerked on the wheel, drifting out of her lane toward the median and then overcorrecting so far she almost crashed into the ditch.

Easing up on the gas, she did the swivel back and forth another time before straightening the Tahoe's wheels.

Her lungs gasped to fill with oxygen after the scare. Her phone was still ringing. In anger, she snatched it up to answer, but instead of the expected silence on the line, a high-pitched noise pierced through the speaker.

Eve closed her eyes to block out the sharp pain in her eardrums and lost her grip on the phone.

She didn't have time to swerve before the world exploded around her. The other vehicle appeared out of nowhere. There had been no beams from the headlights to warn her.

The brutal impact on the passenger side was the first thing that registered, followed by the imminent collision of the airbag with her skull, igniting a white flash behind her eyelids. Then came the sound of metal on metal and the clash of glass shattering in her face.

Eve didn't know up from down anymore. Her truck flipped, and everything inside that wasn't glued down went flying. Shards from the windshield shot out at her, littering the interior, and through the gaping hole in front, she got a glimpse of the highway's guardrail.

At last, the Tahoe slammed to a stop on its roof. Dazed, her head throbbing from the blow, she heard a woman's voice utter something she couldn't track. Then a man spoke with a thick accent. "You take her. We get rid of the truck."

A few moments later, the latch on the driver's door released, and her body was pulled out of the truck. As her eyes focused on her surroundings, she saw the other vehicle.

The last thought on her mind before her consciousness fizzed out was that it looked just like the black Dodge from earlier.

CHAPTER

24

He watched Caleb crack his knuckles. "Piece of cake. Let me know when you have a real challenge for me."

The boy hunched over his laptop on the couch, looking almost bored as his fingers swept over the keys.

Nessa rolled her eyes at him. "Feckin' show-off."

"She still hasn't noticed that I hacked her, and I got her phone too," he remarked over his shoulder without taking his focus off the screen.

Kjartan hung back to make the call, Askja eying him quietly. She did not approve of the plan. Despite her efforts to appeal to his patience or make him reconsider tonight, he remained resolute.

"…I'm just finishing up. I'll be on my way in ten, I swear… Tanya? Hello?"

"We move now!" He nodded at the rest of them, leading the way to the trucks.

Kristján shoved the cigarette pack back into his pocket when he saw them coming and straightened from his lean against the Suburban. He had quit the habit but held onto the memento for some strange reason Kjartan did not understand.

"How do you want to play it?"

"I take the Dodge with Askja and Caleb. You two take the Chevy," he ordered with a jerk of his head toward Nessa.

Kristján was his right hand and one of the vampires he had turned in Iceland. He was the oldest of them, which was why he trusted him the most to get a job done right. Besides Askja, of course. The two of them were the backbone of the coven, but unlike her, Kristján never questioned his decisions.

Before turning the engine, he dialed Eve's number again. This time, she did not pick up on the first ring.

"Hello?" she answered, no longer cheerful. Wariness spread through her tone.

He waited for her to end the call, then exited the loft's parking lot. "Keep tracking her phone," he told Caleb in the backseat.

Askja continued to scowl as he pulled the truck onto the road.

"She's headed northeast and should be passing us any minute."

The white SUV flew past them, and he took up pursuit with Kristján and Nessa trailing them. He followed Eve's Tahoe for forty minutes before slowing down.

Askja looked at him from the passenger seat. "What are you doing?"

"Traffic! We will not make it through with the trucks and might miss her." An even better opportunity just presented itself to him. He dialed Kristján. "Change of plans. We wait by the dark stretch."

Kjartan flipped the truck around and circled back a few miles. They pulled off the road and hid the vehicles from view of the highway.

"Jam her phone. She will leave if she cannot find her friends," he determined. "Let me know when she is getting close."

"You got it," Caleb shot back.

Askja voiced her skepticism with a huff. "How do you know that she will turn back?"

"I just do!"

He had not told her about his passenger. She could draw the conclusion that he was feeding on his host's memories on her own. He had also withheld the fact that there were gaps in his own.

Out of the first seven chosen, he had only taken Askja home to Iceland with him, leaving Nessa in charge of the kids in Portland, who had been his eyes and ears in the city for months. Kjartan had never actually caught sight of Kjan or Eve himself until the night he confronted the man in the alley. His orders had been to lie low, and Askja's mate had made sure that everyone stayed in check during their absence. After turning Kristján and the other three, she had flown back to join Nessa.

The kids, as he referred to them, were Lucas, Emma, the twins Parker and Claire, and Caleb, the baby of the coven at only 19. They had been the first ones to be turned after Askja and Nessa. All five of them were from Portland and knew their way around like the back of their hands, making their addition useful in aspects other than maturity. Caleb, for example, had proven himself to be an exceptional hacker. How he had acquired the skill while living on the street was hard to comprehend.

Kjartan's jaw ached from the pressure of his clenched teeth. He hated waiting. Closing his fist tightly, knuckles cracking, he kept his eyes on the clock as time went by. He sensed Askja's worry without glancing at her face in his periphery. It spurred greater frustration.

"An hour till sunrise," she reminded him. She was concerned for Nessa and Caleb.

He had taken the veins of all his acolytes to see into their minds and assess their strengths as well as their weaknesses. Yet Kristján and Askja were the only ones he had shared his blood with more than the initial time to turn them, therefore making them already able to tolerate daylight. It had been necessary for the travel. It would take the rest of them a few more years without his help.

"She's on the move," the boy reported from the back. "Traffic has died down. She's ten minutes out."

Showtime.

Kjartan called Kristján. "I will cut her off. You stay behind her. But keep your distance."

He waited for Eve's truck to get closer and then floored the pedal, peeling out in front of her. He heard the tires screech, but kept his foot on the gas until he lost sight of her in the rearview mirror.

Two miles down, he pulled off the road again. "You two get out," he uttered with a sharp edge.

Caleb complied, unlatching his door, but Askja hesitated as though she was going to open her mouth to protest.

"I am not doing this with you in here," he jabbed back, facing her.

She sighed in surrender and followed his order.

When Eve's Tahoe approached again, he killed the headlights, and his thumb subconsciously worked the redial on his phone.

'Please, don't do this. I'm begging you.'

He ignored the pleading voice in his head and closed his eyes.

Punching the gas pedal a second time, he braced himself for the crash. Eve stood no chance.

He felt numb, right until the inevitable collision. The sound of crushing metal and shattering glass tore through the silent emptiness in his mind. The violent strike deployed the airbag in his steering wheel, blowing him backward against the headrest

In the short distance in front of him, he heard her truck skidding through the guard rail and flipping onto its roof.

His boot found the brake.

As his airbag deflated with a soft hiss, he saw steam rising out of the Ram's busted grille. The front wheels hung suspended in the air above the ditch.

Kjartan drooped forward and shook off the throbbing ache in his skull while the ringing in his ears continued at a high pitch.

He was met with a curse from Askja as he scrambled out and used his shirt to wipe the blood off his face. His balance was slightly off, but his wounds had already healed, leaving him perfectly unscathed.

The sight of the Tahoe's mangled wreck in the ditch sent an icy wave over his skin, literally freezing him in place.

What did I do?

A blurry picture of a different wreck overlayed the scene in front of him like an echo: a light blue Beetle, struck head-on by a large black truck.

Kristján appeared in his hazy vision, shaking him by the shoulders. "You take her. We get rid of the truck."

Kjartan blinked, refocusing his eyes on the tall blond. He handed his second-in-command the keys to the messed-up Ram, then slid down to the wreck of the Tahoe.

Popping her door open, he fumbled with the seat belt for a second before her semi-conscious body slipped into his arms.

He brushed the hair from her face to give it a scan, confirming the cuts and scrapes were superficial. The pulse at her throat was a little sluggish but steady. She was more resilient than she looked. She felt so small in his arms, like an injured bird.

She winced, eyelids fluttering, hands feebly shoving at him. He tucked her against his chest and rose to his feet.

Back at the top, Nessa opened the rear of the second truck and turned to him. "Want me to drive?"

He shook his head.

She made no further argument and hopped into the passenger seat next to him. Caleb slipped into the backseat with Eve.

They made it to Mount Hood with half an hour to spare. She was still unconscious.

"Give me ten minutes before you bring her in," he told Nessa, cracking his door. "You and Caleb will stay here until sundown. Let me know when Kristján and Askja return."

Inside, he sagged back against the door, his breath tearing up and down his throat. The pounding in his head, merged with the sharp pain behind his eyes, made him violently ill.

He slid his back along the door to sit down on the floor.

Closing his eyes, he rubbed his temples with the heels of his hands in a desperate attempt to make it go away. He had not anticipated the crash to be that harrowing.

For a moment, he wished he was numb again, not able to feel anything physical at all.

How do mortals deal with this? If the cuts on his face and hands were already healed, why did his head still feel like it was about to explode?

'I'll make you wish you were dead!'

Of course. The torment was caused by his host's anguishing rage.

Kjartan clenched his fists to keep them from shaking and leaned his head back against the door. Caging the crazed animal inside him, he felt his muscles relax and his breathing ease.

Much better.

Renate Rowland

E ve groggily opened her eyes. Then blinked. She was staring up at the ceiling, stretched out on the backseat of an unfamiliar truck.

Instantly, the fog lifted from her mind, and her memory came rushing back.

The crash!

She recalled someone pulling her out. She had seen his face too.

That son of a bitch kidnapped me!

She pushed herself upright. Nerve endings prickling, her body went on full alert. The truck was parked in a driveway, and she heard voices outside.

Eve scurried back as the door opened.

"Rise'n shine, lassie. Get out," a female vampire with curly red hair ordered her in a thick Irish brogue. "Walk, or I'll carry ye," she added with a smirk after Eve didn't comply.

She was trapped. She had no choice but to proceed if she wanted to find out why he'd brought her here. After all, it was what she wanted. Though she would've preferred not to do this on his turf. He did not only have the field advantage; he also had minions to keep her here for as long as he wanted.

She did have one choice, at least. She refused to let him prey on her fear.

Eve lifted her chin. "Ever heard of a *please*?" she shot back while scrambling out.

The woman emitted a derisive laugh and seized her by the arm the second her feet hit the concrete. Eve squirmed in her hold, but she didn't let go and dragged her toward the house.

As she was shoved through the front door, the giant stone fireplace that stretched to the top of the vaulted ceiling captured her attention. Then her eyes found him. Kjartan stood in the center with the same stupid grin on his face.

He must feel so *superior. So damn smug.* Eve swallowed the bile rising in her throat.

His stance wide, arms crossed in front, and authority oozing from every pore of his body, he looked even bigger now. Downright enormous. She watched him in the light of the room, his massive chest swelling with every vile breath he drew.

Well, she'd been looking for a confrontation with him, hadn't she? Here was her chance.

Shaking herself free from the woman's grip, she charged at him like a rabid dog let off the leash. "What the fuck is wrong with you?"

He cringed at her coarse choice of words, like he hadn't expected the graphic language from her mouth. Then he gave the female vampire a nod to beat it, and she closed the door on her way out.

"Is that how you address your former lover?" He raised his eyebrows in mocking anticipation.

"How DARE you—" *You self-righteous, arrogant prick,* she wanted to add. Who did he think he was?

Okay, she should probably cool the attitude. Despite his wryly amused tone, his powerful energy radiated from him like the heat of a bonfire. Or that fireplace, were it lit. It took all her willpower not to cower right there.

"You're not Kjan," she barked, jabbing her finger at him.

He gave her a humorous laugh. "But I am. This is his body, is it not?"

Eve snorted. "You're nothing like him."

"How so?"

Is he serious?

A rush of adrenaline gave her courage a sudden boost, and she went off. "Well, let's see, um, you purposely tried to hit me with your motorcycle, then you ran me off the road and caused a massive crash, and now you're holding me here against my will." She recounted the recent events dramatically on three fingers to make sure they hadn't already slipped his memory. He'd mentioned problems in that department, after all.

"Kjan was kind… and… and selfless," she paused again, tears filling her eyes. "He was *good.* You're nothing but a twisted, evil version… and you'll never be like him." She jutted her chin, curling her clammy fingers into her palms.

As if her words had struck a nerve, he uncrossed his arms and turned his back.

Eve watched him plod toward the fireplace, head bowed in thought. His hair had grown another four inches. The slim braids of his ponytail were adorned with beads and hung down in between his shoulder blades.

Kjartan came to a stop at the mantel. With an unhurried spin, he sagged against the solid beam, angling his head in her direction. "You do not even know me," he claimed with a shrug.

Her arms went rigid at her side. The muscles in her shoulders flexed. "You fucking abducted me!" she yelled, her face flushed with fresh rage. Through narrow eyes, she added, "That tells me everything I need to know about you."

"Would you have heard me out otherwise? Your lover painted you a picture of me that you blindly accept at face value."

"I trust his judgment."

"Then your mind is made up by prejudice."

"Ha! You've been terrorizing me for weeks just for the fun of it. You're a complete psychopath from what I can see with my own eyes." She remembered the lore. Kjan had called him a monster. The mere sight of him was suffocating her.

"Give me a chance to prove you wrong. Teach me how to be like him."

Never. Kjan's tone of voice had been like honey, warm, and smooth, but his evil twin had an arrogant edge that never left his tongue. When he spoke, the words scraped down her back like nails.

He also carried his nose a little too high. And the way he assessed her with his unrelenting stare... *ugh!*

Eve shook herself to get the image out of her head. "I can't... I can't do that."

"Why not?" His question seemed genuine as he stared at her calmly, his eyes searching hers for God-knew-what.

She stomped toward him. Slouched as he was, resting against the wood, hands in his pockets, she was at eye level with him, and she wanted him to see her clearly as she spoke.

"Because when I look at you, all I feel is hate. You're destroying his memory."

Kjartan cocked his head and scowled, keeping his cold blue eyes locked on her. "I do not seek to destroy him. I want to *become* him. Is that not what *you* want too? Do you not wish to feel his touch again?"

The unnatural light in his eyes flared a little brighter with the abhorrent suggestion. He straightened to full height, all staggering 6 feet 4 inches bearing down on her. "I can give you what you want."

Eve caught her mistake before he made a move. He took one step around, and then he had her backed into the fireplace.

She opened her mouth, but her throat turned dry and was compressed by an invisible force, smothering her response. She'd walked right into his trap.

He put his right hand up on the mantel next to her head with a menacing smile, revealing fully descended fangs like they were meant to be a threat. Would he resort to forcing her into submission with his bite if she didn't comply? He had nothing to gain from biting her other than intimidation.

And it worked. She found herself shrinking more under his close examination. He was studying her with those irises that appeared to be powered by raging lightning storms. A nearly imperceptible hum rolled off him as if he'd been rubbing his feet along a carpet.

Eve bristled. She could feel the faint brush of energy against her own skin, raising goosebumps. She was anticipating the electric shock when he reached out to touch her.

No zap of pain occurred.

He brushed his thumb tenderly over her cheek, his focus on her mouth. "You speak crude words with such delicate lips."

Eve ignored him. She clenched her teeth when his hooded gaze dropped several inches lower, lingering at the low-cut front of the shirt she had ignorantly chosen for the party.

The heat behind his stare burned a path over her skin, the flush rising with the swell of her chest as she breathed him in. He stood too close. She couldn't help it. Couldn't fight the twitch in her thighs or her body's arousal at his proximity.

He turned his smug grin up a notch.

Can he tell?

"Help me remember," his voice rasped.

Raw fear stirred in the pit of her stomach. How exactly did he expect her to jumpstart his memory?

∫

The center of his chest burst with heat. Before him stood, not a girl, but a grown woman whose every need he ached to satisfy.

Eve swallowed audibly, swiping her hair behind her ear to rein in her emotions.

He sensed her confusion. Her eyes were no longer storming. There was something else.

Kjartan filled his lungs with her scent. It flowed through him like a drug, steeling every muscle in his body. His arm flexed against the beam of the mantel. Every inch of him strained to know more of her. *Touch* more of her.

Averting his gaze, she nibbled on her plump bottom lip, leaving a soft indentation. Full and lush as it was, he wanted to take it between his own teeth now that he had her trapped.

Scrutinizing her reaction, he trailed her jaw with the tip of his finger.

It coaxed a twitch from her mouth.

Emboldened by her response, his gaze wandered over her body again. "How badly do you want to be with him?"

The only reply that reached his ears was the rapidly pounding drum of her heartbeat.

He skimmed his finger slowly over her lips, down her throat, and even lower to the deep plunge of her shirt. "Teach me," he enunciated, following the trail with his eyes.

She swallowed again, burying her reply deeper.

Rage pulsed at his temples as her silence started to vex him. He hooked the neckline of her shirt with his finger and tugged her toward him, his tone soft, his threat subtle.

"I could take whatever I want, Eve." His goal was to nudge her in the right direction—his direction—not force her. Yet the connotation of his words was very clear.

"Then what exactly are you asking of me?"

"Compliance," he replied dryly, his eyes snapping back to hers. "I want you to stay here. With me. But I am *asking* for your consent."

"How generous of you!" she mocked him, then nodded toward the door. "You already have an entourage. Why do you want me?"

His left hand released her shirt; the other remained braced against the fireplace at her back. "Because you have something they lack. You are the only one who truly knew him."

Kjartan had to use all the honey he had to catch this fly, and he would tell her whatever she needed to hear. She was feisty, like a wild horse. It would be so much fun to break her.

He let his hand slip off the mantel. "You look tired. You should rest. No need to make rash decisions." He pulled away from her to give her space. "Choose any room you wish," he offered, heading for the stairs. He was not opposed to sharing his own, either.

"What if I don't want to stay?"

He exhaled a sharp breath, turning halfway back to her. His jaw tightened as he pressed his lips into a thin line, but he forced his voice to remain gentle. "The sun is up, so for now, you are stuck here. Get some sleep."

"I don't care about the sun."

He froze with his hand on the banister. He was not accustomed to being so openly disobeyed.

"But *I* care," he said over his shoulder as calmly as he could, his grip around the creaking wood tightening. "No one is going to take you back to town. So, unless you wish to walk, I suggest you make yourself comfortable. I have things to take care of."

It took everything he had not to slam the door. Maybe this would not be as easy as he had hoped after all. He really had to keep his temper in check. She was certainly stubborn, but that should not have come as a surprise. It was way too early to regret his decision.

∫
⟨HAPTER

26

He checked his phone for a text from Kristján. He and Askja had disposed of Eve's mangled Tahoe, but his Ram had still been drivable. The pair would stay at Kristján's place in Nob Hill for the day, and Nessa and Caleb were safe here with him.

The house was practically a vault.

The windows had no shutters, only black-out curtains, since he enjoyed flooding a room with daylight now and then. But all doors were secured by a high-tech system he controlled through an app.

Nobody went in or out, or even opened a window, without his knowledge. Unless Eve was determined to crash through the glass wall downstairs, which would still set off the alarm on his phone, she was locked in.

Caleb had set up the loft downtown where the rest of them crashed with the same security features. After checking in next with Emma, Lucas, and the twins to confirm their whereabouts, Kjartan activated the system.

Having a coven split up instead of contained under one roof was rather impractical, but the old-fashioned living conditions were outdated; everyone preferred their privacy. And sometimes, when they were all together in one place, his empathic connection to his neophytes became simply overwhelming. He needed the break.

Kjartan changed out of his clothes. Conveniently, the blood stains had been mostly invisible on the black-on-black ensemble.

Bracing his palms against the cool tile in the shower, he hung his head and replayed the disastrous night. It had been too close. He had endangered Nessa and Caleb by making the call to wait, yet Askja had been the only one to question his orders.

'Your impatience makes you careless and selfish.'

Right. One other had indeed objected.

On a violent impulse, Kjartan swung his right fist full force at the wall. Bones in his hand and forearm shattered on impact.

But it was not the injury that raised concern.

Ignoring the sharp pain, he watched the blood trickle down the black tile. While the fractures in his arm healed almost instantly, the brutal blow left a crack in the granite.

What if, next time, the damage done by him was something he was not adept at fixing? Something a little more terminal?

He rinsed the blood off his knuckles without inspecting them and got dressed. When he caught his reflection in the long mirror above the vessel sinks, he stalled.

As much as he had been intrigued by the torture of his victims, it had never been fueled by bloodlust. He was a creature driven by simple curiosity. His nails had caused deep gashes in their skin, which had never healed cleanly after their ultimate initiation. The marks left behind had always been permanent, much like the one on their chest.

He had eventually resorted to using their own weapons against them, gutting them like the prey they were, and then reanimating their nearly dead bodies just before their essence crossed over. With a single breath left on their lips, he had brought them so very close to the gates of Hel's kingdom. He wanted them to taste death before he ripped them back from the verge.

As his last neophyte, Kjan did not sustain any additional scars at all. His magnificent body was a nearly flawless specimen. That was why he had used the dagger during the ritual. To prevent any unnecessary new blemishes or ruin the tattoos. He liked the ink. He felt as if it connected him not just to his vessel's past but also to his own. The images depicted the sagas of *his* family, after all. His father's brother *Þórr*, battling the mighty *Miðgarðsormr*, and brave *Týr*, sacrificing his hand to *Fenrisúlfr*.

All names on his skin were inscribed using the ancient runes he had learned from his mother, instead of the Younger Futhark alphabet humans later replaced them with. Magic still flowed through the old symbols. Was that why Kjan had chosen them?

Other than the names of Gods and Monsters, there were three more on his arms. The two on his right, Kjartan recognized as the man's parents. The one on his left forearm, meanwhile, had not made a connection until a few weeks ago.

ᚦᚢᚱᚾᛏ

Images and related emotions he could draw from the blood of his victims, but never words. He had seen her face so many times and never known her name.

Thórunn. His fingers traced the shapes carefully. The human had kept her a secret from him as well as Eve. What else was he hiding? And how much did she know?

Lifting the deadlock on the house, he descended the stairs hours later. The sun was just setting, and he expected Kristján and Askja to arrive shortly.

His feet came to an involuntary stop when he reached the bottom and found his new houseguest sleeping on the couch. This girl's—no, this *woman's*—brazen defiance was astonishing.

Kjartan pressed his tongue to the back of his teeth, then veered hard left around the newel post to join Caleb and Nessa in the kitchen. It was an open concept with modern cabinets and appliances that accented the rustic flair of the great room's high cross-beam ceiling. A large, square-shaped island sat in the middle, four wooden stools on each side. The ones with the low back.

Nessa and Caleb both looked up as he entered.

"You look stressed," her sharp eyes observed from her seat across the concrete slab. "Din get no sleep?"

He was in no mood to elaborate on his mental state. Luckily, he was saved from having to reply. The back door opened, and Askja strolled through.

"Hey, Love." She greeted Nessa with a kiss.

"What is the verdict on the Ram?" he barked at Kristján, who came in right behind her. He kept the conversation in English for Caleb and Nessa's sake instead of switching to the giant's native tongue.

His massive shoulders heaved in response. "It has seen better days, but it drives. How's the girl?"

"Fine. Go keep an eye on her," he told Caleb to his left. He had no desire to chase Eve through the woods behind the house if she decided to give it a try. And a little voice in his head told him she might just. "Where is the Tahoe?"

"At the docks."

"Good." He addressed Askja next. "You two head home while we go check on her truck." He had no further need for either of them tonight.

"I shall be right out." She handed Nessa the car key and watched her leave. When she turned back to Kjartan, her usual warm eyes were hardened by criticism. "You think it's wise to leave the boy alone with her—"

Wham!

His fist slammed down on the kitchen counter, making her jump. She took a step back and bumped into the 48-inch, 8-burner gas range that would never be used.

"*The boy can handle it,*" Kjartan growled, switching the language on reflex. Sometimes Askja took her motherly role toward him a little too far. She still saw him as the 12-year-old who needed her protection. He was *not* a child.

And neither was Caleb. He understood the punishment for failure.

The wariness in Askja's scent prickled up his nose. Kjartan was trying to control his temper, but the impulse for violence was always there. Right beneath the surface. At least the blow to the 3-inch-thick black concrete countertop left no crack, as it had in the shower earlier. He was improving.

Something else tripped his senses. He knew Eve was awake... and probably listening.

Addressing Kristján, he continued in Icelandic. *"I left her phone behind. You and I are going back to the docks."* He pulled the man's key fob from his rear pocket and tossed it across to him. *"I follow you on the bike."*

He swung around to leave the kitchen. "Just go home, Askja. Caleb stays here until Kristján and I return."

Crossing the great room in long strides, Kjartan locked eyes with Eve for a split second and then descended the stairs to the garage. He hated having to leave the boy with her, but he had to get his hands on her phone before someone else did.

CHAPTER

27

Eve woke to the sound of voices. She opened her eyes and rolled over on the couch.

A face appeared in her still fuzzy view, and she had to blink a few times to clear her vision. Recognizing the boyish grin, she jumped back.

"Remember me?" he asked, cocking an eyebrow at her.

The golden sunburst in his brown eyes was much brighter now that she got a close-up. It was the vampire who had been following her. The same one she'd almost run over with her truck on New Year's.

Over his shoulder, Eve could see Kjartan standing with two other vampires in the adjoining kitchen. He said something to the freakishly tall male that she didn't understand, tossing him a set of keys. The female next to him wasn't the same woman from last night. Her hair was dark blond and stick-straight. She also looked older. Mid-thirties maybe?

He'd really done it, hadn't he? He built himself a coven. How many of them were there? Eve knew of one other female who was with this one the first time she'd seen him. So, including Kjartan, that made at least six.

"Just go home, Askja," Kjartan said to the woman. "Caleb stays here until Kristján and I return." He nodded toward the other vampire and then cast a look over his shoulder at Eve before disappearing down a set of stairs. Probably a garage.

The tall blond, *Kristján*, opened the door, but the woman hesitated. "You heard him, Askja. The boy can handle himself," he said in a deep baritone voice with the same thick accent Eve had heard at the crash site. More clear-headed now, she immediately recognized it as Icelandic. "Förum!" he pressed with more emphasis. She couldn't be sure, but the way he said it had an air of *'Let's go'*.

Askja didn't seem convinced. "Watch her!" she ordered Caleb, and then the two of them went out the front door, leaving them alone.

"Yeah, I got it. Like I'm a fucking babysitter," he added under his breath after she shut the door.

He stretched out, crossing his feet on the coffee table. "Man, what a night. I could use a drink."

"You can't drink alcohol."

"Thanks for the reminder, sweetheart."

"I'm not your *sweetheart*," she bashed him, but instead of returning another retort, he rolled his eyes in annoyance, then slid a big pair of those noise-canceling headsets over his ears and returned to the video game on his laptop.

Eve expelled a long breath, letting her weight sink into the cushions. After catching only a few hours of sleep, she had to admit she felt more rested than she had in months. *Can it be…*

No. It had nothing to do with Kjartan's proximity. She'd simply been exhausted after the crash. That had to be it. She needed to get out of here.

Eve canvassed her surroundings from her seat on the couch. She could only partially see into the open-concept kitchen. It was huge, with a massive island in the center and lots of extra counter space lining the walls. The style was a mix of modern and rustic. Outrageously expensive, she guessed.

Her eyes traveled up to the second-floor landing that overlooked the front room. The place was more like a lodge than a simple cabin. It could easily fit four bedrooms. Maybe more.

When she cranked her head around the other way, she could look right out to the back of the house. An entire wall made of glass faced a large stone patio with a fire pit.

Eve's heart skipped with joy. Just past the half-wall was a line of trees… and freedom.

She wasn't familiar with the mountain range but assumed they were somewhere around Mount Hood. How far could she make it until he caught up with her? Were there any roads nearby?

Restlessness niggled through her as she looked into the distance, and her focus didn't stray far from the boy. The occasional profanity burst from his lips into the mic, along with other heated insults gamers threw at each other like they had a case of Tourette's.

After a while, Caleb was so engrossed in his game that he didn't even notice her slipping out of her seat. She moved over to the window wall and managed to unplug a desk lamp from a side table without making a sound. She wound the cable around the stem and closed her grip tightly on the length, her eyes burning a hole into the back of his skull.

But when raising the lamp to hit him over his head from behind, she was not as stealthy as she'd hoped, and they both caught a glimpse of her reflection on the computer screen at the same time. Without a second's notice, he chucked the laptop onto the cushions, hurtled the back of the couch, yanked the lamp out of her hand, and tackled her to the ground.

Eve crumbled under his weight. With the wind knocked out of her, she found herself face down, cheek pressed into the polished flooring. His lithe body settled on her legs as he tied her wrists with the wire from the light behind her back.

"Get off me!" she shouted.

"It's payback. You hit me with your car."

"I did not!" She writhed under him, boobs squished, her hip bones grinding against the wood. "I stopped in time. You're the one who walked into the street."

"CALEB!"

His head snapped in the direction of the guttural roar, and he jumped off her so fast, you'd think his ass was on fire.

Or maybe it was about to be. He jerked the wireless headphones down and hid them behind his back. Eve got the notion he wasn't supposed to wear them while watching her. Probably not one of his better ideas.

Kristján hulked out in the open door, his shoulders heaving.

"Self-defense, I swear. She came at me first." Pointing at her on the floor with his free left hand, cheeks blazing, the boy looked frantic.

A second later, the walls of the house shook as Kjartan pulled his motorcycle into the garage.

"I'm so fucked," Caleb whispered to no one in particular.

Eve was still on the ground, wrestling her way out of the cable, when he trudged up the stairs. All focus shot to him. His glances hurrying around the room, he tried to make sense of the scene. Nobody said a word until Kristján broke the silence, and Kjartan's eyes shot to Eve.

Rising to her feet, she ran her fingers through her hair in an attempt to straighten the mess. She felt utterly disheveled in front of him and instinctively tugged on her clothes, even though everything was still on straight. His overbearing presence robbed her of the ability to speak. His hard features were a mask, giving her nothing of his thoughts.

"Take Caleb home," he replied apathetically, as if it were none of his concern, then disappeared up the stairs.

Eve wasn't sure what exactly she'd expected, but certainly not that. Even Caleb had anticipated some repercussions.

She wondered how Kjan would've reacted in his stead if someone had laid a hand on her. Something told her he wouldn't have been so lenient. Kjartan shrugged it off like he couldn't have cared less. And for a reason she couldn't explain, that bothered her. A lot.

The room stayed dead quiet for another second, and then Caleb beat feet, hanging his head. Kristján took off after him, and Eve was left alone in the house with Kjartan.

Renate Rowland

ᛋ
⟨HAPTER

28

H e took Eve's keys and her phone out of his pocket and discarded them in the desk drawer. The battery was dead, and without the right charger and Caleb's help to unlock it, the thing was useless for now.

Kjartan closed his eyes, rolling his head side to side to stretch the tense muscles in his neck. His body felt stiff, and a tingling sensation crawled along his spine like an itch he was unable to scratch.

The scene with Caleb wrestling the desk lamp out of her hand was not something he had expected to walk in on. The boy had defended his actions to Kristján, and at the moment they seemed justified, but something stirred in Kjartan at the thought of the kid's hands all over Eve.

He had underestimated her willfulness again. She had guts. And she was tenacious.

Like a damn dog with a bone…

The words rang in his mind with a sense of déjà vu. Why? What was he missing? What could he not remember?

A scene flashed in front of his eyes, appearing out of thin air: Voices… a penthouse… Eve… her touch…

He was inept to decipher the vision. Pictures blurred. Sounds muffled. His mind clawed at the image, digging deeper, trying to—

And then it was gone, wiped clean. Knife-like pain erupted in its place, toppling him to his knees. He fought the anguish, pressing the heels of his palms against his eye sockets until it subsided.

Peace returned to Kjartan in the vast darkness of the study downstairs. He did not require sleep. Skull throbbing or not, his thoughts raced uninterrupted, and he had yet to locate the off switch. Furthermore, he was not entirely sure what would happen if he fell asleep and gave up control of his body.

'I dare you,' the voice in his head mused in challenge.

"Speak of the devil." Kjartan chuckled while lifting the whiskey glass to his lips. "I told you she would be fine. She is tougher than you accredit her."

'Let her go before you put her at risk again like you did with the others.'

"She is free to go if she chooses to. She is not my prisoner." Per se. He had not even bothered setting the alarm for the night.

'You gave me your word that you would stay away from her.'

"I lied. Sue me," he taunted, taking another sip. He had developed a taste for the smooth burn of the liquor. "You kept her a secret from me."

'Because I didn't trust you.'

"Thus, neither side held up their end of the deal. The way I see it, it renders her fair game. I am not forcing her any more than I forced you. The decision is hers."

He sensed Eve's movements upstairs. She had capitulated and settled in the guestroom farthest from his own, on the opposite end of the long hallway.

"We shall see how long she can keep up her resolve. Continue to defy me, and I swear I will take it out on her. Because we both know that sooner or later I *will* bed her."

When he received no further response, Kjartan leaned back in his seat victoriously.

ſ

Eve was restless. The house was too quiet. But she knew Kjartan was still here, or else she would've heard the motorcycle start.

Her pathetic escape attempt had failed miserably, and now there was no way she'd get another chance.

Does this cabin have a security system?

She opened the window to lean out, but she couldn't glimpse any cameras. Sneaking out of her room was her only option for getting an idea of what she was up against.

She held her breath, opened the door without a sound, and peeked around the corner. The long hallway was only lit by the dim glow of wall sconces mounted on the dark wood paneling. She kicked off her sneakers before tiptoeing her way to the handrail, listening for any noise from downstairs.

She had given the house a broad sweep before settling on this room. There was a third story with two more bedrooms in addition to the three on the second floor. The ones on top shared a large deck that wrapped around the corner to the front of the house and overlooked the driveway. None of the rooms appeared lived-in.

Is there really no one else?

Except for the drum in her chest, she was wrapped in dead silence. Like the star in her very own horror movie, she crept down the wooden steps, incredibly grateful they didn't creak.

Turning in the opposite direction of the front room, she slipped down the hall toward the study while keeping her ears perked with every soundless step. No lights were on, and even the heavy drapes were drawn shut to block out the remaining hours of moonlight.

She rounded the large armchair and tugged on the dark curtain—

"So, what exactly was your plan?"

Holy shit!

Eve froze with her palms up. Her heart jumped out of her chest as she spun around. Kjartan stared at her from the sofa by the wall, right next to the door she'd just come through.

"Incapacitating the boy and making a run through the woods? On foot?" He raised a mocking eyebrow, hinting at her current lack of shoes.

"Uhm, I didn't really think that far ahead," she confessed.

Right hand up to his chin, fingers at his lips, a wicked gleam sped across his expression, intensifying his stare. His non-existent aura was freaking her out. She was never able to sense his presence unless he wanted her to.

Eased back in the dark leather seat, knees wide, he continued spotlighting her with his attention. His all-consuming confidence dripped with sex appeal. She hated to admit that it made her feel more alive than she'd felt in months.

A seductive fire smoldered in his eyes, and she found herself wrapped up in the fantasy of straddling his lap.

"Sit."

Her thoughts swung back to reality at the commanding tone of his voice. He nodded his head toward the seat across from him.

Riiight. The armchair. Eve swallowed the lump in her throat, resisting the urge to face-palm herself, and took his suggestion.

"You are agitated," he observed, circling his index finger around the narrow rim of the Glencairn glass in his lap. She recognized the familiar scent of Bourbon.

"Yeah, well, I was in a car accident yesterday, and then I got kidnapped," she snapped, crossing her arms to hide her balled fists. She had a lot of reasons to be agitated.

"You need to feed."

Eve shook her head. She'd rather starve. "I'm not taking your vein."

"And I did not offer," he said with a sly grin, taking a stab at her misunderstanding. "I do not share my blood with just anyone. No matter how pretty."

Just anyone? Was that how he saw her? Her ears burned hot from a mix of embarrassment and rage.

He let his words hang in the air for a moment. "You want to leave," he continued calmly. It was another observation, not a question.

"Of course I want to leave. You can't keep me locked up in here like a pet while you go out and do whatever it is that you do. Where *did* you go?" She narrowed her eyes at him, wondering what kind of activities he pursued. Did he have hobbies? Or a *day job?* And how exactly was he paying for his expenses? Kjan's accounts ran through her.

"That is none of your concern." He set the glass down on the table next to him, momentarily freeing her of his unnerving gaze.

"Speaking of concern. So far, you don't seem to care an awful lot about whether I'm here or not."

His brows pinched as if he wasn't sure what she was referring to. "You mean earlier?" His eyes suddenly flared brighter, the blue lightning dancing frantically in his irises. He was doing it again. That stare.

Leaning forward, he rested his elbows on his knees and clasped his hands loosely in front. "Why would I care? Caleb is part of my coven. Every one of them is free to do as they please. I do not control them." He glared from beneath his dark lashes, studying her reaction.

Free to do as they please? What was he implying? That he didn't mind passing her around?

Eve pushed out of her chair, her anger rising. "Like I said, I'm not your fucking pet."

She turned on her heel and stormed back to her room, slamming the door. He'd made it look like it was her choice to be here, but that wasn't true. She had no idea what he'd do if she opposed him. She should never have agreed to this. This was a trap. Again. Everything was a game to him. She wasn't here of her own free will. She was a prisoner, wasn't she?

CHAPTER

29

She kept pacing around the small space of the bedroom until a knock on the door snapped her out of her rant. Kristján opened it without waiting for a response.

Jesus Christ! He was huge. Eve instinctively took a step back. His shoulders went from jamb to jamb as he filled the frame with his solid muscle. He had maybe three inches on Kjan's height, plus another inch and a half with his short blond hair spiked. He had a faint shadow along his jawline, and Eve estimated him to be somewhere in his mid- to late thirties. His eyes were glacial blue, but much kinder than her abductor's. Despite his imposing size, he didn't appear threatening.

"He wants me to take you back to your place, so you can pack whatever you need," he said in a low, almost bashful voice.

He also kept his eyes toward the wall as he addressed her. From his height, it would be so easy for him to stare down her cleavage, and yet he made no attempt to take a peek.

What do you know? Her respect for the guy just went up two points.

"So, I am allowed to go home under the condition of returning afterwards?" she asked, ascertaining the terms of her agreement for staying, which she had never officially given, and becoming his... what? *Personal therapist?*

Kjartan required professional psychiatric help from a shrink. Her minor degree in psychology did by no means qualify her for that.

Mouth pressed into a thin line, Kristján nodded.

Fine. She would play along. She had no alternative. She needed to feed.

He stepped out of the frame, waiting for her to lead the way, his eyes unreadable. He was an accomplice in this. Was he sorry? Did he agree with it? Or did he simply not care either way, like a good little soldier?

His blind compliance frustrated her, but she wasn't going to turn down her chance of getting out of here. It was likely the only one she would get.

The dark blue Suburban in the driveway was the same one that had brought her here. To her surprise, Kristján opened the front passenger door for her to get in, not the rear.

Eve hopped in and noticed that the windows weren't tinted. Dawn was creeping over the horizon, the pretty pink hues already visible above the dense tree line.

"You're okay with the sun?" Eve asked, buckling her seatbelt.

He grinned sideways. "Don't worry. I shall be fine. Askja and I can tolerate daylight."

"But not the others?"

"Nei."

"That doesn't make any sense," Eve deliberated. "Why would Mr. *I'm-so-high-and-mighty* choose to turn all of you and then not share his blood with them."

Kristján shrugged, putting the truck in reverse. "We do not question his decisions."

"That's horseshit. I don't understand how you can follow him so blindly." She would be a hypocrite if she let prejudice cloud her judgment, but Eve was beginning to paint her very own picture of the guy, and it wasn't getting any better.

"He is not like that." The giant chuckled next to her. "He does not bully us around, you know? He is not as bad as you think."

"Speak for yourself," Eve mumbled under her breath, then turned her gaze on the scenery outside the passenger window. "He took the only person I cared about from me."

"I know," he said, and Eve's head snapped back to him. "In the catacombs. Askja told me. He was an honorable man… and very brave."

She felt her lip quiver. "What are you talking about?" her voice choked out.

What catacombs? Why had he been brave? *How exactly did Kjartan take over his body?*

"I should not say anymore. It is not my place." He focused his eyes back on the road ahead.

Eve got the sense that Kristján felt like he'd already said too much and wouldn't elaborate more on the subject. She leaned back in her seat and didn't say another word for the rest of the drive.

At the condo, he handed her the keys to the penthouse, which she assumed he'd taken from her Tahoe after the crash. She wondered if they'd taken her phone, too.

229

Kristján waited by the door while she made a straight line for the fridge. The familiar taste of the O-negative hadn't felt that good on her tongue in months.

After she emptied the cup, she disappeared into the bedroom to pack some clothes and her laptop. She was hoping that Kjartan would let her keep it. It was the only thing that could keep her sane in his prison.

∫

Kjartan plugged the little copper earbuds in before dragging the helmet over his head. He had to force it over his braids. Each time, the discomfort had him wondering why he even bothered, but the purpose of the device was more about the dark visor than the damage his skull could possibly sustain in a crash. He would endure.

Queuing *Dominate* by Beartooth on his phone to psych himself up, he started the bike and flipped the visor down.

He had waited until sunrise. Since Caleb, Parker, Lucas, Emma, and Claire had to stay indoors for the day, they would all be home by now. Perfect time to pay them a surprise visit downtown.

He cut the engine early and let the Harley roll out the rest of the way. When he came to a full stop in front of the rundown warehouse, he kicked the motorcycle to a tilt and freed himself from the contraption around his head. Without his view impaired, he glanced up at the vacant windows and smiled. Everything was quiet.

Kjartan lingered for another second, then dismounted the bike and charged up the iron stairwell on the side of the building, two steps at a time. He heard them scram inside like rats, the thumping of his boots serving as an announcement of his arrival.

"Where is he?" he growled as Claire opened the door.

Her hazel-green eyes bulged, and her expression lacked the usual quirky grin. She nodded over her shoulder into the front room, where the kid in question froze expectantly the instant his sight landed on Kjartan.

He strode past the young woman and kept right on going. "Out!" his voice hollered.

The order was meant for everyone but Caleb. Despite feeling the boy's fear rippling over his own skin as much as he could taste it in the air, he was smart enough not to run. He knew it would only make matters worse. The immortal commended the kid for that.

He watched the boy's Adam's apple jerk nervously before he opened his mouth. "It wasn't my fault. I told Kristján. I only defended myself," he reasoned with his hands up.

He was right, but Kjartan had no intention of letting him get away without a proper reprimand for laying a hand on Eve. If he appeared lenient or weak in front of them, he would risk losing their respect for him as their leader. And that was unacceptable.

Kjartan's palm launched forward, clamping around the front of the boy's throat, and he glared down into his face. He had the urge to squeeze harder and crush the fragile windpipe in his clutch.

Instead, he dragged him to the window and ripped down the heavy curtain. Sunlight flooded the room. On reflex, Caleb shielded his face. Kjartan pressed his body against the glass, so there was no escaping it, and his victim accepted his punishment without a fight. Not that he would have stood a chance.

His strong grip held the boy in place for only five seconds, but it was efficient enough to cause third-degree burns all over his exposed skin. The air turned thick with the stench of his blistering flesh.

In spite of the visible anguish, the boy never screamed or even made a sound.

"Put a hand on her again, and I will make this permanent," Kjartan threatened before dropping Caleb to the floor.

It would only take him a day or two to heal, but the warning burned into his memory was less temporary.

CHAPTER

30

When Kjartan returned home, Eve was already asleep in her room. He had received a text from Kristján confirming that everything went smoothly and that she fed at the condo. It was not exactly a revelation that she refused to take his blood—not that he had actually offered, of course—but he had felt the unexpected pang in his stomach from her rejection nonetheless.

Leaving the earbuds in, he went upstairs. He loathed the dead silence of the house. It made him itchy. Sounds were a distraction he needed, and music worked especially well. It kept his mind focused.

He remained in his own room all day, not licking his wounds from her taking a stab at his pride. No. He was not sulking. He was contemplating. Revising his strategy.

Maybe he had come on a little too strong. He had to avoid spooking her again, as he had at the club in Reykjavík.

That was it! Their connection. Something they had in common.

The solution finally came to him. She loved music. He could use that to his advantage. Evidently, they shared the same taste. Why else had she picked that particular club? There had been so many others to choose from.

He would lure her out of hiding. Make her come to him.

One arm up, pinned behind his head, he leaned back on the pillow, scrolling through his phone to find the right song. Nothing that would drag her into the past. He was looking for something new. Something with… meaning.

Swiping his thumb up, he gave the list on the screen a spin like it was the Wheel of Fortune.

No.

No.

Not that one.

Or that one.

Not that one either.

Definitely not—

Bingo!

He removed the plugs from his ears and pressed play, turning his phone speaker-side up for good measure. Stretched out on the bed, door to his room wide, he waited. It took mere moments for the soft click, followed by the sound of her footsteps, to reach his ears.

So predictable.

Her face emerged around the corner of the frame. Her long hair was pulled back into a ponytail, and the top teased up, making her appear two inches taller than she was. He noticed that she had changed into a different shirt. The neckline was so high, that it could almost be considered a turtleneck. A pity, really. But the black fabric left her arms bare as it stretched over her curves, which were not the least bit diminished by the formfitting style.

Her demeanor timid, she kept her distance and refrained from crossing the threshold, like she expected him to devour her. And he certainly wanted to.

Eve leaned her shoulder against the wood, crossing her arms over her chest, her disapproval of his choice of music apparent. He let the first run of the chorus play through, then switched the song before the second verse.

The next one he picked started equally brutal. She scrunched her cute little nose in distaste. "That's an awful lot of screaming."

The prejudice is strong with this one. "Patience," he scolded.

Her eyes darted to his at the reproach, and he was uncertain how to interpret the reaction. "Listen to the words before you judge."

Brows pinched tight, she humored him and continued to listen. The tiny muscles in her forehead eased, and her eyes widened in surprise. He could tell when the chorus took effect. Right at the one-minute mark, he watched her skepticism melt into curiosity. Her mouth hung slightly open. She. Was. Hooked.

"Do not let prejudice cloud your mind."

Regarding her lasting awkwardness, he sat up and crossed his legs. "Sit with me," he said, offering her the corner of the bed two feet in front of him.

"I'd rather not."

"Afraid I will bite?"

Her mouth twitched but revealed no smile. When she swallowed nervously, his eyes lingered on her long, delicate neck. Unfolding her arms, she pushed away from the door and took a few uncertain steps along the wall toward his desk.

She moved with such grace. It was mesmerizing. The parts of her hair that had been braided earlier now fell in curls down her back, bouncing ever so slightly.

Her fingers skimmed the top of the desk briefly, and then she lowered herself onto the edge. Pleased with her choice, her mouth curved into a self-satisfied grin.

Halfway was tolerable. One step at a time. He was happy to meet her in the middle, for now. She would make the entire stretch on her own eventually.

Letting the music play, he rose from his seat and crossed the rest of the distance to join her. Subsequently to her declining his offer, he got to choose exactly how close he wanted them to be. She had turned down the two-foot space on the bed. Now he would give her even less. She was uncomfortable with his proximity, and he could not have that now, could he?

Kjartan saw her eyes shift away as she regretted her move. She looked mortified. And he could not get enough. He would continue to find a way to trap her with her own decisions, just for another taste.

He put his phone down beside him and settled on the edge of the desk to her right, so close his arm brushed up against her bare shoulder. She dropped her gaze into her lap, and his eyes followed the path to her hands, where she was spinning a white gold ring around her thumb.

He abstained from asking about its significance. He was ambivalent about knowing details about her past. He rather preferred to focus on her future. Specifically, her future with him.

He picked up his phone again. Once the purple album cover appeared on the screen, he scrolled to the bottom and selected the last song. He wanted to finish strong with his final choice.

"You call that music?" she said sarcastically to tease him about his bad taste.

But when the halftime bridge dropped at 2 minutes and 15 seconds, he knew he had her. He could tell by her little smile that she liked it too. Somehow, he had known that she would.

"Who is this?" she asked, her interest piqued at last.

"Beartooth."

"Never heard of them."

"Then you are missing out," he replied with a proud grin.

Her eyes downcast, she nibbled on her bottom lip again. Kjartan's fingers twitched. Her scent was intoxicating. Blackberry shampoo, green tea body wash, and jasmine deodorant.

Before he realized it, his left hand reached up to lift her chin toward him. The final lyrics of the song began to repeat at the end as he watched her lashes flit up, then down, then back up again, while her glance went back and forth between his eyes and his mouth.

The line continued to repeat, the lyrics ringing in his ears, and he felt himself crumbling under the weight of the words. He saw it. It was right in front of him. The fruition of all his efforts…

…and *he* was the one stalling.

He caught the reflection in her eyes. *Kjan's* reflection. Because that was who she was seeing. He would have to prove to her first that he was not that man.

The last run of the lyrics was choked off by an incoming call. Kjartan looked at the screen and frowned.

Renate Rowland

CHAPTER

31

L ucas was supposed to gather information on new dealers, and the boy's call finally came, informing Kjartan that the men were eager to schedule a meeting with him in person. Tonight.

The out-of-towners had kept the details vague; that alone made him suspicious. What kind of merchandise were they trying to push? In his current 'line of work', it could be anything. Donovan Morgan invested in a variety of goods.

Kjartan hated going in blind. Not to mention, the unscheduled meeting disrupted his primary plans. He contemplated leaving Eve with Kristján at the house and handling the deal alone with Lucas, but he much preferred the giant as his backup. Having his guest stay by herself was out of the question. She had to tag along.

Kjartan chose the time and location himself, as always. His cabin was off-limits for any kind of business transaction, and he refrained from meeting new clients at the warehouse. He wanted a public place for that, whether Eve was coming or not.

The dive bar downtown would have to do, although he disapproved of the establishment's notoriety. It was perfect for small dealings and first contact, but not a place where she belonged. It did not meet the South Waterfront standard she was used to. Not to mention, his bad company did her reputation no favor. Generally speaking, it was bad for her to even be seen with him. It could put a target on her back. Kristján would have to keep a close eye on her while he took care of business.

He rolled up to the bar in the Harley, where Lucas awaited him at the curb. The boy always looked like trouble with his dark eyes and buzzed hair. Maybe unapproachable was exactly the look he was going for.

Pulling the bike to a stop, he took his helmet off and set it down on his lap. "What did you find out?"

"Nothin'," the boy replied bleakly, hands buried deep in his jeans.

Kjartan frowned. It was not the answer he had hoped for. Lucas worked as a bouncer at a local club and had all sorts of underground connections. He had been a military brat until the age of sixteen, then made Portland his permanent home, scavenging the streets and surviving on his own. His intel was vital and always reliable.

"They're from Vegas, that much is true. Other than that, I don't know who they're in contact with. I've been asking around, and Caleb did his thing on the web, but we couldn't dig up any dirt on either of 'em. That *never* happens," he stressed. "I know everyone, and these guys popped up out of nowhere. I wouldn't trust 'em."

SOUL BOUND

Kjartan had an equally bad feeling about the two men showing up in Portland. It was quite possible that they had simply been drawn to the alias he was using.

"Then there will be no deal," he affirmed, hanging the helmet on the handlebar and getting off the bike. No one was going to touch his Harley. No matter how shady this part of the city was.

As far as he knew, it was the only one of its kind. The denim black paint job with the red accent stripe and bronze-colored pipes was practically infamous. In the short time he had been here, he had already built himself a reputation not to be messed with. The guys that had to learn the hard way, were either never heard from again or quickly passed their less than pleasant experience on to others.

"That's what I figured you'd say. I could've handled this myself; you didn't have to come down here."

"But you said they insisted on talking to me in person."

"So? Who gives a shit if you're going to turn 'em down anyway?"

The kid always had a rough edge, but tonight he seemed extra twitchy. He was the only member of the coven who had committed actual cold-blooded murder. He had killed a man twice his size when he was a mere teenager, taken his time mutilating him bit by bit.

"Are you stable, or are we going to have unnecessary problems in there?" Kjartan sensed emotional unrest in him and wondered when he had fed last.

"I'm tight. I fed two nights ago."

"Are you sure you can control yourself in a bar full of humans? Because it might get ugly if they do not take my *no* for an answer."

241

Lucas opened his mouth, but before he could respond, the Suburban approached with Kristján and Eve. Kjartan glanced over his shoulder, then stabbed his finger at the boy's chest. "You better not cause problems again," he warned through clenched teeth. He could expect a similar punishment to Caleb's.

"I won't," he gnashed, his navy blue eyes meeting him with a level stare.

Lucas did not respond well to authority and was known to be a wildcard. Kjartan could have sworn he detected contempt in his tone.

"On second thought, I think you should sit this one out altogether. I will handle it alone."

"But—"

"Go home, Lucas," he ordered, bumping into his shoulder as he pushed past him toward the bar's steps.

He trained his field of vision on the entrance, meeting up with Kristján, who held the door open. Eve slipped in after. She seemed less than thrilled to be in this part of town. He did not blame her. A girl like her was lucky to only get mugged in the alley, even with enhanced strength from her precious blood. Predators here hunted in packs.

Inside, he shoved a path to a high table in the corner, from which he could keep an eye on the only way in. Her back to the door, Eve stayed across from him, elbow on the tabletop, chin defiantly propped on her knuckles.

Kjartan leaned his shoulder against a post and stuffed his hands into his pockets. Flanking him, Kristján asked, "Where is Lucas?"

"I sent him home."

"When will they get here?"

"They should be here shortly."

"Any idea what the deal is about?"

"I am not even sure how they tracked me down. They might be using fake names; the kid could not find anything on them. All they told Lucas was that they wished to work the deal out in person."

"What deal?" Eve snapped.

Focusing on the door behind her, he had watched her eyes zip back and forth, following the conversation like a wild tennis match.

There was a long pause when neither of them answered her question, and then her eyes bulged. "Oh my God! You're a drug—"

The rest of her words were muffled by Kristján's massive hand over her mouth. "Shush, girl. We don't need people around the block to hear you."

Her little fists flailed violently in the air, as if she were trying to lunge at him from across the table. The giant behind her had to tighten his hold around her waist, lifting her off the ground and pulling her back further into the dark.

Her lips were still moving, mumbling incoherently, eyes hardened in outrage, feet kicking. She was too cute, Kjartan could not resist the urge to humor her. If she wanted a piece of him, he would indulge her.

He stepped closer, giving her a few feeble hits at his chest. "Do not worry, Love," he said flirtatiously. "I am not a drug dealer. Now calm down, and he will let you go so we do not draw any unnecessary attention."

Eve huffed in surrender, and Kristján dropped her to the ground, removing his hands. Then he nodded his chin toward the two guys entering the bar. They were casually dressed, and their attire blended right into the scene, but their body language gave them away: they were nervous. They scanned the crowd until their eyes landed on Kjartan.

"Stay here. This will not take long."

"You're dealing weapons, then? Is that it?" Eve muttered, her face twisted in disdain.

He flashed a quick smirk and spun on his heel to work his way to the back of the bar.

Her second guess was right on the money. Only antiques, however, no modern weaponry. He had not even bothered strapping on the small firearm he owned himself. Opening fire in a crowded bar served no purpose. Kristján was the only one packing tonight.

Kjartan had only agreed to meet with the new dealers because he was looking for something particular from further up north for a change. Possibly Viking-related. Black market deals with the Russians were lucrative, but he wanted to expand his personal collection, and his usual sellers were unable to deliver.

The two men took their spots at the very end of the counter. One of them lowered himself onto the barstool at the edge, the other one stayed standing next to him like a bodyguard, hands clasped behind his back.

They both looked to be somewhere in their thirties, clean-shaven, with a steady build and wide shoulders, but Kjartan was hardly intimidated; they were like college football players compared to his pro status. He planted himself right in front of the taller one, elbow casually propped at the ledge of the countertop.

The one seated addressed him first with a slight tilt of his head. "Donovan Morgan?"

"The very same."

The good soldier leaned over to speak into the other man's ear in a hushed tone. "He looks different."

Indeed, he does. Kjartan chuckled to himself. "What can I do for you, gentlemen?"

The one who had been elected to do the talking put his forearm up on the bar. His other hand rested on his hip. "We heard you're in the *relocation business.*"

There was something familiar about his features, although Kjartan did not specifically recall his face.

"And you need something moved?" The man nodded. "May I inquire what type of item you are looking to re-home?"

He shifted on his seat, and his tongue did a quick swipe across his lips. "We're not exactly pushing antiquities," he said, dabbing the tip of his index finger nervously on the polished counter.

"So you lured me here under false pretense?" Kjartan kept his calm composure, not letting his rising temper show. He was better off making deals with the Russians; at least, they never wasted his time.

"We thought you might still be interested in what we can offer."

Drugs, he figured. "I am not."

Kjartan straightened, ready to walk off. The young man rose from his seat to regain his attention. "We make it worth your while."

"I am not dealing in drugs," he enunciated.

"Since when?" The quiet one finally found his voice. It was burlier than he expected for the man's age.

This was beginning to feel like a setup. A name clawed at the back of his head. "Who sent you?"

"An old friend."

Cooper! Kjan provided him with the rest of the intel to put the pieces together.

The younger one must be his son.

CHAPTER

32

E ve's eyes regarded his strange ensemble from a safe distance. Kjan had only cared about appearances to blend in. He'd never been vain. This guy was on another level. He wore a titanium gray button-down shirt with a plain black vest and black jeans over black leather Timberlands—Kjan's black leather Timberlands—the 8-inch shaft fully laced.

How proper.

Only the top button of his shirt was undone, and the cuffs were neatly folded over, flashing his inked forearms. He wore a very similar watch to the Hublot that was locked in the penthouse's safe. But Kjan's had a black dial on top, whereas Kjartan's was all rose gold, other than the leather strap.

The rustic-chick combo with his goatee, mohawk, and skull tattoos was odd, and yet somehow he didn't just pull it off. He freakin' rocked it. He looked so damn irresistible. Eve's mind drifted.

His conversation with the two men went on for a few minutes before the air took an abrupt turn, with the second guy pushing to his feet. Kjartan's hands were stuffed into his pockets, arms loosely bent at the elbows. He didn't appear braced for physical confrontation.

Without further warning, the guy pulled his fist back and swung out…

Missing by less than an inch when Kjartan leisurely tipped his head to the side, as if anticipating exactly how far the human's arm would reach. His boots didn't even move. Chest puffed, spine as straight as an oak, and stance wide, he stared down at the man stumbling from the momentum of the swing.

Bewildered, the human looked up, and before he could recover, Kjartan's arm shot forward, open palm colliding with the front of the guy's throat.

The instant he made contact, his fingers clenched, lifting his victim up by the neck so that his feet kicked nothing but air.

The altercation was marvelous to watch. The human was only slightly smaller than Kjartan, and yet he manhandled him like a toddler. With legs dangling, the guy clawed at the hold on his windpipe and got nowhere.

Kjartan's grip still biting deeper into skin, he slammed the man's back to the ground.

Eve's hands clasped over her open mouth, and she turned to Kristján. "Aren't you going to do something?"

The tall blond threw his head back with a bellowing laugh, and Eve took that as a *no*.

"What if someone calls the cops?"

Kristján shook his head, still laughing. "No one is going to call the police." He directed her focus back to the scene at the bar. "Just sit back and enjoy the show."

Everyone was watching now. The second guy jumped out from the bar, assuming he would fare better. He threw a punch at an upward angle, aiming for Kjartan's jaw, but he caught the fist in his palm and twisted the man's arm like a rope. The human let out a scream and crumbled to his knees.

Eve saw the first one scramble to his feet to come to his buddy's aid, and he promptly received a boot to the chest, thwarting his admirable attempt. He had the wind knocked out of him a second time by being slammed backward into a table.

He didn't recover.

Still holding the other man's fist in the vise of his right hand, Kjartan's expression never changed. He was completely unfazed as he forced his prey onto his back and then straddled him, closing his hands around his windpipe.

As his victim's panicked kicking slackened, Kjartan turned his head over his shoulder toward Eve to make sure she was watching. The hint of a fang showed. He *was* putting on a show. For her.

Eve didn't know what came over her. She couldn't let him kill the man using Kjan's body. She leaped around the table, only to be immediately cut off by Kristján.

Hooking her waist, he swiped her up before she got past him. "He told you to stay put. What do you think you're doing?" His annoyance registered in her ear above the noise in the bar.

"If you won't intervene, then I will."

She squirmed and shoved at him, but he didn't budge. His tree-trunk arms encircled her upper body, pinning her arms down. Luckily, he didn't cover her mouth this time.

"Stop!" she yelled.

Kjartan's attention snapped to her, and that was when the human beneath him took his shot. His fist struck out at his jaw again, only this time there was definite contact with a loud *CRACK!*

The sound of the collision still rattling through the air, Kjartan's grotesque expression was utterly foreign to her. His chin tucked, eyes two solid black pits beneath heavy brows, she saw the fearsome soul dwelling within Kjan's body. She saw the God for what he really was.

Darkness incarnate.

Eve had seen his irises glow red in anger before, but never this solid, depraved black. She'd made matters worse.

Kjartan's head turned in slow motion back around to his victim, and then his brutal right hook came down on the defenseless human's temple in one ruthless blow. Unable to block the punch, his head flung violently to one side, and his body immediately went limp.

Hovering over him, Kjartan clenched the collar of the man's shirt in his fists and yanked his forehead toward his own. With a sickening crack of bone on bone, he delivered another fierce strike to the man's skull.

The guy's body stayed lax as he blinked slowly, and Kjartan gave him a subtle shake, waiting until he recovered enough from his injury.

When he began to move again, sluggishly lifting his arms, feet twitching, he pulled him up close to his face, and it looked like he was relaying some sort of message.

Once Kjartan's lips stopped moving, he dropped the poor human back to the ground like a sack of potatoes. Satisfied, he rose to his feet and stalked toward Eve, wiping the blood off his lip with a casual swipe of his thumb. It was already healed, not even swollen.

"I got it from here," he told Kristján while nailing her with a hostile glare.

His wingman made himself scarce without so much as another word.

"What the fuck was that?" Eve was a live wire. She didn't restrain her tongue from offering him a piece of her mind he didn't ask for.

"Self-defense," he replied blatantly.

"I think you took that a little too far."

"I got excited." He shrugged, throwing both hands wide in jest. "I thought you would be happy. Those guys actually *are* drug dealers."

"And you're a monster!"

He scowled and glanced back over his shoulder as if he had to double-check that they'd been watching the same show. "I left them alive, did I not?"

"Barely."

Kjartan laughed coldly with indifference and then grabbed her elbow with a harsh grip. His hold on her arm never letting up, he escorted her through the parting crowd in front of them and out the door.

"Get on," he ordered in a gravelly voice, pushing her toward his motorcycle. The same motorcycle he had tried to run her over with twice.

He let go of her arm and took the helmet off the bike's handlebar. Eve threw up her hands before he could nail her in the chest with it.

To her surprise, there was a passenger seat. What were the odds? He didn't appear to be the kind of guy who would give someone a ride. Not on his bike anyway.

"What if I don't?" Using the black object he'd tossed at her like body armor, she kept her eyes steady on him, standing her ground as she provoked him. She knew she was playing with fire, but what the hell.

He made a skeptical sound and nudged his head in the direction of the dark alley. "Suit yourself."

It was a few miles back to her condo. Alone. In this neighborhood? She wasn't even sure exactly where they were.

Kjartan knew that. He called her bluff.

He swung his leg over the Harley and punched the key into the ignition. As he twisted it to start the engine, Eve expected him to burn rubber and literally leave her in the dust.

But he didn't. He waited. Chin slightly tucked, a wry smile crept across his face. "What is it going to be?"

Eve weighed her options, staring down the chilling alley and then back at the immortal. A dark tunnel of misery and loneliness with no light at the end of it? Or him?

She tapped her nail against the side of the helmet. The weight of it suddenly felt much heavier in her hands.

With little resolve, she slipped it over her head and fastened the buckle under her chin, but before she took a step off the curb, panic briefly paralyzed her.

His body so close to mine…

Reaching for his shoulder to steady herself, a familiar comfort flooded her as she mounted the bike behind him. It was still there. The connection between them. It rekindled the moment she made the conscious decision to touch him.

Overwhelmed by the realization, her hands skidded across his upper back. Her palms roamed his frame, both familiar and new.

Beneath her touch, his rigid muscles relaxed. With what she assumed was self-satisfaction. As she caught only the profile of his face, his features gave a subtle twitch. She could picture his smug grin when he fed the throttle more gas.

Eve leaned into him. Her arms wound around him, and not entirely out of fear of falling off. Her coat unzipped, she took in the warmth of his body against hers.

Then they were off.

With the dark visor down, she watched the city lights zip by. They were glimpses of her past. All the places they'd been together.

Fleeting memories of Kjan and her came and went too fast to hold onto. It wasn't enough time. The reel of film ran out too soon. The movie had barely started.

By the time they reached the large house in the woods, the whole world around her had turned to black.

Renate Rowland

CHAPTER

33

He pulled the Harley to a stop in the garage. The engine was still running when she leaped off. She shoved the helmet at him and stormed upstairs, her hair whipping around her in her hurry to put distance between them. He had very much liked her legs around him, her warm body pressed against his backside, arms holding on tightly.

He wanted her to touch him again. Wanted her hands all over.

Alas, Kjartan was more than disappointed with tonight's unfortunate turn of events. His most recent attempt at seducing her had been foiled at the first sign of bearing fruit. Now he had to start over from scratch. Maybe he could coax her back out once she cooled off.

He walked out onto the patio to light the firepit. After all his time alone in his icy prison, he still found solace in solitude. Comfort in darkness.

Well, almost. The bright glow of the fire was his companion. His one constant.

It made no difference that it was barely five degrees outside. He was probably the only one crazy enough to ride a motorcycle in these temperatures. Eve had not appeared to mind the trip either, but she had also been wearing a coat. The cold, of course, did not bother him. Perpetual winter was his element. He almost dreaded the summer.

Kjartan watched the wood catch flames, splitting and splintering in the heat. No gas. No tacky torches. *This* was his refuge.

Only the lake and mountain view from the master suite managed to rival its serenity. Private and secluded, the sizable cabin in the mountains stood like a stronghold, surrounded by 30 acres of nothing but trees and rolling hills. It had a rustic charm that fused with modern, contemporary elegance, creating a masterpiece of the two opposing styles. The former owner had built it himself, and there was even a small forge detached from the main home.

The back wall of the house was completely made of glass and overlooked the stone patio with the massive outdoor firepit. At close to 4,000 square feet, the entire home featured five bedrooms and an equal number of baths. Not that he needed the space. His acolytes were free to take residence wherever they chose, as long as they remained readily available for him.

His objective before the merge had been simple: making a new home in Portland with his coven—his chosen family. The plans for that had been in motion before going back to Iceland. He had felt the urge to return and see the place where he was born by day just once. Perhaps confront the one who had imprisoned him there. But upon his arrival, he had lacked the courage to approach the glacier. What if the magic trapped him anew?

Truth was, he had been stalling. For two months, he had been battling his fears. Then she had found him and given him a new goal to pursue.

He threw another log onto the pile already aflame, the heat pressing on his face. The crackling of the wood grew angrier, snapping and popping, the sap drowning out the peaceful song of the wind sliding through the trees.

A large raven sat on the branch, cocking its head almost as if it were watching him. The presence of small animals rustling in the underbrush reminded him that he was no longer isolated. No longer living a parallel existence. Like the wildlife around him, he was a part of this world. But the loneliness had sunk its claws so deep into his soul he could never escape it.

Eve stirred in her room an hour later, and he heard her quiet little steps approaching, finding their way to the patio.

To *him*.

She opened the door behind him slowly and hung back, as if testing the waters. He kept his eyes on the flames. "Still so timid? Am I really that frightening?"

"The jury is still out on that," she replied, taking a seat on the wicker chair next to him and tugging her knees into her chest.

A throw was draped over her shoulders, and in his periphery, he could see that her hair was down. It fell in thick, dark waves around her head, resting against the stark contrast of the arctic fox fur.

"Thank you for letting me go home this morning."

"As long as it sways the verdict in my favor." His eyes fleeted toward her, and she tried to hide a smile. The wind ruffled her unruly locks, wafting her subtle floral scent in his direction. He caught a hint of wild berries.

She was wearing a slim-fitting purple t-shirt, the modest neckline depriving him of getting another glance at her goods. He got the feeling she was not accustomed to flaunting what she had.

"Where are the others?"

He forced himself to focus. "At home."

"You mean they don't live here with you?"

"No. They have their own place."

"Then why do you need all this space? What's with the Fortress of Solitude?"

Fortress of Solitude? It felt like a reference of sorts. "I do not like to be confined."

As the crackling of the burning wood filled the air between them, she looked up at the full moon, and the fine features of her perfect profile turned into a scowl, that lovely smile of hers slipping from her expression.

"What is it?"

"I thought total lunar eclipses were supposed to be rare."

"They are." Kjartan wondered what else was going through her head.

"Apparently not that rare. This is the third one I have seen lately. There was one a few weeks ago, and…" she hesitated for a moment, "and another one before that."

He knew there would be a fourth one before the six months were up.

So, that was the matter on her mind. *Him.* Kjartan sighed through his nose. He wished he could distract her.

Jaw tense, he got out of his chair and strolled over to the half wall surrounding the patio's edge. "Some religions believe that they hold special power."

"Like magic?"

"Yes, like magic," he humored her, leaning against one of the pillars. "How much do you know of our Gods?"

She rose too and followed him like a moth drawn to a flame. "Only what I read in books. Kjan never talked about them."

And why would he? A man like him would never willingly share his trauma. "He did not choose this life. This existence."

Of course, unlike his new ones, none of his original neophytes had. But what about Eve? Where did she fit in?

The velvet liner of her throw shifted over the bare skin on her arms with her subtle movements, and he could not help imagining her body naked, tangled with his in the soft fur.

His craving for her was reaching a critical state. He needed to get her out of his system. She was an obsession that took over his mind, poisoning him from the inside. He could feel it working its way through his veins, his blood thickening.

"Tell me, could you go back and change things… would you? Would you choose this, knowing the outcome? Knowing you would end up right here?"

"I would!" she said without delay. "In a heartbeat. Kjan didn't make a mistake by siring me. People say it's better to have lost a love than never to have loved at all."

"I wonder if he saw it the same way?"

He received a second, immediate reply. The defined voice in Kjartan's head rang loud and clear. He stifled a smirk.

His eyes roamed over her taut skin again as goosebumps rose just above her neckline. She was feeling the chill now that they had stepped away from the fire, while he was still burning up.

What he would give to wrap his arms around her to keep her warm.

"What did he tell you about me?" Or exactly how much damage control was needed to reshape her opinion of him?

She hugged the blanket closer around her arms, letting the plush mass of white and tan swallow her up. "That you are the son of Hǫðr. But that wasn't in any of the stories I found."

"No, you would not find that in a book. The Gods made sure my story would stay a secret."

Kjartan turned his gaze to the sky. "When I turned twelve, I was no longer considered a child, and my mother abandoned me; either to save herself from getting caught sneaking around or to protect me, I do not know. The other Gods learned of my existence nonetheless, and with my father joining his twin in the underworld, Frigg wanted me out of the picture."

"Why was she so harsh on your father? Loki wasn't punished, and he had a hand in the tragic death of Baldr too?" She raised her voice, and birds ruffled their feathers in the trees.

The *Word Smith,* as he was known, had indeed whispered in his father's ear and directed his aim, but he had not launched the wretched mistletoe. "Loki was different. He got away with a lot of things. The Æsir Gods tolerated him, but he was not technically one of them. And he was punished for his crimes eventually."

"But you were INNOCENT!"

They both looked up at the same time as a flock of small birds burst from the branches of the tree.

The large, black one was not among them.

When Kjartan drew his gaze away from the sky to focus back on her, she bashfully turned her head, embarrassed by her outcry.

"They cursed you and locked you in a cave for something you had no control over. You must hate them," she continued in a softer tone.

"Actually… I do not." He was stunned by her unexpected display of empathy.

Her brows pinched together, Eve stared at him in surprise. "You don't?"

The second her blue eyes found his, he felt the rays of the sun on his skin. Or rather, in his blood. The surge of heat flooded his veins like magma beneath the earth.

"They did what they thought was right. It was the way they perceived the world," he rationalized. "Maybe that is what caused their downfall in the end."

"How did you get out?"

"I am not sure. I felt the magic of the spell that kept me locked up weaken. I did not know the reason. Nor did I care. I simply took the chance I had been given."

The raven, still left behind in the crown of the pine, croaked noisily, as if it were no longer interested in his sob story, and took off in the opposite direction the flock had taken.

"Yet the curse persisted, never granting me the freedom I so longed for," Kjartan went on. His story was meant to sway Eve's opinion of him, not the raven's. "I remained vulnerable to the sun until Kjan's sacrifice. Thanks to him, I found a way to beat it."

Kjartan picked his phrasing carefully and with intention. He had to eliminate every shred of doubt in her that the merge had been coerced. She had to believe Kjan voluntarily made the choice to leave her.

"You sired more than just Kjan. Why him?"

"He was the only one left. I discovered later that most of them had died trying to sire others while they were still fledglings themselves, too young and weak to tolerate the physical exertion it took."

All true so far...

"I had warned them not to make the attempt within the first decade, time would only make them stronger, but they disregarded my advice."

And there is the lie. He had never warned them, but he needed Eve to believe in his compassion.

"It is not hard to understand why. I know all too well what it feels like to have no kin. To feel that loneliness."

"How... how long?" There it was again. The empathy in her eyes. He knew he had her hooked.

"868 years before Kjan's arrival. And Nearly another 800 after."

"You turned him on New Year's Eve in 1067," she said absently and in a low voice.

"I had no knowledge of the date. He was the last one I sired. That is why I chose his name as my own."

Eve was quiet, and her stare dropped back to the floor. Kjartan's eyes focused on her lips, refusing to be redirected. He envisioned touching them, kissing, sucking, and biting. He imagined the taste of her—no, not imagined...

Remembered.

Out of nowhere, the scent of apple blossoms filled his nose as he recalled the sweet, magical fruit that had nourished him as a child. The memory nearly suffocated him.

"What happened to your own body after the transfer?"

"It is gone," he choked out, turning back to the fire to hide his face. "Burned."

⟨HAPTER

34

She clenched the edges of the throw, her fingers digging into the gorgeous faux fur. Despite the brisk air, Eve wasn't cold. She didn't feel temperatures the way she used to when she was human; she hadn't even put shoes on. The blanket was more for comfort. Kjartan made her feel exposed. Like he could see right into her soul if he tried. She always got chills around him. The extra plush layer was a buffer.

And she needed something to hold on to. Keep her hands busy. She wrestled with the urge to reach out and touch him... comfort him.

"Your mother never came back for you?"

His face stayed grim as he shook his head. The way the shadows played with the light of the flames in the sharp angles, his somber features looked so much like Kjan, it hurt.

He smelled like him, too. The overwhelming blend of charred wood and smoke from the fire wasn't enough to smother the traces of him. Her heart fluttered in her chest. His distinct nuances were all there, mixed with the pine and earthy moss that surrounded the edge of the patio.

She wondered how long it would take for the Stockholm syndrome to kick in.

Or maybe it already had.

Kjartan wasn't the monster she'd thought him to be. He had his reasonable moments, and she could definitely empathize with him. She knew what it was like to be stuck in a role or place you didn't want. She'd gotten out. Why shouldn't he get a chance?

Hearing his story in his own words had a deeper impact than hearing it from Kjan's point of view. Unfiltered through another's emotions, he stood before her—her own ears, her own eyes passing judgment.

And she saw him. Not as Kjan. But as a different man entirely.

He wasn't born evil. Forces beyond his control had shaped him that way. He was a victim of abuse through neglect. So he'd built himself his own family. Like Doctor Frankenstein. Did that make the coven his monster?

She almost found herself feeling sorry for him, but then she remembered that he had sacrificed Kjan's life for his own good. His unfair treatment didn't give him the right to inflict the same on others.

As if he'd read her mind, Kjartan reduced the meager inches separating them, his hands suddenly skimming along her waist. Eve felt like her skin was on fire all over. His touch lit her up.

She tensed but didn't flinch away when he parts the blanket further and gently pulls me into his chest. Chin angled toward her, he inclined his head, his goatee grazing her jaw.

"Lie with me, Eve." His lips brushed her cheek as he spoke, his voice so low and affectionate. "I want you to share my bed."

Her heart thumped even harder in its cage at the cajoling rasp in his timbre. The words wrenched at her conscience, but the muscles in her thighs twitched. She hated how they responded to him.

The air caught in her throat. There it was. The request she'd been dreading. But it wasn't really a request, was it? Kjan had been a control freak, never a bully. Kjartan, on the other hand, didn't ask permission. He didn't tolerate being refused; he took what he wanted, when he wanted it.

For someone who'd spent his entire life confined to a cave, the man had no patience.

And then, to confirm her intuition, one of his hands slipped around the small of her back while his other one dragged through her hair to the back of her neck in a claiming act, compelling her to submit. Rejecting him was not an option.

Slanting his mouth over hers, he kissed her. Eve expected him to be rough, but the caress of his lips was soft and tender. She felt her body relax in his embrace, the same way it had always been with Kjan. His arms still felt like home. Even without his soul, they remained physically linked through his body and mind.

Does Kjartan know?

It caught her off guard how easily he manipulated her. She tried to fight it. This wasn't right; he wasn't Kjan. She had to keep reminding herself that no matter how much he looked like him or felt like him, he was not the same person. She needed a distraction.

Eve broke away. "What about Askja?"

His brows furrowed. "Askja?"

"The two of you seem close. What is she to you?"

"She is loyal," he replied flatly. "And the closest thing I have to a friend."

He skimmed his hand around her waist, his fingertips brushing over the sensitive parts of her belly. She blocked him from wandering under her shirt. "I can't."

"I will not hurt you, Eve. I swear by the Gods; you have my word." And then he pressed his mouth to hers again, more demanding this time when his tongue breached her parted lips.

Did he really think that was going to sway her? She tried to pull away, but he wouldn't let her. His grip didn't relent.

Eve tasted blood. A sudden panic shot through her. His blood was not like Kjan's. With the effect of it already kicking in, she felt the warm and fuzzy sensation not just under her skin but in her head.

"Relax. It will not last long," he whispered in her ear, holding her steady.

Kjartan's blood wasn't just more potent; it was like a different kind of drug altogether. Instead of giving her a high, it hit her like the Lorazepam in Jordan's tequila. Her muscles started to relax on their own volition. Eve was incapable of stopping it.

"I told you, I can take whatever I want." His fingers fanned through her hair, and he tugged her head back to look into her eyes. Sensual flames flickered in his. "But I want you to trust me."

"This is not going to help your case," she assured him with a tremble in her voice. A tear rolled down her cheek, and he wiped it.

"I know," he paused, studying her face. "That is the only reason we are still standing here. I want your consent."

266

"You're blackmailing me to get what you want."

He chuckled. "You are not the first one to accuse me of that. I am just trying to persuade you, Love."

"Don't call me that," Eve spat back. He'd used the endearing term at the bar earlier, too.

There was a subtle twitch at the corner of his mouth. Her defiance amused him. "I have no doubt you will make the right decision on your own. Either way, I will get what I want. I always do."

He tilted her chin up and leaned down as if to kiss her, but stopped short just before his lips touched. Then he drew back, flaunting a self-assured grin.

"You know where to find me," he said with a wink, leaving her alone outside.

Eve watched the door shut and balled her hands into fists. The effect was already wearing off. She was angry at herself for letting her guard down and for walking blindly into each one of his traps. Even with Kjan gone, she couldn't help but wonder what he'd think of her now. Would he judge her for wanting to hold on to the only thing that was left of him?

The way Kjartan talked was strange. He'd adopted Kjan's distinctly American accent and drew on his mind for general knowledge of everyday things, but he refused to use his vernacular. He enunciated the word *either* like *aye*-ther, where Kjan had used the long *ee* sound. And she'd never heard him use contractions. Ever. Like he thought it was beneath him.

Eve sat down on the cold stone wall. The smoke stung her eyes as the wind veered. She wanted to scream at it. Scream at the sky if that made a difference. He'd told her she wasn't a prisoner, and she wanted to run as far away from him as she could, but his touch was what she craved. What she needed to feel alive.

She couldn't bring herself to follow him upstairs. At least not as long as the moon was taunting her. It reminded her too much of that first night alone when she'd waited for Kjan to come home.

She'd been waiting still. This whole time, she'd hoped for a miracle that would bring him back. But that miracle would never come.

Kjan had left her.

He was gone.

Eve didn't want to rush the closure. Watching the blood moon against the black sky, she drew out every second. She hadn't been with anyone in five months. Hated the idea of someone other than him touching her.

She'd waited this long. She could wait a little longer.

CHAPTER

35

H e had shared too much. Given her a piece of himself that he had not meant to divulge. His mother was a sore subject. One that he never even spoke to Askja about. The grown man did not want their pity, and the broken little boy, who needed his mother, no longer existed. Never had, according to the perception of the world around him.

Kjartan sat at the foot of the bed, elbow resting on the one knee that was pulled up. His other leg was tucked under, and he absentmindedly fidgeted with the hem of his jeans. He had stripped the rest. The inside of the house was too hot. He was five seconds from peeling his skin off.

Forehead resting against his palm, he worked his temples in a small circular motion with his thumb and middle finger. Had he really misread her signals? The sun was already high in the sky, and Eve had not shown. Spurning his request was a direct slap to the face. It stung.

As irritating as it was, Kjartan had to stay patient. He knew waiting for her to make up her own mind instead of pushing her was the right approach. It would be worth it. He would win and reap the reward—

His attention snapped toward the door.

He sensed her advancing on hushed steps, and when she entered, her skin was slightly flushed. She had stayed out on the patio until the rays had become too much, but yes, she had come. Just like he predicted.

He would not harp on his pride. She looked plenty uneasy walking up to him; the wrong words might send her running.

Eve's bare feet halted at the edge, and Kjartan rose from the bed. She did not meet his eyes. His hands itched to touch her, but he resisted the urge, giving her all the time she needed.

Apprehension lingered in her movements. Timidly, her hands reached for him, the tips of her fingers exploring each ridge of his abs as if for the first time. They grazed along his pecs, tracing the sharp lines of solid muscle with her hands as much as her eyes.

He watched the rise of her chest, her pulse quickening with every breath, and his glance traveled up her neck to the subtle jerk in her throat. She was wrestling with her emotions, but she *was* here—with him—of her own will, dangling on his hook. All he had to do was reel her in before she slipped free.

Moving in for the kill, he took her clammy hand without a word and placed it in the center of his chest. His own hands were steady. There was no trembling or pounding headache. He relished the silence in his mind, his heartbeat in harmony with hers, and then she looked up at him at last.

Eve caught him off guard once more when her hands slid up his nape, pulling *him* in instead.

Kjartan felt the cold ice melt in his heart, thawing from the radiating warmth of her confidence. He exhaled a shuddery breath. Enclosing her to lift her to him, he deepened the kiss.

The attraction was inexplicable. An unparalleled phenomenon. She bewitched him with her siren song… manipulated him into compliance… commanded his body…

…and he lacked any form of aspiration to resist.

How does she do it?

He could feel his host's emotions toward her and knew they were not his own. They were two minds in one body, ever out of sync, but his vessel was responding to a link it shared with the woman.

The sweet fragrance of her pheromones magnified his hunger. He was starved all of a sudden. Ravenous. Reveling in her passion, he feasted on the soft moans that poured from her lips.

One arm around the small of her back, he stretched her out on the bed and lowered himself down on her, his huge frame covering her entirely. Her lips parted for him with a soft sigh, and he reclaimed her mouth with more fervor, his fingers dimpling her thigh through her jeans.

Eve was no longer tense. Hiking her legs at his sides, she countered his movements with her hips, increasing the friction.

He rolled into her body. The muscles in his back drawn tight, Kjartan surrendered the jarring groan building in his chest.

His grabby hands slid under her t-shirt, and he pushed himself up to pull it over her head, regretfully breaking the connection to her delectable, plump lips.

Kneeling between her thighs, he made quick work of her bra as well, but it was far from sufficient. Her pants had to go next.

He undid the front of her jeans, and she bridged her body off the mattress impatiently while he tugged them down.

He edged off the bed, his skin tingling from her watching him undress through the space between her legs. The desire in her eyes was glorious. The view of her sublime.

Naked before him, he urged her back onto the pillow, dragging his mouth down the front of her body. His fingers pinched the tender pink nipple adorning her breast, and it pebbled under his attention.

Eyes closed, Eve arched at his touch. He could not withdraw his gaze. He found immense delight in seeing her squirm in sweet agony, hands clenched around the sheets up by her head, whimpering. He wanted to push her to the brink and watch her armor shatter into pieces, leaving her bare and unguarded in front of him.

As he eliminated the distance to her mouth, her body moved like molten glass in his arms, her soft, rounded shapes rising and falling in restless motion. Her heated form was moldable but fragile nonetheless. He held back. It took so much self-control not to hurt her accidentally. Not to snap her like a twig. At last, she had made herself vulnerable because she trusted him to keep his word.

Nudging against the heat of her core, she allowed him a small taste of the blaze within. Kjartan felt his skin aflame, but he did not breach the threshold. He kept them both on the verge of what they craved so deeply, savoring the seconds leading to imminent gratification. He had won, and Eve was his prize.

Triumphantly, Kjartan wound his arm around her waist, sweeping her up to straddle him, then pulling her down in a single thrust. With a sharp cry, her nails dug into his chest, and her body shuddered through the convulsions of her climax. Her legs quivered against him, the sensual spasms gripping him tighter.

It was nothing like all the other times he had satisfied this desire. This need. Their connection reached deeper somehow. His mind threatened to split.

After the wave of pleasure released its hold on her, she began moving on top of him. The way she worked him—her hands tangled in her hair, abs flexing beneath her skin when she leaned back further—his muscles tensed up again. Clenching his teeth, he held back the rumble building in his throat.

Hands firmly grasping her hips, he kept them rocking together until she came once more, and he let himself go with her. His eyes rolled back as he arched off the bed, little fireworks exploding behind his lids in bursts of white.

Funny, Kjartan thought, while their ragged breathing slowed to its natural pattern. He had expected Kjan to put up a fight, but he had not sensed any resistance from him since the night he put a muzzle on the feral dog. Almost as if he had finally given up and crawled into a dark corner of his mind to succumb.

It seemed that Kjartan had killed two birds with one stone: his host had accepted defeat, and he would have Eve all to himself.

∫

The aftershock coursed through her. Kjartan kept his grip firm as he dropped her down beside him. The set of rings that hung from the leather string around his neck slipped to the side and disappeared in the crease of the pillow. Eve never got a good look at them.

Catching her breath, she let her eyes wander over the tattoos on the sides of his head. "Why Óðinn's ravens?"

"You are familiar with them?" His face was open, his smile sincere.

"Only by name. Huginn means thought, and Muninn means memory. What do they mean to you?"

He raised himself onto his elbow, and the twin set of rings around his neck slipped free, dangling right in the center of his jugular notch as he leaned over. Each one was made with three individual iron wires, hand-forged into a simple braid. The two rings were identical in style, though one of them was significantly larger. They looked like wedding bands. *Whose are they?*

Kjartan hovered above her, tracing the thumb of his left hand from her temple to her chin. Eve's gaze dropped from his eyes to his mouth as his tongue swept across his lip.

"Ravens are believed to bestow transformational energy," he began to explain in a sultry voice, "revealing the path to freedom from your deepest fears by illuminating your darkest parts. A raven can show you how to reach within to heal inner conflict and bring out your true self."

"Heal inner conflict? Is it about recovering the memories you can't access?" Particularly, the memories of her. Eve wasn't sure she wanted him to.

"For one. I also hoped they would connect me with the past."

"And they didn't?" She felt a sense of relief. What she had shared with Kjan was private.

"I am still working on that," he asserted firmly.

Her eyes landed on Kjan's old scar at the tip of the raven's wing feathers. She brushed her fingers over the prolate irregularity in the center of his chest. "Do you know how he got the scar?"

"He did not tell you?"

Eve shook her head. "He said he stabbed himself, but I didn't believe him. It would have healed."

"He lied."

Kjartan's words stunned her. Kjan had never lied to her before.

"It happened when he was still human," he elaborated.

Blood rushed from her face with a tingling sensation. "How could he possibly have survived that?"

"He did not. Not technically. I had to kill him before I could bring him back. And then I repeated the process for the possession in the same manner."

Eve met him with a furrowed brow. *What manner?*

"He never told you the whole story? He left out the best part, then. His initiation was not as painless as yours." Kjartan took her index finger and ran it slowly down the center of his chest while he said, "I cut him open, reached into his chest, and directly fused my blood with his heart."

"WHAT?" she sputtered. Kjan had been so desperate to kill himself that he'd agreed to physical torture?

A frigid wave of horror crashed over her. Eve tried to pull her hand back, but he held on like a vise.

"It was a necessity," he said as casually as if he were talking about the weather and not the fact that he had tortured the man she loved. "I am not a vampire, Eve. I am a God."

He kissed the tips of her fingers, and the electric blue of his irises flashed through his dense, black lashes, studying her reaction. She tried not to let her horror show, but his smug face was proof that he knew exactly how to get under her skin.

Kjartan pulled away and reached for his jeans. The sun had shifted, and light was now flooding the room through the clear balcony door. It gave his silhouette a bright backdrop as she watched him.

She'd noticed a subtle tan on his skin before. He must spend more time outdoors. He was utterly invincible, and his body was even more majestic in daylight. With the tattoos densely covering his torso and arms, he had all the splendor of a Norse God.

He caught her squinting. "You should get some sleep," he suggested, closing the heavy curtain.

"What about you? This is *your* bed," Eve pointed out.

"I do not sleep. But you are welcome to stay."

The rings swayed toward her when he leaned back down to kiss her, beaming like a kid in a candy store. "Then I know where to find you," he added with a cheeky grin.

He swiped a shirt off the desk chair before heading out the door.

Words echoed through her mind in Kjan's voice: *'The rules don't apply to him.'*

He was not a vampire… didn't feed… didn't sleep…

Well, he was something else, alright. *Terrifying*, for example, was at the top of her list.

She couldn't get what he'd said out of her head. How could she stay here, knowing what he was responsible for? What he had done to Kjan?

Twice.

CHAPTER

36

The vibration against his hip nearly took the bounce out of his step on his way downstairs. Direct calls were never a good sign. They suggested urgency and immediate action on his part. He liked texts. They were easier to ignore.

Kjartan snapped up the phone. It was Kristján. *"Speak!"*

"We have a situation," the man's dark voice relayed in Icelandic.

"Who?"

"Lucas."

His nostrils flared as he growled into the speaker. The boy's name was all it took to get his temper into gear; he was on his bike and down the driveway, not sixty seconds later.

On the ride to the loft, Kristján filled him in on the developments of the night: Lucas had tried to pull off a deal on his own and ended up getting shot.

Unfortunately for him, Kjartan was not the good Samaritan type. The kid had gotten himself into the mess; he would have to get himself back out.

25 minutes later, Kjartan breached the warehouse's front door. His vision locked on Lucas, who was pacing the front room and rubbing his palms aggressively over his shaved head. His breath heaving, eyes wild while mumbling to himself, he looked like a mental patient.

"…blindsided me… never saw him coming…"

"He's stable, but the bullet is still lodged in his skull," Claire explained from her seat on the couch, hugging her knees into her chest.

Her brother Parker was sitting next to her, his bright eyes so very unusual for his dark complexion. The features of his face showed the same worry as his twin's.

"And what exactly do you expect me to do about it?" Kjartan weighed in. He was good at cutting things open, but that did not qualify him as a surgeon.

None of them met his glare as he scanned the group.

Friction prickled the air. The dreadful mood in the room was so very familiar; they already knew how this would play out. They had been in a similar situation shortly after their transition. The girl had been a bad choice. Weak-minded. But they had found a more suitable replacement. A simple swap. They were better off for it.

"It's not like we can take him to a hospital." Caleb, whose face still showed the fresh marks of his recent punishment, opened his mouth with a bitter edge. For some reason, he had always considered himself Lucas' keeper, even though he was seven years younger. "The wound's already healed up. There's not even a scar. They'd raise some questions." And the boy knew the immortal would hunt each one of them down for drawing that kind of attention to the coven. "He needs help."

Kjartan sensed Kristján shift behind him. The giant hung back to let him handle things his way. When glancing over his shoulder, he got a peek at him cracking his knuckles, and judging by the intense expression on his face, he seemed eager to lunge himself at the ignorant boy for the disrespectful tone.

Emma, the second female in the room, beat Kristján to the punch. "What he needs is to keep his ass in check. Why do you always defend him?"

Caleb shot her an annoyed glance. Small in stature, she made up for it in attitude. She was always quick with a retort. Indeed, she had proven herself to be a strong replacement.

Kjartan's fingers twitched. He had no intention to help, but he was not entirely indifferent to the kid's condition either. He considered Lucas an asset, not a weak link, despite his much-needed attitude adjustment. The loss of him would be unfortunate. The dilemma was that he saw no way to handle the problem without cutting his cranium open. Lucas was already a mental case; the last thing he needed was a brain injury that healed wrong and made him damaged goods. Kjartan had enough problems with his own neurons to know what that was like.

"*Aaargh!*" Lucas let out a violent howl and dropped to his knees. Fists pounding at his temples, he writhed in pain. "Fuck! It burns. I can't take it. Get it out. GET IT OUT!" he yelled, squeezing his eyes shut and battering his skull to no avail.

Kjartan crouched down beside him. Reaching into his back pocket, he pulled out the 6-inch Italian stiletto knife he recently acquired and flicked its switch. At the sound, black eyes full of hatred opened to meet his.

Clasping the dark horn handle lightly, he waved the slim blade in front of the boy's face. "Dig it out yourself."

Maybe he would stick it clear through his brain and end himself right here.

Lucas' stare remained steady on him, not following the taunting motion.

"No? I guess that means I will have another vacant slot to fill. You are of no use to me in this condition." Letting his ranks dwindle over this minor inconvenience was unacceptable. He needed a total of twelve.

He sheathed the blade and stowed it back in his pocket. Hands braced on his thighs, he pushed to his feet.

"You tried to pull a deal without my knowledge. I think it is only fitting that you suffer the consequences. And if anyone helps you, they receive a bullet in their head as well. Courtesy of me," he threatened with a nonchalant smile while addressing the rest of the group.

It was better they feared him. He was their leader. Not their friend.

The emotional turmoil in the air became palpable. Fear. Anger. Hate. He fed on all of it, and yet it did not fill his appetite. He knew they were not meant to be his source of nourishment. He was their Sire. They depended on him for protection.

Kjartan had to get out before he actually started feeling guilty. He swung toward the door, then paused and looked back. One last thing burned on his mind. "What was the dealer's name?"

"C-Cooper," Lucas' voice rasped in physical agony.

The old man himself?

Kjan's body did not carry the resilience of Kjartan's own former shell. Shots would not bounce off his skin the way weapons used to. The kid had caught a bullet that had most likely been intended for him. It almost made him feel a little sorry.

He would have to take care of the problem before it got further out of hand.

He gave the security app on his phone another check before getting on his bike. All doors were still locked and armed. He had to make it back to the lodge before Eve realized she was alone at the house. The cameras showed no movement. If he was lucky, she was asleep.

Once Caleb had done a little bit of digging, he identified Cooper's current whereabouts as a little cabin not too far from Mount Hood. How ironic. After his mishap of shooting the wrong guy at the meet, the coward tried to hide outside of the city, and now here they were, practically neighbors.

Kjartan fought a laugh while driving up the gravel road. Rocks popped beneath the bike's tires. Making a stealthy approach was not his concern, but he was not going in guns blazing either. He had a plan. Diplomacy. And in case that failed, there was always a plan B.

Cooper's eyes nearly popped out of their sockets as they landed on Kjartan. The importance of reputation was never to be underestimated. The man already knew he was dealing with the devil. He had been Donovan Morgan's business partner in the Las Vegas scene for over a decade.

He did seem to be taken aback by the not-so-subtle difference in Kjartan's appearance. Mostly his luminous blue eyes. Demonic possession had to be the only logical explanation for the devout Christian. Though, how sincere could a man's faith really be if he did not care to uphold the simple Ten Commandments?

But Kjartan was no demon. Nor the infamous fallen angel. He was a God in his own right.

"Jesus Christ!" the human yelped, fearfully taking a few steps back into the room.

"No," Kjartan replied. He was not that one, either.

Eyes still wide, mouth agape, he stumbled into the dresser at the far wall. Various items on top started rattling. A cologne bottle tipped over with a soft *clank*. The former all-star athlete had gotten fat in his old age.

"You tried to have me killed and shot one of my men instead," Kjartan started off in a level tone as he planted his boots inside. Hands casually tucked into the back pockets of his jeans, he puffed his chest out to let the man take in the full size of him.

"I-Impossible... I shot you... I saw you," he stammered.

"Then your eyes must have deceived you. And lucky for you, my man is still alive," he went on, ambling toward the cowering man. "And that is the only reason why I am willing to let the attempted murder slide."

Kjartan stopped and leered down at Cooper. There was barely any black left in his gray widow's peak.

He pulled his hands from his pockets and drilled his left forefinger into the large man's chest. "But if you ever come after one of my own again, I will end you. There will be no more leniency. Do I make myself clear?"

The flustered human's lips twitched, his eyes full of fear. Kjartan's lungs inflated, and he gorged himself on the mouthwatering meal he was handed. He did not expect Cooper to find his voice, so he accepted his silence and turned to walk out.

"This will never be over, Don. You ruined me. I'll kill you for that," the warning threat shot after him.

"No, you will not." The immortal scuffed over his shoulder. "I am unkillable."

"Maybe you are. But I bet *she* is not."

Did that wretched piece of human garbage just threaten Eve?

Kjartan stopped in the open door, facing Kristján, who had waited out on the porch.

"She was seen at the bar with you. I have pictures of her. She's a local. I can have hired guns on her ass with one phone call."

Yup, he sure as hell did.

He felt Kristján's eyes on him. His giant shadow knew exactly what was going to happen next, and his hand twitched in response, but Kjartan was faster. His finger found the trigger at the small of his back as he spun, locking onto his target. The round went through Cooper's right biceps, and the gun he had drawn from who-knew-where dropped by his feet.

Kjartan had upgraded Kjan's classic Colt 1911 to something new and flashy. The Sig Sauer P320 AXG Scorpion was a little more his style, and he had clocked enough hours on the shooting range to hit his mark at a distance of 100 yards dead center each time. Once he took aim, he never flinched.

"I gave you a chance to walk away, but you could not leave well enough alone. You just had to go there. All because of your precious reputation?" Kjartan sneered, advancing on the son of a bitch, his weapon still drawn.

The gleaming gold watch on the dresser caught his eye. Ambition and arrogance had made Cooper greedy long before Kjan had taken the club away from him.

His hand went behind his back to shove the gun into the holster. "Let me make my point clear. You threaten her. You die. No negotiation."

This time, Cooper made an attempt to open his mouth in response, but Kjartan gripped his shoulder and rammed the long blade of the stiletto through the bottom of the man's jaw. It went to his brain before he mustered a single sound.

He leaned down, fingers of his right hand biting into the muscle of Cooper's shoulder as he twisted the knife just for fun. "I'll do whatever it fucking takes to keep her safe," he whispered into the dying man's ear.

Neither he nor Kjan had killed anyone in cold blood for a long time. An odd calm washed over him as the human's blood ran freely down his left hand, soaking the sleeve of his shirt. For the first time since the transfer, it felt like every cell in his body was in sync—mind and body aligned by the same objective.

Kjartan watched the life drain out of Cooper's dark brown eyes, death coating them with a hazy sheen. With a firm grip on the now-slick horn handle, he ripped the steel free from the man's skull. His large body slumped into a heap at his boots.

"Burn him," he uttered with indifference. "No one hears of this."

Kristján gave him a terse nod, then slung the dead man over his shoulder.

Kjartan could not watch. It had been an odd sensation to observe his childlike body lifeless on the ground. Askja had wept over the empty husk as the flames swallowed it up. He had never seen a body burned to ash before. The image still haunted him, and he was grateful that Kristján would take care of the old man.

Leaving the cabin, Kjartan recalled the sense of someone watching him after the meeting with the Russians. Had it been Cooper himself or one of his lackies? How long had the man been scouting him out? If they had followed him to her apartment, they knew where she lived.

Renate Rowland

CHAPTER

37

She tossed in his bed for hours, but it was useless. Eve wasn't going to get any sleep. She'd heard him leave on the Harley shortly after making his exit from the bedroom, and he hadn't returned yet. She didn't want him to find her still in the sheets where he'd left her, as if she were desperate for a continuation of their coupling.

That was not happening. She felt so ashamed for throwing herself at Kjartan. All she could think about was washing him off her.

Eve grabbed a change of clothes from her room and took a shower in the guest bathroom down the hall. Turning the heat as high as she could tolerate, she scrubbed her skin until it was bright red and raw.

Once she finally felt clean again, she returned to his room. She opened the curtain a few inches and was instantly taken aback. Before her stretched a large wooden deck that faced the same direction as the patio on the ground floor. The sun was just setting behind the trees, and the view of the lake was breathtaking.

Mesmerized, she almost forgot the nightmare she found herself in.

Eve didn't sense his approach. Her muscles steeled at the shock of him brushing her hair over her shoulder.

When did he get back? She hadn't heard his bike come up the driveway.

His rock-solid chest, among other things, made contact with her back as he engulfed her, the gesture so intimate, so familiar. His face came close enough for her to feel his breath feathering her cheek. "How did you sleep?"

His voice made her skin crawl. "Fine," she lied.

She hated it when he sneaked up on her like this. Hated herself for staying with this monster—this God—who commanded Kjan's body.

Yet she still craved his touch. There was no denying it. That was why she hadn't tried to run while he was out.

He had to know about the Sire-bond, but did he know about the addictive nature of marking a mate? Eve couldn't imagine him ever pledging himself to another person.

The enticing bouquet of Four Roses Single Barrel whiskey, Kjan's favorite, bloomed in her airways, but the guilt that swelled in her heart threatened to drown her. A lump lodged in her throat, thick and heavy. She couldn't breathe as he leaned down to kiss her neck, his lips lingering over her exposed skin.

She could still smell the charred wood and smoke from the fire on him, even though he'd showered and changed his clothes. The earthy undertones and hints of pine lingered as well.

Is this him? His natural scent overlaying all that was Kjan? There was something new to it now. Something rich, but unlike chocolate.

Fresh coffee grounds, Eve noticed. Everything about him seemed dark and bitter.

"Does my precious bird not enjoy her golden cage?" he asked.

The air hitched around the persistent lump in her throat at his unexpected choice of words. *Bird—Dove*, the term was too similar; hit too close to home. "Why would you call me that?"

"It fits."

"I'm not your *bird*." Eve turned her face to prevent him from discovering what she struggled with in her heart.

She was saved just in time by the sound of a truck pulling into the driveway, and Kjartan backed off.

"Those are Kristján and Caleb," he said over his shoulder, retrieving something from his desk drawer and shoving it into his back pocket.

He was wearing a different dark button-down than last night, sleeves halfway folded up.

How many gray shirts does he own?

"They will stay here with you. I have an errand to run, but I will not be long," he added, and then walked out.

Eve waited until she heard him leave on the bike, and then she went downstairs. She found Kristján at the bottom and saw Caleb around the corner in the kitchen. He didn't even look at her. He sat silently at the island with his eyes glued to the laptop in front of him. Something about the color of his skin was off.

"What happened to him?" she whispered, turning to Kristján as he lowered himself onto the couch in the front room.

"What do you think?" he said in his deep Icelandic accent. Eve was confused. "He got hung out to dry," he elaborated to clarify things.

He rolled his *r* as pronounced as the Irish woman she'd met on her first night here. His tone was nonchalant, suggesting that this kind of stuff happened a lot and was no big deal.

"He burned Caleb in the sun?" she whisper-yelled, keeping her voice well below indoor volume. Was that why Kjartan kept the others vulnerable to sunlight? So he could use it against them?

"*Yow*"—*Já*, Kristján confirmed in Icelandic.

Yes, was one of the few easy words Eve remembered from her trip. She was also familiar with the two different th-sounds. Þ—*Thorn* was usually at the beginning of a word, and ð—*Eth* was used in the middle or at the end.

The giant stretched his arm over the back of the couch. Eve's eyes were drawn to the titanium button-down shirt that was draped over the chair next to him. It was the one Kjartan had worn last night and also when leaving her this morning.

The dark red stain up the left sleeve captured her focus. She stared at it in horror. It was blood. She could smell it from where she stood. And it wasn't his own.

It was human.

CHAPTER

38

K jartan turned the key to the condo and stepped through the door. He found the charger for the dead cell in the kitchen and plugged it in. Giving it a few minutes, he took a closer look around the suite.

His eyes were drawn to a few pieces of opened mail on the counter. He picked up one of the envelopes and flipped it over, scanning it for Eve's last name:

Brooker.

He still had no recollection of it.

He crumbled the paper in his fist. He felt like he was trying to remember a dream but consistently failed to put the pieces back together properly to make sense. The memory he glimpsed days ago had slipped through his grasp the instant he got too close.

He rubbed the sides of his head as if the tattooed ravens could jog his mind. He had hoped to fill in the gaps by seeing the place with his own eyes, but now he felt even more frustrated.

His browse took him on a loop around the front room, the shaggy white rug, an odd set of gothic furniture that matched nothing else in the penthouse.

His fingers twitched, itching to clench around something.

He scanned the random array of books on the shelves, but nothing particularly stood out. The only thing that triggered a reaction was a hunting knife. The large blade pulled him back to the conversation with Eve about Kjan stabbing himself.

Nothing else registered.

Kjartan ended up in the bedroom, eyes darting over the tousled sheets. He sank onto the edge in disappointment. He had the distinct notion that his interest in Eve would not fade as quickly as it did with shiny new toys. She was not something he could check off a list and move on from. Instead of extinguishing the flames of his desire with the conquest, he had merely fanned them. She was far from out of his system. She had burrowed herself deep into his bones.

Dropping his head into his palms, he scrubbed them across his face. He should have remembered her sooner. He had forgotten Kjan had a mate. Clearly, he had known about Eve before the merge, even if he never laid eyes on her, but then every connection to her had been erased. Exactly like the images of Thórunn he had held on to for a thousand years had slipped his mind. All memories of them washed away, deleted like files on a computer.

Kjan kept them both hidden from him. How was it possible for his feeble host to put up this kind of resistance?

Kjartan tucked his head lower, dragging his hands over the top, fingertips wedging between the braids. He was struck by the urge to dig deeper, all the way into his brain, to shake something loose.

He tugged the large tie free and then detangled one of the braids, his fingers skimming across, delving between the weaves. He did the same with the second and then the third, unraveling them like strands of a rope that could lead him back to his past. Guide him home.

His fingers grazed through the roots on his scalp to scratch at the memories beneath. He watched the long waves tumble down his shoulders, and as his eyes focused on the dark shade of brown, he was reminded that it was not his own hair. Not his own body. It was the body of a man he hardly knew. Barely scraped the surface of.

Kjartan felt like all the key details about Kjan's character revolved around the two women. Everything else had been pretend, a façade, and only with them had he truly been himself.

All that was lost to him. Unreachable.

Rage exploded out of him. He went back to the phone. The screen flickered, but it was access-protected via fingerprint, just like he had assumed.

A thought occurred to him. *Can it really be that easy?*

He pressed his thumb to the display and smiled as it unlocked. Alas, his delight quickly faded as he stared at the picture on the home screen. No doubt, there were more photos of the same saved on it.

He opened the message app and scrolled through the recent ones. Most of them were from her friend Tanya, checking in, and there were also missed calls. After a moment's hesitation, Kjartan clicked on the texts he was really interested in.

Reading through them, he felt his anger rising again and decided he had seen enough. This was not getting him anywhere, and for an instant, he contemplated shoving the wretched thing down the garbage disposal.

His eyes caught sight of another laptop. Not Eve's. Kristján already told him she took hers the last time she was here.

He turned it on, but his progress halted at the required password. Knowing Kjan's concern for safety, this would not be as easy as getting access to Eve's phone. Surely Caleb would have fun with the challenge.

He went to the closet in the bedroom for a backpack. Grabbing the one he found crammed into the corner, he paused, staring at his reflection in the floor-length mirror.

A smile replaced his irked expression, and he swung the mirrored panel wide. He would not leave empty-handed after all.

When he returned to the kitchen, he slid the laptop inside the bag. Then he powered down the cell phone and took the charger as well before heading out the door.

On his way back, he let the 114 V-twin engine of the FDXR loose and pushed the torque to the max. The thrill of the speed was exhilarating, and it was one of only two things that truly freed his mind of the continuous rage. He felt peace as long as he kept going.

Reaching the lodge, Kjartan pulled the Harley into the garage this time; he had pushed it up to the front door earlier to keep Eve oblivious to his arrival. He immediately felt the weight on his shoulders return. He could sense that she was still upset, and it affected his own mood.

The three of them were seated in the front room, and he handed the backpack to Caleb without a word. He kept his eyes on her as the kid pulled the black laptop from the bag.

"Nice!" Excited about the assignment, he flipped his new toy in his hands.

An expression of shock swept across her features while tracking the exchange. Eve jumped off the couch, lunging at it in a presumptuously daring move.

Kristján was quicker and seized her upper arms to hold her back.

"You have no right to take that," she barked, struggling in vain against his grip.

"Make it a priority." He shot the kid a glance before refocusing on Eve. She was livid. Her usual delicate scent ignited in a sharp, prickling sensation he could taste in the air.

Caleb slid it back into the bag. "Gimme 24 hours."

"What else did you take?" The spicy kick of her temper flared in her tone.

Kjartan made a quick judgment call. He nodded to Kristján to let her go and clear out with Caleb. She did not settle down, but at least she refrained from jumping at his throat.

"Your phone," he revealed with a satisfied smile, crossing his arms. *And a forty-thousand dollar watch.* He should thank her for shaking the memory of the code for the safe lose.

"Why do you want my phone?"

"I do not want it," he teased, closing the distance between them at an amble pace. "But I do not want you to have it, either."

He hovered an inch from her face, and Eve stood her ground, glaring up.

So precious.

Then she spun toward the chair. Clutching the gray silk in her tiny fist, she flung his ruined shirt at his chest.

"What did you do?" she demanded to know, as if he owed her any kind of justification.

He made no move to catch the shirt. Rounding his gaze in a wide arch, he let it drop to the floor. "Do not worry your pretty little head."

"What did you do to Caleb?"

The question took him by surprise. Kjartan's eyes darted rapidly back and forth between both of hers as he tried to decipher her meaning. Then it clicked. The burns on his face.

"He crossed a line, and I reprimanded him for his behavior."

Eve cocked an eyebrow. "That's all?"

"That is all," he sneered in exasperation, his patience running as thin as his energy.

"So you consider burning him an acceptable punishment?"

Her challenging tone triggered a nerve. His shoulders flexed. He seized the back of her hair in a fist and pulled her head back a few extra inches.

"Watch your tongue. You are walking on thin ice," he warned. "You do not get a pass just because you spread your legs for me." He had already gotten what he wanted. He no longer needed to hide behind a mask. She would see his true face. Undisguised.

Her throat jerked, but she didn't back down. She held his eye contact without a flitter of her lashes. "You get off on the torture because you have always felt powerless, and now you can finally turn the tables. You want to be worshiped, is that it? Is that what all this is about?"

He had been angry with the boy, yes, but he did not enjoy inflicting pain. It was a means to an end. "You think I am the monster? Do you know how many people your beloved Kjan has killed? Humans, just like you?"

Then he saw it. That flicker in her glare he was aiming for, and the little quiver of her lips.

"I never asked," she admitted, the sharp edge in her tone wavering.

"Why not? Because you did not want to know? Or because you could not handle knowing the number?"

Kjartan let the question drift, watching it weigh on her conscience.

"He did not simply kill. He tortured. For fun. Kjan loved what he was. What *I* made him," he gnashed, tightening his grip. "I gave him immortality. I gave him a gift. And he enjoyed it. I know he did. He kept that little detail from you because he feared you would never look at him the same way if you knew the truth."

He felt the heat behind his eyes as he defended his actions to her. "Let me be eminently clear. I do not '*get off*' on torture. I simply gave Caleb a lecture that he would remember even after his skin healed. I do not expect you to approve of my methods."

Eve flaunted a pout. "You don't?" she huffed sarcastically. "I could have sworn that's exactly why you wanted me here. Or was that a lie? I'm not going to just stand by and watch this."

Kjartan's jaw punched down, muscles taut as his nostrils flared. He swallowed his reply. She had hit the nail on the head and thrown his own words back in his face.

He ground his teeth and let go of her hair. He was too close to the edge already. He tried really hard not to lose his temper completely.

Clenching his fists down by his sides, he remembered the cracked tile in his shower. Eve had no idea of the danger she was in.

He walked past her and made a beeline for the study, where he shut himself in to calm down. But it was not meditation he sought. He was a God, not a monk. He needed aggressive medication to subdue his violent impulses.

CHAPTER

39

E ve held her breath until she heard the door slam and then exhaled in relief. She might have appeared tough on the outside, but underneath, she'd been scared to death.

Fire had ignited behind his eyes, making them burn with a bright red glow she was very familiar with but no longer feared. Better than black. And that wasn't a conclusion she'd ever expected to draw.

Kjartan had been to her condo. He'd been inside her *home*.

Eve pictured him waltzing through her private space like he owned it. He was obsessed with Kjan. Fixated on taking his place. What had he been looking for?

And did he find it?

She'd searched the penthouse herself multiple times, but then they weren't looking for the same thing, were they?

Eve began pacing the front room, giving them both space. He was so goddamn full of himself it made her want to strangle him. She couldn't stay here if they continued budding heads every time. She'd need to feed again in a day or two.

But if her body still reacted to Kjan's, then maybe his did too, and she'd be able to calm him down. Not that she was planning on touching him.

Eve took a deep breath, gathering her courage, and hoped he wouldn't bite her head off. Then again, she didn't know anything about him. He was a God. Maybe biting heads off was his thing?

He'd hurt someone while he was out today. Or worse. Killed. Were there sponsors for murder or just alcoholism and drug abuse? What else was the point of keeping her as his live-in 'counselor'?

Either way, she'd have to take the risk and approach him. She wasn't going to give him the upper hand to seek her out whenever he had the need for *entertainment*. She was neither his pet nor his toy, to be cast aside as soon as she didn't meet his expectations anymore.

She opened the door slowly without bothering to knock since she didn't want to give him the chance to turn her away. But she still hesitated before crossing the threshold, wishing she had a white flag to wave in front of her. She did come in peace, after all.

He lounged in the armchair in the darkest corner across the room, slouched low, and for a moment, Eve was propelled back into Bobby's frat house. The guys at her ex's had usually been high or drunk. Or both.

Her eyes fell on the bottle of Four Roses on the table beside him first; no glass this time. A lit cigar rested on the ashtray next to it. Immediately reminded of the rank stench of cigarettes, Eve wrinkled her nose before the smoke even reached her.

"I want my keys back."

"No," he grumbled like a defiant child. Unmoving.

"Are you planning on going back?"

"Perhaps." Kjartan straightened somewhat, squaring his ankle over his knee, and the slight movement made the smoke waft her way.

It wasn't like cigarettes at all. The aroma was surprisingly pleasant, deep, and complex. Most profound were the peppery spices, but she could pick out rich earthy notes of espresso, dark cocoa, and leather. It fused into a sinful combination of his own scent, finishing with a lush trace of cherry.

Something carnal ignited in her lower belly.

As he raised his chin in her direction, Eve noticed the toothpick in his mouth.

"You really are bizarre," she noted.

"How so?"

His curious expression was encouraging. She leaned against the built-in bookshelves, crossing her arms and keeping a respectable distance. "First of all, I didn't expect you to enjoy sitting alone in the dark. What's that about?"

He cocked his head, and a soft chuckle found its way to her ears.

Good. He seems a lot more relaxed and personable. Almost human.

"Second," she continued, "for someone who's been stuck inside a cave for eons, you lack patience."

As he licked his lips, his tongue made a quick appearance under the skinny piece of wood. She tried to read his eyes, but it was too dark.

"And third?" he asked.

"Third, you like being in charge... control things. Well, that one really wasn't a surprise. You don't want people to question your decisions, but you drag me here against my will and think I'm going to *play house with you*. Did you really expect me to blindly comply like one of your minions?"

He smirked, keeping the pick firmly between his teeth, flicking it with his tongue. Eve couldn't tell if he was still amused or getting pissed at her accusations. Which were all true, by the way. "And fourth—"

"There is a fourth?" His brows jumped up.

"Oh, I can go all night—" *Wait, that didn't come out right.*

"Is that so?" He narrowed his eyes, his tone dryly amused. His long fingers toyed with the toothpick, his gaze darting over her body as if he were envisioning her 'going all night'. "Prove it," he goaded, pointing the little stick at her before returning it back to his mouth.

Her cheeks burned. There was something about the way his hands drew her attention to his lips. "You have a temper," she blurted, distracting from her blush. "When people do question you, you act out. Like a child throwing a fit."

"You are quite blunt." He dramatically snapped the toothpick in half with his thumb and index finger, suggesting he could do the same with her neck.

Eve shrugged, not feeling offended.

Kjartan discarded the piece of wood in the ashtray, then dropped his foot to the ground and rose out of his seat. Her pulse picked up when he made his way to where she stood, the books suddenly poking into her back like some form of Iron Maiden torture device.

His left hand reached for her face, but instead of touching her cheek, he twirled a lock of her hair around his finger. Eve thought back about him handling the toothpick. That had been with his left hand as well. Was Kjartan left-hand dominant?

The punch he'd landed on the guy at the bar had been a right-handed one because he was using Kjan's fighting skills, but there had been other times when he'd acted left-handed on instinct instead of right.

Icy-blue stare fixed on her, Kjartan pursed his lips. "Why can I not remember you? You should be all over his memories, yet there is nothing."

He watched her curiously, his eyes darting back and forth between hers. "There is something there. A link. I can feel it."

"It's not between *us*," Eve emphasized. The needle of her compass was attracted to the magnetic pull of his body, not his soul.

"No, but there *is* something. You know what it is. Tell me."

Nope, he had no clue about the profound bond of their DNA, and she wasn't going to tell him. It was the only defense she had against him. If he realized that and rejected it, she was doomed.

"Tell me what you want with Kjan's laptop," she prompted.

His hand dropped abruptly, and he took a step back, anger flashing in his eyes again like a bolt of lightning. "I need to remember. I cannot find myself until I unlock his mind. All of it. You cannot possibly imagine how frustrating it is to feel like you are losing your own identity."

His temper flared as he raised his voice, glaring at her. "I have to know what he knows. Why did he sire you? Why did he choose you? Was it really fate, or was it something else?"

"Are you suggesting he subconsciously attacked me because I look like his wife?"

"*Attacked?*" he repeated, appalled.

Whoops. She probably shouldn't have divulged that. Talking to the moody prick was a balancing act, like walking a tightrope. "He didn't mean to. He slipped up."

His expression promptly softened. No more sneer. No more anger. "He attacked you, and you still went with him?"

He made it sound a lot crazier than it was. "I trusted him. Well, not at first. It took a while. But I wasn't afraid of him. I'd known him for a long time." She perfectly recalled her attempt to make a run out of Kjan's studio in broad daylight.

"How long?"

"Eleven years," she stressed. And then her actions didn't sound so crazy anymore.

The reply surprised him. The muscles in his jaw ticked as he mulled it over. He knew he didn't have the patience for that.

"How long do you expect me to stay here?" She needed a finish line. A goal to keep her focus on.

"Do you believe it will take me equally as long to sway you?"

Eve couldn't pin down his personality. It was all over the place. He could go from the threat level of a ticking time bomb to a sensual stare with the flick of a switch. Is that what he meant by losing himself? Or was there something more juvenile about this identity crisis? She'd seen this behavior in college kids all the time. They didn't know where they fit in or what they wanted in life. She included. Even though technically adults, they were still trying to find themselves. Kjartan was somewhere around 1700 years old, but what did that really mean for a God?

He reached out and touched her again, left hand, letting his fingertips drift along her jaw and then travel down to the flickering pulse at the side of her throat. "You value your freedom. Your independence. I respect that. Maybe you and I are not that different."

"I highly doubt that," she snorted. Her shoulder blades bumped into the books, reminding her she had no way of backing up further.

Kjartan tipped his chin at a condescending angle. "How is it that out of all the places in this world, you walked into the one where I was? *You* found *me*, remember? We obviously have something in common."

Gaze dipped, a sneer tugging at the corner of his mouth, he waited for an answer.

Her sight caught on the tiny copper headphone buds that nestled in his ears. There was no more sound coming from them, and the color made them nearly invisible. Had he been listening to music?

Damn. Eve tried not to let her discomfort show. Kjan was a recluse who shunned large gatherings and preferred books.

"So we both like crowds and loud music. Big deal. That was a total coincidence. It was my first time in Iceland, and I had to check out the infamous nightlife."

"He never took you?"

Eve shook her head, avoiding his eyes. Kjan had been running from his past for too long. Always been so overprotective when it came to her. He wouldn't even let her borrow his Charger. Definitely wouldn't have taken her on a motorcycle.

She had to admit that it was totally hot. Kjartan was a rebel, reckless, and impulsive…

Crap. He was right. They were a lot alike.

He took her hand and teased his thumb across her palm. "You are like a song stuck in my head, Eve. The lyrics, so familiar, repeating over and over, and yet I cannot recall the title."

Her eyes flitted down to his lips when he spoke, and then quickly back up. *That cocky smile of his… and that stare…*

He knew he had her. They both did.

His blue gaze remained level, and she recognized the desire raging through the lightning as he drew her wrist to his mouth, his warm lips caressing the sensitive skin on the inside. His tongue licked along her tattoo like a shark who'd tasted blood and couldn't get enough.

With his other arm pressed possessively to the small of her back, she melted in his embrace. He ventured higher toward the crook of her elbow and then linked it around his neck. Eve closed her eyes, attaining only a clipped breath before his mouth was on her, nudging her lips apart with gentle demand, his tongue seeking out hers.

She couldn't fight him. Didn't want to.

Tasting the Bourbon in his kiss, sadness exploded in her chest. But she swallowed it back down. She couldn't let it continue to consume her. Drown her. When his hands slipped under her shirt, his touch was everything she ached for. There was only him, and she was in desperate need of his lifeline.

Her mind went blank. Maybe it was the fumes from the cigar. Eve focused on the warmth of his hands while they moved up her back and around her sides. Her pulse sped up in anticipation.

He pushed under her bra, and she gasped as his touch aimed for the hardened tips, the suede pads of his thumbs teasing right where she wanted him. Tendrils of desire unfurled deep in her core, spreading through all the little cracks that had formed by the longing to make her whole again.

He rolled both nipples simultaneously in a sensual rhythm with the motion of his tongue, which had her moaning against his mouth. It came out like a plea. And it was. Her body undulated, begging to feel more of him.

His lips parted from hers on the soft sound of their inhale, and he started to sink in front of her, kissing a heated path down between her breasts. Eve's arms lifted. Her fingers grasped at strands of her own hair in need to clench around something.

With greedy moans, he breathed her in. His mouth and his hands worshiped her body, roaming her curves… the hills… the valleys…

His knees hit the ground. His tongue brushed across her stomach where he'd pushed up her shirt, and her skin caught fire. Panting, she arched against the bookshelf, willing her legs to keep her upright.

He went lower. His lips pressed to the most sensitive stretch of her belly as his thumbs hooked over the waistband of her jeans. Her breath caught. He flicked the button, releasing the zipper gradually while the slick tip of his tongue chartered the path of lace he freed in maddening little circles.

He lingered at the dead end, fingers tracing the top edge of her jeans. His hands rounded her hips, squeezing her ass, and his deep, hungry groan hummed through her, throbbing fiercely between her thighs. Eve burned with need until no shred of thought remained in her.

Then a different kind of vibration went off. He ignored it at first, but when his phone continued to buzz, he growled in disapproval.

Sitting back on his heels, he pulled it out of his pocket and frowned. His face looked grave as the light of the screen illuminated it from below.

"Tala!" he barked into the phone. Eve didn't know the word, but from the tone and context, she assumed it was the command to talk.

A woman's voice erupted from the little pieces in his ears, her tone agitated. She spoke Icelandic, as far as Eve could tell, but it was too fast and too muffled for her to track a single clue.

Kjartan seemed disturbed by the news. He rose to his feet, eyes darting frantically, processing information.

The conversation did a rapid back-and-forth while he inquired about the who-when-where-details, then he hung up and switched to English. "I have to go," he uttered, already in motion.

Without looking back at Eve, he stormed out.

The Bourbon still lingering on her lips, her eyes followed him out the door of the study. Left alone in the dark, the high from her quick fix faded, and the inescapable feeling of regret kicked in.

God, he tasted exactly like him. Kjan had pledged his body, mind, and soul to her. He had no right to give that away.

Resentment and anger threatened to swallow her up. Sadness returned like a bomb, bursting out of her, and this time she didn't battle its force.

Eve slid to the ground. Dizzy and hungry she let her tears fall.

CHAPTER

40

H er eyes flew open at the sound of voices arguing. She didn't know how long she'd been out, but the sun wasn't up yet.

Eve got off the floor and straightened out her clothes before leaving the study. Pacing the front room, Kjartan was talking to someone on his phone. Askja and Kristján were the ones arguing in the kitchen. Nobody was speaking English, and she couldn't make heads or tails of the conversation.

When Kjartan hung up and joined the other two, she followed him on instinct. She noticed that he spoke in a different dialect than Askja and Kristján. He turned the muted *g* in *ég*— the pronoun *I*, which was pronounced something like *yeagh*— into a harsh *eck* sound. He threw that around a lot. And his soft th-sound at the end of words was a sharp *t* instead. It reminded her a little of the German she'd overheard on Kjan's call.

Eve focused, trying to catch the smallest details in his speech. "Nei. Ek hóndla þat sjálfr." *No. I handle it...* "Ekki til umræðu." *Not to... discuss!* Maybe? "Ek fer til þeirra." *I go to them.*

"Go where?"

Eve didn't mean to interrupt, but all three of them suddenly looked at her, and she realized that she'd absently asked the question out loud.

"Home," Kjartan answered, sparing her a quick glance, then turned back to Askja, who seemed to avidly object to his decision.

"NOG!" he roared through the kitchen like a fire-breathing dragon.

His outburst shook the floorboards beneath their feet. Askja shrank back. She was probably half a foot taller than Eve, and yet she suddenly looked like a terrified child.

"Ek fer," he went on in a sharp tone. "Þit tvo dveljit. Ek þarf fjora daga. Í mesta lagi." *...four days...*

"Did Kría say who was following them?" Kristján asked, kindly switching back to English, obviously for Eve, but it also seemed to dampen Kjartan's temper.

"They never saw a face. It does not matter. If they have been exposed and someone is really hunting them, they are no longer safe. I am not going to risk their lives."

Eve was putting the pieces together now. There were more of them still back in Iceland. "Why did you leave them behind in the first place?"

Kjartan stared at her as if he couldn't believe she was questioning his authority after he'd just knocked Askja down a peg. Fists balled by his sides, his eyes darkened with a purple tinge.

"They cannot tolerate sunlight," his voice grated out. "The flight would have been too dangerous."

"And whose fault is that really? If you had let them take your vein, they wouldn't still be vulnerable to the sun." She refused to endorse this selfish power trip he was on. She wasn't a suck-up.

Shoulders squared, he turned his full attention on her with a glare that drilled through the back of her skull. "I do not need to justify my decisions to you."

Eve wasn't just accusing him of being a bad leader. She was deflecting her own anger at him, and then the words she had been wanting to scream for months finally broke past her lips. "*You* sired them! *You* are supposed to protect them!" she blurted before she could stop herself.

Big mistake. She regretted it as soon as the words slipped out, but it was too late. Her words struck his pride, and the flames in his eyes ignited like laser beams.

Pure fear had her scrambling backward when he charged for her with strides she couldn't match. She backed into a countertop. Her slippery hands fumbled with the edge on her turn into the living room, and Kjartan caught her. Seizing hold of her hair, he yanked her back hard, preventing her from getting much further.

The trauma to her spinal cord from the sharp pull left her disoriented. Her field of vision spun. Before it could refocus on the room, her hips slammed into solid contact again. Her palms shot out to brace for the impact but were pinned beneath her rib cage when he repositioned his heavy hand like a vise at her neck and bent her over the kitchen island.

Cheek pressed into the cold slab, her warm breath appeared in fast, short huffs against the matte black. Her heart battled the unforgiving surface with each desperate beat. Between the concrete and him, there was no freedom to be had. He crushed her vertebrae in his grip. Eve felt paralyzed as he leaned down to her ear.

"Disrespect me one more time, and I will make you tremble in my grasp," he threatened in a low rumble, gripping the back of her neck tighter still. "Do you understand?"

It was the first time that she felt his full power thrumming through his voice. She nodded, too terrified to make a sound. From her peripheral vision, she could see the crimson flash of his eyes, and the air crackled around him, ready to lash out at her.

"You will learn your place like the rest of them," he promised, then turned his glare on Askja and Kristján. "Sjait um hana."

His weight lifted off her body, liberating her lungs, and he released her neck, but she didn't dare take a deep breath with him so close.

"Four days!" he repeated while storming out.

Eve drew an unsteady stream of air through her nose the moment he was out of sight. Her muscles ached from the tension they'd been under.

Askja and Kristján slipped out the backdoor of the kitchen to give her a chance to pick up what was left of her pride after the humiliation. Confronting him in private was one thing, but had she really just antagonized an ancient immortal being in front of his disciples?

He'd warned her that he wasn't playing favorites with her. If she got on his bad side again, she would not end up with a harsh sunburn. No. His imagination would likely cook up something special just for her.

Eve couldn't let his looks fool her. There was nothing left of the man she loved. He was the monster she needed to run from the first chance she got. She had to find a way out of here.

∫

Her accusation ripped a gaping hole into his chest. Eve's bitterness was warranted. As her Sire, he *was* supposed to protect her, but Kjan had been powerless to stop his own damn hand from closing around her neck. No matter how much he screamed, no matter how much he writhed beneath his skin, the chains around him only tightened. He remained nothing more than an observer. He had heard everything. Felt everything. And she had no idea.

"I will crush her spirit yet... I will break her defiance... I will beat it out of her while you watch!"

With a tilt of his wrist, the immortal gave more fuel to the twin-engine, weaving in and out of traffic at nearly max speed. Rage was still pumping in his veins. Better he took it out on the bike.

"She believes you would make a better leader than me. That you would not leave behind the ones who count on you. Do you concur with her high opinion of you?"

"*No.*"

He had failed her. He had broken her trust and left her vulnerable to *him*, serving her up to the God like a lamb to the slaughter. All he could see were the bastard's hands on her— *HIS* hands... but not *himself* touching her...

He had been relieved when his Sire returned to Iceland after the merge. Of course, Kjan never anticipated Eve going on the fucking trip of her life.

He had sensed her first. The second she stepped foot through the door, despite the sensory overload, her presence had woken him up. Kjan had drawn attention right to her before his Sire caught her scent.

Now, every time he fought back, he opened his mind up a little more. The parasite could use his body any way he seemed fit, but Kjan refused to give up his most cherished memories. He wouldn't share them with the leech. What he had with Thórunn and Eve belonged to him alone!

He wanted to scream again. Staying quiet took everything out of him. Kjan felt exhausted. How much longer could he really keep this up?

Eve was still holding on to the bond. She didn't hate him enough for betraying her. He needed her to break her vow.

She had to reject him.

And kill him.

CHAPTER

41

E ve stared out the window across the woods, watching the sun set. The uneven tree line suggested there were various cliffs and sharp drop-offs along the hillside. The straight drop down in front of her was also over twenty feet, easily. And there was no way to climb down. The smooth brick provided no ledge for even a small toe.

Like a princess locked in a tower, she was royally fucked. She wished she'd slept on the ground floor instead.

As if she'd actually done any sleeping. She felt exhausted and longed for a cold shower to clear her head. She needed to come up with a plan. It scared her how easily Caleb had overpowered her. She was no match for his strength, even after everything Kjan had taught her. And then there was the giant.

Maybe she'd have better luck taking down one of the females, as long as they didn't outnumber her.

From the hallway, she overheard Askja and Kristján, her designated babysitters for the night, in the front room. Eve didn't like to lurk, so she figured she might as well make her presence known as she came down the stairs.

"Who was Kjartan talking about? Who is he going to see?" She was sure she had gotten her translation right. He'd used the word *þeirra—them*.

They both got quiet and simply looked at her as she joined them on the couch. Then Kristján cleared his throat and finally spoke. "Kría, Dynja, and Erik stayed behind in Reykjavík. Temporarily. He wanted to make Portland his home. Caleb and the others are from here, so I guess that made sense."

It did. But how had he chosen them? And where did the two of them fit in? "Why had he gone back to Iceland?"

"I think he needed closure of sorts now that his body could tolerate sunlight," Askja answered.

Staring off at the empty space in front of her, she dropped her chin into her hands, elbows propped on her knees. "I'm sorry. I should not have blamed you," she said to Kristján. "They are your friends, and I know you care about them. But he was right, you know? There was no point in you going. Kjartan is the only one who can protect them."

"Who is hunting them? Why would they be in danger?" It was 2021. Were vampires still hunted?

"Humans," Askja bit out dismissively. "And it's not like they hurt anyone. They only feed on the willing—"

"Wait, what? They feed on people?"

Askja avoided Eve's eyes, and that was all the answer she needed, but Kristján apparently felt no shame in the matter.

"There is nothing wrong with that. It is what we are. It is how we live. We never take by force, and we most certainly do not kill."

"Well, how honorable of you!" Eve commended him sarcastically.

His tone remained stern, without anger. "I'm not going to apologize for it. You have your way, and we have ours."

Great. Now Eve was the one feeling bad. Though Kristján was clearly on Kjartan's side, she'd perceived him as a mediator and not a threat. "I'm sorry. I have no right to judge you, and I shouldn't be so condescending."

He accepted her apology with a simple nod, and Eve hoped they could all just forget about this whole damn day. She rubbed her hands on her thighs, then tried to change the subject. "I was wondering if I could get access to the Wi-Fi on my laptop. Kjartan took my phone, but I haven't checked in with my job in days, and I need to log into my college classes too."

"Sure. I will hook you up," Askja offered, hopping off the couch. She had an accent too, but it wasn't as pronounced as Kristján's or the redhead's. "I don't think he would mind. And Caleb has already hacked into it."

"Caleb did what?"

She ignored the irked expression on Eve's face and led the way back to her room.

"Why do you stay with him?" she asked Askja, her voice more timid than she wanted it to be. She meant no offense to the woman, but the question had been burning in her mind for quite a while now. Kjartan seemed more like a dictator than a leader.

Askja turned over her shoulder with a slightly bewildered look on her face as she bent over the laptop on the desk. "Is it not obvious? We are a family." She straightened but shifted her weight uncomfortably on her feet. "None of us ever felt that before. We were alone. Some of the others were orphans, living on the streets before Kjartan found us. He promised us a better life. A home. Kinship. I think he identified with them most as someone who had always felt unwanted himself. Like he did not belong anywhere, you know? We were all outcasts. Misfits. He brought us together."

"I'm sorry. I never thought of that." Street kids, she could understand. They would probably jump at the opportunities he offered, but Askja and Kristján were much older than Caleb. Eve had never considered that they could've been outsiders. And who would willingly leave their family behind for a life like this?

"Sometimes, I get the feeling he still believes that he is alone. That no one really understands what he's been through."

Askja's tone carried a heaviness that showed how deeply she cared. Eve's suspicion had been right. There was more between her and Kjartan than he'd let on.

She tucked her hair behind her ear. "You seem close with him. How did he find you?" she asked casually, trying not to make her nosiness too obvious.

Askja's smile came back. "I found *him*, actually. In Iceland. Totally by chance and in the middle of nowhere. Like it was meant to be. We have been traveling together for almost fourteen years, passing as siblings and then mother and son."

"Mother and son?" Eve baffled. There really wasn't anything of a romantic nature between them?

"He was stuck in the body of a twelve-year-old. Well, his own body, but still stuck." She shrugged. "The curse, you know?"

"He mentioned that he was twelve when he was cursed. I didn't know he stayed that way." Eve raked her mind, going back to their conversation on the patio. How'd she missed that detail? Or had he purposely avoided clarifying it?

"I looked a bit older than I was, so it just made a good cover story. Then I fell in love with Nessa in Ireland two years ago, and the three of us have been our own little coven ever since. But he did not turn me until now." Askja gave her a pained expression and directed her eyes back to the laptop.

"He used Kjan's body to turn all of you," Eve murmured.

She assumed Kjartan had not wanted to put Askja through the same painful ritual he had put Kjan through. His coven was sired the same way she'd been. And Nessa? That was a woman's name. Was she the other female?

"Can I ask you a weird question?"

"Anything," Askja replied, keeping her gaze on the screen and clicking through the tabs.

"What does he smell like to you?"

"Smoke!" she chirped with a grin. "Not in a bad way, like burning tires or anything. It's more like charred wood. Oak, I think. Pine and cherrywood, too. It reminds me of a bonfire."

Oak suited Kjan. So did the softer cherry note. No chocolate, and whiskey, or ground coffee for Askja? "Has it always been that way?"

"I do not recall it from before he turned us. My human nose was not that acute." She gave another half-shrug.

So he hadn't lied. They were close, but not together.

"What does he smell like to you?"

Eve felt herself blush. "Different."

She realized with loathing that his scent was indeed specific to her, a personal trigger, just like she had feared.

"Well, there you go. You are all set. Let me know if you need anything else. Kristján and I will be here all night, and I will stay for the day as well."

"Thanks." Eve smiled at her as she left.

She couldn't stop picturing the twelve-year-old boy. Abandoned. Alone.

CHAPTER

42

E ve had fallen asleep after doing a lot of catching up. The classes weren't a problem, but she was lucky she hadn't gotten fired for being AWOL for days.

Askja had left around sunset to go home to her girlfriend, and Kristján had taken over the second night watch from there. Eve had spent the entire time downstairs with the Icelandic giant, who'd become less intimidating by the minute once she got past his fearsome exterior.

He hadn't talked much, but he loved classic American sitcoms. Among *The Fresh Prince, Home Improvement,* and *That '70s Show, Friends* was his favorite. Her uncle Joe had made her watch it too and used to quote the show on a daily basis, so Eve was more than familiar with it.

Kristján and she had binge-watched the entire night on old sitcoms, while he emitted the occasional deep, bellowing laugh at some lame joke. It reminded her of the quiet nights with Kjan, both of them working side by side.

When Eve woke on the third night, she heard loud voices and laughter coming from the ground floor. It wasn't the sound from the TV.

What the hell?

She sensed the presence of three vampires. Apparently, Askja and Kristján were not continuing with the one-on-one watch system.

Maybe she could use the cover of a crowd to her advantage. But if she wanted to find a way out of here, she'd first have to figure out what she was up against. And what better way to get to know your opponents' weaknesses than by fraternizing?

Eve blew out a breath as she stepped softly into the hallway and closed the door behind herself. She followed the voices into the kitchen, and found Caleb and Askja with the Irish woman.

"Eve, this is my girlfriend, Nessa," Askja introduced her.

The red in her hair was a lot brighter in the light of the kitchen, and her curls bounced around her head when she moved.

She greeted Eve with a broad smile. "Good to see ye again, lass."

"Yeah, I remember you," she replied wryly. She was still a little bitter about being manhandled by her. The woman had a surprisingly strong grip.

Nessa grinned sheepishly. "Sorry 'bout the rough first impression. I promise I make it up to ye."

Aaaaand there were the heavily accented *r*s Eve remembered. Her tone was firm, almost a little deep, yet perfectly charming in combination with her grin.

Caleb, on the other hand, acknowledged her with a frosty nod and tightly drawn lips. Hands in his pockets, he rocked back and forth on his heels. Eve still felt guilty about getting him into trouble.

"I thought it was time ye met the rest of the gang. I talked Askja into cutting ye some slack," Nessa said, nudging her girlfriend. "They're all itchin' to get out. I'm sure ye feel the same. Ye ready?" She cracked the back door of the kitchen. "Unless ye'd like to change first?"

Caleb didn't wait for her reply and immediately slipped out. Considering the opportunity to finally leave the house, Eve took only a split second to evaluate her blue jeans and simple red t-shirt.

"No, I'm good." She didn't want to go upstairs for her coat. She couldn't believe her luck.

The boy was already in the front passenger seat when they caught up with him in the driveway. Eve climbed into the back, and Nessa slid in beside her.

"Askja and I have a house in Goose Hollow. The others share a place downtown," she said. "But don't let the kip fool ye."

Whatever that meant. Eve's heart jumped at the idea of being so close to her own home. What was the chance of her actually making it there? She didn't have the keys, and the fridge was empty too.

Askja parked the car around the corner of an industrial-looking building and killed the engine. Eve was momentarily pulled back to the night at the warehouse with Jordan seven months ago. The horrific scene played out in front of her eyes with the flickering strobe lights, the cold concrete, the chains around her wrists, Jordan's blood pooling on the ground, Andromeda...

The only light at the end of that nightmare had been Kjan coming to her rescue in the tunnels. He had felt so guilty for leaving her.

The parallels between the events lit up like neon signs. He had left her again, and she was alone among strangers. There would be no light at the end of this tunnel. He would not come for her.

Eve's heart turned colder in the brisk air, and she focused her eyes on the building as they approached. They were in a crappy area downtown somewhere, that much she knew. Paint was peeling off the brick walls, and she counted three smashed-in windows.

They live here while the BIG MAN stays in his cozy mansion in the mountains? What a dick.

An old iron staircase spiraled up the side, but Askja and Nessa led the way to the large warehouse doors on the ground instead. Eve finally saw a chance to pull Caleb to the side.

"I'm sorry—"

"Don't be." He cut her off and kept walking in long strides. "I got what I deserved."

"No, you didn't. I attacked you," she argued, trying to match his pace.

"I've been through worse. Not everyone had it as easy as you. Let it go, Eve. I'm okay with it."

"You're *okay* with him torturing you?"

"He told me off, that's all. He had every right to. I should never have touched you."

"How could you possibly be okay with this?" Eve couldn't fathom how Kristján and he admired Kjartan so much. Was it the Sire-link that made them so obedient? Was it influencing their willpower?

She had accepted Kjan of her own free will. Had they all accepted Kjartan's authority over them too? Did not even one of them retain some form of opposition?

"He's chosen *us*!" Caleb stopped in his tracks and turned to her, no kindness in his golden eyes. "We were nothing before him! He could easily take that away. We are all replaceable, Eve. All but *you*," he stressed the distinction. "A God makes you an offer, you don't reject him. You don't ask questions. You take it. Gratefully," he added, stalking off.

Eve hesitated for a moment to let his words sink in, but she wasn't ready to let this go. Kjartan wasn't here now. Maybe, with him out of range, she could get through to them.

She took a chance and grabbed his arm to pull him back. "Take my blood."

Caleb shook her off. "Girl, have you lost your damn mind?"

"The effect is only temporary, but at least he can't burn you again."

"No. But he can still kill me," he hissed, getting right in her face. "And he would. Thanks for the offer, but I'd rather end up with a suntan than dead." He gave her a shove to catch up with the others.

Eve was the last one through the door. She forced herself to blink, and her eyes refocused on the interior.

First of all, *wow!* It was fully furnished, and not in a couch-grabbed-right-of-the-street kind of way. Everything looked new. And not cheap.

Second, the place was huge. Probably big enough to have one bedroom for each of them. Possibly multiple bathrooms, too.

There was no need for a kitchen, obviously. The décor was modern with function in mind. No unnecessary frills or knickknacks to collect dust, yet Eve assumed everyone had their own personal touch in their private space.

The main room was basic but clean. She saw a big-screen TV mounted on the wall and a massive stereo system.

Maybe they kept it rundown-looking on the outside to deter thugs from breaking in? Nobody would ever expect anything worth stealing inside.

"Why is she here?" A small girl with long black hair glowered her way.

Eve recognized her. She was the one who'd been with Caleb on New Year's. She looked about Eve's age, but her cold blue eyes didn't make her very sympathetic.

"Watch it, Emma," Askja scolded her. "If she matters to Kjartan, she matters to us."

She gave Eve a respectful nod that didn't make her any more comfortable. She noticed three more vampires in the openly spaced room now, too.

"Don't mind her." The other female approached her. She had a mixed African-American complexion and beautiful hazel-green eyes. "I'm Claire. That's Lucas and my twin brother Parker over there." She pointed to the two young men seated on the floor.

The resemblance to her brother was obvious, even if she hadn't pointed it out. He had the same perfect cheekbones as her, down to the little crooked smile he threw at Eve.

"What's her problem with me?"

"She's just protecting Caleb. Don't worry, she'll get over it." Claire shrugged. Her smile was non-judgmental.

"She knows what happened?"

"Everybody knows," she explained with indifference. "There are no secrets between us."

Eve swallowed hard as she looked around the group. She'd have to remember that.

The young man she identified as Lucas had a faded buzz cut and rubbed the side of his head like a dog with an itch.

Parker jerked his chin in his friend's direction. "Hey man, you good?"

He shot his friend a hostile glare in response, then jumped to his feet. "I'm starving. Can we go now?"

His tone was annoyed, and his abrasive attitude gave Eve the impression that he didn't like being told what to do. His eyes appeared black, and his face was grim as he addressed Askja.

"Two groups," she directed them. "We meet back at Mount Hood at 3 a.m."

The second the female in charge let him off his leash, he barged across the room. The rest of the peculiar bunch didn't linger far behind. Eve brought up the rear, watching him with caution while retracing her steps. She felt an instant aversion toward him. His aura screamed danger.

Why would Kjartan choose someone like him?

She met up with Caleb at the door. He held it open, motioning for her to go ahead of him. It was for safety reasons, not chivalry. He knew she was a flight risk.

When she squeezed past him, she saw Lucas already halfway through the parking lot. His head snapped around, eyes caught on something across the street. Eve thought she saw a figure vanish in the shadows of the alley next to the strip club.

"I need to take care of something. I'll catch up with you guys," he said, his gaze still focused with intense concentration on the corner.

Without waiting for clearance from Askja, he made a sharp turn and beat feet in the direction of the dodgy alley.

Eyebrows drawn in a high arch, Nessa gave her girlfriend a look that communicated a clear telepathic exchange between the two. Eve had to agree. Lucas' action seemed offensively bold.

Will he be punished for disobeying orders?

Nessa slung her arms around Askja in a comforting hug, and the taller female tapped her forehead to her girlfriend's, completing the affectionate gesture. Eve overheard the words "lost cause" and "cannot save them all" muttered quietly.

Askja sighed, and her shoulders dropped. When she lifted her face, her subtle smile resurged, facing the group.

"See you at the cabin," she said, and then both of them pivoted toward the street, still locked in an embrace.

Claire rushed to join them. Eve instinctively took a step forward, but an arm shot across her chest like an I-beam, stopping her dead.

Caleb turned to face her, the sunburst in his irises suddenly sparkling with sadistic glee. "You're on my watch tonight," he growled at her.

Rotating his body, he led the way in the opposite direction of Nessa's auburn bobblehead. Emma and Parker followed suit, and so did Eve, her heart thumping uneasily.

It's gonna be a long night, she thought as she wondered where exactly they were headed. But at least she wasn't grouped with Lucas.

ᚼ

Lucas' fine-tuned threat antenna tingled like a *Spider-Sense*. He was drawn to the green flash of light that was not part of the sign out front. He figured it must've come from inside the club when someone opened the back door to the alley, but for a second, it had looked exactly like the flash that had compelled him to check out that damn warehouse at the port. He was beginning to think someone was fucking with him.

The sound of motion above made him look up. He still saw the tail end of a black coat disappear from the edge of the roof.

Without thinking, Lucas charged the wall in front of him. He kicked off the ground, planting his boot flat against the brick, before he straightened his leg and pushed his body higher to reach the lip of the wall.

He pulled himself up to the ledge and immediately turned around, leaping toward the fire escape ladder across the alley. His fingers curled around the rungs, feet following like second nature, and he pushed on, rapidly ascending to the top of the roof.

As he jumped to the next building and the one after that with the agility of a cat, his boots crunched on the gravel on each landing. His natural awareness of danger kept him on edge. He couldn't establish if he was doing the hunting or *being* hunted. There was someone else on the roof with him; he could feel the powerful presence.

His eyes pierced the darkness, canvassing the perimeter. He got nothing other than the usual scattering of rats.

What am I not seeing?

He couldn't shake the feeling. Lucas scouted the rest of the surrounding buildings without success, then circled back. From the street level, he watched the regular crowd of people. He recognized the individual groups: the pimps with their hookers, the dealers and their customers, and then there were the dancers just starting their shift at the club. One face, in particular, drew his attention, and his hand twitched. He rubbed his palm across the side of his head. He couldn't shake the phantom pain.

"Fucking asshole," he muttered to himself. *HE doesn't care about anyone. Doesn't even know what it's like.*

Or was it just the ones here he couldn't care less about? He'd left them all vulnerable in a heartbeat to go rushing back 'home'. *This* was their home, dammit. *Portland.*

And what he did to Caleb for touching his precious little toy...

He wanted to make the immortal bastard pay. Or at least make him hurt.

Lucas drew back from his vantage point, turning south toward Everett Street. He needed to see someone else tonight before catching up with his half of the group. They didn't need to know about it. This was *his* business; no one else's.

Passing the tattoo shop, he kept thinking about the presence on the roof. It had been as potent as Kjartan's. Maybe more—

A crunch behind him made him whip around, then he gasped in relief. "It's you!"

∫

⟨HAPTER

43

Kría's shoulders were drawn forward, her hair falling loosely around her face as she hugged herself.

Kjartan had them gathered in the living room of the cottage outside the city within less than an hour of landing. He was lucky there had been a charter jet available at short notice.

His gaze caught briefly on Kría's delicate hands. It was hard not to think of Eve in that moment.

"It happened in the middle of the day," she recounted, her soft brow creasing. "We were staying at my old place in the city center after feeding. Someone must have followed us. There was a rap at the door, so loud it woke me."

Kjartan recalled every word of her frantic phone call but needed to hear the details again in person.

"Then more banging on the windows. The curtains were drawn, I didn't dare open them, but I knew it wasn't just one man. There were others. I heard voices shouting, they had the house surrounded."

Her voice shook. The fear in her tone was genuine, even two days after the incident.

Erik draped one arm over her, pulling her into his chest. Being just slightly below six feet, he was not as tall as Kristján, who would have towered over her by almost a foot.

Kjartan felt their turmoil. Saw it in their tense postures, too.

"Then something came crashing through the glass. Smoke grenades!" she cried. "All windows at once. We dodged the light, but we couldn't get out. Not while the sun was still up; it was hours until sunset. We were trapped—" Her words faltered, and she stifled a sob by dropping her face into her hands.

The lump in Kjartan's throat swelled with guilt. He should not have left them unguarded.

"I don't know what sort of smoke it was," Erik added, taking over for Kría. "She was the first to faint. I managed to drag her and Dynja down into the basement before I passed out myself." He bowed his head, and his heavy features twisted with shame, though there was no need for it. He protected the females as best as he could.

At only twenty-eight, Erik was the youngest of the three, but more reliable than Dynja, who occasionally acted ten years younger than she was. He had left Kría in charge as the oldest. Being 34 when he turned her, she was just two years shy of Kristján's and Askja's age.

Dynja shifted in her lean against the wall, drawing his attention. She was wearing a black leather mini and a shear blouse over a pink lace bra. Naturally, she was dressed for a night out, unlike the other two in their casual street clothes.

"When we came to, it was dark," she said with a shrug. But her composure was far from indifferent. She was rattled too, and disappointed with herself, as he could tell. She was a tall female, built to put up a good fight if not unconscious. "Everything upstairs was smashed, not a single pane left in the frames, the door off its hinges... It was terrible." She shook her head, her fingers working the ends of her long, blonde braid.

Kjartan met her pale green stare. On closer observation, he noticed that her makeup was smudged, meaning she had not applied it recently. And if he had to guess, the outfit was the same one she had worn the night of the attack.

A fresh wave of anger rolled over him. *Hunter's? Here?* Kjartan had not encountered any since gaining his freedom. He had been unprepared for their attack. They could have set fire to the house while the three of them were trapped in the basement.

He swallowed, then reined in his emotions. "I am sorry for the loss of your home, Kría. I will replace everything you and Kristján lost," he promised. It was a trivial gesture, but it was all he had to offer as consolation. "Tell me where you went that night. I will start looking there while you hide out here."

Kjartan waited until daylight, then took Kría's car. Parking it in the general vicinity, he made his way down the city center on foot—not a yellow-brick road but a rainbow-colored one, which ended in the square of Hallgrímskirkja.

The church's distinctive design rose above the buildings ahead. The architectural marvel had become an inspiration for movies, and he fought a smile at the irony in that. If the church were a representation of Ásgarðr, then he was now crossing

Bifrost, the rainbow bridge that linked the world of mortals to the realm of the Gods. His father's world.

Will I ever be welcomed? Kjartan wondered, glaring at the church. It was his home by blood, even if he was born on Miðgarðr.

As he ambled down the street, the sky met him with a flawless blue canvas that once again threatened to distract him from his task.

He needed to get back—

There! He almost missed it; that was how fast it flicked past him. But he *had* caught the subtle *ping* of a presence that was not of human origin. Someone else was out here.

Kjartan set off in pursuit, his stride switching into a more determined pace without appearing hurried. The street was filled with shoppers pouring out of stores on both sides, and he wanted to avoid drawing attention to himself.

Keeping a respectable distance, he weaved through the masses of tourists and locals to stay on the presence in front of him until he sensed it gaining speed.

His breath accelerated. It was pulling further ahead.

He picked up his pace. Either his target was trying to shake him or lure him away from the crowd to get him alone. He knew it could be a trap, yet he gave chase. He could not risk losing it. Not now that he had found it. That he had found *someone*... like himself.

Shoving through the throng of people, he pushed into the open square in front of the church.

His feet came to an abrupt stop. It was gone. The presence had simply vanished, as though someone had flicked it off—

No. His spine stiffened. It was behind him now.

His head whipped around, but then another *ping* registered to his right. His heckles rose. He was outnumbered... only he could not see anyone.

Kjartan's fingers twitched, and a faint crackling sound reached his ears. Adjusting his stance, he braced himself for an attack. Since his eyes failed to identify the source of the inhuman powers, he was forced to rely on his instincts.

His feelers locked onto the two entities, tracking their movements with the utmost vigilance while the mortals around them went ignorantly about their business. They had no idea what was lurking among them.

But then again, neither did he.

Kjartan's focus remained on the strange visitors. They circled him slowly before stopping on opposite sides of the square, trapping him in their midst.

Dread twisted his gut. The tension rose. Despite being unable to see anyone, a mix of emotions wafted his way. He felt anger, resentment, hate, and right when the rage flared so hot he expected a burst to come his way, everything went black.

A darkness so dense his eyes could not penetrate crashed down on him, cutting him off from his surroundings. A push against his chest forced him back a step. It was less the touch of a hand than it was a kind of shockwave. Something without substance.

Like magic.

Once the blackness lifted from his eyes, Kjartan found himself alone in the square. The strangers were gone.

No. One of them remained. But something powerful was blocking his feelers from getting a read. He sensed no more than a black void and a sense of cold.

Kjartan's breath stalled. He had felt this before. At the warehouse. There *had* been someone in the shadows.

Perhaps it had never been Cooper following him in the first place.

CHAPTER

44

She felt uneasy knowing they were technically out hunting. Hunger gnawed at her too. Eve wasn't sure that she actually wanted to know the details of how they fed. She kept reminding herself that Kristján had assured her they didn't force anyone. If they did this regularly, they probably had a pretty good grip on their self-control and wouldn't need much blood either. She admitted it was kind of kinky, and no doubt there were plenty of people with that kind of fetish. Eve herself had known one, but she quickly pushed the thought of Charlotte from her mind. As the past had proven, feeding like this was still dangerous.

The four of them cruised down the somewhat-busy road, Caleb throwing her an occasional wary glance. Her eyes kept shifting all over the place to find an escape. She wondered if he knew what she was thinking. He flanked her left, cutting off her path to the curb. Emma and Parker dawdled behind.

At the intersection, he nudged her toward the right. They came up to a club Eve had heard of but never actually gone to herself. It was one of those factory-style places with plenty of dark corners. It reminded her of the one she'd been to in Iceland.

"So, is this what you guys do for fun? Hang out and *drink*?" she asked her babysitter when they shoved through the crowd at the door. "I can't believe the bouncer fell for your fake ID. You look nowhere near twenty-two."

He scrunched his face in a snarky grimace. She wouldn't give him more than nineteen. "Like you're one to talk."

Though she'd technically turned twenty-one last Halloween, she'd never look much older than twenty. Maybe twenty-four if she tried harder.

"No," Parker replied, taking the conversation back to her question. "We do a lot of free running along the rooftops, actually."

Eve's jaw went slack. "No way. You do parkour? I wanna go."

Caleb snorted a laugh. "Like we'd take you."

"Why not? It sounds a lot more fun than this." And it would definitely increase her chances of escaping.

"Duh! You could get hurt. And I'd be dead meat," he added under his breath.

Emma shot Eve a glare over her shoulder as she marched ahead.

"Claire does it," Parker threw in, giving a subtle shrug with his shoulder. "She's pretty good. Not as good as Lucas; no one can catch up with him."

A shiver crawled up her spine at the mention of the guy's name, and she couldn't help but picture his abrasive exterior with those black eyes. *Urgh!*

"Thanks for having my back, bitch." Caleb groaned.

"I'm just sayin', if the woman wants to go, we should take her."

"Ya, the woman wants to go. So, thanks for having *my* back... um, not-bitch," Eve winked, pointing a finger gun at him.

The handsome smile she got in return probably made her night. Unless she actually made it out of here.

They finally managed to push their way through the herd to the bar. "You ever tempted to have a drink?" Eve asked, tipping her head toward the row of shot glasses on the counter in front of them. "Other than... you know?" She didn't want to say the word *blood* out loud in a cramped place like this.

Kjan had said that alcohol was a poison their system couldn't handle. Maybe if she got her security detail to pass out, she could make a break for it.

Caleb grimaced. "Nah. Just smelling tequila gives me heartburn."

Damn! There goes that idea.

But Eve couldn't blame him. She had a bad experience with that one too.

In her periphery, Parker shook his head, replying to something Emma had asked him. "He went on his own. Said he didn't want to get anyone else in trouble since it was his fault and all. Not sure what happened exactly. He's not talking about it."

Eve hadn't caught the question over the noise. Nor did she know who they were talking about. Leaning back against the bar, she pretended to scan the shimmying mass with indifference when she was really looking for an escape plan.

Are there any backdoors to this place?

Caleb kept a close eye on her, much to Emma's dislike, but she soon went on the prowl and left them with Parker at the bar.

"What about you? Not hungry?" Eve probed.

"Nice try, but you're not gonna shake me," Caleb replied, leaning back against the counter. "I already fed."

"Speak for yourself," Parker chimed in. "I have my eye on the cute blonde at the far end."

Naturally, Caleb's head snapped in that direction. "The guy or the chick?"

"Either," he winked. "Or both. The night's young."

Eve snickered under her breath, teasing Caleb for turning his head. "He made you look. So much for not letting me out of your sight."

She hopped smugly onto a barstool next to a guy with a black mohawk and accidentally knocked her elbow into him. "Sorry—"

"Eve?" He turned to her, his eyes wide, before pulling her in for a hug.

"Colby! Hi!" She craned her neck for blue hair. Was he out alone? "Where's Tanya?"

"Working. I'm here with a friend. Where have you been? We never found you at the party. We've been trying to reach you for weeks." He paused and narrowed his brows, giving Caleb and Parker a suspicious look over her shoulder. "Who are your friends?"

"Oh… ah… nobody. I mean, they're not… never mind." Eve shook her head awkwardly. "I'm so sorry. I really didn't mean to ghost you guys."

"So, what have you been up to?"

"Um…"

Before Eve could think of an answer, she felt Kristján's giant presence appear next to her. She bristled. He wrapped his arm around her shoulder and affectionately pulled her into his chest, keeping his eyes on Colby, who was six-foot-one himself, but even he had to crane his neck to get a good look at Kristján's face.

"Sup?" he greeted Eve's friend in his deep voice, and a flush rose to her cheeks.

"Yeah, I think I'm gonna go find my friend," Colby said, visibly uncomfortable. "See you around, Eve," he tacked on and then disappeared back into the crowd.

Kristján leaned down, mere inches from her face. "You tell him anything that jeopardizes us, and I will personally rip his throat out. Are we clear?"

"He's my friend—"

"And we are your blood," he growled back. "Your coven. We choose each other above anyone else."

Eve felt the ice in his voice down her back. His threat made it very clear why Kjartan had picked him as his right hand. He didn't seem like the same person she'd shared laughs with last night.

"Man, that was kind of a buzzkill." Caleb cut the tension. "Can we go somewhere else? Where is Parker?"

"I saw him take off with a couple when I came in. Let's give him a minute. Or two," Kristján snickered, which sounded as pleasant as a bear foraging for a snack.

Damn. Eve kept her eyes peeled for an opening to slip free, but neither he nor Caleb took theirs off her again.

A while later, Claire's brother returned to the bar with Emma in tow.

"There he is!" Caleb shouted, clapping him on the shoulder. "You look satisfied."

"I wouldn't mind a challenge next time. This is getting too easy." His eyes sparkled as he grinned, still licking his lips. They were a brighter shade of green than his sister's, but not quite like Kjan's. No doubt he slayed with the ladies. And guys, apparently. His voice also had that deep, seductive timber going for him.

"I'm ready to leave," Emma faked a yawn. "Let's go."

Nobody argued with the tiny girl as they made their way to the door.

When the fresh night air hit her lungs, Eve saw Parker clutching his chest. "What's wrong?"

"It's nothing." He waved her off.

"The truck is just a block down." Kristján nodded in the direction.

The whole way, she watched Parker meticulously. His breathing was just a little uneven, yet enough for her to notice. It was hard to tell in the dark, but she could have sworn that his skin was flushed too. If he got worse, he might just become the distraction she needed.

Eve swayed on her feet.

♩

"What the fuck is wrong with you, man?" Caleb eyed him with worry while bracing him up. By the time they made it to Kristján's Suburban, he was supporting most of Parker's weight. His heart rate continued dropping rapidly, and he collapsed against the truck.

342

"Can't… breathe," he wheezed. "The chick from the club… feel weird—"

Beads of sweat gathered on his brow. He looked like he was running a fever, but that was impossible.

Emma opened the door and helped pull him in. "What's going on?"

Caleb shook his head. "No idea, but we gotta go now or he's not gonna make it. Call Askja." He shut the door and climbed into the front.

Kristján turned to him from the driver's seat. "Uh, where is Eve?"

Panic seized him. Caleb's head snapped around.

"FUUUCK!"

His heart slipped into his stomach as he jumped out of the truck and started sprinting back down the alley. His lungs were immediately on fire. He wished like hell Lucas were here. The guy lived for this shit. Caleb fucking hated running. He did his best work sitting down.

He didn't slow as he passed by the club. It was the last place he'd laid eyes on her, but Eve was long gone now. A small crowd poured out of the bar further down the street, and he averted a collision with a clumsy swerve that had him nearly tripping over his own feet.

Caleb skidded to a halt at the fork, looking left, then right… then up.

Motherfuck. What are the odds?

He'd come to a halt right across from the shitty apartment building Lucas had pulled him out of ten years ago. He'd been just a kid himself, barely sixteen. When everyone else had evacuated to escape the fire, he'd traced the screams back to their source. Only his courage had not led him to a child trapped by flames.

Caleb would never forget Lucas' dark blue eyes staring back at him in horror through the wire of the cage in which his captor had locked him. No doubt, the sick bastard had hoped his dirty secret would perish in the fire.

Caleb's breath burned in his lungs just like it had that night. If he didn't find her, he was a dead man.

He bent over, bracing his palms on his thighs, forcing himself to calm down and think. Which direction could she have gone? She knew the city, but so did he. Maybe even better. He'd lived on these streets for years. She couldn't outrun him. And she couldn't hide. He'd find her. Had to.

Drawing the air back into his lungs, Caleb finally caught her flowery scent. It was still etched into his mind since he'd tracked her that first time to the med clinic, but it was fading fast.

He hung a right and picked up his pace, following her trail for a block. He stopped short when he saw her red shirt disappear into a building.

Why'd she stop running?

Did she believe he wouldn't find her in there? He was going to drag her out if he had to. Even if it meant getting burned again for touching her.

He sneaked up to the smashed window and climbed in the same way she'd done. He found her crouched behind the counter in the far back of the shop, digging through the shelves with her back turned. Her shirt did not make good camouflage; she stood out like a sore thumb. She should've kept running.

Without making a sound, his grip clamped around her upper arms, and he jerked her up toward him.

"Let go of me, Caleb." Eve yelped as she fought to get free.

"Did you really think I would just let you run off?" He gnashed his fangs in anger. "You know that my head is going to roll if I don't bring you back."

She abruptly quit struggling and went lax in his clutches. "I wasn't running," she explained. "I was looking for this." She held out a little glass vial and a syringe.

"Drugs? Really?" Caleb said, surprised. *Could her metabolism tolerate it?* Olivia, Lucas' friend, had overdosed despite the vampiric mutation in her system. Maybe Eve's blood really was stronger than theirs.

"Guess you're not that pure after all. Kjartan will be *soooo* disappointed. Whatever. Move it." He shoved her out of the large window they'd climbed through and kept his grasp on her elbow just in case she decided to make another break for it.

"Please hear me out. It's not what you think."

"Thinking is above my paygrade, sweetheart. I don't care about your addiction," he shot back, dragging her along behind him.

He had no experience with that shit. After his own mom sold him for drug money, he'd never touched any of it.

Lucas, on the other hand, that guy had traded one addiction for another. Got rough with the girls when he fed sometimes. Caleb was usually his wingman. He owed him his life, even if neither of them ever spoke about it. They'd buried that memory so deep, no one knew.

When he'd bounced around foster care, Lucas had become somewhat of his shadow, watching over him on the streets. So, yeah, having his friend's back was his way of returning the favor, but tonight he'd switched with Claire, and now he was failing her, too. If her brother died because he'd let Eve give him the slip, he'd never forgive himself.

"Caleb, please listen to me."

"Look, I'll keep your little secret if it makes you feel better, but do you mind walking a little faster? I'm kinda in a rush. There's a storm rolling in." He sincerely hoped Parker was still breathing.

Eve zipped it tight the rest of the way. Back at the truck, Kristján opened the door to the backseat for her, and this time, Caleb made sure she was buckled in before getting in the front passenger seat.

"Where was she?"

Caleb shook his head. "Doesn't matter. Just drive."

What the hell were they going to do? Without Kjartan's blood to heal him, Parker was already dead. And even if he were here, the chances of him helping were slim to none.

CHAPTER

45

The storm was quickly catching up with them when they pulled up to the cabin. Eve skipped her finger over Parker's wrist. His pulse was low.

"I texted her again," Emma said, looking up from her phone. "They're almost here."

"Let's get him inside before it starts pouring down," Kristján hollered over the sound of thunder.

Car doors slammed shut in sync with flashes of lightning that lit up the sky above the trees. The storm was nearly on top of them.

With his arms across their shoulders, Kristján and Caleb braced Parker up in between them. They dragged him inside and laid him down on the couch in the front room. His complexion was paler than before, ashen compared to his black shirt.

"PARKER!"

Eve leaped sideways. Claire burst through the door with the others and ran to her brother's side.

"What the hell happened?" She looked up at Caleb for an answer.

"The chick he fed from must have been on something. Her blood wasn't clean. He's not recovering."

"What are we going to do? Askja, you have to help him. There has to be something we can do?" Tears rolled down her cheeks as she pleaded.

Askja and Kristján exchanged looks. Neither of them seemed hopeful. "He is not going to make it," he said quietly.

CRACK-BOOM!

A bright flash shot across the sky with a thunderous clap, and lightning struck the tree line just past the patio.

The tension in the room erupted into voices shouting, finding someone to blame. Nessa was holding Claire back from lunging at Caleb, who was trying to defend himself with more arguing. Kristján had taken his side. Emma was cowering in the corner, arms wrapped around herself, shaking. Askja didn't know what to do. Even Lucas looked shaken, his expression tense, eyes on the ground. Eve couldn't tell if he was breathing.

Everyone was panicking.

Except for her.

Feeling like an outsider, she'd stayed back to give them space, and still, no one was paying any attention to her. They all knew she didn't belong.

She glanced over her shoulder at the front door, shuffling her feet. Nobody would notice her slipping out.

Why was she still standing here?

For the same reason, she hadn't run downtown.

She cared.

Friends or not, if she had the means to save Parker, she couldn't just turn her back on him. She wasn't selfish like that. She'd given up her only chance at escaping to get the atropine sulfate, and she wasn't entirely sure her idea was going to work.

Eve calmly took the vial from her pocket and inserted the needle into the top. *2mg*, she remembered Kjan telling her.

Once she'd prepped the syringe, she pushed her way through. "Move!"

She pulled Caleb out of the way and kneeled on the floor beside the couch. She could feel everyone's eyes on her. It had been a long time since she'd done the med training in college before settling on her psychology major, but she still remembered the basics.

Parker was coherent, though too weak to move on his own. His weary eyes tracked her movements. The veins in his arm were clearly visible, and Eve had no trouble aligning the needle with the most prominent blood vessel protruding from the crook of his arm.

"What are you doing?" Claire asked in between sobs.

Eve didn't meet her eyes and kept focusing on the syringe. She drew the plunger back a smidge, watching his blood swirl inside the plastic cylinder and mix with the clear liquid. "This should raise his heart rate," she supposed as she sent the entire contents into his bloodstream.

"Where did you get that?"

"The pharmacy downtown," Caleb answered for her. "How did you know?"

"Personal experience," Eve replied dryly.

She withdrew the needle from his arm, putting pressure on the insertion point, and then addressed Parker. "You have to feed. You need to take someone's vein."

"What?"

"No!"

Eve didn't track who had asked the question, it seemed like a combination of voices under the sound of the ongoing thunder, all meeting her suggestion in the same appalled manner. But she knew they needed to buy Parker time. Just a day. Long enough for Kjartan to get back. And then *he* would—

"We can't," Caleb said. "We're not allowed to."

"This is hardly the moment to worry about what you're *allowed* to do. He is going to die unless you save him."

Claire buried her face in her hands at the harsh comment.

"Kjartan will punish us for trying. We abide by his laws or we die," Caleb hissed over her shoulder. His tone sounded more scared than angry.

Eve couldn't believe her ears. "What's wrong with all of you?" She looked around the group, waiting for someone else to speak up, but they all avoided her glances. "Claire! He's your *brother!*"

The boy's twin broke out into another sob.

Cowards, Eve thought. "Kjartan is not here. He won't have to know—"

"Our blood won't work." Lucas' voice was low and hoarse as he spoke. "We can't heal each other... I've tried."

Caleb's expression turned bitter. "What do you mean '*you've tried*'? When?"

"When *he* refused to help her," Lucas bit back.

Eve's eyes searched their faces. "You mean Kjartan let someone die?"

"Olivia shot herself up with heroin two days after she was turned," Caleb said, his eyes glaring at his friend. "She didn't follow the rules, and she had to suffer the consequences."

Lucas scoffed. "You sound just like him."

"Look, whatever," Eve interrupted their quarrel, "Parker made a mistake. It wasn't his fault. And he doesn't deserve to die for this. We have to do something. We have to at least try."

"You heard him," Emma snipped from the back. "Our blood won't work."

Eve locked eyes with Parker. "Take mine, then."

Caleb's words popped back into her head: '*We're all replaceable... all but you*'. Their blood didn't work, but maybe hers was slightly different. She'd fed on Kjan dozens of times. That had to count for something, right?

She carefully sank her lower fangs into her wrist, then brought it down to Parker's lips. More bright flashes lit up the sky outside, shaking the cabin with thunder from the impact.

"What makes you think yours is any better than ours?"

"I don't know," Eve answered the mouthy girl. "I can't guarantee this is going to work, but it's the only option we have. It only needs to tide him over long enough."

She wanted to believe that Kjartan wouldn't let him die. He cared more now, didn't he? He cared enough to fly home to protect the others.

She watched Parker's throat bob, keeping her fingers crossed as he swallowed her blood. If her theory proved to be wrong, no one had to tell Kjartan anything. But if it worked...

His pulse began to pick up the pace, and deeper breaths inflated his chest. It was working. It was *really* working. She could see the change in his dark skin tone already.

Another bolt of lightning struck, and a crazy thought crossed Eve's mind. Maybe her blood was strong enough to heal him after all. She could feed him again tomorrow. Maybe Kjartan never had to find out about any of this.

As long as everyone keeps their mouth shut.

The crackling on top of them became louder, and her heart pounded under the deafening rumble of thunder. He would punish her for going against his orders. Caleb was wrong. Kjartan might not be able to replace her, but he wouldn't put up with her for long, either. He *would* kill her if she provoked him, and he'd given her his final warning before leaving.

'There are no secrets between us'. But what if it was a matter of life and death? Would they keep a secret? Would they protect her for saving Parker, or would they throw her under the bus?

No. No, they wouldn't do that. They were too afraid of his wrath. They would surely lie. And Parker looked almost normal already. They were fine. Everyone was fine. By tomorrow, he'd be back to his usual handsome self, and then all the attention would be on him, giving her a chance to make her escape. Everything would work out. Just one more day.

Eve exhaled in relief just as another white bolt streaked through the glass and thunder roared again, rattling the cabin like an earthquake. This time, lightning struck so close that the lights flickered and then went out.

Her heart made a jump up to her throat from the blast, and everyone's heads snapped around in unison.

A drastic drop in the room's temperature registered on her bare arms as the air turned suddenly frigid. Nobody moved. Everything was dark. Even the exterior lighting on the patio had gone out.

Turning her head slowly in the direction the others were staring, Eve could see the little puffs of her breath. She flinched back the second her eyes found the source of the red glow behind her, and all her chances for another escape vanished into the thin, icy air.

She had been so close to freedom. Had felt it at the tips of her fingers.

Renate Rowland

CHAPTER

46

He had told them four days at most, but he made it back in a little over three. After a 15-hour flight, including the weather delay, and another two hours of driving well below the speed limit under the wet conditions. The Harley was in need of a complete check. He should have replaced the tires sooner. New brakes would be a good call too.

Kjartan stood at the top of the stairs that led up from the garage, dripping wet, his mood palpable.

All power to the house was gone.

His eyes shot from Eve to Kristján and then landed on Askja for an explanation. "What happened?"

His fingers twitched while she filled him in on the entire night. He felt the charge tingle across his scalp as he pictured Eve downtown. He was itching to unleash. Someone was going to pay for this.

Kristján jumped in to add his side of the story, and they finally arrived at the crucial part, where Eve had taken charge of the situation.

"She did what?" Teeth locked tight, his words snapped through the air like the crack of a whip.

From the corner of his eye, he noticed Eve cringe and take two steps back toward the kitchen. His fingertips flew to his temples to alleviate the pressure behind them.

"What's wrong with your head?" His confidant's warm eyes were once again full of concern for him.

"Nothing." Kjartan diverted with a long exhale, dropping his shoulders. Naturally, she was the one to get through to him. He relaxed. Mildly.

"You are supposed to watch each other." He glowered at all of them, not really accusing anyone in particular. Then he pointed a sharp finger at Eve. "She was not supposed to leave the house."

Askja straightened in front of him. "It was my fault. I made the call, and I take full responsibility."

"Nae, Love," Nessa butted in. "I'm the one who talked ye into this brock. Ye did nae want to take'r out. 'Twas *my* idea."

"She was on *my* watch." Caleb rose to his feet and stepped forward, his eyes level. "You want to blame someone, blame me."

For the second time in mere days, Kjartan felt respect for the kid.

"This was no one's fault but mine." Parker struggled to sit up on the couch when all eyes turned to him. "Nobody is taking the fall for me. I wasn't careful."

"You made a mistake. That could've happened to any of us," Claire piled on.

All hell broke loose as they started arguing with each other. Bickering like children. All of them. Kjartan pinched the bridge of his nose.

"ENOUGH!" His deep growl shook the walls and finally put an end to this.

The room fell dead quiet, but something was off. He felt it in his gut.

One particular heartbeat was missing.

His head snapped around, and his eyes immediately shot to the kitchen, where Eve had stood a minute ago. He bared his fangs. "She is gone!"

"Not again," Caleb groaned, rolling his eyes.

Kjartan's hand shot out and fisted the front of the boy's shirt, yanking him up close. "AGAIN?"

Kristján had skipped right over that part of his narrative.

Lips flapping like a fish, Caleb struggled to find his words. It made no difference, he would not be around to catch the response.

Kjartan raced after her out the back through the kitchen door. The storm was still in full swing, and the rain made it impossible to trail the scent. No wildflowers. No apple blossoms. He had no Sire-link to Eve. Her connection to his host had been through the man's soul, not his physical form. He had to resort to alternative means of tracking her.

There was only one other way: the draw Kjan's body shared with his mate.

Though his blood had changed after the possession, this elusive bond remained. Kjartan was unable to explain it. As much as he loathed the idea of channeling his vessel's link to her, he was running low on options.

Heart pounding, adrenaline surging, he closed his eyes to focus. Then he felt the tug in his chest, his body's instinctive response to the mating call of his little bird.

Twigs snapped under his boots as he took off, the direction of the pull steering him over the uneven ground pitted with roots and rocks. Leaves rustled where he pushed through, branches scraping at his skin. He pressed on. Faster.

∫

Run!
Don't look back!
Don't let him catch you!

Eve's thoughts ran wild with the frantic beat of her pulse and the pounding of her feet against the rough terrain. She pushed more speed from her limbs, arms pumping like the wheels on a locomotive. Branches ripped through her hair. Dark greens and blacks blurred in front of her. She couldn't see past the dense forest. Couldn't find a path.

He's right behind you.

Pure terror flooded her body with a cold sensation. Her fingertips were numb as she clenched them in her fists. She didn't slow. Didn't glance over her shoulder.

More trees rushed at her with increasing velocity. Then her view cleared, the vegetation coming to an abrupt end—

And so did the ground. She was headed for a sharp drop.

Eve put on the brakes. Feet kicking out in front of her, she went into a slide. Tree trunks gave way to roots and twigs, filling her field of vision on her way down. Rocks scraped her arms, tearing skin with her momentum. She clawed for traction in the soil, getting nowhere while the burn of fresh cuts lit her body up with pain.

Legs dangling over the edge of the cliff, she skidded to a full stop. Her hands had found hold on a root at last. Her fingers wound tightly around the feeble thing that was barely strong enough to hold her weight. She knew her elbows were bleeding. Her shirt had ridden up her stomach, too, causing more abrasion along her front.

Hip hinged on the ledge, she dug her toes into the vertical hillside to get a grip. With a heavy grunt, she braced her palms in the dirt and pushed up. First one knee and then the other, she hauled herself from the precipice onto the solid ground.

Eve kicked back into a sprint, skipping over stones, not letting the brush with death get the best of her. There were likely more dangerous landslides out here, but she feared him more than dying. A fall was quick. If he caught her, the punishment would be much worse.

She felt him getting closer already. The pull toward him sucked the air out of her lungs. He was so fast. Her muscles weakened. The soles of her sneakers sank into the muck, slowing her headway, and diminishing the distance between them with each passing millisecond.

He was right on her heels.

Renate Rowland

CHAPTER

47

He finally caught sight of her between the trees ahead, a defenseless deer's meager attempt at escape. The thrill of chasing her drove him to pick up speed again, the air whipping past him.

Like a predator closing in on his prey, he did not restrain his assault. He took her down, tackling her with all the force he had at his disposal.

Her back took the brunt. Limbs tangled, she tried to wrestle her way out of his clutch, screaming, kicking, and clawing, but he refused to let up. He employed the whole weight of his body on her hips to pin her to the ground and restrained her wrists by trapping them on either side of her head in the wet soil.

"Stop it, Eve. You are not going anywhere," he snarled, struggling to force air into his body. His lungs burned as they inflated. "Did you really believe you could outrun me? There is nowhere in the world you could hide."

Kjartan's eyes flared red, illuminating the forest around them and reminding her of who he was—a God—and she but a mere mortal, vampire or not. His power was undeniable. His wrath inescapable. No one dared to challenge him. He would always be superior.

The sound of Eve's terrified heartbeat resonated in his head, pounding like a drum. She continued thrashing, gasping, and heaving to catch her breath. Tears rolled down the sides of her face.

His gaze skated over her naked arms, marred by deep scratches and cuts from thorns.

His rage evaporated into the waning storm, and he relaxed his body with a deep sigh. Loosening the grip around her wrists, his hands slid upward, entwining with her fingers, and he dropped his forehead to hers. He exhaled, closing his eyes, his thumb teasing the inside of her palm.

"Breathe with me," his words implored her.

They stayed like this, chest to chest, with no sense of time, while he waited for her to ease up. Eve was weak and starved, all fight drained from her. Kjartan felt exhausted himself, and not just from the run. The ordeal had taken a toll on him.

He sensed the sun creeping over the horizon and lastly pulled her up. Not giving her a chance to argue, he scored his wrist, then forced it to her lips.

Her body went lax in his arms within seconds, and the gashes in her skin healed in front of his eyes.

Satisfied, he withdrew his wrist. He shot Askja a text to confirm everybody had cleared out before sunrise. He had no interest in making a big scene.

Eve was conscious but still weak when he brought her back to the house. Her arms linked around his neck, she let him carry her upstairs into the shower.

He set her feet on the ground and held her steady as he turned on the water. His body on autopilot, he absentmindedly chucked her muddy clothes, then pulled her under the hot spray with him, boots and all.

The sleek strands of her hair flowed in between his fingers like satin as his hands fanned through the glossy mass, rinsing out the dirt. It felt so familiar.

With his cognitive perception suddenly back on full alert, he fought the urge to brush over her flushed skin. Delegating the task of worshiping her body to his eyes alone, he regarded her with adoration. In the heat of the moment and the haste of that first time, he had not taken her vision in properly.

She was stunningly beautiful. Her skin, smooth and fine as silk, was unmarred, besides a tattoo on the inside of her right wrist. A warm, dark chestnut in color, her hair was as soft to the touch as it looked. It cascaded over her strong shoulders and sharp collarbones.

A perfect curve shaped her rear, perky and taut, matching her ample breasts, which were nestled inside a lacy bralette in a color that reminded him of a young Cabernet.

Eve was indeed not a delicate little bird. She had a distinct definition in her deltoids. Her frame, yet small compared to his, was fierce and graced with hard muscles from her neck to her calves, ready to put up a fight. Underneath her clothes, she was tougher than she looked, and she had given him a delectable taste of it tonight when her body had squirmed ferociously beneath him.

His gaze followed the trail of water running down her contoured figure, yearning to catch the steady stream mixed with the salt from her skin on his tongue. He saw himself on his knees, savoring the taste of her, each drop a precious gift.

Foreign thoughts emerged in his awareness, carving out memories from nothing...

...rising steam...

...their bodies locked in a slick embrace...

Buried deep inside her, I give her everything. Pour myself into her soul, my own in a tailspin, plunging toward certain doom. There's nothing slowing my descent. I'm fated to crash and burn.

And that's fine.

Because within her, I'm alive. A part of me tucked away. Safe. Untouchable by death.

Cradling her cheek, he burrowed his face in her hair, gorging himself on the sweet, blooming plethora of her natural perfume emanating from it. The volcano inside him stirred, heat rising to the top, threatening to erupt. His vessel was answering her song, and he was helpless to fight it. His body craved her even more now that she had shared his bed. Three days away from her had been torture.

Kjartan wanted her again—now—despite his own weariness, and he had to painfully remind himself that this was not the time. Eve was still subdued by his blood. He would not take advantage of that. She had vastly approved of his touch in the study, but that had been before his outburst in the kitchen. Hurting her was not his ambition. His rage made him blind and unpredictable.

Would she forgive him for attacking her? She had been deathly afraid of him in the woods.

He shut off the water, then braced her against the wall and reached for a towel to wrap around her. Unconcerned about his own wet clothes, he carried her over to the bed.

After tucking her in to keep her warm, he forced himself away from her. His body protested. But as much as he longed to stay, he had more pressing matters to take care of than his personal desires.

Renate Rowland

CHAPTER

48

She recalled being in the shower. Either that or some dark cave with a waterfall. It had been a walk-in with smooth black stone tile on two sides and a rough-cut wall at the end. Blue light had flooded the space as the water rained down on them from not one but two square heads, each one as wide as her shoulders.

The haze lifted, and Eve was finally lucid again when Kjartan returned a while later. He was wearing an actual t-shirt this time—not a button-down—plain, with a snug fit on his upper body. It was black, like his jeans. This guy never wore any colors, only blacks and fifty shades of slightly different dark grays.

"Is that blood?" she gasped on closer observation. Her heart started to beat a little faster. *Not again.*

The streak on the front looked like he had wiped his hands on it. He had punished them because of her, hadn't he? And she was next.

The hard shove he gave the door made her flinch. "My own," he huffed, dismissing her concern.

He reached up to pull the shirt over his head and dropped it by his feet. The pair of rings around his neck bounced as he moved. She didn't see any marks on him, but they probably would've healed by now. Why had he been bleeding?

Sliding into bed with her, Kjartan aimed for the space between her legs. He kept his body low, so his chest was even with her belly, and laid his head down right above her heart.

There was something freakishly familiar about the way he moved, almost like second nature. Her pulse picked up speed as his arms wound around her waist.

God, he smells like him too.

Eve breathed him in. Dark chocolate, hints of cherries, and the burn of Bourbon inched down her throat. If it weren't for his choice of hairstyle, she could have mistaken him for Kjan.

Except it wasn't braided now. His long hair was tied into a sloppy bun that seemed to have been done in haste. Her hands slid along his bulging shoulders, and she ran her fingers through the loose tangles draped down his neck.

He was so big. Easily twice her size. Eve felt like she was trapped beneath a massive fallen oak, crushed by its unmovable trunk. Would she make it out of this, or would she die here without anyone hearing her scream? Would anyone even care?

He'd been irritated, but whatever the cause, it had melted away at her touch. Like she'd just defused a bomb. Either he knew how it worked or he was doing it subconsciously.

Of course, it only worked if he opened himself up to it. He could just as easily shut her out as he could switch off the resonance of his aura.

She was caught in some kind of crazy inverted funhouse mirror. Eve couldn't figure out the enigma in front of her. Kjan, though rough in the sheets, had a kind and gentle nature. This guy—this God—had a violent temper, yet in his bed, he touched her with a tenderness that seemed impossible to comprehend. As if he were afraid to break her.

It was funny that she was the equalizer that brought balance to them both.

Eve drifted off again. Her subconsciousness clung to the memory of Kjan and their first time together back in Seattle. It was the night he'd forged his half of the bond, bitten her with the sole purpose of embracing her as his only mate and establishing the chemical dependency in his DNA.

She'd reciprocated the pledge and marked him as her mate in return months later, when he'd sought her out here in Portland. Sinking her fangs into his shoulder and not the vein at his throat to draw blood, Eve had acted on instinct without understanding what it meant. All she'd known was the all-consuming need to surrender her mind, her body, and her soul to him.

The images behind her eyelids blurred as her dream changed to a different scene: the night after Eleanor's fundraiser. Eve was wearing the infamous green dress, and the two of them were curled up together on Kjan's bed.

Eve realized that the new dream was not a memory when his fingers skimmed along her nape and drew her into a kiss. In reality, nothing of the sort had happened that night.

She felt his lips brush over her skin as he led a trail down to her collarbone, sliding his hand under her skirt. His touch was so real. Cradling his head in her hands, Eve pulled him closer, and then his fangs grazed the column of her neck.

She braced herself for his bite, but the moment his teeth sank into her skin, Eve's eyes flew open in a panic.

Braids! His hair had been braided.

It took her a second to shake the dream and clear her head. She looked down at the heavy weight on her chest. Keeping her breathing low and even, she tried not to rouse the dormant beast between her thighs, slumbering like a tiger after overindulging.

"'I don't sleep—*my ass*", she snorted.

Passed out cold on top of her, his heartbeat was slow and steady. Eve frowned. Their fingers were laced. His right hand with her left—

Kjartan woke with a start and jolted upright, seemingly confused, as if he didn't remember where he was. His frantic, electric blue eyes locked onto Eve, and he rolled off her, rubbing his temples.

Flustered herself, she inched away to give him space.

The distinct palette of his scent returned, the earthy tones of pine and moss pulling her right back into the woods. She'd stopped resisting him before he'd force-fed her his blood. She recalled the taste on her tongue. Much stronger than the single drop the first time. It had started out sweet like Kjan's, but there was a smoothness about it that reminded her of creamy black cherry and chocolate Bailey's rather than red wine. The bitter espresso finish was what had sedated her instead of delivering the cocaine-like rush she always got from Kjan's blood.

Eve clutched the towel to her chest. She felt so conflicted. The lines between them were beginning to blur. Where did Kjan end and Kjartan begin when it came to their bond? He hadn't hurt her in the woods, but that didn't mean he wouldn't still choose to punish her for breaking his precious rules. And just because the blood on his shirt was his own didn't mean he hadn't hurt anyone.

"How did you know?" he said abruptly. Her gaze jerked to meet his as he looked back at her over his shoulder. "How did you know what to do?"

Eve just stared at him, hesitant in her response. It was obvious he didn't remember their mutual history with the deadly nightshade, and she wasn't sure how much she was willing to share.

"Caleb came clean about your little adventure to the drug store. How did you know about the atropine?" The question rasped from his lips, but it sounded more weary than hostile.

Eve blinked. "I didn't," she lied. "Not for sure, anyway. I just know that it's used to raise the heart rate, and I hoped that it would work on him, too." At least not all of it was a lie.

"I am in your debt. Parker would have died without you." He paused briefly. "Thank you."

Eve was shocked. Kjartan was grateful? Did that mean she was off the hook?

∫

His focus caught on her face, with the perceptive little frown between her brows.

"I'm just glad I could help," she said, smiling back at him nervously.

He had fallen asleep on top of her? *Unfathomable.* But having eight vampires take his vein in less than three days had been enough to wear him out. Although it should have been nine, Lucas had been a no-show.

Kjartan did not even remember the ride home from the loft downtown; his body had resumed its autopilot routine. The vial of atropine had been sitting on the coffee table in the great room. Something about it had struck him with a strange déjà vu.

Scouring her closed-off expression, it was still on his mind when something else hit him out of the blue. Her scent! Eve was aroused.

He inhaled deeply. Her pheromones, which hung thick in the air, were the reason he had snapped out of his slumber. And now, with the little hairs on his overstimulated skin raised, all his senses were cranked up to the maximum.

Scrutinizing eyes on her, he saw her swallow and noticed the blush creeping onto her cheeks. The image of them in the shower together returned sharply to his mind. Drawn like a moth to a flame, he abruptly remembered that she was wearing nothing but her lingerie and a towel. She was practically naked.

Without warning—or further regard for any proper etiquette—he tugged on the front of the terry cloth covering her. Her hold on it fell away. Overt desire sparked in her eyes, and Eve parted her thighs for him to nudge in between.

Gathering her into his arms, he bent down to press his lips to her belly. His tongue led the way, closer and closer to the hollow of her breasts, while his hands mapped her backside. They grazed higher. He pinched the clasp of her bra, then slid the deep red lace down her arms without lifting his kiss.

He let his touch whisper across her skin, really taking in the feel of her this time.

Eagerly, she sank into his embrace. Her fingers tangled in his hair, pulling on the tie to free it and delve deeper.

A prickle darted up his neck as she dragged a lazy nail up and down. He inched higher up her body until his still fully clothed hips found hers. Eve arched her back to meet him, her skin warm, and her soft breasts squished against his bare chest. He could feel her heart pacing his own.

Working herself against him, she bit her bottom lip and tipped her head back further, her hands keeping him close. When she exposed the exquisite front of her throat, he gave into the impulse to drag his fangs along her skin.

The ripple of the shiver that the lethal points forced from her passed through his body in an exhilarating thrill. Her scent flared. A smooth burn chased the distinct fragrance of her lust, inflating his lungs.

His nose traced the curve under her chin, seeking out the plush velvet of her lips. He kissed her tenderly, caressing her mouth with his own, when her strangled moan sparked a steep hunger in him.

Kjartan deepened the kiss, his hand cradling her head, fingers splayed in her hair in a claiming act.

She tensed abruptly beneath him as his touch grazed her nape, and on instinct, he pulled back. "Did I hurt you?"

"No. Don't stop," her rough voice choked out, deflecting from whatever had been on her mind.

Without elaborating, she cupped his face in her hands to guide him back, whimpering while she rocked into him with more urgency. He matched her rhythm, his hand slipping to the small of her back, rounding her hip, and squeezing her thigh until her breath billowed and she climaxed.

Her craving unfulfilled, her hands wandered down his chest to the fly of his jeans with a clear target in mind. Her nimble fingers moved swiftly; the button popped, the zipper released, and then his constraints were gone.

He groaned, squeezing his eyes shut. The muscles in his back strained at her touch, as did his firm grip on her thigh.

Compelled by her soft wail, Kjartan eased off but kept his motion deliberately unhurried to demonstrate his patience. He twisted the skinny sides of her G-string around his fingers and pulled them slowly down her legs to strip her of the single piece of clothing separating them.

With her legs hiked at his waist, he lowered himself and brought his mouth back down on hers, gradually inching his way inside her molten core.

"You are mine, Love," he growled into her throat, swallowing her moans.

The tips of his boots dug into the sheets for traction while he ground his hips to stroke her on each deep thrust. With his grip hooked underneath her shoulder, he pulled himself deeper, working her inside and out.

Eve splintered apart in his arms again, shuddering through blissful tremors, and the most beautiful sound reached his ears.

As she cried out, he welcomed his own release, but Kjartan did not let up. He was voracious. His arms still molding her into him, he filled her core, temptation tickling his jaw. He had already gotten under her skin, and in between her legs, he wanted to be in her head, too. Needed to *see* into her mind.

Baring his fangs, he aimed for her internal jugular vein in his endeavor. The electric charge went up his spine the instant he drew her blood, and the first picture he saw sliced through his heart like a knife.

374

The emotion fueled him. He kept going, swallowing in greater gulps, releasing memory after memory of hers with each drop he took—

A jolt ravaged through him, abruptly reversing the perspective he had been viewing. Like a door had flung open in his mind, visions flooded in that were not his but Kjan's. Visions of Eve smiling back at him, the sound of her laughter resonating in his head... yet all little more than an echo of the real thing.

His steel cage around her body tightened. A sudden surge of jealousy he had never felt before came over him. *He* wanted to be the one to bring this feeling out in her.

The sweet taste of her blood down his throat turned sour, and a deep rage incited him. Every fiber of his being wanted to erase Kjan from her memory and wipe her slate clean.

Kjartan withdrew his teeth from her neck, then punched his eyes shut, fully aware that they were burning red. He was reluctant to face her this way. His former inclination had shifted. He no longer wanted her to see him as a monster.

Breathing hard through his nose, he gathered himself and noticed Eve was no longer trembling.

She was not moving at all. Her body lay completely slack.

Renate Rowland

ᚠ
ᚲHAPTER

49

His eyes flew open in alarm. His hands shook as he scurried backward, mortified by what he had done. So preoccupied with himself, he had lost control and taken too much. Eve was unconscious. Her pulse low.

His tongue swept across his lips, still coated with the taste of her. How could he have been so careless?

Kjartan scrambled off the edge of the bed and snatched up his shirt at the foot end before darting out the door. Reaching the bottom of the stairs, he shot straight for the garage. He grabbed the helmet and mounted the bike, but when he turned the key, the ignition sputtered.

The irritation provoked him, bringing his rage back to a boil. Lips curling off his fully descended fangs, he locked his jaw and flexed every muscle in his upper body, from his chest to his forearms and fists.

Curving his spine forward, his anger unloaded with a thunderous roar as he forced the electrical charge back out of his body.

The engine kicked to life.

Power returned to the cabin.

In his current mood, being in his presence was so toxic that he snuffed the spark out of every object in the vicinity without even trying. He needed to get out of this house. Needed to get away. The garage door was only halfway up, and he ducked under it, speeding around the tight turn of the driveway.

Dark clouds blackened the sky. It gave the late afternoon the appearance of twilight. The storm had gathered a second wind, and the rain had continued all day. Large drops blurred his view through the visor. The road beneath the tires was slick, and he knew the winding stretch would get treacherous, but Kjartan refused to slow down. The compressing force behind his eyeballs was back.

Revving the throttle, he fed the engine more gas, ignoring the thumping inside his skull that battered like fists against bulletproof glass. The trivial blows were futile.

The indistinct greens and browns of the pines streaked by, and the steep side of the mountain tore through his periphery. He caught sight of the turn-off, but it came up too soon... he took the sharp corner going too fast.

Swerving at the last second to avoid the collision with the tree, his right hand slipped from the wet throttle, and the overused tires lost traction in the dirt. The bike skidded sideways on the unpaved road, crushing his leg under the weight. The muddy gravel slammed into the left side of his body, then a blaze of agony streaked up his arm where his skin was exposed.

The physical injuries were insignificant. His wounds began to heal, tissue pulling and straining to stitch itself together despite the unfavorable conditions. It was the white-hot pain of nuclear proportions that nailed him to the ground as it exploded behind his eyes. Spasms stirred in his muscles. He roared and twisted in rage, fighting the enemy within.

If her former lover was looking for retribution, he would be met with stark disappointment. "You will not get rid of me that easily," he growled inward. "Eve is mine."

His hand went for the visor and flipped it open. Deep, rapid breaths shot through his lungs but failed to make much impact. The limited amount of oxygen did not reach its destination.

He ripped the helmet off his head one-handed and hurled it into the bushes. Collapsing back onto his bad arm, he winced. His shoulder was dislocated and his knee shattered. He felt little shards of bone moving like shrapnel while they tried to shift back into place.

He shoved against the motorcycle's seat, freeing his leg from under the pile of steel, and scooted backward through the muck. It began to mend instantly on its own, leaving only one injury for him to fix by hand.

Rain pelting down on him, he reached for the back of his right shoulder. With a sharp *crack*, he ripped it forward into the proper position, relieving the piercing discomfort.

Kjartan gave the rest of his body a quick assessment, then pushed to his feet. He stormed toward the temple's entrance, nearly taking the gate off its hinges.

On his descent into the grand chamber, he was welcomed by the familiar darkness. The warm glow of the torches had died since his last visit, but he did not require them. He was so accustomed to the layout that he could easily find his way, as if still able to see in the dark, an ability he had lost by taking this vessel.

His steps echoed as he crossed the floor to the altar and pulled the offering bowl into the center. Hovering his left arm steadily above it, he took the ritual dagger and made a deep cut along the inside, all the way from his wrist to the crook of his elbow.

"Gods of Old, behold, my blood runs true. In my time of need, I call on you," he prayed while the red liquid sprung from the wound and spilled into the dish.

"Huginn and Muninn, winged emissaries of the realms beyond, teach me your tricks of thought and memory." He paused and took a deep breath, drawing on the meaning behind his words. "Undivided in my purpose and bound by my blood, I stand before you to dive into darkness and return with knowledge."

The cave stayed quiet. Nothing but the reverberating sound of his heartbeat and the hammering in his head breached the silence.

Bracing his hands against the altar, gripping the edge of the stone top, he sighed in disappointment.

"Lead me to quench my flames in the cool well of wisdom and grant me strength, so that I may persevere in my efforts," he begged, his voice nearing a tremble.

Nothing happened. No words penetrated the veil between the worlds.

Kjartan swung out his arm, swiping the bowl off the altar in a violent motion and sending his blood spewing. It clattered to the ground, the high pitch ringing on as the rim gradually settled on the stone.

"You shall not find peace…"

His head snapped up when the female voice spoke softly in his mind.

"...as long as the fire of Fenrir's rage burns deep within your soul...," a second one added.

"...bound you will be by the same tools," the third concluded.

The Norns, Kjartan thought. Urðr, Verðandi, and Skuld, the Shapers of Destiny and voices of the past, present, and future.

"Strongest chain ever built...

...light in appearance...

...soft to the touch," the three echoed in order.

"And share his fate you will, to be banished into exile," they finished in one voice.

"I am a child of the Gods," Kjartan objected, balling his fists. "I shall not suffer defeat. I will not be overthrown." His voice boomed through the hall, shaking the mountain's base before it fell silent again.

The Great Wolf, Fenrir, was a son of Loki, the Trickster God. The beast had been raised by the mighty Gods, and then imprisoned once they grew fearful of his alarming size. According to the Ragnarok prophecy, he was to unite with his siblings, Hel and Jǫrmungandr, to bring about the end of days by swallowing the sun and everything else in his path.

The magical chain to hold him had been made by the dwarves, well known for forging great weapons like Þórr's hammer and Óðinn's spear. The specifications of his bindings were just like the Norns described them: strong, light, and soft to trick the monster.

He failed to understand how the prophecy related to himself. He was not that easily fooled. He would crush any threat to his claim.

The trickle of blood from his nose caught his attention, and he wiped it.

Kjan was still meddling, was he not? And he had deliberately caused the bike to crash. Kjartan was sure of it.

CHAPTER

50

E ve jerked off the pillow, her heart pounding, neck feeling sore and stiff. Her hand shot to the throbbing area, still tender to her touch.

Blinking the fog from her brain, things came back to her: his harsh hand in her hair, pain swelling at her throat.

The moment Kjartan had driven his fangs into her vein, her survival instinct had taken over, sending her into panic mode. He'd ignored her distress, and she'd been helpless against him, eventually losing her battle with consciousness.

Considering the dried blood under her fingernails, she'd fought back, though she couldn't remember the details. His hold on her had never softened, and within seconds of struggling against his vise grip, her muscles had ceased, leaving her paralyzed by fear. Then everything had gone fuzzy.

He hadn't marked her. His bite had been possessive in nature. Marking a mate was not about claiming them as property. It was about giving yourself over wholly and without reservation. A characteristic totally uncanny to the immortal.

Why had he done it? He had everything he wanted. What more could he possibly gain from her?

Or had this been her punishment for defying him?

She wanted to believe that it was an accident because the alternative was too terrifying for her to accept. All the same, his conduct still left her with the affirmation that he was not in control of himself.

Eve yanked the blanket off and stood up so fast the loss of blood gave her a headrush. Dropping to the floor, she stayed there for a moment until the dizziness faded and her body stopped shaking.

Where were her clothes?

Oh right. Still in the bathroom.

She rose and stumbled back toward the shower, where she remembered him dropping them. Blinking hard, her eyes fell on the bathtub first. It was huge. Big enough to comfortably fit two NFL linemen. It was made of black granite to match the design of the walk-in shower. While the inside was smooth, the outside had a rough stone texture. It was gorgeous.

The giant bowl sat in front of a clear glass wall. It offered a very romantic scene at night and, no doubt, a breathtaking view of the outside during the day as well. Unlike the dark shower, the rest of the bathroom would be bathed in sunlight. Various switches on the wall led her to believe that the clear appearance could be changed to an opaque setting, ensuring a little more privacy.

Eve avoided her reflection in the large mirror above the double vanity, but she couldn't peel her eyes away from the tabletop sinks. *Is this guy for real?*

Two square vessels in the same rough granite style as the bathtub and shower sat on the slate counter. The color on the smooth inside was a bright blue, giving them a mystical appearance. She had a hunch that the open waterway spout on the fancy matte black faucet would light up just like the shower.

Can you tell there's a magical waterfall theme in here somewhere?

Eve had to get out of there before supernatural fog started rising up from the ground, trying to swallow her up in some otherworldly fantasy.

Uh-oh! Too late. She was already stuck in one.

She retrieved her muddy jeans, shirt, and shoes from the floor, then went to change into clean clothes in her own bedroom. She sensed Askja, Nessa, and Caleb's presence downstairs, and even though she didn't feel like making small talk, she eventually joined them in the front room.

Askja looked surprised to see Eve descending the stairs alone. "Where is Kjartan?"

"I don't know." She shrugged.

"What do you mean?"

What am I, his babysitter? "I mean, he left before sunset and didn't say where he was going," Eve enunciated as if she had to explain it to a child. She wasn't sure how she could be any clearer than that.

Askja blew out an exasperated breath and pulled out her phone. "This morning he said he wanted all of us back here at sundown."

There must've been a change of plans on his agenda since then.

Caleb grimaced. "The fuck's up with your neck?"

Eve uncomfortably adjusted her hair and draped it over her shoulder without a reply. Avoiding his eyes, she took a seat on the couch.

Askja's cell chimed not a minute later. "He is at the temple," she called out. "He wants us to wait for him here. Kristján is on his way with the others. He will want to hear the news as well. Kjartan said it concerns the entire coven."

News?

And there's a temple?

Eve wondered if she'd be allowed to sit in on their talk.

The back door opened, and all four of them, including Nessa, moved at the same time toward the kitchen. Kristján appeared in the frame first, Emma, Claire, and Parker right behind him. Eve was glad to see him on his feet again. He seemed to have fully recovered from last night's events.

"Where is Lucas?" Askja asked, annoyed.

Damn, bad attitude really was contagious, spreading from Kjartan to her to Askja. *Who will catch it next?*

"He said he's on his way," Emma replied. "He should be here any minute."

"He better hurry the feck on. Kjartan shan't be happy if the lad comes 'round late again."

As soon as Nessa had spoken, Lucas strolled through the door... with company.

Eyes bulging, Askja went off on him first when she saw the vampire female by his side. "Who the hell is this?"

"This is Bayley." He introduced her by giving her hand a soft tug. "She is with me."

Nessa fake-sneezed the word *"Ijit"* into the bend of her elbow.

"The hell she is!" Askja puffed her chest like an angry mother hen, and it became clear to Eve why she was the one in charge.

Lucas' *friend* was tiny but had a set of knockers on her that made Eve wonder how she didn't tip over. Her long blond hair was gathered in a big, fluffy ponytail at the back of her head. Maybe it redistributed some of her weight. She looked like a perfect little doll next to him while coming only up to his shoulder. And yet she didn't seem intimidated by the crowd.

"Hey, ah know you," the young woman shot across the kitchen at Eve, making her instantly uncomfortable. Everyone was now staring at her instead of Lucas.

Her heart gave a sputter. She'd never seen the female before in her life. How'd she know her?

"You Jordan's friend. Ah seen pictures o' you," she went on to explain in a melodious southern drawl. "He talked 'bout you every tahm he came by the clinic."

Right. Crap. Eve's ex, who wanted to drain her valuable blood like a battery to charge himself so he could walk around in the day—

"No one's heard from him in months. You haven't seen him, have ya?"

—*Aaaand* the same guy, who ended up getting mauled by Kjan's ex just for fun.

"Uhm, nope. Not at all." Eve diverted quickly. "I think he mentioned something about Alaska."

"Have you lost your damn mind, boy?" Kristján finally interrupted their merry exchange, stepping in front of Mama Askja, glowering down at the accused.

Victim number three of the infectious disease.

Eve had never seen him this scary. Not even at the club in front of Colby. "What are you thinking? Get her out of here now before she ends up dead."

"You were told to keep a low profile. Not fraternize with other vampires," Askja poked at him.

"Why? What the fuck's the big deal? Aren't we all on the same side?"

"They are nothing like us," Kristján growled. "Nobody is."

His eyes shot to Eve, and she felt a drop in her stomach. Wasn't he the one who'd reminded her that she was part of their coven now?

"He isolates us. I HATE IT!"

Yep, Lucas caught it too.

"Keep your voice down." Askja shushed him, wagging a stern finger. "If he finds out, he's going to kill her, and then he's going to kill *you*."

"This is bullshit! We're all stuck inside during the day while he gets to do whatever the hell he wants."

Now Lucas was the one glaring at Eve, making her more uncomfortable by the second. What had she ever done to him? She'd known him for five seconds.

"What makes the two of you so special?" He turned back to Kristján and Askja, who exchanged uncomfortable looks.

"Their loyalty!" The deep timber in his voice cut through the friction like a knife.

Eve's mouth fell open, and she forgot how to blink. She couldn't believe what she was looking at. Kjartan loomed at the corner to the front room, wearing a deep red raglan shirt with long black sleeves and a pair of dark blue jeans she recognized immediately. He'd been back to the condo. He was wearing Kjan's clothes.

Arms crossed over his chest, his posture appeared relaxed as he casually leaned against the end of the wall, but Eve could've sworn somebody had opened a window to let in the cold air because the temperature in the room seemed to have dropped below freezing.

"Where were you last night?" His powerful aura on full blast, Kjartan's sharpened eyes glared at Lucas. "You were the only one unaccounted for. And you neglected to answer your phone."

"I-I was with her."

"You expose us, and you dare to bring her into *my* house?" *A rhetorical question.* "What exactly did you tell her?"

"N-nothing," Lucas stuttered again, choking on his trash talk from a minute ago. "I swear."

His glance switched back and forth between Kjartan and Bayley, like he was hoping she'd confirm his story. Then something shiny streaked through the air past his head with a sharp *hiss.*

Eve's eyes went wide as she followed the sound of the thud of the metal object now stuck in the wooden pantry door behind Lucas.

Kjartan had picked a small paring knife from the unused block on the counter beside him and hurled it clear across the kitchen with deadly precision. The blade had nicked just the tip of the guy's ear. A perfect throw.

"Any more surprises I should know about?" he asked while twirling a second knife between his fingers, ready to launch it at anyone.

Bam! Full circle back to patient zero, Eve thought. His tone was so calm, it was frightening. Nobody even breathed in his direction.

"Good." He flipped the knife in the air once and caught it again by the handle before sliding it back into the block. "The four of you, take her back to wherever she lives, then go home," he continued, still glaring at Lucas. "And let last night be a lesson to all of you. There will not be a repeat."

Eve thought his eyes didn't look as bright as usual. They seemed abnormally dark and muddy. His hair was now tightly woven into a single braid.

Caleb stayed behind in the kitchen, and Kristján waited for the group to clear out before he spoke. "What of Kría?"

"I relocated them and told them to lay low. She assured me that they were not followed."

"Did you find out who was tracking them?"

"No. Whoever it was, kept themselves hidden from me."

"Who could do that?"

Yeah, seriously, WHO was so powerful he or she could hide from a God? Eve pondered.

"I have no idea, but they should be safe there for a few days." Kjartan pushed off the wall and turned to the front room.

"And then?" Askja asked as they all followed.

"And then the three of them will join us here."

"You have decided for them to come to Portland? What's changed your mind?"

"I want all twelve of us in one place," he announced in another clipped reply. His curt tone made it clear he wouldn't accept any more questions regarding his decisions.

Is that it? So much for having a big coven meeting. Lucas' surprise guest had canceled tonight's program. He wasn't going to discuss things in front of a stranger.

Or was it Eve's presence that had disrupted his private briefing with the coven? Was there something he didn't want her to know?

He addressed Caleb with a short nod. "What do you have for me?"

Eve watched the kid grab his backpack and silently hand him Kjan's black laptop.

"Go home. Tell everyone to stay put until you hear from me."

He marched off without another glance at either one of them, including Eve. Kristján and Caleb went straight for the door, but Askja hesitated, shooting her a sympathetic look.

"Don't antagonize him," she advised before following suit.

Something in him had changed, and they'd all sensed it.

Eve's eyes trailed upstairs. He no longer felt the need to disguise the commanding presence he carried. It gave the entire house a haunted-mansion vibe, and she didn't feel like spending the night to win a prize.

The overfamiliar chill skipped across her spine. *'There is nowhere in the world you could possibly hide.'*

∫

The taste of her blood sent him into a fury. Kjan pictured her face lighting up his darkness. He allowed himself to draw up every little detail of her features to fuel his fight.

Trapped in his eternal hell, he exploited what little slack he had temporarily been given…

And failed.

The chains that restrained him pulled tight once more, biting deeper into his skin. On his knees, he pried and ripped at his shackles, screaming his voice hoarse. It was of no use. Like an iron boa, the links constricted his movement, locking his hands behind his back and wringing the noose around his throat.

His captor's emotional distress had caused the unique opportunity. For the first time in his existence, the immortal felt remorse for his actions, and it made him vulnerable.

Kjan sensed his fear.

His Sire knew Eve would never truly belong to him. She could never love him. He was unworthy of her. Defective. Everyone would leave him eventually. If his own mother couldn't love him, no one else could. In the end, he would be abandoned again.

Kjan felt it all.

The cut along his forearm burned brightly, then voices began to echo in his head. Voices he didn't recognize spoke of the old prophecy. A parallel.

Hands pushed at his chest, casting him back into darkness. The immortal was forging a plan, and he wouldn't reveal his next move to him.

Kjan was running out of time. Every day that passed, he grew weaker, and the lunar tetrad was nearly over.

Sightless, bound, and gagged, he felt himself being dragged under water, the air draining from his lungs as the level rose above his mouth and nose.

Cut off from all his senses, his consciousness drowned in absolute numbness.

CHAPTER

51

I t wasn't until hours later that he came to her room. His temper had cooled, and Eve wondered what in the world had gotten into him. *He* was the one who bit *her*. What reason did he have to be so irritable?

She ignored him, her eyes glued to the 17-inch screen in her lap, as he approached and sank onto the bed across from her.

Was he bored? Looking for a playmate?

Stretched out on his side, knuckles at his temple, he watched her with intent. She felt the heat of his glare on her forehead, her fingers sweeping across the keyboard, relying on the buffer between them.

She couldn't focus. And it didn't help that she kept reading the same line over and over just to avoid glancing in his direction. She would have to rework the entire essay. It was littered with typos or plain gibberish, but that didn't matter as long as he didn't turn the screen.

She wouldn't engage in his selfish games. Wouldn't indulge him—

The screen snapped shut, giving her only a split second to save her fingers.

Her eyes lifted from his hand pressing down on the lid to his face. With a look of exasperation, he removed her shield and tossed it aside.

He was like a cat, knocking over a vase to get attention.

Fists slowly digging deeper into the mattress on either side of her, he shifted his weight. He leaned closer, decreasing the distance between them, his eyes roaming, prowling before the pounce.

His hand reached out, and Eve winced. Brushing her hair back over her shoulder, he frowned at the puncture wounds on her neck.

"You need to feed. Your body is not healing."

He didn't sound apologetic, merely pointing out the facts.

"You've been back to the penthouse." Eve acknowledged his outfit with a quick glance. She wondered why he suddenly felt the urge for a wardrobe change.

Kjartan stalled his reply. Lips slightly parted, he tapped the tip of his tongue against one of his upper canines, reminding her of how frightening he was.

"I needed a change of clothes," he said at last.

And that wasn't all. He had also showered. She recognized the fresh scent of Kjan's shampoo and body wash.

Bullets of rage fired through her veins. "What did you find on the laptop?" she blurted.

Damn. She should be heeding Askja's advice, but Eve just couldn't help herself. "You could've asked me anything you wanted to know."

His breathing was calm, but she knew better than to trust his temper. She had a clear view of his irises, and there was a slight purple tinge in the center, as if the red was trying to break through. He was out of control and his mood dangerous.

"I much rather see it with my own eyes than take your word for it."

Eve scoffed. "You still don't trust me? You don't trust anyone, do you?"

"I have no reason to trust you. I do not know you. You are the final page of the book I have yet to finish writing."

The look in his eyes was unreadable. His face didn't show any emotion. And his mood swings were unpredictable at this point. Every time she thought she had him figured out, he did a complete 180°.

"You think I would lie?"

"I *think*"—he stressed the word—"you need to feed."

"No!"

Eve shoved off the bed past him and moved closer to the door. Better to have an exit strategy. Though there was nowhere for her to go.

Kjartan's gaze narrowed as he came to the same conclusion and charged for her. His steps precise and focused, he backed her up, and then her sweaty palms were flush with the door.

With one heavy blow, his hands slammed down on either side of her head simultaneously, trapping her inside. Nostrils flaring with each vigorous breath, his chest expanded and contracted at her eye level.

His nails scraped at the wood while he scowled at her defiance. The intensity of his stare was no less demanding than his physical conduct.

"Why did you do it? Why did you bite me?" Her voice was as weak and shaky as her body, but she needed to hear the answer from his mouth.

Cocking his head, he lowered his left hand to cup her jaw. His thumb swept over her bottom lip. Eyes stone cold, he flashed a cruel grin. "Because I could. I take what I want."

Eve's hands balled into fists to give the door a soft *whack*. "Urghhh! You're so arrogant."

"I am self-assured."

"There's a difference," she sneered up at him.

"And what is that?"

"Knowing what you're good at versus believing you are better than everyone else at everything." Like the prideful way he spoke, for example. And another thing she had noticed was that no one, besides her, cussed around him. Did foul language offend him?

Kjan had been the image of confidence. The man in front of her was a tyrannical prick.

Dammit! Eve growled inward again. She hated comparing the two.

Icy stare drawn into slits, Kjartan regarded her with a mix of anger and curiosity. He knew what she was thinking.

"You *will* feed. Do not make me force it on you again."

That was it. No one forced himself on her. She would never be a victim again. She jerked away, and then her open hand shot out, her palm slapping him across the face before she could stop herself.

Shock forced a whimper from her throat, her eyes wide in fear. Shrinking into the door, she clasped her hand over her mouth.

What had she done?

The ground beneath her feet started to shake, rippling from his fury. The light from the desk lamp flickered.

He didn't meet her eyes. Still facing away from the force of her slap, the muscles along his jaw twitched, clenching hard.

Without a word, he snatched her wrists and shoved them back against the door, pinning them above her head. Lips curled into a snarl, he hovered over her, seething with anger. Heat of his wrath radiated from his body.

When his gaze lowered to her lips, her determination dwindled. She hated what he did to her. Hated how he made her feel. Her breathing trembled, and she didn't know what to do.

Eve turned her head away, but he wrenched it back toward him, releasing her wrists. Palm against her chin, he crushed his lips to hers, his kiss more vehement, more impatient than before as he asserted his demand.

Pressing her hand against his sternum, she could feel his heart pounding inside his rib cage. Her breath fell as erratic as his, and heat coiled through her, flaring between them.

With their bodies inches apart, the passion of his impulsive behavior drained the fight out of her. She let him have his way.

Renate Rowland

CHAPTER

52

E ve woke before sunrise with the taste of his blood on her tongue and both of them still fully dressed.

Kjartan had stayed with her, one heavy arm tucking her hips neatly against his own. His goatee brushed along her shoulder as he trailed his lips up her neck to her hairline. Properly fed and completely healed, his warm breath tickled the highly sensitive tissue of her repaired skin, where the puncture marks had been.

He'd refrained from making any further advances, but his blood had knocked her out cold. She'd lost hours this time. The bitterness of strong, black coffee and charred wood whirled her senses, making her head spin again.

Askja was right. He *did* smell like a bonfire. Or rather the morning after.

"Why does your blood do that?"

"Because of who my father is," he explained. "His rune is Eihwaz, the yew tree. It is highly toxic and therefore considered a symbol of death. Consuming any part but the red arils leads to cardiogenic shock. The effects of my blood are less severe in comparison. It only lowers your heart rate temporarily."

He eased back, diminishing the suffocating intimacy, and propped his head up on his right hand. The fingers of his left tucked gingerly at the hem of her shirt that had ridden up her waist.

"Kristján will take you back home at sundown."

Eve stiffened. "You're letting me go?" she asked, barely glancing over her shoulder.

"Under one condition." He rolled her over to look into her eyes. "Agree that you will only feed from me, and you are free to leave." He paused. "If you go back to the clinic for human blood or take anyone else's vein, I *will* find out. And I will make you stay. Indefinitely."

"You call that a choice?"

"I call it trust." He swept the hair out of her face and stroked her cheek with his thumb. "I will not force you to stay here. Swear you will honor the arrangement, and you can go."

"Fine, I agree," she said through her teeth.

"No. I want to hear you say the words."

What he wanted was for her to swear an oath to him—a God—so he could bind her to it. Eve understood the meaning behind his strict request. He wasn't exactly subtle.

She wavered. She could live with his stipulations, but she didn't approve of his blackmail. "I swear I will only take *your* blood."

"Thank you."

Content with her reply, Kjartan pulled away and left. Eve noticed that, for once, he didn't look smug after getting what he wanted.

Kristján knocked on her door two hours later to take her back to the city. The awkward silence on the long drive was almost unbearable; he didn't bothered fishing for small talk, and Eve hated goodbyes.

It was just as well. She wasn't sure if she'd ever see him again. Or any of them. They were back to being strangers.

"He wanted me to return this to you," he said as he pulled up to the front of the condo.

"My phone!" She'd forgotten all about it. It was surreal that she hadn't touched it in over a week. "Thanks."

He returned a tight-lipped smile that seemed forced, and she got the distinct notion he was holding something back. His cryptic expression made her wonder if Kjartan's generosity was too good to be true. What was his endgame?

She stared at Kristján for another second, and just before the silence became uncomfortable, she reached for the latch.

"Take care," she told him, pushing the heavy door open and hopping out.

"You too."

Eve gave the door a shove and watched from the curb as the dark blue Suburban pulled out into traffic. Her fist clenched around the set of keys in her pocket. She was finally back home, but instead of being overjoyed by her freedom, she felt like a reject.

∫

Kjartan's fingers curled around the low back of the chair as he spun it around and straddled the seat. The man on the other side of the table twitched in alarm, ready to jump to his feet, but Lucas' firm grip on his shoulder advised him not to.

Arms crossed in front of him, Kjartan gave the younger Cooper a long look. "Stop searching for your father. The only thing you will find is trouble."

His bodyguard buddy was still in the hospital here in Portland but was going to pull through the injuries he had sustained in the brawl.

Cooper raised his chin, keeping his hands flat on the table on either side of his drink and in clear view. "Did you kill him?" he asked, hatred flaring in his voice as well as in his eyes. They were the same dark brown as his father's.

"I did. And I will not apologize for it. He threatened someone he should not have threatened."

His mouth twitched with recognition, then his stare narrowed spitefully. "Wouldn't happen to be the pretty little thing that was with you, would it? Be a real shame if someone were to take your toy."

The chair's backrest creaked in Kjartan's grip. He unclenched his jaw and kept his tone level. "I will give you the same warning I gave your father before he forced my hand: Do not threaten what is mine. Do not hunt for anyone under my protection."

"Why not just kill me now and be done with it? Why take the risk?"

"Because I want to trust you."

"What if I don't agree."

Kjartan lowered his voice to a whisper without shifting his eyes. "The man your father shot in the head is standing right behind you. By killing your father myself, I cheated him out of getting his own revenge."

And Lucas was itching for it. He could feel it rippling off his taut muscles in his periphery.

"I might just let him take it out on you instead. I know how much he enjoys drawing out the end. He will make you beg for death."

Lucas' fingers bit deeper into the man's shoulder, his knuckles turning white. His victim let out a stifled cry as his body folded to one side.

Kjartan rose to his feet. He swung the chair around and pushed it into the table. Bracing his palms on the top, he leaned in. "You do not understand the powers you are challenging," he snarled.

Cooper shrank back in his seat, his eyes large as they beheld Kjartan's fully descended canines. "If you set foot back into Portland, if you come back looking for me and mine, you will meet the same fate as your father. So heed the advice. Let it go. Forget about me and live."

The young man's head bobbed, his face still a mask of terror. The taste of his fear, laced with credence, permeated the air. *Smart boy. Smarter than his father.*

Satisfied with that, Kjartan pushed off. Lucas followed suit, giving the man one last shove into the table. They would have to employ Caleb's skills to keep an eye on him.

He sent Lucas on patrol downtown, then mounted his bike. Before turning the key in the ignition, he checked the text he had received from Kristján two minutes ago:

It's done.

Eve was safely back in her penthouse. And none the wiser. It was time to move into the final phase of his plan.

CHAPTER

53

Almost two months had passed since Eve took his vein. The stretch was a far cry from her twelve-day fast during the Iceland trip. But as the first signs of withdrawal began to kick in, she was becoming increasingly anxious and irritable. She wasn't ready to make the dreaded call.

At the end of May, the first weekend of Portland's annual Rose Festival rolled around, and though she resented the crowds, she found herself drawn to Waterfront Park for the fair.

The sun was sitting low when Eve ambled through the carnival grounds, and the Ferris wheel caught her attention. With a sharp ping in her chest, her eyes followed it all the way to the car dangling at the top.

She couldn't possibly set foot on it. Painful memories threatened to overwhelm her, and suddenly everything became too much. The flashing lights, the smell of the food, the noise, the crowds. Her head was spinning from the excessive clutter.

Eve whipped around so fast it made her dizzy. She leaned against the steel barrier of one of the carnival rides to catch herself.

Her stomach churned. She forced more air into her lungs to fight the nausea. Her limbs tingled with dread.

She inched backward. Running her hand along the brightly colored makeshift walls of the rides to keep herself steady, she escaped the onslaught on her hyperactive senses and slipped into a crevice.

The music from the fairgrounds dulled, but as the fireworks soared above, every boom reverberated in her chest.

Cowering in the darkened space, she waited for it to end.

The following morning, she mulled in her closet, trying to pick a dress for the Grand Floral Parade. None of them sat right with her, but the fit wasn't the problem. She'd emotionally outgrown her wardrobe.

Eve needed a change. If she wanted to move on with her life, it was time to clean out her old stuff and spring for something new. For now, she settled on a strappy white dress that was formfitting and short but still casual enough to pass as a spring dress.

Completing her look with a pair of sunglasses, she blended right into the attending crowd. The parade started at 10 a.m. from the Coliseum and traveled across the Willamette River through downtown. The potency of Kjartan's blood had increased her resilience to sunlight, and she'd been spending more time outside during the late spring days without getting the urge to peel her skin off.

The floral floats were exquisitely decorated, and numerous dancers in costumes filled the ranks of the parade. Squished in the herd, Eve watched band after band go by, losing count sometime after fifteen-ish.

While disassociating from the colors and sounds, a familiar face amidst the spectators across the street caught her eye, and her stomach dropped. Before she could focus on his features, a horse in the parade passed in between them, and when she looked back to the place where the young man had stood, he was gone. She searched the nearby area for him, but he was nowhere to be found.

Eve wondered if the lack of sleep was getting to her. For a split second, she could've sworn he looked like Lucas.

She shook off the thought. It couldn't possibly have been him. It was the middle of the day, and as far as she knew, none of them could go out in daylight.

After the parade, she went home and collapsed onto her bed, ignoring the gnawing hunger that had picked up some time during the day. When she couldn't take it anymore, she decided to find a different solution to distract herself from the thought of having to feed.

Hitting up the mall downtown on foot, she browsed through the individual boutiques, not really looking for anything in particular. She was still wearing the dress from this morning, but it was looking a little worse for wear now that she'd added a few wrinkles by taking a nap in it.

She tried on a handful of other dresses in different lengths and colors, narrowing it down to a black one with a plunging neckline and a backless red number. Glaring at her reflection in the mirror, she knew damn well that she would probably never actually wear either of them.

Eve sighed. *What the hell.* She grabbed the red one again and put it back on. She would be damned if she didn't at least wear it once.

She paid for the merchandise and left the boutique, feeling no better about blowing money on her ridiculous purchase.

"Eve!"

She'd barely taken a step out into the main area of the mall when she jumped at the call of her name. As she turned toward the familiar voice, she was immediately pulled into a hug.

"Claire?" She blinked in surprise. "Are you here alone?" Eve instinctively glanced over her shoulder for more familiar faces.

"Oh, Caleb and Emma are around here somewhere," she said with a dismissive motion of her hand, her bubbly expression never faltering. "It's good to see you."

Eve returned an incredulous smile. Truth was, she barely knew any of them. "Um, you too. What brings you to the mall? Shopping or food?" she asked jokingly.

"A bit of both, actually," Claire snickered and looked embarrassed. "But I'm really glad I ran into you. I never had the chance to thank you for saving Parker."

"Don't mention it."

There was an awkward pause, and then Claire's eyes shifted nervously. "I should go and catch up with them. I totally lost track of time." Her body turned, but she threw Eve another glance over her shoulder. "We miss you," she added quickly before taking off in the direction of the large sporting goods store.

Eve looked after her for a second, feeling jealous at the fact that they all had each other. She remembered the hot minute she'd been part of their family too.

She'd eventually scrolled through all the voicemails and unanswered texts from Tanya on her cell, but Kristján's threat from the night at the club made her decide not to reply to any of the messages. She didn't know what to tell them about her mysterious absence and didn't want to lie to her friends again after everything she'd already been through with Kjan.

Dismissing the trip down memory lane, Eve turned toward the exit at the end of the food court, and once the fresh air hit her face, she felt the hunger again.

The mall was only a block from the med center where she got her blood supply, and the thought of disobeying briefly crossed her mind.

No matter how she played it out in her head, the scenarios all ended badly. Kjartan had assured her that he would find out.

Her cell phone chimed in her pocket, giving her a start. She pulled it out and glared at the screen. The number the message had been sent from no longer came up as unknown. He'd saved it in her contact list under *K*.

The text was equally short and sweet:

WHERE ARE YOU?

Eve snapped around to check her six. She was paranoid again. She sensed eyes on her, practically felt his breath down her neck. *How the hell does he know?* She hadn't even considered it until a few moments ago.

Her heart leaped out of her chest at the thought of having been followed. Running into Claire might not have been a coincidence after all. She could've been a scout, Eve figured. And Lucas, too. It *had* been him at the parade this morning.

Kjartan has spies all over this damn city. THAT'S how he knows.

Eve hurried home, feeling queasy, and her hands trembled as she turned the key. When she flung the metal bunch onto the granite counter in the kitchen, it landed with a loud *clunk* that pounded behind her eyeballs. She exhaled and took a few more deep breaths, rubbing her temples.

Don't freak out, she repeated in her head, trying to calm herself down.

She didn't want to call him. Not tonight. Not ever!

Storming off into the bedroom, she knocked the door open wide and stumbled back in another start.

Her hand shot to the wall to catch herself as she tripped over her wedge sandals from the abrupt stop, twisting her ankle in the process.

"Goddammit!" Eve yelled, stomping her foot in anger, which only made it throb more.

His dark six-foot-four shape stretched out on her bed, Kjartan looked mighty comfortable with his ankles crossed, hands behind his head, watching her hobble.

Oh, the sheer arrogance of him…

She slipped the sandals off her feet and fired them at him— "You. Don't"—one at a time—"Live here"—like she was shooing off a pesky raccoon that couldn't catch a hint. "You have no right to barge in whenever you feel like it."

He dodged them, nonplussed by her outburst. "I thought we had a deal. Where were you?"

Crap! She'd forgotten to reply to his text.

"Shopping." Her arms relaxed by her side. "But I'm sure Claire already relayed that information. Are you here to confirm my story?"

She dramatically swiped up the bag that had dropped to the ground and held it out for him to inspect her alibi.

He ignored it, making no motion to get up. Instead, he cocked his head, looking her up and down in a dreamlike manner, no doubt picturing all kinds of things he would like to do to her.

Eve suddenly felt naked in front of him, but she knew the ridiculous red dress had not magically disappeared. She refused to take her eyes off him to check, but her fingers tugged apprehensively on the short hem.

Her breath accelerated slightly as she scanned the tight black t-shirt over his chest, and her gaze traveled lower down his black jeans. Her stare froze on the boots.

The goddamn half-laced boots.

She didn't acknowledge the signals her body was setting off, but the walls of the bedroom edged inward, with the two of them essentially eye-fucking each other. He needed to go.

"What do you want?" She flung the bag onto the floor and went back to the kitchen, hoping he would follow. Which he did. It was one room closer to the front door and one step closer to getting him out. "And how the hell did you get in?"

It wasn't like he could climb up the fire escape and enter through the window the way Kjan had done in her old ground-floor apartment downtown. This was the penthouse.

Eve heard his condescending laugh over her shoulder before she turned around. "Did you really not expect me to keep a spare key?"

Hands stuffed in his pockets, he leaned his hip into the countertop and crossed his feet. He had no intention of leaving.

"I am only here to remind you of your promise to me," he stressed.

"I'm fine. I don't need to feed." That had been mildly true until she'd started freaking out tonight.

He didn't buy it, either. Folding his arms over his chest, he stayed steadfast, eyes low, studying her. "I gave you my trust. Do not break it."

Eve glanced at the large void of ink that stretched up the outside of his left arm. It looked like someone had taken an eraser to his tattoo. The entire midsection of Jǫrmungandr was gone. Had he gotten hurt?

Though his body healed, she assumed his tattoos did not. The renewed epidermis would remain blank. She couldn't imagine another explanation.

"If I take your vein, will you leave?"

Straightening from his lean, Kjartan dropped his arms by his side and stalked over to her, his eyes even more hooded, focused on their target.

"Why are you making this so hard, Eve? Why do you continue to resist?"

His hand came up. He tilted her chin and roughly stroked his thumb over her lips, forcing them apart. "Yes. I will leave," he answered her question and paused. "*After*." His eyes flashed brighter at the insinuation. His stare was pure lust.

Eve shook her head free and put her hands on her hips. "That's not what I meant. And that wasn't part of the deal."

"I allowed you to come back home, but I never agreed to let you go. I will personally make sure you will not stray."

He wasn't teasing. He meant it. He would drag her back to the cabin himself. Again.

"I want you. And you want me too. No matter how hard you try to hide it. I know you do."

She rolled her eyes. "Don't flatter yourself. You're vile."

His grin came back even wider. He leaned in closer, and Eve heard the amusement in his tone as he nuzzled her cheek. "Would you like me to prove it?"

Kjartan slid his hand under the hem of her dress, slowly inching it up the inside of her thigh to call her bluff. "Just say when."

Eve swallowed hard, and her fingers closed around the edge of the granite countertop of the island behind her. She knew without confirmation from him that she would be wet to his touch.

Her hand darted out to block his from going any higher. "Stop!"

"Are you sure?" he drawled provocatively, underlining her blush.

"I hate you."

He gave the corner of his bottom lip a quick tug, flashing the tips of his fangs. "You only hate me, because you cannot help wanting me."

It's not you I want, Eve thought, glaring, her eyes burning a hole into his skull. She really did despise him. And despised herself for the way her body responded to his touch.

"You proved your point. I can't control my body, but I can still control my mind."

Kjartan diminished the inches between them, looking proud, and Eve felt her meager armor crumble.

Drawing in a breath to argue, she made one last attempt at resisting everything he was stirring in her, but he clasped her neck on either side roughly enough to make her heart skip.

With his thumbs hooked below her jaw to force her chin up, his mouth swooped down to claim her, and they both knew this time he had her. He was the fix she needed, just like she was his, and she wanted to keep using.

Eve couldn't bear to admit the truth. She closed her eyes and held back the tears, but her mouth softened against his on its own accord. His hands moved along her throat to cradle her jawline, and when he eased his head to the side, his lips were warm and soft like velvet against her own.

Nudging her lips apart, he growled with fierce desire, his tongue pressing urgently, teasing. His fingers weaved through her hair. He tipped her head back to accept him, and she gave into the pull, swallowing his moan and arching her hips toward his.

Braless, her hardened nipples strained against the thin texture of her dress, making contact with his solid chest.

Her awareness followed his right hand as it strayed from his possessive hold on her, lazily drifting down between them to the tingling tips aching for attention. Engulfing her breast, his large palm squeezed, while his thumb went back and forth, stroking her through the wispy fabric, rubbing, and pinching.

He knew how to torment her.

Eve's mind wandered. She thought of Kjan, the way she always had, but as his movements became progressively bolder, it was so much easier to imagine him now. She wanted him to be rough. That was why pinning her against the door had been such a turn-on. She loved this savage side of him.

As her panties dropped to the floor, courtesy of his impatient nature, she focused on the dark cocoa scent instead of the bitter coffee, blocking out the woodsy pine completely to keep the illusion going. In her mind, there was only Kjan.

With her arms firmly wound around his neck, she didn't open her eyes when he wrenched her legs apart and lifted her onto the granite top. Gripping her tight, he nudged her core, and she tensed briefly, cursing with a moan.

"So vulgar," he snickered wickedly darkly against her lips.

His hands smoothed over the sensitive backside of her thighs as his nose grazed the curve of her neck, his heated breath against her throat stoking her own fire.

"Who are you really trying to fool, Love?" His mouth moved along her skin as he spoke. "You will not tell me *no*. Not now. Not ever."

Renate Rowland

CHAPTER

54

He pulled back only far enough to catch her reaction. Eve glared with defiance as her dress parted for him, insistently between her thighs. She was herself again after the momentary lapse in the woods. Unwavering. Unyielding. That crack in her armor fixed.

But he would find a way through it somehow. Wildfire blazing in her eyes, Kjartan had never desired her more.

He had tried to distance himself from the pull she had on him, but he knew there was no going back to being without her. After taking someone else into his bed, it became clear he would never get the same high he did with her.

His hands skimmed her exquisite figure, the soft curves, the firm muscles. With the switch in position, they were at eye-level, and she kissed him harder, nipping at his lips.

Frustration prickled in his chest at the ceaseless resistance of her mind when her body so evidently sided with him. Over and over, it betrayed her. He wanted more, and she wanted him too. He was sure of it.

She had stilled only for a second, face flushed bright red, and then given herself up to her lust. With her eyes closed in ecstasy, she drew scattered breaths, writhing and spasming beneath him while her heels dug brutally into the small of his back.

Her passion made him feel alive, and it confirmed what he already knew. He never wanted to be a God. Or be worshiped. All he ever longed for was to be accepted. He was an orphan, desperate to have a family. A place where he belonged.

He could have that with Eve.

Kjartan had hoped that if he let her go, she would choose to come back to him of her own volition, but he had maintained an invisible leash. He had been keeping tabs on the GPS in her cell, tracking the usual trips between the park and home.

The first time she had deviated from the routine, he had followed her to the fair merely out of curiosity.

An odd sensation had struck him in the midst of the commotion, and his hearing had sharpened to a painful degree. Something about the lights, sounds, and smells had triggered him, and he had closed his eyes for a moment to shut out the overstimulation of his senses.

When he had reopened them, he found Eve hunched over at one of the spinning rides, looking particularly unwell.

Why had they both been overwhelmed by the same triggers? Or had he somehow projected it onto her unintentionally?

Her need to feed had already been so evident to him, but she was too stubborn to admit it. She would rather starve than accept his blood. He had to offer her something that was greater than her desire to live.

To avoid another unwanted trigger, he had sent Lucas after her the second time she deviated, but of course, the careless fool had been made.

Claire had been the next logical choice until Kjartan took matters back into his own hands.

Eve's breath had caught in a panic when she found him on her bed. But the instant their eyes met, her air had changed into something carnal.

His presence had rattled her composure.

While readjusting her own lustful thoughts, she had avoided his eyes.

That dress…

He did not trust himself to pull the delicate silk over her head. He was tempted to rip it off her body, but it would be a shame to ruin it. No, he made sure that it stayed intact when he took her on the countertop, devouring her desire and feeding his own hunger.

After, Kjartan picked her up with one arm, thighs split around his waist, and carried her over to the couch, where she ardently straddled his lap.

He guided her mouth to his vein, but she broke the skin herself for once, sucking and licking at his throat with audacious fervor.

Eve took what she wanted. Her body rocked on top of him with the same confidence as that first night, and the slick fabric covering her skin moved readily beneath his touch while he adored her.

Within seconds of feeding from the rapid flow at his jugular, her heart rate slowed. Peacefully stretched out on the couch, she fell asleep, and he watched her for another moment.

Her long brown hair cascaded over her shoulder like the smooth waves of a river. She looked so much like Thórunn.

The memory of the woman he had never met stayed with him in his prison long after the man who had shared her left. For centuries, he had drawn up the image of her face in his mind. If Kjan had forgotten her, was it possible he could too? Could he make him forget the guardian angel he had embraced as his savior in his loneliness?

There were moments when Kjartan was unable to differentiate between his host and himself anymore. The deeper he dug, the blurrier the lines became, and yet he could not stop himself from going down the rabbit hole.

His limbs felt sluggish. Muscles rigid. He lacked all motivation to leave. Her nearness soothed the restlessness that gnawed inside him. He would hold up his end of the bargain, however. As she had done her part.

Before departing, Kjartan brushed his fingertips over the tattoo on her wrist, admiring the beautiful design of the wing. A spike of warmth hit the center of his chest, and acting on impulse, he gently pressed his lips against the ink on her skin.

"Kjan…," she sighed in her sleep.

The name was spoken softly, almost like a whisper, but the weight of it hung heavy in the air. Kjartan felt the blow to his gut.

Grinding his teeth, he released her hand from his grip and rose to his feet. His eyes flared red. With the swelling anger in him, a current of electricity crawled up his spine.

He clenched his fists and forced it back down as he stormed out. Painful thoughts raced through his mind:

She will reject you…

…leave you…

…abandon you like your mother…
…you will lose them all and end up alone…
…again.

But he was not a child anymore. He was not helpless. And he would never let Eve go. He needed her. He had let one slip through his fingers. He would not lose the other one too.

Kjartan remembered everything now: every single detail, all the gaps in his memory filled in. There were no more secrets his host could hide from him.

It had taken Caleb longer than 24 hours to crack the laptop, but the wait had been worth it. The computer wiz even recovered all the deleted files. Kjartan had been digging through them for weeks and finally stumbled upon the ones that had triggered it all, giving him not just access to Kjan's mind but also restoring his own missing pieces.

There was so much about Eve on the hard drive, like the future plans he had made for the two of them. But one thing had struck him the most. A letter. Kjan had penned it to her after he made the deal and then chosen to delete it. Reading the words, as the man had poured his heart out to Eve, the jealous monster had seethed within him.

Kjartan had taken the liberty of deleting the letter permanently, leaving no trace of the truth. She believed Kjan had discarded her, and it would stay that way. She would never know his sacrifice. Never know how much he had loved her. Never know how hard he had fought to hang on.

He knew she was willing to give her body over to him, but he would never possess her heart. She would never truly be his unless he bound her to him.

Now that Dynja, Kría, and Erik had joined them here, he was just waiting for the right moment. The number twelve, considered perfection, was believed to be most in touch with the energy of the universe and signified all things whole, complete, and final.

Eve's initiation would be on the night of the last eclipse, and with the power of the lunar tetrad, he would bind her to him for all eternity. With all twelve of them present, his plan was truly *perfect*.

HE WOULD HAVE HER.

All of her.

CHAPTER

55

E veryone was making a big deal out of it. They called it a *trifactor* on the radio. This year's Blues Festival happened to coincide with the July 4th fireworks and a total lunar eclipse.

Which is only the fourth one in less than seven months.

Eve didn't get the hype. She was totally over this 'mysterious' and 'rare' blood moon bullshit. But she *was* excited for tonight's concert.

The Bowl, the informal amphitheater of Waterfront Park, was already packed and probably had been all day. There were people drinking, smoking, and holding up their phones to record the show as far as the eye could see. Considering the mass of couples huddled together on blankets, Eve fell back. She had no desire to squeeze into a tight space with strangers. Instead, she took a spot leaning against a tree, singling herself out. Per usual.

She'd chosen her latest purchase, the little black dress, for the occasion and already regretted her decision. She was drawing more attention than she was comfortable with. There had been a guy with a goatee earlier whose gaze had lingered just a little too long, and now even the woman behind her seemed to size her up. It made the hair on the back of her neck stand on edge.

Though Blues wasn't usually her cup of tea, the music was good, and the band really kept the audience going.

As the announcer took the stage and drew the crowd's attention to the sky, everyone started cheering. Except for Eve. She scowled at the full moon. It would be a few more hours before it started its disappearing act.

The fireworks show kicked off shortly after, and everybody joined in with their *oohs* and *aahs.* Giant spotlights shining onto the crowd blinded her eyes, and the overwhelming reek of marijuana assaulted her nose. It instantly reminded her of Bobby.

The two of them used to go to concerts together regularly back in the day, though his taste in music had been a lot tamer compared to her Metalcore preference.

Kjan hadn't cared for music at all. He'd sat in silence for hours… brooding. His mind, always lost in the past, had never reached the future. Never made it further than the present.

Like a shiny diamond, Eve had watched him from a distance. Admired his infinite, brilliant facets that reflected the world around him, but let nothing breach the impregnable surface.

For Eve, music was a lifeline. She couldn't imagine living without it. It was what kept her going. She looked toward the future now and the things she could still affect. Not the unchangeable past.

The noise from the huge speakers flanking the stage picked back up again at an insanely loud volume, and she had the urge to draw back further toward the walkway. She felt the bass vibrate through the air, raising goosebumps on her skin.

While assessing her options, she caught two familiar faces in the crowd that made her heart sink. Tanya and Caleb sat together near the shore of the Willamette.

Eve waved awkwardly at them, but only received a tight smile in return. The empty gesture made her feel more isolated than she'd felt in months.

Maybe it was the stench of the pot, but her heart was suddenly heavy, almost sluggish. As the tightening in her chest built on her sense of dread, she considered heading home and crawling into bed.

In her absentmindedness, she didn't notice the dark shape approaching until she felt the tiny pinch at her neck. She spun around too late, dazed by the rushing sound in her ears as her heart raced.

The tall, blonde woman grabbed her arm, and she recognized the pair who had caught her eye before. Their vampire presence still didn't register. Eve could only think of one explanation.

Whatever they had injected her with was working fast, counteracting the adrenaline rush. Without resistance, she was being dragged away from the crowd, and no one even noticed. The last thing Eve saw were the merch vendors. She lost consciousness before they even left the park.

When her eyes flew open again, she couldn't orient herself. An earthy scent invaded her nose, so heavy she could taste it.

She was underground, staring at the stone ceiling of a cave while she slowly blinked herself out of the blackness.

Eve had done this rodeo too many times to panic. Her brain quickly put things together: the man, the woman, the festival. The couple hadn't been ordinary vampires like Jordan. They didn't want her for blood. They were Kjartan's.

She pushed herself off the hard stone floor, and more sharp rocks cut into her forearms and elbows. The air was stale and cold, spreading shivers over her exposed skin.

Dang. Drugged and kidnapped again! And she hadn't brought her punch card.

But the stupid dress with the plunging neckline didn't have pockets. She had no phone either. Her one key was... yep, still there. She could feel it on the inside of her high-heeled peep toe bootie.

Eve sat up all the way. Loose stones dug into her hips as she shifted. She braced herself on one hand and wiped the back of the other across her mouth. Her throat was dry from inhaling the chalky dust visibly floating in the air. It made it hard to swallow.

She looked around. The chamber was dimly lit by large black candles. Pools of wax surrounded them as more dripped down along the sides.

The first thing that struck her was the Helm of Awe etched into the ground underneath her. The eight identical arms of the symbol were easily recognized. It didn't seem part of the original *décor*, though. It must've been added more recently.

Against the back wall, Eve could see an altar with an offering bowl in the center and statues of the Gods arranged in a semi-circle around it. Yet the most impressive item in the cave's chamber stood in between the two. It was a large, throne-like armchair made entirely of stone. It looked rather uncomfortable, but Eve assumed its purpose was more to intimidate than provide relaxation.

The piece was gorgeous nonetheless. Intricate designs had been carved into the stone along the armrest. It had a very tall back in proportion to the rest of the seat, and Eve recognized the design engraved in it from a distance: The Web of Wyrd.

The symbol featured nine staves that were arranged in an angular grid and contained all the runes. It represented the past, the present, and the future, as well as their inseparable connection with each other. The Matrix of Fate was also called Skuld's Net, named after the Norn who weaved it. Since they determined fates and lifespans, these ancient Goddesses were considered the Shapers of Destiny.

This is his temple, she realized in shock. *Why am I here?*

Wondering how long she'd been unconscious, Eve rubbed her head when she heard Kjartan approach with Kristján. They were deeply engaged in conversation, and it sounded like he addressed his lieutenant with a question.

Kjartan didn't seem to like the answer. He was visibly irritated, jaw ticking and brows heavy as he frowned. Whatever he was planning, it didn't seem to be going in his favor.

Blondie and Goatee from the festival stopped on either side of her with chains in their hands, which they anchored to the ground. The female pulled Eve up, and her eyes dropped to the blood stain by her feet. It was startling in size and almost blended with the color of the stone.

This was the spot. This was where he had killed Kjan—or *'sacrificed his soul for the greater good'* as he had put it.

This was where he had bled out.

Panic fluttered through her as horrible images flooded her mind. Eve felt sick. Bile rising in her throat like acid replaced the air.

On a new surge of adrenaline, the words exploded out of her. "What is this?" She charged toward him while the woman held her back by her upper arms. "Did you bring me here to boast? You expect me to worship you the way *they* do?" Her body twisted with rage.

Kjartan drew closer, bearing down on her. "Know your place," he hissed through clenched teeth.

A wispy little flame flickered in the dark center of his enlarged pupils. "Your impudence is beginning to annoy me, Eve. I have tolerated it long enough. I am a God and you will recognize me as such."

"Or what?"

"Or I will make you," he threatened in a dark and malevolent tone, utterly void of any form of affection for her. He didn't sound like himself. Something in him had changed.

"Get the others." He nodded toward his minions before returning his attention to her.

The candlelight flickered from all the motion. Eve stood her ground, holding her chin high, once the female released her.

Kjartan's eyes roamed down the deep plunge of her dress, his teeth tugging at the corner of his mouth. "I can see why he did not want to leave you. You really are everything a man could want."

She grimaced in confusion. "Didn't want to leave me?"

She knew something didn't add up the second his mouth twitched as though he'd unintentionally revealed a secret. She tried to back away, but he caught her upper arm, fingertips delving brutally into the muscle.

"You're hurting me. Let go!" Her voice cracked while wrestling in his hold to get free.

His right hand grasped her throat and jerked her toward him. He lowered his face to hers, the tips of their noses touching.

"NO!" Kjartan growled, powerful enough to make her tremble.

The spell was broken. Eve was no longer fooled by his charm; there was no more light in him. Only darkness.

And pure evil.

Renate Rowland

CHAPTER

56

His electric blue eyes bounced back and forth, never blinking, daring her to cave first.

"Do you want to know what I found on his laptop?"

Beneath his harsh hand, Eve's throat narrowed further, dreading his answer.

"Everything!" The word left his lips like a revelation. "I remember it all now."

His grip released her arm, and he reached for the leather string, clasping the set of rings dangling from his neck. "He still loved her, you know? His wife. You were nothing more than a sad little replacement for him. She was the real deal. And he was happy to forfeit his life to reunite with her."

Kjartan confirmed all of Eve's worst fears, and yet his words fell on deaf ears. "No. No. I don't believe you," she choked out, shaking her head vehemently. "You said he didn't want to leave me."

His left hand slipped from the wedding bands. She couldn't look at them.

"He chose *her*, Eve. You know the truth. I can see it in your eyes. He abandoned you. He does not deserve your love. Foreswear him and submit to me. I am all you have left. I will never leave you."

The more he spoke, the clearer it became to her. He'd denied that he hated the Gods for his unjust imprisonment. He wasn't fueled by hate. Abandonment and rejection were his accelerants. It was fear that pushed him, and he would say anything—*do* anything—to claim what he thought he deserved as retribution.

Eve understood at last. "I don't know how, but I know you tricked him. It's what you do. You lie... and you cheat. You killed him."

"I did not lie."

Kjartan squeezed his palm tighter around her throat. The little flicker of hope that had sparked in him extinguished, and his cold mask of indifference dropped back into place. "Just withheld certain details. For instance, how out of the original twelve I sired, five had still been alive. Do you want to know how his predecessors died?"

Eve stayed mum again, trapped in his hold, his fingers biting into her skin. He leaned in, his lips right by her ear. "*I* killed them," he breathed.

Eve's legs went soft. The only thing keeping her from collapsing was him.

"One by one, I tracked them down and drained their blood in hopes of increasing my powers to break the curse. They had not been hard to find, after all, having never left Iceland in the first place. But also because they had been complete."

"Complete? What do you mean?"

"When creating one of your kind, every Sire consequentially leaves a part of themselves within them, a piece they cannot recover until the *unfortunate* demise of their neophyte."

"Like Kjan and Andromeda?" she muttered. He had regained the missing piece of his soul when she died. Eve still had a remaining sliver.

"Yes. But I neither have a Sire-bond with her nor you." His grasp relaxed as he possessively stroked his thumb along her jawline and tipped her chin higher. "The connection only carries over to the one sired directly and not into their next generation. This imperfect state, however, makes them harder to track since parts of them are scattered in different places. The vampires that my first generation sired had already perished, making them vulnerable and easier targets in return. I believed I needed to kill them all to make myself whole again, so I hunted them. I ripped their pumping hearts from their bodies. I felt the last beat in the palm of my hand."

Kjartan sighed, his features hard and his gaze distant, as if he were picturing the past.

"But my theory was flawed. Tracking them down and killing them did not make me stronger," he continued, refocusing. "I knew Kjan was the key. My lucky number twelve. Unfortunately, after turning Andromeda and inevitably splitting his immortal essence, he had simply dropped off the radar altogether. I had been left to resort to other methods of pursuing him and eventually followed the gossip, chasing him to the New World. I found Andromeda and raised her from her watery grave off the coast of Alaska by sacrificing one of my human acolytes. But even with my blood temporarily increasing her powers, she failed to lure him in. Instead, the pathetic wench tried to kill him."

His voice took on a bitter edge for a second. "*'Hell hath no fury like a woman scorned'*. I should have foreseen that. Still, I gave her another chance to prove her loyalty and bring him in, yet she failed me again. I believe you are familiar with the rest of that story."

Eve couldn't believe her ears. Her entire world crumbled at her feet. *He* was the one responsible for Andromeda nearly killing Kjan and coming after her. Eleanor was dead because of him. So was Charlotte. And Jordan… he'd been right all along about the *Ancient One's* presence in the States.

Her lips quivered, but she refused to cry in front of him again. "You told me you believe in fate."

He cocked his head, eyes narrowed into slits. "I do."

"But you were trapped, destined to spend all eternity in a cave, and now you're trying to change your fate. How is that not cheating?"

Still clasping her throat, his lips curled into a cynical smile, and he fanned the fingers of his left hand through her hair. "You are thinking too linearly, Love. Does the thought of a predetermined future scare you?"

"It makes me feel like I have no free will."

"It is quite the opposite," he explained, his eyes burning into hers while he swept a lock behind her ear.

If it weren't for him cradling her head like he was about to snap her neck, his expression seemed almost reverent.

"Your destiny is only limited by your imagination. You do not know the future. You might think you are not meant to achieve a certain goal, but what if I told you that you are supposed to fail a hundred times, only to succeed the hundred and first? If you really want something"—his gaze drifted down to her mouth—"never give up."

"Why are you doing this?" she whimpered.

"You are mine, Eve." Kjartan leaned down, his lips barely brushing hers as he spoke. "And once I bind you to me, you will accept me too. You will do whatever I want."

He kissed her tenderly, but there was no warmth in his devotion. No sweetness. The gesture held a bitter taste, like the dusty silt in the air.

She didn't return his kiss, her lips rigid and unmoving, and he drew back, seemingly irked. "He left you, and still you cling to him? You really are hopelessly pathetic. You leave me no choice. I will repeat the ritual tonight." He tapped his index finger on her forehead. "I would advise you to find your happy place and hold on to it—*real tight*—because this is going to hurt."

Repeat the ritual... ON ME?

Fear shot through her. In a fight-or-flight response, Eve pushed both palms into his chest and was surprised when he let her slip free, but she didn't hesitate. The instant his hold fell away, she reeled her right fist back. If she could get a shot at his Adam's apple, it might stun him enough to follow up with a left hit to his eardrum.

Knuckles aimed at his throat, she kept her other hand prepared to strike next.

Kjartan never even blinked. His forearm came up to stop her attack immediately. He deflected her first blow and then the second, as though he'd read her intentions.

Of course. He knew her combos.

Eve tried again, but he blocked her next attack as well, and then sidestepped before her leg so much as twitched to lift off the ground for a kick with the pointy end of her heel.

He was too fast. Too strong. She couldn't beat him. Each new attempt was thwarted without effort, his expression almost amused.

Kjan's instructions echoed in her head: *'If an opponent is holding on to you, press down on the area between the thumb and index finger.'*

When she swung out again, he caught her wrist mid-air, and Eve saw her chance.

If only I could—

The moment his grip closed around her wrist, a jolt of electricity ran through their connection. It raced all the way up her arm, shoulder, neck, and higher still, where the shockwave exploded inside of her head.

Eve smothered her cry, but her knees buckled from the pain.

He didn't let go. "STOP FIGHTING BACK!"

"Never!" she vowed, thrashing in his grasp to regain her freedom.

Flames burst from the center of his pupils, instantly snuffing out the electric blue of his irises. The fire bathed his eyes in a blaze of red from corner to corner, swallowing every last bit of him that had still appeared human.

Kjartan increased the intensity of the surge rushing through her. She couldn't fight the scream this time.

How is he doing this?

"You look surprised, Love. Kjan never told you about all the little tricks he had up his sleeve?"

"You can create lightning?"

"Not exactly. Think of me as a black hole," he clarified. "In this modern world of yours, there is always some kind of current or energy flow in the air. I simply manipulate it. I am a little more skilled at it than he was."

She couldn't take it any longer. Eve closed her eyes tightly as they started to fill with tears when her wrist suddenly slipped from his grasp, and the current went dead.

She braced herself for his next assault, but nothing happened.

One second went by… and then another… still nothing.

Her eyes sprang back open to find him staring back at her, unmoving, his hands hanging listlessly by his side. Something made him hesitate.

With his defenses down, Eve took her chance. She crouched low, swinging her leg backward to sweep his out from under him, her hair whipping in motion.

Making no attempt to avert the maneuver, his body went lateral. His upper back hit first, and then his head collided with the unforgiving ground of the cavern. He never even tried to break his fall.

She heard the crack of the impact and took off. Heart racing, she ran for the door and pulled with both hands on the iron handle to open one side, then froze.

The giant blonde Amazon who'd brought her in stood guard outside. No sign of Goatee.

Eve had to improvise. Her chest clenched. Her jaw tightened. She cranked her shoulder back to gather momentum and then rammed the heel of her palm into the female's left brachial plexus, dropping her with one blow.

YES! Fists balled, she tucked both elbows toward her body in a cheer. She couldn't believe that had worked on the first try.

As the tall blonde went down, she cracked the back of her skull on one of the large iron floor torches. She was out before she had a chance to make a move. Apparently, Kjartan hadn't wasted his time teaching her how to fight.

"Pressure points, bitch!" Eve resisted the urge to throw in a *Suck It* gesture. She wasn't free yet.

She dug through the immobilized Amazon's pockets and found the key to a Dodge. Another small tremor of euphoria went through her.

As she sprinted toward freedom, her steps echoing up the narrow stairs, she hoped not to run into any more of his henchmen. She wasn't entirely sure she could take on one of the guys.

Luckily, the tunnels were deserted, and she made it through the open gate at the entrance. Hunched over, catching her breath just for a second, she tried to get her bearings. The tunnel she'd come out of was the entrance to some kind of mountain cave, and the surrounding woods were dense and dark, which made it hard to see far. She found the Harley and only one other vehicle in the dirt lot:

A black Ram.

The sound of a car approaching set her body back on high alert. Eve lunged for the truck to dodge the beam of the headlights, her heels sinking into the soft ground.

Crouching behind the front wheel, she hid out of sight. Doors opened and slammed shut, followed by rushed footsteps. Either the female had called for help or Kjartan himself had alerted them.

Eve cautiously rose to glance over the hood and recognized Lucas and Parker. The second their bodies disappeared through the entrance of the cave, she unlatched the driver's side door and slid behind the wheel.

Slamming things shut, she fumbled with the key. The metal skipped around the ignition as she frantically glanced over her shoulder, expecting more backup. Eve clutched the steering wheel with her left hand and finally managed to shove the key home.

When she cranked it, the cruel rumble under the hood was ironic. She was making her escape inside the very truck that had crashed into her Tahoe.

Eve threw it into reverse and floored the pedal. Gravel popping beneath the tires, she gunned for the main road. She had no time to waste. They would be coming for her.

J

Kjartan awoke on the ground with no recollection of how he got there or what had caused him to black out.

He felt the blood drip from his nose and quickly wiped it. The last thing he remembered was holding on to Eve, and then, out of the blue, the current had reversed back into him.

"Kjan!" He growled, grinding his teeth.

From all the times he had felt him writhe beneath his skin before, never had he been able to command his body.

"Why won't you just die? You conceded your body to me. It wasn't supposed to be this way."

A terrifying thought occurred to him. The lunar tetrad was almost over. What if the possession was not permanent?

Dynja burst through the doors first and stopped short at the sight of him, her eyes wide.

"What happened?" Lucas' voice echoed over her shoulder. Parker next to him looked just as puzzled, trying to make sense of the scene in front of them.

"She got away. I'm sorry," Dynja apologized, rubbing the back of her head.

He felt their eyes on him as they anticipated his reaction to the bad news. He should have kept Erik here instead of sending him out with Kristján and Kría. He was too close to let this all fall apart now.

Kjartan took out his phone and called Askja. "How far out are you?"

"We're still at the loft. Claire locked herself in the bathroom. She won't come out."

His grip tightened around the flimsy cell, and it creaked under the pressure. They had less than two hours until the eclipse, and his window was closing fast.

"Leave Caleb with her and bring Nessa and Emma here now." He hung up and dialed Kristján next. "She's at the condo. Get her and bring her back!"

Blind rage seeping from his pores, he rose to his feet and stomped over to Parker. His left fist shot out, seizing him by the front of his shirt. "Get your sister here now. Break down the door and drag her ass out. I don't care if you have to snap her fucking neck. You'll do whatever it takes."

He glared at his reflection in the kid's wide eyes, watching the red consume the green of his irises until it matched his own, eradicating all free will.

Defeat was unacceptable. Insubordination would not be tolerated. And compliance was no longer optional.

Once he had Eve back in his grasp, he would bend her, too. Bend her until she broke.

CHAPTER

57

E ve unzipped her black leather boot and retrieved her key. The skimpy dress really hadn't been one of her better wardrobe choices. Without the GPS on her phone, she'd relied solely on road signs to get her back to the city, never even taking her foot off the gas while flying down the winding mountain road.

At least her key hadn't fallen out during her prison break. She dropped the slippery thing twice before finally jiggling it into the lock. She didn't know how much time she had, but she needed to change out of this ridiculous dress first. There had been no oncoming traffic up to Mount Hood or signs of reinforcements in the rearview mirror, which only assured her that they were already downtown and closing in.

The whole drive back, she'd tried to come up with a plan. She knew she couldn't keep running forever, but maybe she didn't have to. She just needed to buy herself some time.

Eve moved through the living room, aiming for a particular book shelf. It was the one with the hunting knife Eleanor had bequeathed her. The space beside it was vacant. Just like she remembered.

"Where is it? Where did you put it?" Her eyes scanned the rest of the shelves. She'd searched the entire place so many times and never found Andromeda's stake. She knew now that Kjan never used it on himself.

But the narrow piece of wood was gone... and so was her only hope. Eve couldn't let herself get caught before finding it.

The throaty roar of a truck echoing from the parking lot curdled the blood in her veins. She didn't need to check the window to confirm that it was Kristján's Suburban. She'd expected him to be the one sent after her.

Eve swiped her keys off the bed and froze with her grip around the metal objects.

The Charger.

It was the one place she hadn't searched. She'd never even started the engine.

She rushed out of the penthouse and into the building's hallway, flinging open the steel door to the stairwell.

The crisp sound of footsteps carried to the top from the floor below, cutting off her escape route right as the elevator chimed behind her with the acute *ding!*

Shit! She was stuck.

Eve let the heavy door fall shut and darted for the corner of the plant nook between the two penthouse suites. Peering through the bladed leaves, she watched Kristján step off and walk into her place like it was the son of a bitch's own apartment. The stairwell door opened two seconds later, and a pair of vampires followed him inside.

Beads of sweat formed at the back of her neck. Hidden behind the fake shrub, she waited for the door to shut behind them before leaving the shelter of the recess and then sprinted for the still-accessible elevator. She gave the button for the garage a blow and exhaled the long breath she had been holding.

With a stitch in her side and her heart punching up her throat, she ripped the driver's side door of the Charger open. She figured she had about ten seconds until they put two and two together and started looking for her down here.

She checked the center console and rummaged through the knickknacks. Coming up emptyhanded, she reached for the glovebox next. Something toppled onto the floorboard on the passenger side, but her eyes stayed glued to the long piece of dark orange wood sticking out of the compartment.

Jackpot! "I love you," she whispered, as if Kjan were sitting right next to her.

Eve didn't have time to admire the beautiful luster of the stake. She angled it at the small of her back in the waistband of her jeans and tugged her t-shirt down to cover it.

Leaning over the center console again, she fumbled for the item under the seat.

She frowned at the black box in her hand. Her fingers brushed over the smooth velvet, and she hesitated to open it. Why would he hide this in his car?

Now or never, she told herself, flipping the top.

Her heart skipped at the sight of the beautiful bracelet. It was silver in color and in the style of a traditional Viking cuff, but instead of depicting animal heads at each end, delicately twisted wires formed the shape of a wing on one side and an arrow on the other, curving in opposite directions.

She knew without a doubt that it was unique. The design matched the tattoo on her wrist exactly. Kjan had this specially made for her and chosen all the details himself. Even the little triangular emerald that was set into the arrowhead.

Tears filled her eyes as she gently took the bracelet out of its box. The flat cuff was about a quarter of an inch wide at the halfway point, and as she turned it over, she saw the words engraved on the inside:

I will always be with you

Eve felt the sharp stab in her chest and wanted to scream, but her breath got caught in her throat. He had commissioned this after making the deal with Kjartan, knowing he wouldn't be around anymore.

They had pledged themselves to one another, and she'd betrayed him. Given up. She didn't deserve this.

Heavy with guilt, she put the bracelet back in its box and picked up the black lid. A note fell out onto her lap, but she barely got a glance at it.

Eve yelped as rough hands grabbed her arm to yank her out of the car. Kristján towered over her, glaring, and his entourage didn't look any friendlier.

She didn't fight back as they dragged her to the truck, then shoved her into the rear. The male, Erik, she remembered now, stayed with her in the back, while Kristján and the female got in the front. It wasn't the Amazon from the temple earlier. Her hair was a much darker shade of blonde, and she was only about Eve's height.

Pointing up at the moon, she said something in Icelandic to him that had the word *minutes* in it.

The eclipse! That had to be it.

Kjartan himself had told her how magically significant the lunar cycles were in Pagan rituals. That was what he had been waiting for. He was on a deadline.

Kristján pulled the Suburban onto the obscured path to the cave and turned toward the woman next to him, killing the engine. "Join the others. I bring the girl."

Erik slid out and handed Eve over to the giant, then the pair hustled inside. Kristján looked after them over his shoulder, and once they were out of sight, he shoved her hard against the truck.

"You stupid girl. Why did you have to run? You should have known better than to make him angry." He paused and almost looked sympathetic. "If you want my advice, do not fight him, and he might still take it easy on you."

Eve scoffed. "Take it easy on me? What exactly is he going to do to me?" In her mind, she kept seeing the pool of Kjan's blood on the ground.

"It's better you don't know. I'm sorry, Eve... I really am." His lips pulled tight, like he didn't want to elaborate further, and he turned his eyes toward the moon with a heavy sigh. "It's time."

Renate Rowland

CHAPTER

58

Gripping her upper arm, he towed her to the entrance. The light that was thrown off by the single torch didn't reach far; the narrow stairwell remained in darkness. More sweat dripped down her back despite the chill in the air, and Eve couldn't get enough oxygen into her lungs.

She tried to stay calm as they made the descent, the wooden stake chafing at her skin with each step. She felt like the cave was swallowing her up until a warm glow emerged from below. The large doors were flanked by two wall torches, she hadn't noticed in her rush earlier.

Kristján forced her back through the gaping mouth of the grand chamber, where she counted seven figures in heavy blood-red robes standing in a wide circle around their leader.

Eve's heart started galloping in an irregular rhythm, like a horse with a limp, when she saw their glowing red eyes in her peripheral vision. The muscles in her neck were too stiff to turn her head. The only sound in the temple came from a fire crackling on top of the altar.

Yay! More Fire.

As they approached, the group parted to let them through, and her eyes dropped to the unknown bindrune drawn in blood on his bare chest. He loomed over her, his hood pulled low over his face, a red glow emanating from underneath like a heating lamp. The illumination engulfing his head cast a beam down at her, catching her mercilessly in his searchlight.

His scent had turned from the comfort of a bonfire to a raging forest blaze. Eve pictured the burning evergreen trees in his eyes, flames surging, laying waste to all life.

The crippled mustang in her chest thrashed. Hopelessly.

Lucas stepped forward from his place in the circle. With his dark eyes and buzzed hair, he had always been the most frightening of the bunch, but now he was as terrifying as Kjartan himself. His red irises matching the group's, he was following orders without any opposition.

He went around and grabbed her wrists from behind as Kristján handed her off to him. He pinned her right arm to her chest, leaving her left one stretched out by her side while he locked her against his front.

Kjartan kept his watchful eyes on them. There was movement behind him, but Eve couldn't see over his broad shoulders.

"Who's pathetic now?" She provoked him. "You need them to hold me down?"

"I do not *need* them to hold you. Their presence serves a different purpose."

"You're a coward. You will never be half the man Kjan—"

"I AM NO MAN!" he bellowed, his hand shooting out to grasp her jaw in a vise.

Brutal fingers pulled her face up to him, and black exploded in the center of his eyes where his pupils had been. They were once again the dark orbs she recognized from the night of the bar fight. The matte color reflected no light from the candles.

"I am above any mortal," he said in a tone of indisputable superiority. "Next time you speak his name, I will cut your throat from ear to ear. You will pray for death to liberate you, but it will never come. I will not let you die. I will watch you bleed out, and right when you think you are finally free, I will bring you back. You will always return to me, Eve. You belong to me."

He removed his grip and straightened. Then Kristján approached and put something in his hand. "Every time you think of him, I will hurt you until there is no more love left and you associate his name with nothing but pain!"

"That will only make me hate *you*. Not him," Eve hissed, her voice shaking.

"But it will be *his* face staring back at you… smiling as you scream."

Her sight dropped to the long metal rod clenched in his left hand. It had a symbol at one end the size of a silver dollar and looked like a branding tool for cattle. The tip of it was glowing orange.

Panic lanced through her. Her breath caught. Her stomach lurched. She shoved against Lucas, flailing and kicking, when Kjartan grabbed her hand to hold her arm steady.

Her knees buckled.

Fingers curled into fists.

Eve turned her head; she couldn't watch.

There was only pressure at first. Her brain couldn't distinguish between hot and cold. She heard the sizzle of her skin… then felt the prickling, and then…

Eve screamed.

The voice of her pain tore out of her chest without restraint. It rang in her ears as it pelted down from all sides of the cave. No longer a single scream, the sound fractured, and a hailstorm of echoes assaulted her on their return with amplified clarity.

The smell of hot metal and burned flesh clogged her lungs. After seemingly endless seconds, he removed the iron from her skin and pressed his palm against the wound.

The burn surged a second time. Eve's eyelids fluttered as she nearly lost consciousness.

Then, at last, the torment stopped.

She was pulled back onto her feet. Kjartan's crude grip replaced Lucas', and the boy took his place among the others, leaving the two of them in the center.

Her skin itched like it was already healing. Eve raised her arm into view and looked down at the mark of the branding. It was identical to the bindrune on his chest, but it was a bright cobalt blue in color.

She rubbed her fingers over it. The ridges were not smooth like the tattoo on her other wrist, and there was salt in the wound, preventing it from sealing properly. It throbbed with an electric hum, like there was a strange current connecting her to him.

"W-what is this?"

Kjartan shrugged coldly. "A little token of my affection. Do you like it?" His tone had lost its authoritative edge. He sounded more like his sly self now. It was no less frightening.

Eve opened her mouth but realized her reply was irrelevant.

"NO!" Claire's scream ripped through the tunnel. "Parker, stop. Please. Don't let him do this. She saved your life." She dug her heels into the ground, thrashing, as Caleb and her brother dragged her in. "Caleb, listen to me. Don't do this."

Nobody was paying attention to her pleading, almost as if they were under some kind of spell. The boys jostled her to join the other eight and held onto her arms as they flanked her, closing the circle.

Eve felt her hope drain away, replaced by a coldness settling in the pit of her stomach. This was bad. She could clearly see them with her eyes, but she was unable to sense their presence. Any of them. They could turn the radiance of their aura on and off the same way Kjartan was able to, and now he was controlling them with his will alone. There was no getting through to them. He played brother against sister. They were acting like mindless drones. Even Askja and Kristján.

All of them but Claire.

"Seems she's not following you so blindly anymore," Eve taunted.

"The more of my blood they consume, the more control over them I get. She'll eventually come around." Her back toward him, he turned so that they both faced the altar. "It doesn't matter as long as there are twelve of us present."

It was so subtle, Eve nearly missed it. Not one contraction, but two?

Had the crack to the head given him brain damage? His personalities kept switching, like he was trying out different roles to find one that fit.

"Is everyone really replaceable to you? Just a vacant spot in your circle waiting to be occupied?"

His lips brushed her ear. "Not everyone."

Eve stood in front of him, trembling, as he swept her hair back over her shoulder and pulled her close against his chest. She prayed that he wouldn't feel the stake hidden in her waistband. Kjan had carved it himself, and the sentimental value it held was so fitting. Almost poetic.

Her eyes fell to the dark stain on the floor again. A golden dagger lay beside it, reflecting the flickering candlelight.

"Don't worry, Love. Not a single drop of your precious blood will go to waste." He spoke in a husky voice that was too intimate for the circumstances. He didn't acknowledge their audience. The coven was only a fixture of the temple for him.

"*Byrit!*" He shouted his command toward Askja and Kristján, who stood closest, and on his signal, the lot began chanting in a low hum.

Eve didn't fight him. Not this time. She squeezed her eyes shut while his fingers crept up the base of her neck and twisted around her hair. Slowly, he pulled her head to the side, not hard or violently, but in a doting manner that perverted the gesture.

"Can you feel it?" he asked, reverence dripping from his voice. "The darkness swallowing the light of the moon?"

She could tell how much he was enjoying the torture of drawing it out. "Don't fear its power, Eve. Embrace it. Let it elevate you and ascend as a queen by my side."

Pursing her lips, Eve said nothing.

An angry rumble erupted from the depraved hollow of his chest. "I will drain you and force my blood on you over and over again as many times as it takes to bend you to my whim. You will accept me. I will beat the defiance out of you if I must, but I will have my way."

"You will never own me. You can never truly possess someone by force," she said, spitting Kjan's words back at him.

It was all she managed before Kjartan cut her off. His fangs struck. All four of his canines came down on her, slicing through veins and arteries alike.

The seal of his lips fixed on her skin, she felt the life slip out of her, draining her with each pump.

Her body swayed. He dropped to his knees, taking her to the ground with him, and sat back on his heels, his dedication unyielding.

Fear seized her heart. How far would he take it? How far could she let this go until she wasn't able to pull through with her plan?

As she slumped in his arms, his fangs retracted to bite into his own wrist. Still holding on to her from behind, he brought it to her mouth, but she didn't open up. Eve clamped her teeth shut as tightly as she could.

Kjartan didn't take her disobedience well. He ripped her head back hard, and her mouth opened.

The taste of his blood was harsh and bitter. No more chocolate. No more cherries.

"I will watch your defiance unravel as you tremble in my grasp," he growled, trapping her head between his hand and his forearm. The power behind his words rippled through the air. "You will give yourself over to me, Eve. In the end, you will be on your knees, worshiping me. I know who I am now—who I have always been. I *am* the monster."

Eve wanted to throw up. She had that wretched sensation where you were so drunk that you thought the room was spinning, and you knew only expelling the toxin from your body could bring relief.

Only this time, it wouldn't. The cycle would repeat and repeat until HE determined its end.

Was this how it had been for Kjan? A helpless victim? Too weak to fight him?

His voice in her ear lowered back to a murmur, only loud enough for her to hear. "He fought back, too," Kjartan whispered. "Fought back *so* hard. I have spent months with his voice in my head."

He tightened his grip on her even more. "But I found a way to shut him up. I broke him, and I will break you, too."

Tears started streaming down her cheeks. Eve couldn't breathe. Snot and blood blocked her airways while her body convulsed. She was drowning, unable to stop the rush from his vein, but consuming more was the only thing keeping her conscious. The moment she stopped swallowing, it was over.

"You were right. I did lie," he breathed down her neck, making her tense in his hold. "Kjan didn't want to die. There was a letter addressed to you on his laptop. All the things he couldn't say to your face. He did it all for you, Eve. To keep you safe from me. Once I threatened to hurt you, the pieces fell into place. In my favor, naturally."

His fingers at the back of her head weaved affectionately through the tangles at her hairline, mocking her ignorance. "His only stipulation was that I leave you alone. I wasn't allowed to come after you. But you found me, and I had my loophole."

His words cut deep, slicing through her heart like a knife. Kjan had warned her. He'd sacrificed himself for her, and she'd resented him for leaving.

"Do you want to know what his last words to you were?"

She already knew—

DON'T HESITATE!!!

—The words from the note appeared on the inside of her eyelids as she squeezed them harder.

Eve was done listening to him. He could not hurt her anymore. She felt numb. Reaching for her back, she clenched her fist around the fine grain as tightly as she could and slid the stake free. Her mind was made up. Her determination unwavering.

I won't.

Kjartan removed his wrist from her lips, and she felt his body shift toward the golden dagger on the ground beside him. With a steady hand, she plunged the stake's tip into her own chest.

Renate Rowland

CHAPTER

59

After everything he'd done, she still couldn't hurt him. Still couldn't see past the face of the man she loved with all her heart. Taking her own life was her only option to escape the fate of becoming his drone.

She braced herself for the imminent pain.

There was none. No agony. No suffering. She didn't feel a thing.

Eve opened her eyes. Kjartan's acolytes stood still, frozen in their place, no longer chanting. She looked down at the length of wood in her grasp, fingers still curled around it. His hand had gripped the stake, stopping her from driving it through her heart.

His warm breath settled on her neck before he spoke. "That wasn't the plan, Dove."

"Kjan!"

Eve spun around, locking onto his deep green eyes in confusion.

How?

Her mouth hung open, but she didn't get the word out. Their lips collided like the crack of thunder as he crushed her against him.

Enclosing her face with his hands, he silenced the chaos in her mind. They obliterated the air between them with one deprived kiss turning into another and another, his fingers tangling in her hair, while Eve clawed at his chest out of desperation to convince herself that it was real. That she was not imagining him.

Suspended in time, they stole the precious seconds for themselves, neither one of them getting enough.

Panting, he came up for a breath. "I'm sorry... Eve. I'm so damn sorry. I tried... I tried to stop him. I swear I did." His voice hitched, trembling as he touched his forehead to hers.

"Every time he hurt you... that was my fault. I let him take me—" He choked on his words, tears flooding his eyes.

'Let him'? Hardly. No, he'd been forced into this. Didn't have a choice. *She* was the one who'd *'let him'*. And Kjan had been there this whole time. Knew what Kjartan had done. Knew what *she* had done. *Knew* about everything.

Eve's mind rattled with guilt. "I thought I lost you. I thought you were gone... Kjan, I didn't know you were still—"

He dismissed her with a shake of his head. "There is no time."

Kjan picked up the stake and put it back in her hands, the heel of her palm at the butt end, the tip aligned with his heart just above the bottom two ribs on his left side. "Punch it. As hard as you can."

WHAT?

Like the recurring tide, panic flooded up again, pulling her under. "No! No-no-no, I can't do this." She shook her head in protest.

His emerald gaze lifted back to her—

Oh, how she had missed the stunning view. She couldn't imagine his long, dark lashes closing forever. Not by her hand.

"You have to," he insisted. "I can't stop him. No one but you can. This is your only chance. You have to take it."

"I can't…"

Sobs garbled her speech, tears falling like rain. "Please, don't make me do this."

Eve wanted to pull her fingers free, but he cradled her hands in his and squeezed them reverently. "Promise me that you'll live. Don't do what I did. Don't let the darkness swallow you. There's too much light inside you. You have to live for the both of us."

Noses touching, his expression was stern. His tears dried up. "Let me go, Dove. Please."

"I can't lose you again."

"You won't. I promise." He lifted his hand, knuckles tracing the curve from her temple to her cheekbone. "I will always be with you… right here. Never forget that."

Tilting his head, he pulled her in for one last kiss, his touch gentle, deep, and burning with a passion hotter than the flames of hell. A kiss that was all him. "I love you, little dove. So very much."

With a shaky breath against her lips, his hand drifted to the back of her neck, and his grasp around the stake tightened, steadying it for her.

All she had to do was run it through the heart of the man she loved.

"I'm not ready—"

Her words caught in her throat. It happened so fast Eve didn't have time to scream. One hand collared her without warning, then the other released the stake and joined the noose of bone-crushing force at her windpipe.

NO!

Stunned, she stared up at Kjartan, cold blue irises shifting to red as the stone floor of the cavern crashed into her back.

Overpowering her with ease, he laid her out and straddled her hips, pressing his thumb deeper into the notch between her collarbones.

Eve felt her body go limp. The stake slipped from her hands. Spots floated in her vision, blurring the image of him above her. Grip unrelenting, his weight became excruciating. Her pelvis nearly cracked under the pressure.

She would die at *his* hands.

The last thing Eve saw was his twisted face, ruby eyes burning into her, and just as she began to slip away, his grasp loosened. She was suddenly able to drag air down her throat and into her lungs.

When her eyes started to clear, she saw why. The red in his glassy stare was fading, and with the reversion, hope clawed its way to the surface.

Kjan's fighting for control.

Holding her at arm's length, one of his eyes gradually changed from purple back to blue; the other one followed a second later, turning green. In a bursting motion, his palm released and he darted upright, his body rigid, unmoving on top of her.

Eve drew in a choked breath, unable to process what was happening. There was no awareness in his gaze. He didn't blink. His chest didn't inflate.

Her relief was foiled. Joy never gained a foothold in her. Eyes rolled toward the ceiling, and arms slumped by his sides, she watched him slip off. He crashed to the floor, unimpeded.

All at once, as if someone had powered them all down, the rest of the coven collapsed in the same manner around her. They lay there, incapacitated, like their leader.

Eve flung herself back around. "NO!" she called into the nothingness, clawing at his cloak to rouse him. Her fingernails dug into the fibers as they shifted against his rigid muscles.

"No!" she repeated, her voice more desperate now, trembling through tears. He couldn't be dead. He couldn't—

She sensed no life force, no spark of his soul for her to draw on.

It was over…

He was really gone…

The anguishing sound of her grief detonated inside the vast temple chamber, ripping her chest open and shattering her heart along with it.

Wailing, Eve threw herself onto Kjan's lifeless body.

Renate Rowland

CHAPTER

60

K jan slammed flat onto his back. It wasn't as hard as he expected. The ground beneath him was soft and damp. He was no longer underground in the temple.

"Arise, warrior."

His eyes flew open at the sound of the voice, and he sat up. A thick gray fog surrounded him, making it impossible to tell where the sky met the earth.

The silhouettes of two men pierced through the haze in front of him, one bright and the other dark. Kjan blinked at the shapes, clutching his temples. His head throbbed like he had been hit by a semi-truck.

"You have fought valiantly," the one with black hair said with a sullen expression.

"Now choose!"

Kjan frowned. "I don't understand. Choose what?" He slowly pushed to his feet, still clasping his skull to keep it from splitting in two. "Am I dead?"

The blond one of the brothers extended his arm, pointing at the distance behind him.

Kjan turned around to follow the gesture and saw a woman cradling a newborn. Her brown hair was tied in long, intricate braids with flowers in them, and he recognized her before his eyes could focus. He knew her in the dark—her scent, her warmth, the feel of her body entwined with his.

He darted toward the pair, racing like his life depended on it, and the moment he reached them, he fell to his knees at her feet. "Thórunn," he choked out, his voice shaking.

Wrapping his arms around her waist, he pulled her in close, his face buried in the folds of her robes.

"Elskan mín."

My Love, she addressed him in the same affectionate way she had always used, only calling him by name when scolding him.

Her tone, now warm and gentle, could turn viciously sharp, he remembered. She had been fierce. A woman no man wanted to cross, not even him. Nothing but childbirth could have brought her down.

The infant cooed in her arms, sparking something painful inside him.

"Forgive me."

The words spilled out of him in his mother tongue. Clasping her hand, he pressed her palm to his lips, then her fingers, kissing them one by one, desperate for proof that she was in fact real, standing in front of him. *"Please forgive me,"* he begged. *"It is all my fault. I should not have left you."*

"Kjartan, look at me."

Kjan complied, and she wiped the tear off his cheek.

"There is nothing to forgive, my love." She smiled, touching his face. *"All is as it should be now."*

Renate Rowland

CHAPTER

61

The fire on the altar had gone out, and only the faint light of a single candle remained. Eve refused to leave his side. She couldn't bring her body to move. Entombed alongside him, she stayed right where she'd broken down, her head still resting on his chest.

There was no breathing other than her own. No second heartbeat to comfort her in the darkness. Even the last of her tears had soaked into the soft cotton, which retained traces of his scent.

She'd found closure, even gotten her goodbye, but she didn't know how to let go. With her eyes closed, she could see his smile, hear his laugh, feel his touch as if it were real.

She held on to the illusion. Clung to the part of him that was alive inside her. A spark that would never die.

A nonexistent draft prickled across her nape.

Eve lifted her heavy eyelids to the disturbance. Bathed in a soft glow, the shapes of two men appeared in front of her.

Their bodies illuminated the crypt, and she had to squint. Her eyes failed to adjust to the change after too much time in the dark.

"A vow was made, and blood was spilled. Intentionally or not." The one with the golden hair addressed her first, his face kind and open. His irises were as blue as the sky.

The one with the black hair kept his eyes downcast. His tone was glum but not malevolent. "My son broke the oath he made to you and therefore forfeited his claim to the vessel," he added.

Son? The word echoed in Eve's head. That would make him Hǫðr and next to him was his brother Baldr. They were the Twin Gods—light and darkness in perfect balance.

On closer examination, Eve recognized the similarities in their faces. They had the same light complexion, the same straight nose, and sharp jawline. Their expressions, however, could not have been more different.

"We granted the host the power to retake what is rightfully his, and he has fought honorably," Baldr said.

"He has made his choice."

"What choice?" Eve looked frantically back and forth between the two.

Hǫðr raised his gaze and regarded her intently. Eve almost forgot that he was blind behind those stunning seafoam green eyes. "We bestowed upon him the honor of taking his place with his family in Valhǫll alongside the Gods."

"Or return here, to this realm, in his former state," Baldr explained, taking his turn.

"He has made a wise choice," Hǫðr emphasized, his pale eyes sparkling like a pair of diamonds.

His twin placed his hand on his brother's shoulder in agreement. "A wise choice indeed."

Then the radiance of their aura began to fade, and the shadows behind them expanded, swallowing their shapes in a cloud of black.

Eve was alone again.

In the dim light of the last candle, her gaze drifted over the serene features of his face, the strong lines among the shadows.

Kjan was at peace. After all this time, he'd earned his way home. He'd gotten his wish to reunite with his wife and daughter.

Eve tried to be happy for him. No one deserved the honor more. But she couldn't deny the pain of his choice. It tore her in half, and she knew she'd never be whole again.

She forced the stale oxygen down into her lungs, willing her heart to beat and compelling her body to move. He wanted her to live. Had given his own life to guarantee her survival. She couldn't let him down. The permanent imprint of his aura—his very being, his essence—was still alive in her. She had to make it out of here.

But what about them?

Eve peered around at the group of misfits she'd come to care about. She got no read on their heartbeats either. What was she supposed to do? Lock the doors and bury her memory of them deep inside the mountain as if none of this ever happened?

Her shoulders dropped with a sense of inevitable acceptance.

Turning back to Kjan, she took his hand and raised it to her lips, pressing them to his knuckles. His skin was still warm.

Eve's heart fluttered. She hadn't imagined it.

His fingers twitched.

Eyes flinging open on a gasp so abrupt and violent it startled her, he shot upright. His chest heaved with each deep breath he drew, staring at her in a moment of utter bewilderment... and then his face lit up.

Eve's reaction was immediate. A cry of immeasurable joy burst out of her as she hurled herself at him, winding her arms tightly around his neck, terrified that she might be dreaming.

But he was real. He was alive. His strong arms held her protectively, his body enveloping hers, swallowing her up when she climbed into his lap.

It was him. All of him. His kiss seared her lips and set her skin on fire. The taste of him on her tongue, his scent filling her lungs, he set her aflame. Inside and out.

∫

His sigh of relief muffled against her lips. Kjan pulled back. Cradling her head, fingers splayed, he let his thumbs graze the bottom of her earlobes and studied her face like he hadn't seen her in years.

He saw the resemblance now. The immortal had been right. His mind unlocked, he remembered everything. Not only his own childhood memories but also his Sire's.

"I thought—" She choked, weeping again. "I-I didn't think you would come back."

Kjan wiped the tears from her cheek and cupped her chin in his hand. "I will always come back to you. Not even death could stop me."

"But he said you still love her. I thought you would choose to stay with them."

"I saw her. I got a chance to say goodbye… make amends. That's all I ever wanted. She is my past, and she will always be a part of me, but I'm not that man anymore. You are my present, Eve. And my future. How could you doubt that I would choose you?"

She hung her shoulders, dropping her gaze. "I'm sorry, I gave up—"

He cut her off, lifting her chin to meet his eyes. "You have nothing to apologize for, do you hear me? Nothing," he repeated firmly to reassure her. "Now let's get out of here. I want to be as far away from this wretched place as possible."

With a quick up-and-over, Kjan heaved her off his lap and jumped to his feet.

Eve frowned as he pulled her up and tugged her toward the exit. "What about them? You can't just turn your back on them!"

"Why not?"

She stopped dead, and her hand slipped from his. "Because Kjartan made a promise to them."

"That was *his* promise, not mine," he defended himself.

Eve's posture stayed resolute. "They need a leader. They need you."

Seriously? "The hell they do!" he balked. "I didn't sire them. They're not my problem."

Arms crossed in front of her chest, she glared at him. "You could have turned your back on me, but you didn't," she finally spat out. "You chose to save me because it was the right thing to do."

He couldn't believe that he was having this argument with her right now. He just wanted to go home and never come back here.

Stunned, Kjan shook his head. "That is so not the same! How could you possibly compare yourself to them? You saw what he turned them into. How he controlled them. They're a pack of rabid wolves who just lost their alpha."

"Exactly."

"I'm not it." His fists balled involuntarily.

"What about Claire? She didn't want this. She fought him till the end. You're just going to leave her with the rest of them?"

"You don't know if there's anything human left in them. He was the one who turned them. They were connected to him, not me."

"And with him gone, they're lost. They need an anchor. They need *your* help," she pressed, trying to convince him to change his mind. "You are kind, loyal, honest, and just. You take care of others. It's who you are. It's what I love about you."

Eve closed the space between them and took his hand. "I believe this is who you're meant to be."

He let her words sink in before replying, then hung his head with a sigh. "I can't do this."

Eve put her other hand on his cheek. "No one but you can." She threw his own words back at him. "I believe in you. Whatever he took from them to turn them into this, you can give it back."

"You're asking me to choose them over you?"

"Of course not. But I've waited almost seven months, and I will wait longer. I'll wait forever. *I will always be with you.*"

And then she did it again. The message on the back of the bracelet. The last-minute addition he had requested. The words had been meant for her, but now held just as much significance in return. She was so much braver than him.

The group around them began to stir, and they both tensed at the same time. He couldn't be sure how the others felt about their sabotaged plan, but he wasn't going to put Eve at risk until he found out for himself.

"Go!" he told her, taking the spare for the Suburban from his keychain and putting it in her hand. "They'll be looking for someone to blame. I handle them, and then I'll find you."

He gathered her into his arms with a heavy heart and kissed her one last time before sending her off.

Renate Rowland

∫

CHAPTER

62

E ve passed out the second her head hit the pillow. The sun had come up on her drive back, and after everything she'd been through tonight, there had been no fighting to keep her eyes open, no matter how anxious she was to see Kjan.

She sensed his presence on the balcony when she woke up. Her heart skipped at the view of him against the backdrop of the city's skyline. He was like a fever dream. A mirage.

Back turned toward her, hands braced against the railing, he was a sight for sore eyes in his dark jeans and simple burgundy Henley with the sleeves bunched up. He looked like himself again: ruggedly alluring.

His hair hung loose and was no longer touching his shoulders.

Eve stifled a chuckle. She would bet money that it had been the first thing to go. She could picture him taking a knife to it himself. It was probably too soon to tease him about the fact that his hair had been as long as hers, braided and beaded.

Goddamn, she had missed him. Eve stood there for a moment, taking all of him in. She couldn't believe it was true. She'd dreamed of this, hoped for this so many times, and now he was really back.

She opened the sliding glass door and stepped outside. He didn't move, keeping his eyes glued to the sky.

"I see you finally got that haircut," she heckled.

He didn't react.

"Kjan?"

She walked up behind him and followed his gaze to figure out what was captivating him. There was nothing she could see.

"Kjan!" She repeated his name, but he still seemed too engrossed in whatever he was staring at to hear her over his shoulder.

Puzzled, she swung her focus around to him, and then her legs nearly buckled as she caught the blue glow.

"Kjartan!" she gasped. Her breath hitched in her throat.

He blinked and turned to her, smiling, his eyes green again. Slipping his arms around her waist, he kissed her softly on the lips. "I didn't want to wake you."

Eve's heart thundered behind her sternum. Was her mind playing tricks on her, like some kind of PTSD?

It took her a few seconds to recover her speech. "What happened after I left?"

"I told them the truth."

"Then I assume they all hate me now."

"I explained what really happened. None of it was your fault. Trust me, they won't so much as breathe on you without me present. You have nothing to worry about."

His words comforted her, but it was his body she took solace in. The warmth of his skin chased away her paranoia, and her tense muscles loosened in relief.

"Besides, I told them how you stood up for them, and that meant a great deal. After their connection was severed, they were left crazed… irrational. I gave them my blood, and it gave them back the part of their awareness he had replaced with his own will. If you hadn't convinced me to stay, they probably would have turned on each other or killed humans. Who knows?" Kjan swept her hair behind her ear and gingerly caressed her cheek. "They owe you."

Eve had almost forgotten how gentle and tender he could be when he wanted to. She leaned into his touch and covered his right hand with her left.

His eyes flicked to the blue symbol on her wrist, and abruptly, his posture stiffened.

"I can't stay." He pulled away, looking down.

A jolt of panic shot through her like lightning. "What's wrong?"

"Nothing. I'll be back." He kissed her forehead and then withdrew his hands from her waist.

"When?" she asked as he turned away from her.

"I don't know. Soon," he added over his shoulder, sounding irritated.

"It's the mark, isn't it?"

Eve knew she'd hit the nail on the head when Kjan stopped in his tracks.

"I'm fine. I don't care. Honestly, I think I blocked out the whole thing. I don't even remember."

"But *I* do!" Facing away, he stood poised in the middle of the living room, caught between her and the door.

A long pause followed before he turned on his heel with a heavy sigh. "I remember driving the hot iron into your skin... I remember holding you down... I remember everything."

His voice turned ragged, and he grimaced in frustration. "I have all his memories, and no matter how much I wish I could erase them, I cannot. I recall everything I did to you."

"You mean everything *he* did to me," Eve corrected.

Kjan shook his head. "It's all the same to me. There's no difference."

His face grew hard as his eyes raked across the ceiling, and his expression switched from regret to something else. "Why did you have to go to Iceland?"

"W-what?" Eve stammered.

"You were supposed to stay *here*. In Portland." His eyes briefly darted to the floor, chasing the stabbing motion of his forefinger, and then back up to her with bitter reproach. "He never would have found you."

She stared back at him blankly. "You're blaming *me* for this?"

His words struck like a dagger in her heart. She wrapped her arms around herself, the shock of his resentment robbing her of any further words.

Kjan bit his lip as though he wanted to take it back. He took a step toward her, but Eve gave him a dismissive wave of her hand and turned her shoulder, unable to maintain eye contact any longer.

He just stood there in her periphery, rooted to the ground and keeping his distance.

Had she really expected they could just *kiss and make up* and everything would go back to the way it had been? He wasn't the same anymore, and to be honest with herself, neither was she.

Eve pulled her shoulders straighter. "You never talked about what he did to you. You kept yourself closed off." *If I'd known the whole truth sooner…*

"I didn't want you to know."

"You didn't trust me to stand by you. You had no confidence in *my* feelings, either."

"It wasn't about you, Eve." His stance tensed, muscles rigid from head to toe as far as she could see. "I couldn't admit to myself how he made me feel. Weak. Powerless. You have no idea how badly I wanted to wring his little neck when I saw him."

Eve sensed the deep hatred welling in him, lips pulled back over clenched teeth as he spoke. "I blame myself. For everything."

Her voice faltered. It had never occurred to her that he could feel responsible for someone else's action. He was beating himself up to the point where he couldn't even be around her.

His words deflated the anger swelling in her. "I would never blame you for what he did," she whispered.

"I know. But he made you doubt my feelings for you, and you blindly fell for his lies because of my secrets. I drove you right into his arms."

Ah! There it is. Drove her into his arms… and his *bed.*

She'd been waiting for the other shoe to drop. He was not just playing the martyr. There was another reason for his disposition.

Eve felt like she'd cheated on him, and maybe Kjan had come to the realization that it was the same for him. He'd been too quick to assure her that she'd done nothing to feel guilty about, but what if she'd fallen too far from his grace and he could not forgive her after all?

She stayed angled away from him. "I never doubted your feelings. I just thought… I thought they hadn't been enough. *I hadn't been enough.*" *Not compared to her.*

"You didn't believe that I love you?" His tone turned defensive, hands gesturing aimlessly. "After everything… you-you really thought I could just walk away from this?"

"That's what you wanted me to believe. That was your plan, wasn't it?"

He hunched his shoulders as her accusation struck him mute. "You're right. I did," he admitted. "I wanted you to hate me. It would have made things a lot easier."

A tremor ran through her gut. Eve's lips quivered. "I'm sorry to be such a great disappointment."

She spotted the anxious twitch in his fingers. He was deciding his next move. They were both out of ammo to fire at each other.

His back straightened as he settled on a choice.

He was going to walk out.

Shifting his weight, he pivoted toward the door. When he spoke, his voice was strained, but the bitter edge was gone. "I will be back. I promise," he said, tight fists at his sides.

Then he left, and Eve stood alone on the balcony, blinking back more tears.

She stared at the branding again. She would have to live with this memento forever.

CHAPTER

63

Kjan couldn't get the image of her out of his head, her oversized t-shirt hanging off-kilter as her shoulders sagged. She looked so much tougher with the hardened expression on her face. She had aged decades on the inside. Her eyes, the ever-sincere windows to her soul, were darkened by pain and experience.

His fingertips still tingled. He had wanted to hold her so badly. But he couldn't touch her. For seven months, he had wished for nothing more than to be with her, and now here he was, alone, back at the damned temple.

She had doubted his love. She had truly believed that he took his own life. What was wrong with him that he hadn't been able to show her how much she meant to him?

Kjan stood in the heart of the chamber and closed his eyes, listening for the voice in his head. It didn't speak to him, yet its silence was deafening. Crushing him even.

He was a fraud. And a coward. Because in his heart, he knew that he had not really defeated the immortal. In that last moment, right when he had been about to kill Eve, something had shifted, and he had chosen to yield, handing the reigns back to Kjan willingly.

He could keep telling himself that he was in control, but it was still a lie. The oath to relinquish his body was still intact. He had given his word, and thus remained bound to it, terrified that his Sire would overpower him any time he wished. They were forever linked to each other. How could he look Eve in the eye, knowing he couldn't protect her?

Kjan sat down where he stood. The hours ticked by, and he could sense the impending sunrise far above him. Legs crossed, he didn't move from his spot in the center of the Helm.

In the temple's familiar darkness, he focused his eyes on the snake's head biting its tail and fought to keep them open until he lost the battle. When he woke, his worst fears were confirmed.

Staring at the same stone ceiling, he immediately felt the weight in his hand. He was sprawled flat on his back with the dagger in his left hand, the sleeve on his right arm pushed up to the elbow.

What did he do?

His eyes searched the floor first and were then drawn to the altar. The small copper offering bowl was not in the same place it had been last, and a single candle burned beside it.

Hesitantly, Kjan rose to his feet, the dagger in his hand becoming heavier with each step he took, dreading what he would find.

As he slowly approached the altar, he read the words on the stone plate, written in his own blood.

The dagger slipped from his grasp, clanking to the ground, and he left it where it landed. He forced his mind to calm down, wondering if there was another way to interpret the message. Then he reread it, again and again, until it sank in.

∫

Recognition struck Kjartan as he watched Eve drive the wooden stake toward her heart. He had been so focused on Kjan being a threat that it had left him blind to the truth.

Now he understood the meaning of the prophecy. It was *her*. Eve had been the answer all along: *light in appearance, soft to the touch*. His restraint—the strongest chain ever built—was love. He had fallen for her and was now bound by the instrument of his own forging. He himself had put the very shackles in her hands.

But Eve did not return his love. She was in love with someone else, and the reality of her choosing death over him had made him snap. He had directed all his rage at her, lashing out, ready to oblige her wish.

That was when he had crossed the point of no return, ultimately breaking the oath he had no knowledge of making.

His ignorance did not grant him an escape. The punishment was still death. And to add salt to his bleeding wound, his own Sire had been charged with carrying out the sentence. Kjartan had felt the cold tendrils of his father's shadows coil around him, prepared to rip him out of Kjan's body like he was no more than a chore.

But to his surprise, he had been offered a plea bargain instead. The question of whether to concede or die was an easy one. The God of Darkness' power to snuff the life out of any living creature would have sealed Kjartan's fate in a heartbeat had he refused to yield.

He was granted clemency… through imprisonment.

But there was a bright side to his punishment.

CHAPTER

64

The suite was quiet when he turned the key to let himself in. He found Eve in bed, clutching the sheet to her chest. She didn't open her eyes, but he knew she was awake.

Kjan quietly slid in behind her. Pulling her up close against him, he kissed her shoulder.

God, he needed her just as much as she needed him. Her emotional grid was a tangled mess. It set his skin on edge.

"I told the coven that I have no desire to be in charge," he said, nuzzling the crook of her neck. "I made it plain that they're free to follow their own path."

He had promised Askja to check in on all of them again, and he had every intention of making good on his word. Kría was staying with Kristján in Portland Heights, but Dynja and Erik had moved into the cabin with him. Well, Erik was supposed to. Apparently, he had switched places with Parker. He had found out by walking in on the guy going down on Dynja. Kjan wished like hell his Sire hadn't opened that door.

"How did they take it?"

Eve's question shattered the images forming in front of him, but her words came out flat and emotionless. Even her natural bouquet of spring flowers was faint.

She's pulling inward... ripping away the morsels... my breath...

Kjan swallowed to find his voice. "Kristján stepped up. He's going to take on more responsibilities. Dynja and Askja have been the hardest to accept it."

Askja wouldn't even look him in the eyes.

"What about Claire?"

Face turned away, Eve's tone remained aloof. He couldn't read her. The tangle of emotions he had sensed was slipping from his feelers.

Did his touch even sooth her?

He didn't dare adjust his arm to hold her tighter. What if she pulled away?

"I kept my distance," Kjan replied, trying to hang onto the fraying tether between them. "I don't blame her for being bitter. She's still giving Parker the cold shoulder. From what I hear, she's taken a shine to Erik, though."

Eve fell quiet after that. Too quiet. The moment stretched into another, and then another, choking him with her silence.

With a tremble, she dragged in a slow breath, but still, she didn't speak.

Kjan brushed his fingers through her hair, sweeping strands from her forehead, when he noticed that she was fighting back tears. The heavy scent of spring rain hovered in the air, burning his lungs.

"Talk to me," he begged. "Please." Her silence tore him open. He would rather have her scream at him than endure her retreat.

Her breath hitched. "I let you down. I hate myself for what I did." Tears streaked down her cheeks, and she hid her face in the pillow.

Yes, the agony had been too much to take, and he had nearly given up right there, but he could find no flaw in her.

Kjan propped himself up on his elbow. "Eve, please, look at me."

She hesitated, but then answered his plea and met his eyes.

"You did *not* cheat on me. *I'm* the one who left." He wiped the tears from her face. "He swore he wouldn't hurt you, and I was foolish enough to believe him. I never thought that he would use his powers against you. When he did, I fought with everything I had to take over and reverse the current, but I never should have let it come that far. I gave up when I should have tried harder."

His voice cracked, and he had to pause to gather himself. "You almost died at my own hands. I'm the one who let *you* down."

"That's what the two Gods meant," Eve blurted, like she had an epiphany. "Baldr and Höðr said he'd broken his blood oath to me, so they intervened and gave you back control."

"I don't recall swearing a blood oath."

Eve scooted around and sat up straight. "Back at the cabin after the altercation at the bar, the night of the third eclipse, he swore that he wouldn't hurt me. He cut his tongue when he made the promise. The Twins called it *unintentionally.*"

"I remember." Kjan huffed in disbelief. "He had no idea. He wanted to prove what he was capable of, not swear an oath. He never even realized his mistake. He trapped himself."

"I think until he used his powers against me in the temple, he never actually meant to hurt me. Physically, anyway. He preferred psychological abuse." She knit her brows in anger. "It was all just a game since I first laid eyes on him in Reykjavík."

"He didn't know who you were," Kjan explained. "He mistook you for someone else."

"I know." Eve slouched back down next to him and put her head on his chest.

Kjan stretched toward the nightstand and reached for the little black case he had dropped there. "I should have given you this sooner."

He flipped the lid of the box open with one hand and flicked it off the side of the bed. As he lifted the cuff from its velvet nest, his glance shot to her hand wedged under her chin. Not the one with the matching tattoo.

Maybe the shiny platinum will distract from the bright blue eyesore.

He slipped her tiny wrist through the opening and rotated the solid part to the inside, so the designs were facing out, the wing curving up and the arrow down. Then he gave it a light squeeze to keep it from slipping off her delicate hand.

"It's beautiful." Eve brushed the tip of her index finger along the outside of the arch. "How did you think of this?"

"You're my inspiration," he whispered. Laying his head back against hers on the pillow, he took her left hand and entwined their fingers.

"How did he do the color?" Eve asked as Kjan grazed his thumb over the bindrune on her wrist.

"Cobalt pigment, mixed with salt. It heals blue, transferring the color to your skin permanently."

"What does it mean?"

"*Life in Death.*" He traced the two individual runes to point them out to her. "Bjarkan and Eihwaz. It's his signature."

Lowering their linked hands, Kjan stalled for an instant before sharing the next detail. "I have the same. He carved it into my heart when he turned me."

Eve tensed. "That's what you meant when you said you were different from me."

"It doesn't matter. It's in the past." He pressed his lips to her temple tenderly, reassuring her.

Slipping his fingers out of her grasp, he brought his palm up close to hers without letting them touch. "Watch this."

Kjan concentrated on the rippling sensation in the center of his back. As the current gathered in his vertebrae and crept along the length of his spine, he forced it down his arm to flow through his hand over her skin.

Little blue sparks discharged from his fingertips and passed onto hers.

"Woah!" Eve's eyes widened, watching in amazement as he trailed the miniature lightning bolts up her arm, raising goosebumps in their wake. "Why did you never tell me you could do this?"

"I used to only draw it out in anger. It's *his* power. I always hated it. Besides," he shrugged, "I could never control it the way he did."

Her hand came up to his chin. "You're controlling it just fine now."

Fingers grazing through his goatee, she transfixed him with her gaze, fangs biting into her bottom lip. He didn't need to read her mind to know what she was thinking.

I will not interfere!

Kjan visualized the message on the altar. He had made the mistake of believing him once. Could he really trust him to keep his word this time?

She looked up at him expectantly, her eyes sparkling, so brilliant, so sure. She was ready to leave it all behind, and he wanted to be there with her. Wanted her so badly it was torture. But he stalled. He was scared. And relieved. And hopeful. And anxious. With so many emotions bubbling up inside him, he felt broken and overwhelmed. All confidence in himself was gone.

"I love you," she said softly. "Always."

Her voice was his beacon in the storm, guiding him safely through the rough sea. Eve paved the way, just like the first time, nudging him to find his feet.

Her fingers twitched, and he captured her hand before she could pull it away. "Touch me again."

Her lips curled with the smallest gasp. "Where?"

"Anywhere," he begged, his breath ragged.

Kjan took a leap of faith. He pulled her underneath him, his hips sinking into her familiar shape with a fierce need, aching to be sated.

Their tongues clashed. Her mouth fully open to him, she matched his ravenous hunger. Her legs quivered around his waist while her whimpers chanted inside his head.

"Come for me, Dove," he coaxed. "I want my name on your lips. I need to hear it."

Grinding hard against the wet heat of her, nothing but the thin barrier of her underwear between them, he held out for that sweet sound of validation, teasing wail after wail from her, each one more agonizing than the last.

And then his name seeped from her lips in a plaintive groan. Jutting up, her spine arched, Eve welcomed her first release.

Watching her, Kjan nearly burst from satisfaction. He eased up just enough to give her room to catch her breath. "Weak," he scolded with a mischievous chuckle.

His mouth found the dip of her throat and continued drifting down her front. The flimsy fabric of her shirt was no match for his fangs. Her perked nipples ached to meet him.

Eve's fingernails bit into his back when she felt the sharp points scrape against the sensitive skin of her breast.

Her soft moans turned urgent, her tone pleading. Nothing could keep him from giving her what she craved. What her body begged him for.

He skimmed his hands along her thighs and dragged her thong down as he kissed his way across her hip, trailing the crease inward.

Yes! Her taste… her scent… undiluted…

"Mine," he growled, dipping in between.

Squeezing the muscles of her legs in his palms, he draped them over his shoulders. As much as he craved to be inside her, right now he needed this.

They needed this.

Thighs spread, eager to receive him, her hands came down to the shaved sides of his skull, making him shudder.

More scraping of her nails, more needy little moans falling from her lips once he sealed his mouth to her. He lapped at the irresistible nectar dripping from her bud, luscious and fragrant, a succulent flower blooming only for him.

Her hands flew up, thrashing above her head, while she complimented him with a string of curses from her finest collection.

Goddamn, how he worshiped this woman. Eve was divine. She rocked herself against him, encouraging him as he licked up her pink seam and flicked across her clit, his tongue persistent like the inferno inside her.

He led her to the brink, watching her contort her body from the intense pleasure until she stopped writhing against his mouth.

But he wasn't done. Not yet. He needed one more before he would answer her plea. Needed to pull her apart before he could put her back together.

Kjan slid his fingers up her tight passage, the glide so smooth, so easy.

Curling them toward him, he found the distinctive texture of her G-spot. He moved over it, again and again, much harsher than he should, while her hips bucked in rhythm, eagerly ferocious.

Neither of them could stop. His tongue thrashed across her clit as he sucked each drop that gushed from her with another orgasm.

Only then did he release her.

Eve started fiddling with the buttons on his shirt as soon as he came up. Her hands didn't delay yanking it over his head. She wasn't having any of the *slow-and-gentle*. Squirming in relentless desire, she pulled him back up, her kisses greedy and desperate.

Kjan didn't object. 203 days, he had ached for her. He was never leaving her side again, come hell or high water.

She explored his torso with her alluring touch, skating her hands over his bare chest and down to his abs.

Fuuucck! Her fingers grazed his belly button, and an electric shock bolted through his body. Like he wasn't already painfully close to bursting.

Eve answered his distress. She released his constraints and freed his throbbing cock.

On a groan, he captured her in a kiss. Mouth slanted, tongue dipping past her teeth, his hand covered hers, and he worked himself against her palm, stroking the entire length in steady rhythm together.

When she nudged him at her entrance, his patience dwindled. Both panting heavily, he cuffed her wrists and pinned her hands up by her head.

"Eyes on me, Dove," he prompted, threading his fingers through hers.

Eve complied, her lips parting in anticipation as he aligned himself. Watching the light in her eyes ignite, Kjan rolled his hips into her until his spine cracked.

A sob queued in her throat. But he knew it wasn't from pain. Her emotions were threatening to overwhelm her.

Her legs tightened around him, reassuring him that she was okay, and he kissed her through the tears streaming down her cheeks, swallowing the turmoil brewing inside her.

His breathing short and fast, he took it slow, searching for their connection, that missing piece of himself inside his soulmate.

Each deep thrust prompted a jarring moan from her lips. She felt so damn good meeting him, the tight, slick fit of her forcing him deeper.

Keeping the momentum going, he pressed down on her arms, his teeth wandering the edge of her jaw. Her muscles tensed beneath him with each prolonged whimper.

"Louder," he rasped into her ear. "Let me hear you. All that built-up frustration... I want to hear it, Dove."

With the growing need to feel her come apart for him, he picked up his pace and wound her body up. His aching canines roved the column of her neck expectantly, taking in the little cues of her body as the intensity peaked in her—the quivers, the broken breaths, the little squeals.

"Your sweet cry is mine. No one can have it. You don't hold back. You scream for me when you come," his voice grated out.

His hips railed into her, driving her higher, and then her cry of ecstasy detonated inside his head like a grenade.

As she climaxed, the pulsing of her core gripped him, but it was the sound of his name on her lips that set him free.

Caught in the swell of his own orgasm, the urge to sink his teeth into her rose like a growl in his throat. Buried to the hilt inside the woman he loved, Kjan found his way home. *You are mine, and I am yours*, the words repeated in his head as his fangs locked into her shoulder, and he pledged himself to her all over again.

Kjan released her wrists as he retracted. Dropping his forehead into the crook of her neck, he took in the warmth and scent of her skin that mingled with the aftermath.

Eve wrapped her arms around his neck and held him tight.

The simple gesture carried so much meaning. Whenever he was in a free fall, she would be there to catch him, wrap him in her immaculate wings, and soothe the storm inside him.

Eyes closed, he waited for the tremors to subside. A strange sensation washed over him. There she was, naked in front of him—physically and emotionally—bare in every sense of the word. She felt the same against his skin, yet everything about him was different. Like his mind was splitting in two, he was completely aware of the other presence.

And it scared the living hell out of him.

Renate Rowland

CHAPTER

65

E ve was curled up next to Kjan, resting comfortably in the
crook of his shoulder. His soft snore and the light and
steady rhythm of his heart confirmed he was still asleep.
He looked peaceful for once, and she wanted to keep him that
way.

Without shifting her weight, she traced the eight staves of his
tattoo, dragging her fingertip along the lines back and forth
between the crest of his pec and down the sides.

On the last one, her finger came to a stop at his scar while
she pictured the horrid scene in the cave.

His heart hiccupped at her touch, and the rate increased
slightly.

"I know you're awake," she teased, picking up her
explorations and drawing a big circle around the oversized hill
before stretching her entire palm across his chest.

He didn't respond, nor did he acknowledge her. The flush drained from her face.

Not this again.

"Kjan?" Her voice trembled. He still didn't reply, and she jerked up in a panic.

"I'm sorry," he said with a weary smile.

"What's wrong?"

He kissed the inside of her palm and pulled her back down to him. "It's nothing."

"Tell me." Eyes trained on his face, she refused to back down.

His chest heaved on a long inhale. "He is still here," he confessed, expelling his breath. "He's still a part of me. I can feel him."

HE, as in his Sire, the God, who tried to kill them both, was still in his head?

Eve stiffened, and he read the concern on her face, quickly shaking his head. "He's no longer fighting. He's... content. At peace. We have come to an agreement."

"What do you mean?"

"A truce." He hooked a finger under her chin. "We will both do whatever it takes to protect you. He's in love with you too."

She scoffed, raising her eyebrows. "I don't believe he even knows the meaning of that word."

He nudged her chin higher. "You don't trust me?" Holding a wicked grin on his lips, a streak of blue flashed over his green eyes when he leaned in to kiss her.

Eve flinched. *Trust him?* A knot formed in her throat. She wasn't even sure who she was talking to right now.

"Take my vein," he whispered against her lips. "You know me better than anyone."

Kjan! Definitely. "It's not *you* that I don't trust," she countered. "How can you believe him after everything he's done?"

"I have faith. I wouldn't be here right now if I didn't. That's why I left. I would never put you in danger, Eve." He caressed her cheek while he spoke, and his eyes were the same bright emeralds she had fallen in love with.

"I went to the temple, and he swore a blood oath of his own volition. I know you're scared, but I believe him. I can feel everything he feels. Take my vein, and you will know." He pressed her hand to his heart as he urged her again.

Eve raised the fingers of her free hand to his temple and then brushed over the bare skin of his head, trying to find her resolve.

Slipping her hand from his hold, she repeated the same motion on the opposite side, framing his face with both hands.

Kjan leaned into her touch with a soft exhale. "I can feel you in my head."

She wished she had his conviction.

Trusting his instincts, she let him guide her to his throat and prayed that she would always be able to tell them apart. Not just by the color of their eyes but by who they were at their core.

Her fangs drove into his skin, and as soon as the first drop touched her tongue, all her doubt vanished. The taste of his blood was overwhelming, rich, and sweet, more intoxicating than before, and the more Eve took, the more alive she felt. Only an insignificant dark trace of coffee remained, while Kjan's wildfire raged through her veins without subduing her.

Her tongue flicked across her lips, savoring every last bit of the divine bliss he brought out in her as his steady palm cradled her head. She could feel the warmth of him on her skin before his mouth pressed against her temple, his breath jagged.

And then he kissed her, passionately, fiercely, making her toes curl, and setting her soul ablaze. His growl, primal and possessive, stirred an insatiable desire in her. Everywhere his hands touched, sparks of electricity jolted through her nerves.

The pleasure shot to her core, blooming in a warm haze that spread through her limbs. Goosebumps prickled over her skin. He was everything she needed, and she recognized him with her eyes closed.

Weaving her arms around his neck, Eve surrendered to him. Bodies molded together, chasing that delightful spark, they clung to each other for dear life. He knew her—knew what she needed.

He was rough. He was savage. He was hers.

EPILOGUE

Nestled into the corner of the chaise lounge, Eve fiddled with the stake in her hand. She was admiring the bindrune etched into the butt-end that she hadn't had time to acknowledge before.

The single Algiz had been sufficient to bind Andromeda, in a way protecting the world *from* her, but Kjan had obviously not trusted it against Kjartan. He'd used additional Elder Futhark to invoke ancient magic. She recognized the infamous Eihwaz merged with the vertical stave underneath and Tiwaz on top. The warrior-rune represented self-sacrifice, order, and justice.

"I always thought of yew as a soft type of wood used for longbows, not really ideal for a stake."

Kjan stood across the room, leaning back against the kitchen island, left hand propped on the edge. A dark curl dripped over his eyes as he scrolled through his phone. Kristján had texted him just to check in.

"It's flexible, yes, but strong," he said, barely looking up from the screen.

He was wearing loose-fitting gray sweatpants and a plain navy t-shirt that stretched across his pecs and shoulders. With his ankles crossed in a familiar pose, the sight of him was one of comfort to her.

Eve brushed her fingers carefully down the rough edge of the shaft. It wasn't exactly smooth, and she didn't want to end up getting a splinter. "Your choice makes a lot more sense now, with it being the tree of death and the personal connection to the God Hǫðr."

"It's not just the tree of death... but life as well," he drew out. "Since it has a lifespan well over three thousand years and remains green throughout winter, it's considered a symbol of eternal life that conquers death. Eihwaz represents Yggdrasill and signifies rebirth, regeneration, the cycle of life, etc.," he gestured lazily with the phone in his right hand. "It's the core of everything, the connection of both worlds, mortal and immortal."

Something rippled inside her at his bringing up the profound link between the living and the dead. The symbol was now on her skin. Permanently.

"Eihwaz was replaced by the Younger Futhark rune Ýr," he went on, still engrossed in his search. It looked as though he was reading off the screen, but Eve knew he had this stuff memorized verbatim.

"It's a predominant symbol of death that looks like a tree trunk with three roots to reference Yggdrasill. But flip the rune upside-down, and you get Elgr—Algiz," he translated into common Proto-Germanic, "the elk, a symbol of protection and life. In return, it sort of looks like a tree with branches."

So, Algiz and Ýr are still representations of Yggdrasill, and consequentially of the outdated Eihwaz?

At his mention, Eve had turned the stake in her hand over to regard the symbols at the end again. When she looked back at him, his lips had stilled and twisted into a pout.

"I'm sounding like a textbook again, aren't I?"

"Not at all." Did he think he was boring her? "I like listening to you ramble on about stuff. And I like the runes."

His brows winged up in an amused note. "Then here's a fun fact for ya," he said, making a jabbing motion with his phone. "Since the yew is viral all year, but at the same time lethal, Eihwaz stands at the center of the 'unfortunate thirteen' myth from its thirteenth position in the Elder Futhark alphabet."

She gave him a weak laugh. "So you're saying it's all superstition?"

His eyes stayed on her, and his mouth tightened with a deflating sigh. "I'm saying a lot of it is up for interpretation."

Eve tugged her knees closer to her chest. His banter didn't soothe her uneasiness. "But you *do* believe in the magic behind the runes?" she prodded again. Why else add them?

His shoulders bobbed, but remained relaxed. "It was the only thing I could come up with. I don't know for sure that it would have worked. My grandmother only taught me the basics, I'm no witch."

Eve rubbed her thumb over the symbol carved into the wood again and then glanced at the mark on her wrist.

In the corner of her eye, Kjan let his arm hang by his side, finally giving her his undivided attention. "The additions were just an extra precaution. The stake immobilized Anne until he removed it because her heart was still intact. When I shot her, there was nothing left to initiate the healing process. The heart is the key. I guess I could have decapitated her too, but I didn't have my axe handy." He snorted a little laugh that brought a smile to her face.

It was so good to see him happy. He had shaved the goatee. Wasn't really his style. The 3-day stubble made him look younger. Almost *her* age.

"You missed your heart when you shot yourself. That's why you survived."

"Yeah, but I couldn't rely on that alone. Her body wasn't as resilient as mine. Then I was thinking about the scars on my palm that never went away from when she ripped the stake out of my hand. I knew it had at least some effect on me, and I bet the bullet left similar scar tissue in my chest after I recovered from the gunshot."

Eve opened her mouth, but he shrugged off her concern before she could get a word in. "It's less of an inconvenience than the damn shoulder that can't seem to stay in its socket."

She tipped her head to the side, waiting for him to elaborate when he didn't. "Is there a story to it?" she asked expectantly.

"Not really. It's been like that ever since I took on a guy twice my size. Gave him a nice shiner. Hurt like hell, but was totally worth it."

"Hmm." *A guy twice his size? Must've been some giant.*

Eve sighed, scratching the blue pigmentation, and he caught onto the reason for her initial inquiry.

"You don't need to worry. It's harmless," he assured her. "He marked you as *his* in the only way he knew how. That's all."

"He branded me like a cow," she grumbled.

Kjan suppressed a grin at her remark by biting his lips. "You know Hindus consider them to be a sacred symbol of life that should be protected and revered, right?"

"Oh, ha-ha, you're so funny." She scrunched her nose contemptuously before reaching toward her back and firing a pillow in his direction.

It landed four feet short of him.

His eyes had followed the trajectory, unimpressed by the pathetic effort. "Pitiful," he declared wryly.

He bent down to scoop it up, then propelled it back full force, flashing a cocky smile.

"Ouch!" She caught it with a thump against her chest, exaggerating sarcastically.

He countered with a jaunty retort, "Don't start what you can't finish."

Okay, maybe it wasn't just his look, he *acted* more her age too. It was refreshingly uplifting.

He gave his phone another glance and finally settled on a song. Eve scowled. "Really? Blues?"

"Why not?"

"Wait!" *That sounds familiar.* "Who is this? I know that voice."

"Yeah, you do."

His bare feet kicked off toward her. He crossed the front room and tossed his phone onto the couch in passing. "You should really branch out more. Some of your favorite artists do."

Yeah, it sounded nothing like Asking Alexandria, but it was still Danny Worsnop's voice.

"Humor me, woman," he pressed, then gently slipped the stake from her fingers and chucked it onto the cushions.

Hoisting her off the chaise lounge, he placed her left arm up on his shoulder, then slid his right hand to the small of her back. His left rested over his chest, clasping hers, fingers tangled.

He lowered his forehead, his handsome features reflecting the true, cordial nature she adored. "You and I… we practically plunged into this hot and heavy—"

"I never complained." She would happily let him screw her six ways from Sunday.

"I know," he chuckled. "I know you didn't, and I love you even more for it. But I want to take a step back. Not start over… just take things slow-*ish*," he smirked with a slight squint.

"I'd like that." Eve beamed, biting her bottom lip. "I like *this* too." He'd only danced with her once, at Eleanor's gala.

"You haven't even seen all my moves yet," he said in a gravelly tone that made her thighs twitch with excitement.

The hand from her back brushed along her outstretched arm as he gave her a push and then pulled her right back toward him.

Lifting her left hand on the tug, he spun her 180°, and she landed backward in his embrace, her arms now crossed tightly in front of her.

He held her close, rocking her to the rhythm of the song, his cheek at her temple.

"This might just be my favorite," she purred drowsily, pretending she wasn't grinding her ass back into him.

The profound fragrance of his aged Bourbon bodywash invaded her nose, refreshing her image of them in the shower together.

"Speaking of brands and signatures." She reminded herself of the new motto to '*take it slow-ish*'—she hated it already. "How did you write your name?"

He splayed her hand out in front and began drawing a long line down the center of her palm. Eve followed the tip of his index finger trace the first one and recognized the Younger Futhark rune *Kaunaz*.

ᚴ—"Kaun," he said, calling it by its Old Norse name.

ᛅ—"Ár," – *Jera*, the Younger Futhark rune for the letter *j*.

ᚱ—"Reið," – *Raido*, which he pronounced like a *t* at the end.

ᛏ—"Týr," – *Tiwaz*, like *tear*drop with a rolling *r*.

ᚬ—"Áss," – *Ansuz*, with the open ah-sound like the English word *us*.

ᚾ—"Nauðr," – *Naudiz*.

He named the shapes one by one, each feathery stroke tickling the sensitive skin on the inside of her hand.

Over her shoulder, Eve watched the tip of his tongue disappear behind his teeth as he finished the soft *th*-sound of the last one. With a light touch, she cupped his cheek and traced his jawline with her thumb. Letting her fingers linger on his chin, she drew him into a kiss.

"Not quite as elegant as your handwriting. But the long branch is way prettier than the short twig chicken scratch."

Another husky laugh tickled her ear when he uncrossed their arms. Kjan reversed the pirouette and bent her backward, supporting her weight, while he dipped down to plant his lips on hers.

Eve's mouth parted effortlessly for him, as if spellbound. "I love you."

"I love y—

His words cut off abruptly as his lips ripped away from her, his head snapping toward the glass pane of the patio.

"What is it?" Eve asked, matching his concern.

His face was tense, and she followed his gaze over her shoulder, craning her neck.

"Jesus! Is that a crow? It's huge."

Kjan narrowed his eyes, his grip tightening around her waist protectively. "It's not a crow. It's a raven."

TO BE CONTINUED . . .

Thank you for reading

Please consider leaving a review however long. A review is always appreciated.

Next in the *Bound by A WEB OF WYRD* Series

BOOK THREE

OATH BOUND

Will Kjartan keep his word to Kjan and Eve? Find out in

Look for book three in the trilogy coming late spring 2025, and check out my romantic suspense novel *OF APPLES AND TREES*.

Bonus Material

Find the official SPOTIFY PLAYLIST to this book on
www.runikpress.com/renaterowlandbooks

While you're there, don't forget to sign up for my
newsletter, so you won't miss anything.

Acknowledgements

I want to thank my amazing beta team — Toni Middleton, Hilary Preston, Hayley Sullivan, and my husband — as well as my growing team of ARC readers.

Thank you all so very much for your continued support.

Translation Guide

Kona
- *Wife/Woman*

Elskan (mín)
- *(My) Sweetheart/Love*

Förum!
- *Let's go!*

Já
- *Yes*

Nei
- *No*

Nei. Ek hóndla þat sjálfr. Ekki til umræðu. Ek fer til þeirra.
- *No. I do it myself. Not up for discussion. I go to them.*

Ek fer. Þit tvo dveljit. Ek þarf fjora daga. Í mesta lagi.
- *I go. You two stay. I need four days. At most.*

Sjait um hana.
- *Watch her.*

NOG!
- *ENOUGH!*

Byrit!
- *Begin!*

Author Bio

Renate Rowland is an author of suspenseful Paranormal and Contemporary Romance. Born and raised in Germany, she grew up with the sagas and mythology surrounding the Norse Gods, but it was her passion for vampires and Viking lore that inspired this trilogy. After being fortunate to have called three different continents her home, she has settled with her family in the US. She is an artist at heart, and although she expresses that in various ways, she held on to her stories until she felt it was time to give them air and let them breathe on their own. Finding much inspiration in music lyrics, she is driven by the desire to create something as powerful and moving as the artists she admires.

Follow me on social media:

Instagram & Threads: @renaterowland

Facebook: @renate.rowland.books

Milton Keynes UK
Ingram Content Group UK Ltd.
UKHW021906230924
448765UK00020B/316/J

9 798330 345151